KT-474-468

TRISKELLI2N
THE BURNING
WILL PETERSON

WILL PETERSON is an award-winning novelist and acclaimed television writer. He lives in London and Kent. Triskellion is his first series for children.

TRISKELLI2N
THE BURNING

WILL PETERSON

WALKER
BOOKS

This is a work of fiction. Names, characters, places and incidents are either the product of the authors' imagination or, if real, are used fictitiously. All statements, activities, stunts, descriptions, information and material of any other kind contained herein are included for entertainment purposes only and should not be relied on for accuracy or replicated as they may result in injury.

First published 2009 by Walker Books Ltd
87 Vauxhall Walk, London SE11 5HJ

2 4 6 8 10 9 7 5 3 1

Text © 2009 Mark Billingham Ltd and Peter Cocks
Cover design by Walker Books Ltd

The right of Mark Billingham and Peter Cocks to be identified
as authors of this work has been asserted by them in accordance
with the Copyright, Designs and Patents Act 1988

This book has been typeset in Fairfield

Printed and bound in Great Britain by Clays Ltd, St Ives plc

All rights reserved. No part of this book may be reproduced, transmitted
or stored in an information retrieval system in any form or by any means,
graphic, electronic or mechanical, including photocopying, taping
and recording,without prior written permission from the publisher.

British Library Cataloguing in Publication Data:
a catalogue record for this book is
available from the British Library

ISBN 978-1-4063-0710-8

www.walker.co.uk
www.triskellionadventure.com

For William, Rosemary and James;
Katie and Jack

Triskellion:
the story so far...

American twins Rachel and Adam Newman have spent a harrowing summer rediscovering their British roots in the village of Triskellion, where their mother was born. But what should have been an idyllic break has quickly become a terrifying adventure.

While staying with their grandmother, Celia Root, they have been befriended by "Gabriel", a mysterious traveller boy. He has urged them to help him find a long-lost amulet, but their quest has made them many enemies. The villagers are willing to do almost anything to protect what is theirs, and the twins soon find themselves hunted by both Commodore Wing – the grandfather they didn't know they had – and his son, Hilary, a dark and dangerous figure who seems bent on their destruction.

The discovery of the Triskellion, an ancient and powerful artefact, has unlocked the dark secret of Rachel and Adam's ancestry. A frightening revelation from the past that will affect every moment of their future…

As they are airlifted from the village – where they are no longer welcome – by their friend archaeologist Laura Sullivan, it seems that Rachel and Adam have finally escaped.

Or have they flown straight into a trap?

prologue

T he helicopter was banking slightly, moving across an
area of flat, black ground, when Rachel heard the
pilot pass a crackly message to Laura Sullivan.

Laura nodded and put away the notes she'd been reading.

Rachel looked across to her mother and Adam, pressed
closely against each other in the seats next to her. Adam's cheek
was flat against the window.

They'd been flying for about an hour, maybe more, she
thought, and she'd watched the landscape waking up as they'd
passed low above it. A patchwork of green and brown fields,
loosely stitched together by threads of irregular lanes, had given
way to clumps of terracotta houses that had become denser and
more tightly packed as they'd approached the city. Lines of traffic had built up and begun to snake slowly along the main
roads. Lights had winked in the windows and then faded as the
sun had struggled up to bleach them out. Rachel had watched
it bathing the crush of buildings and the twist of the river as
they'd flown over the centre of London.

Adam had sat forward, excited, and pointed out the London Eye, the Houses of Parliament and other landmarks familiar from films and pictures. Places they had seen, but never visited.

Rachel yawned. Beneath the rattle of the helicopter blades, she thought she could hear a faint buzzing, just for a second or two, and wondered if a bee was trapped somewhere in the cabin.

Zzzzz … dnk. Zzzzz … dnk.

She looked around and finally located the stowaway slowly walking the glass circle of the porthole just above her head. With the sky behind it, the bee looked like a little man, exploring the surface of a new planet. She wondered if it had travelled with them from the village.

One of Jacob's, come to see them away safely.

Laura turned round, reached across and laid a reassuring hand on Rachel's arm. She signalled to Rachel's mother, told her that they would be landing in a few minutes. Rachel watched as her mother nodded and squeezed Adam's hand. Her mother smiled, but it was thin and weak.

Her mother looked tired.

Rachel was exhausted too: her brain and bones aching in equal measure. The last few hours, the last few weeks, seemed like a nightmare she was waking from. She was wrung out, but at least she knew it was over. That she'd feel better when they were on the plane, and better yet eight hours or so from then, when they were finally home.

Through the window the land stretched out below her, flat as far as she could see. Free of trees, free of anything.

She heard the men up front talking on the radio, its squawk like the noise of some angry insect, as the helicopter turned again.

A complex of buildings came slowly into view ahead and to the left. It was single storey, concrete, and brown, and she could make out the line of a perimeter fence. She looked hard for other aircraft, for a control tower, but could see nothing. It wasn't like any airport she'd ever seen.

"Laura? Where're the planes?"

They came down fast, the large "H" in the landing circle growing bigger as they descended. They hit it dead centre with a bump that made Rachel's teeth shake and she looked across at her brother to see if he was OK.

He gave her a thumbs up.

Then everything happened very quickly...

Rachel was being pulled from the helicopter, out into the roaring wind of the rotor blades. Turning, she watched the same thing happen to Adam, and tried to get close to her mother. But Laura was leading her mother away, putting some distance between Kate and the men who had emerged from a metal door in one of the smaller buildings.

The men who had come to take her children.

They wore headphones and dark glasses. They didn't speak.

Rachel tried to yank her hand away as she was led towards the door, but the man escorting her only increased his grip. Adam cried out to her and they both cried out to their mother, but when Rachel turned to look she could see that her mother was sobbing and shaking her head. Laura was doing her best to keep Kate calm, shouting over the noise of the engine as it died.

Telling her that everything was going to be fine.

Rachel watched, helpless, as Adam was ushered quickly through a door, several metres away to her right. He shouted something which she couldn't catch: his voice lost beneath the wind and the sound of her own grunts as she struggled to free herself.

The nightmare hadn't ended. She hadn't woken up.

The last thing Rachel saw on the outside was a hazy line: the furious arc of the bee as it buzzed around her. She twisted her head to get a last look, to pass a last message, but then it too was shut out as the heavy metal door slammed hard behind her.

part one:
hope

1

Rachel woke up in a bed. In *her* bed.

Not the creaky brass bed in the flowery bedroom of her grandmother's cottage in Triskellion, but in her own bed, in her own room. Her own room in New York City.

She lay still for a moment, letting her eyes travel around the room, afraid to close them again in case it disappeared. Everything was there: the well-thumbed copy of *Where's Waldo?*, a childhood favourite; the china piggybank that only ever held a couple of dollars in change; the furry, glass-eyed cat; and a battered and grubby teddy bear that had belonged to her mother. Everything was in its place, each item a touchstone to memories that now seemed part of a distant past. Rachel's gaze drifted past the Johnny Depp poster to the window, where narrow shafts of light were squeezing their way through the wooden slats of the blind. She could hear the low rumble and honk of traffic on the street outside. The sounds of Manhattan coming to life...

Rachel blinked.

The room was still there. She was not dreaming. But how, she wondered, had she got here?

She remembered the helicopter ride – the flight from Triskellion with Adam, her mother and Laura Sullivan – and the landing, somewhere grey and misty, miles from anywhere. She remembered being separated from Adam and bundled into a building, feeling weak with exhaustion from the day's events.

Her thoughts began to spool back in fast rewind...

Rachel shuddered and felt a fearful lurch in her stomach as she remembered what Gabriel had revealed to them. That they were like him. That she and Adam were human but had ... *something else* in their blood. In their genes. Something that made them very different. Her stomach knotted as she realized that *one* fact would inform every moment of the rest of their lives: their bloodline had been created centuries before, by the union of a human and someone from another world. Rachel felt a wave of nausea and, for a moment, thought she might be sick.

She breathed deeply and closed her eyes until the feeling passed.

Whatever had happened, at least she and Adam had been reunited with their mother. At least they were home. She just couldn't remember how she had got here. She must have slept for days. Maybe she'd been given something to *help* her sleep...

But she took comfort from the fact that, however she had got here, she was a safe distance from England, from the village where it had all started. It would be a huge relief to talk to her mum about everything; to Adam...

Then Rachel realized that, for the first time in her life, she couldn't hear her brother's voice in her head. Nor Gabriel's voice, or any voices at all. Not even the insistent humming, like the drone of bees, that told Rachel she was on their wavelength; that she was ready to receive their thoughts.

Just silence.

She felt a little panicked and climbed out of bed. She needed to find Adam and see if he felt the same. Her head was fuzzy, and her tongue was thick and heavy inside her mouth. She felt unsteady on her feet and, guessing that she'd stood up too quickly, she reached out for the desk beside the bed to steady herself.

The desktop was as tidy as she'd left it a month or so before, with pens in the plastic pot, a stack of CDs and the little round red mirror on it. Rachel picked up the mirror and stared at herself. She looked terrible. Her curly chestnut hair was greasy and matted and her face looked pale and puffy, as if she had been crying for days. She put the mirror face down and, as she raised her head, another thought struck her. This room – her room – looked and felt and sounded like it should, but it didn't *smell* right.

It smelled synthetic, like the inside of a new car.

Rachel slipped on her red plastic flip-flops and walked

over to the door. The handle felt unusually stiff. She gave it a jerk and let out an involuntary cry as the door flew back. It didn't open on to the carpeted hallway that led to her parents' room but on to a brightly lit, white corridor.

And somewhere near by an alarm went off.

2

Stepping from the shadows of her room, Rachel squinted up at the harsh white light flooding from the fluorescent tubes that ran the length of the passage. The corridor resonated with the faint, low-level buzz given off by the lights and with the distant beep of the alarm that had started the moment she'd opened the door.

The alarm that she had activated.

Rachel was frightened and confused, but more than anything, she was astonished by the bizarre feeling of stepping from her own room into an institutional hallway.

She felt as if she was a figure in a Surrealist picture (one of those her mom liked so much) walking from one room to another in a dream-like landscape with the *"slap-slap-slap"* of her flip-flops echoing like a ticking clock.

There were other doors every few metres or so, and Rachel began to push gently at each one, as much to confirm their existence as anything else. She glanced up in alarm as a man passed quickly in front of her, a few metres ahead, where the corridor met another in a T-junction. He stopped and looked at her briefly before hurrying on.

Rachel stood, frozen. He'd been wearing white overalls and she'd seen a flash of panic pass across his features when he'd spotted her. She'd watched him fumbling to push in small earphones before walking quickly away.

He'd looked scared of her.

Rachel moved on past another two doors, stopping at a third, which had something written on it. She looked closely at the small printed label and her heart lurched once again. It read:

ADAM NEWMAN

Rachel tried the handle. The door was unlocked. She opened it and walked into her brother's room.

"Hey, Rach," Adam said. He was sitting on the bed and looked up briefly from the games' console he was busily punching away at. "You just woken up?"

Rachel was too stunned at her brother's nonchalance to answer immediately. Instead, she looked around the room. Like her own, every single thing was in its normal place. Unlike her own, everything was strewn across the floor and spilling out of drawers: the old catcher's mitt that had been their father's; the wall plastered with thrash metal posters; an electric guitar with two strings still missing; the TV in the corner, draped with odd socks. Business as usual, Rachel thought. It was perfect in every detail. But quite *unlike* Adam's room at home, it didn't smell … boyish.

"I had a fantastic sleep," Adam continued. "Feel like I slept for a year. Didn't dream about a single thing. Didn't wake up with voices in my head."

Rachel dropped down on to the bed beside her brother. "Don't you think that's strange?"

Adam shrugged and looked down at his screen. "If getting the first good night's sleep in weeks is strange, then give me strange."

"But the voices are you and me," Rachel said. "You and me … and Gabriel. We know each other's thoughts."

Adam looked his sister in the eye. "You know what? In the last few weeks I think I've had enough of knowing what you're thinking, and as for what Gabriel thinks, well, look where that got us." He'd suddenly lost interest in his game and there was something steely in his voice, something that Rachel found hard to argue with. "To be honest, he's totally freaked me out. I wish we could just go back to normal, but I guess we've gone past that point. I'm trying as hard as I can to forget about it."

Rachel understood his opinion perfectly; understood that he was finding it tough to come to terms with what he had found out about himself. She could see that he was scared. But she still failed to understand why he was not more fazed at being in his own bedroom … that *wasn't* his bedroom at all.

"But what about this place?" she said, gesturing at the room around her.

"They just want us to feel at home," Adam said. "They made me a BLT. I was starving."

Rachel began to feel a tingle of panic in her limbs. "They? *Who* made you a BLT?"

"Some guy knocked on the door when I woke up, asked if I was hungry. It was weird, 'cos I'd wanted a BLT for days. Couldn't stop thinking about it."

Rachel wanted to shake her brother. Of all the weird things they had experienced, his desperation for a bacon, lettuce and tomato sandwich didn't even register on the scale.

"Aren't you worried about where we are? What this place is?"

"I know it's not that village." Adam went back to his game. "I feel safer here."

"We were supposed to be going home. With Mom. Have you seen her?"

"She's here too, I guess," he said, without looking up.

Adam's acceptance was beginning to rattle her. She sat on the bed and prodded her brother in the ribs. "Do you know where we *are*?"

"Not exactly," Adam said, wriggling away from her. He gestured towards the window. "But it looks like New York, kind of…"

Rachel stood up and opened the blind, letting light stream in. The view certainly looked … American. Not the

New York that they knew, but a built-up town of tall build-ings, their rows of windows glinting in the sunlight. Rachel sat back on the bed, her head in her hands, trying to gather her thoughts.

"Why don't we switch on the TV?" she said. "The news should tell us where we are … or which country we're in, at least."

She picked up the remote and turned on the television, scrolling through the channels. There were cartoons, and Adam wanted her to stop when they saw Homer Simpson's yellow face beaming out at them. But Rachel kept scrolling, stabbing furiously at the remote as yet more cartoon channels appeared and, dotted among them, some live-action American sitcoms; the actors' faces as familiar to them as those of their own family. The canned studio laughter was momentarily re-assuring: a reminder of evenings tucked up at home with family and friends. Rachel reached the fortieth channel and threw the remote control across the room in frustration. There were no presenters, no weather reports, no current affairs…

No news.

"That's weird." Adam shrugged, going back to his game again.

The panic tightened in Rachel's chest. "They don't want us to know where we are," she said. She watched as Adam, despite appearing to concentrate on his game, began to chew his trembling lip and push at the tears welling in the corners of his eyes.

"Do you think Mom *is* here?" he said, swallowing hard. The confidence he'd shown moments before seemed to be draining away.

Before Rachel could answer, there was a knock at the door and she found herself automatically telling whoever it was to "come in".

The door swung open and Laura Sullivan stepped into the room. Rachel took her in at a glance, amazed at the difference in her appearance since the last time they'd seen her. Laura looked scrubbed and clean. Her long red hair was tied back in a ponytail and her clothes were smart and businesslike.

"Hi, you guys," she said. "How are you doing?" Her tone was calm and friendly, but her eyes darted nervously between the twins. Rachel registered the look and felt adrenalin surge through her. Her thoughts raced. She was looking for someone to explain everything, someone to *blame*…

Laura Sullivan had stumbled upon their secret by digging up the chalk circle in Triskellion. Was that what archaeologists did? Dig into the past only to mess up the present? Rachel felt a powerful jolt of rage at the fact that Laura had dug up *their* past. If only they hadn't gone to Triskellion, if only Laura hadn't excavated the Bronze Age tomb, they'd have been none the wiser. They could have spent the rest of their lives as ordinary Americans. They could have grown up innocent and had kids of their own. How could they now, knowing about their gene pool?

If only. If only…

"Where are we?" Rachel shouted. "Mom said … we thought you were taking us *home*." Her voice was getting louder, almost a shriek. "Where *is* Mom? You tricked us."

Laura held her hands wide, imploring. "Rachel—"

But something in Rachel snapped and she threw herself across the room, launching herself at Laura Sullivan, her hands grabbing at the tall Australian's face and hair.

Sullivan's strong, sinewy hands grasped Rachel's wrists and held her fast. They stood face to face and Rachel saw that, despite the effort of restraining her, Laura's eyes brimmed with sympathy. Suddenly the fight drained from her. Her limbs felt weak and she fell sobbing into Laura's arms, while behind her Adam hovered awkwardly, not knowing whether to defend his sister or to try and break up the fight.

Laura held Rachel close and stroked her hair. "Let me at least try to explain a few things to you," she said.

Rachel loosened herself from Laura's embrace and looked her straight in the eye.

"This had better be good," she said.

3

"This place is called the Hope Project," Laura said. She had sat down between the twins on Adam's bed. "It's part of a bigger organization called the Flight Trust."

Adam threw Rachel a look, none the wiser.

"What is it?" Rachel asked calmly, like a patient about to receive bad news from a doctor. "A hospital?"

"No," Laura said. "It's an archaeological research centre."

"And you work here?" Rachel was shaking her head, trying to get things straight.

"I do at the moment…"

"So what about the TV stuff?" Adam said. He sounded more than a little disappointed. "I thought you were a TV producer?"

Laura took a deep breath and let it out slowly. "Listen, I'll try and answer as many questions as I can, OK? I'll be honest with you."

"Meaning you haven't been so far, right?" Rachel said.

Laura sighed and lowered her head for a few seconds.

"Look, some questions I can answer, some I can't ... and some I just won't have a clue about. Right, the TV thing. Yes, I *am* a qualified archaeologist and I *was* producing the show with Chris Dalton, but it was also a good cover for my research work here."

"Cover?" Adam's disappointment hadn't lasted long. "You sound like a spy."

Laura smiled. "Dalton makes such a song and dance about everything that nobody notices me getting on with my *real* work. The Hope Project made sure I got the job with him because they knew that TV was a good way of getting close to sites of special interest."

"What sort of 'special interest'?" Rachel asked.

"Well, anything that has potential ... extraterrestrial connections."

Rachel felt herself shudder. Glancing across, she saw Adam do the same. "And you thought Triskellion had that connection?"

Laura nodded. "I knew it was an interesting site; that there were lots of things going on in the area that didn't quite add up. But I never expected the tomb to reveal anything so ... conclusive. We've excavated tombs all over the world but none have actually produced *remains*."

"You mean that there are other places like Triskellion?" Rachel voiced the thought as it came to her, but even before she'd finished asking the question, she was afraid of hearing the answer.

"Let's put it this way," Laura said. "There are thousands and thousands of tombs and sacred sites all over the globe. The Hope Project believes that *some* of them mark the landing place, or the burial place, of *visitors*."

"From another planet?" Adam whispered.

Laura swallowed and studied the pattern on Adam's duvet for a second or two. "What I can tell you is that we have growing evidence that there have been visitors for thousands of years. They are very similar to *Homo sapiens*: they're human, but their DNA is quite different. Actually, I think we now have proof."

Rachel stared at the floor.

"So, where do they come from?" Adam asked.

"Wish we knew," Laura said. "But if they've been coming here for a long time, like they did to Triskellion thousands of years ago, I think we can safely assume that they're more sophisticated than we are in all sorts of ways."

"Like how?" Adam was breathing hard. He needed more information, and fast.

"Well, these guys were getting here centuries before we even had bicycles. Maybe before we even had the wheel. But apart from the ability to travel, we think they're a lot more sophisticated in terms of their ability to communicate using their minds – to make things happen through thought alone." Laura looked from Rachel to Adam and back again. "You've got to agree, that's a pretty powerful skill to have. Imagine what humans could do if *we* had it?"

"But some people already have it," Adam said. "They can read thoughts, see things in the future, you know? People like—"

"Twins?" Laura nodded again and turned to Rachel.

"Yeah, but not *just* twins," Rachel protested. "There are other people who can mind-read too."

"Yes," Laura said. "There are. And we're starting to believe that people with skills like that are all descended in some way from these visitors. They all carry a little bit of their DNA, though watered down over the centuries."

Rachel felt the hairs prickle on the back of her neck. "Like us," she said.

"Yes, like you," Laura said. "But you and Adam are a special case. Everything that we discovered in Triskellion stacks up: the two bodies in the tomb were your ancestors. One human, one from … elsewhere. The generations that followed did not generally intermarry, didn't even leave the area until your mother came along. This means we've got an almost completely undiluted genetic connection from you to that original visitor to Triskellion. Do you see what I'm saying?"

"It makes us freaks, I guess," Adam said.

"No. It makes you incredibly interesting. You're human, of course, but there is a strand of DNA within you and Rachel that is totally, well … *other*." Laura put an arm round Adam and hugged him close. He did not resist. "You are the closest thing we have to knowing what the visitors were like. What they *are* like…"

"What about Gabriel?" Rachel said.

Laura Sullivan looked blank. "Gabriel?"

Rachel realized in a flash that Laura had absolutely no memory of the boy who had guided their strange adventure through the village. She wondered if this amnesia had been Gabriel's doing: a demonstration of the mental powers that Laura herself had just been talking about. Powers that Gabriel clearly had in abundance. Or had she just not noticed him? Either way, Rachel decided to keep quiet.

"No one, really. Just a kid." Rachel pressed on quickly, ignoring the questioning look from her brother. "Listen, we thought you were taking us home. Mom said…" Rachel's stomach fluttered as she thought of her mother, desperate to ask where she was, but afraid of what she might hear.

"*I* never said that, Rachel. That was a risk I couldn't take." Laura looked her straight in the eye. "I told your mum I'd get you somewhere safe, and I have."

"Why do we need to be safe?"

"Well, you've already seen what the Triskellion can do to people. Hilary Wing hardly had your best interests at heart, and it turned Chris Dalton into some kind of lunatic. He became totally obsessed by it. He would have killed for it."

"Like the ring," Adam said. "In the movie … what happened to Gollum!"

The Triskellion!

Rachel suddenly realized that she didn't know what had happened to it. She'd been clutching it tightly in her fist aboard that helicopter but didn't recall seeing it anywhere in her room when she'd woken up. She tried to keep the panic from her voice as she spoke. "Where is it now?"

"It's in a safe place," Laura said. She took both their hands and squeezed. "But it's not just the Triskellion that needs keeping safe. It's you."

"Why?" Rachel asked. "Are we in danger?"

"You're not in danger *here*," Laura said quickly. "But people are interested in you. In what you are. In what you can do." For a few seconds nobody said anything and only the rumble of traffic outside Adam's window broke the silence.

Laura got to her feet. "OK, that's enough questions for now," she said. "We have plenty of time. You must be hungry, Rachel."

Rachel nodded, suddenly starving, and Adam announced that he could manage another BLT if there was one going.

"Right, let's get you something to eat and I'll show you around."

They took a step towards the door, then Rachel caught Laura's arm. "One more question," she said.

Laura nodded. "You want to know about your mother, right? Look, we'll get to that, I promise."

4

Kate Newman sat on the edge of the bed, flicking through the pages of a magazine, trying and failing to distract herself. Every time her thoughts began to drift elsewhere, just when it looked as though she might forget for a few precious seconds, she was pulled back into the nightmare of her current situation. A jolt that felt like a fist in her stomach.

She had tried to piece together the blur that had been the last few days and the chaos and grief of the month that had preceded it. She felt sick with guilt at the thought of having let her children down. When they had needed her the most, she hadn't been there for them.

The situation with Ralph, her husband, had been brewing for a long time, and the split had been inevitable. But some of the ugly things he had said – his reasons for not being able to stay – had shaken her to the core. Her duty, first and foremost, was to the twins, but back then things had been falling apart. She had thought her head would burst if she tried to cope with anybody's feelings but her own. She had felt like she was in no fit state to look after her children: to protect them. The only place she could think of where they might be able to get away from it all was at their grandmother's, in England.

She had made a terrible mistake.

She had sensed it in her mother's terse note acknowledging their arrival. She had heard it in the tone of the brief calls she had received from the kids. Her fears had been confirmed by the bizarre and cryptic email from Jacob Honeyman, the old beekeeper she had known as a child. Then the worries had blossomed into full-blown panic when she'd taken the call from the Australian archaeologist in the middle of the night. When she'd been told that she must come straight away. That Rachel and Adam needed her.

That they were in grave danger.

Laura Sullivan, or someone close to her, had arranged everything. Within hours of the call, the taxi was outside on the New York street and the British Airways ticket was waiting for her at JFK airport. After a sleepless and anguished flight, Laura Sullivan had met her on the tarmac. She had been driven to an outlying aircraft hangar, where a helicopter had already been warming up, ready to whisk them down to the West Country. Whoever Laura Sullivan was, she clearly had powerful resources at her disposal.

It must be the TV company she works for, Kate had thought.

Like the twins, Kate had assumed that the aim of the

exercise had been to get them all home. Instead they were here. In this place, somewhere in England, in a room that looked like her own, but was not. She felt like a guest in a comfortable but featureless hotel. A hotel in a nightmare, where the door was locked from the outside.

Since she'd arrived her conversations with Laura had been brief, and mostly conducted over the ear-splitting clatter of rotor blades. The kids had been involved in an archaeological dig, Laura had said. There had been one or two unexpected results and it had been important to get them away from the site. Kate had had questions, many of them. Were they sick? Had they been contaminated in some way? Laura had been vague, had told her that it would all become clearer in the next couple of days.

And stupidly, Kate had believed her. *Stupidly…*

The guilt was worse, biting harder, because deep down Kate believed that what had happened was because of her: was something to do with the hidden feeling that had eaten away at her since she was a child. Feeding off her: curled in the pit of her stomach like a malevolent black worm.

The feeling that something bad had happened, and was about to happen all over again.

It was a feeling that had driven her from her mother; one that had made her leave England, but which had stayed with her even in New York. It was something she had tried to hide, to bury, like the shameful fact that she didn't have a father. But it had become woven into her personality and infected her with an all but permanent state of fear and melancholy.

Kate looked down at her chewed fingernails. And now she had been separated from her kids. Her babies. She had been tricked into letting them go. Laura Sullivan had tried to reassure her; had said that it would only be for a short time, until the experts – whoever they were – had checked that they were OK.

"Just until they're acclimatized," she had said.

Kate almost felt as if she had been sectioned in a psychiatric institution for her own protection. For the protection of her children. Her mind began to race. Maybe she had? Perhaps that was what this place was. As her brain began to fizz and bubble with bizarre and worrying thoughts, Kate threw herself back on the bed and buried her face deep in the starchy pillow.

And then she heard the door being unlocked.

She sat up as a man and woman came into the room. They were smiling, but their smiles were fixed and there was no warmth in their eyes. The woman offered her some medicine on a tray: a couple of pills and a small cup full of liquid. To make her feel better, the man said. Kate politely refused and then a coldness crept into their voices, and the man took Kate's arms, restraining her, pushing her back on to the bed.

Then the woman took a syringe from her pocket and Kate felt the needle prick...

5

Rachel and Adam struggled to keep up as Laura Sullivan strode down the endless white corridors of the Hope Project. They passed door after door, most of which were solid and closed. Others offered tantalizing glimpses through small, round windows into semi-darkened rooms. Rachel and Adam saw people, illuminated by bright work lights, hunched over desktops or computer terminals. Some appeared to be labelling fragments of wood and other material.

"What are they doing?" Rachel called after Laura.

"They're labelling up some of the Triskellion dig: carbon dating it. I'll show you later," Laura said. "Plenty of time."

They turned right down another corridor and, when she'd reached the far end, Laura opened a large, metal door with a passkey. They entered another passageway, though this one was darker and warmer, with some kind of matting underfoot and orange lights along the walls.

Laura smiled and winked at Rachel. "We're here." She

pushed open a pair of swing doors on their right and the smell hit them immediately. Rachel and Adam rushed forward and found themselves standing in a very familiar kitchen.

"Why am I not surprised?" Rachel said. She and Adam stared at the pots and pans, the chalkboard that Adam was forever drawing stupid faces on, the worktops they'd watched their mother preparing dinner on countless times…

"Not my idea, Rachel," Laura said. "Someone thought it would make you feel more at home while you're here."

"I appreciate it," Rachel said. It was a perfect facsimile of their kitchen, but still, it was *only* a facsimile. Same as her bedroom, she guessed. She wondered what was really outside the window. Some kind of projection? A hologram, even? "But I've never felt less at home in my life."

"Oh, I don't know," Adam said. He hoisted himself up on to a stool in front of the breakfast bar. "It's got to be better than Gran's."

As he sat down, a Chinese man marched in from another set of swinging doors on the other side of the kitchen. He was wearing an immaculate white chef's jacket and hat. He beamed at Rachel and Adam.

"Hi!" he said.

"Ah, Mr Cheung," Laura said. "This is Rachel and Adam, our guests. Rachel, Adam … Mr Vincent Cheung."

Mr Cheung hurried across to shake their hands, nodding and grinning from one to the other. "Let me see… Adam …

eggs over easy, crispy bacon, sausage links and hash browns, hold the ketchup … toast and OJ. Am I right?"

Adam nodded enthusiastically, almost drooling. Mr Cheung had rapidly described his favourite breakfast, detail by detail. The chef turned, grinning, to Rachel.

"And Rachel … I think, pancakes with maple syrup, yoghurt, wholemeal toast with peanut butter, mango smoothie and a decaff latte?"

Rachel could only nod, amazed, as her breakfast wish list was reeled off. She felt her stomach gurgle and realized just how hungry she was.

Mr Cheung tossed a steel spatula into the air, spinning it fast and catching it in his other hand. "Anything for you, Laura?" he said.

"Just a coffee, thanks, Vincent… Oh, go on, maybe one pancake wouldn't hurt. Syrup and whipped cream, obviously."

"Obviously," Mr Cheung said.

Rachel and Adam stared as the chef went about his work; a clatter of pans, the hiss of steam and an occasional crackle of flame providing counterpoint to his cheerful, if slightly tuneless, whistling. Minutes later, the breakfast bar was heaving with fantastic-looking food. Mr Cheung smiled as he watched Rachel and Adam dive in and begin devouring their meals. Laura smiled too, seemingly delighted at the improvement in the children's mood.

"Laura," Rachel said, through a mouthful of pancake. "You still haven't told us where Mom is."

"She's here," Laura said. She glanced across at Mr Cheung, who gave the children a thousand-watt grin and delivered a small bow before scuttling off into the larder.

"Where?" Rachel pressed the point.

"Here ... but in another part of the building," Laura said. "She'll be there for a while – just for a while, OK?" Laura seemed unwilling to say more, until she saw the look of alarm on the twins' faces. "Listen, there're a couple of things you have to understand. Your mum's been through a tough time at home. I know you have too, but your mum is really quite ... fragile."

Rachel and Adam did not need Laura to explain. They knew only too well about the black depressions that seemed to grip their mother for months on end. The herbal remedies, the pills, potions and therapies she had tried in an effort to quash her anxieties. Their dad had never really been much help. He was a scientist, not prone to self-analysis, and while his wife had lain curled up in a ball on the sofa, he had watched her as if she were an animal in a zoo and tried unsuccessfully to figure out what might be going on in her mind.

"But if Mom's in one of her moods, surely she's better off being with us?" Adam said. He cleared his throat and stuffed a forkful of food into his mouth, but the pleading in his voice was obvious enough.

Laura placed her hand on his and Adam blushed. "Of course she is," Laura said. "And she *will* be. But, you know,

she's only just been told about some of this new DNA stuff
... who you are, who *she* is. It's a big deal and it's come as
a bit of a shock to her, and it's going to take a while to sink
in. Also, we really need to keep you apart while we do some
preliminary tests on you guys..."

"Tests?" Rachel looked worried suddenly. "What kind
of—?"

Laura jumped in quickly to reassure her. "No, no, nothing
to worry about... You remember when I took DNA samples
from you? Swabs and a bit of hair. Just stuff like that, and
a few mental tests to see where your heads are at. You see,
your mum, being your closest relative, is of great interest to
us. Basic tests have shown that, although a lot of her genetic
make-up is the same as yours and Adam's, she doesn't carry
the ... *different* gene."

"You mean the *alien* gene?" Rachel asked bluntly. Laura
flinched slightly at the word.

"We don't know that," she said. "But what we do know is
that this different gene is probably what we call a *recessive*
gene; something that has lain dormant for many years and
only surfaced again when two other sets of genes – those of
your grandparents – came together. It's like a family of dark-
haired people suddenly producing a redhead, or a white
couple producing a black child.

"Or twins?" Adam said.

"Precisely," Laura continued. "And although the gene
seems to have skipped your mum, we still need to see what

similarities you share with her – thought patterns, emotional responses and so on – so we can see where the real differences lie. And to do that we need to run the same tests on her. But until we know how far your mental powers stretch, we can't let the three of you too close together, or it might interfere with our results. Does that make sense?"

Rachel shrugged. It didn't make any *less* sense than anything else. "So how long will these tests take?" she asked.

"Probably just a few days," Laura said. "We'll start tomorrow and see how we go. Then you can see your mum, I promise."

Rachel nodded slowly, but she was instinctively worried by the idea of tests, no matter how harmless Laura said they might be. She tried to project these thoughts on to her brother, to see if he shared any of them but, as hard as she tried, she could make no contact. He didn't even raise his head from his breakfast. He suddenly looked sleepy.

The lines of communication between her and Adam were down. Rachel wondered if there had been something in his food … in *her* food?

She was about to take the last mouthful of yoghurt, then stopped herself. She looked across at the worktop where Mr Cheung had been cooking.

There, apparently lapping at a spilt drop of maple syrup, was a large bee. As Rachel stared, she saw the insect's antennae twitch, watched as it moved round to face her…

Suddenly, Mr Cheung reappeared from the larder, and

hurrying across the kitchen, he brought the spatula down with a *"splat"* on the stainless steel worktop before Rachel or Adam could stop him.

He grinned at the twins as he wiped the bee away with a cloth and flicked the crushed body into the steel bin.

"Dead!" he announced.

6

The car is driving through the dark. Diagonal droplets of rain rush through the beam of the headlights and explode on the windscreen. The man at the wheel leans forward, trying to see better as the car tears round the tight bends of the hillside road. The woman next to him wipes in vain at the misty screen with a tissue. In the back seat the twins hold on tight to each other for comfort.

There are lights behind them, milky and blurred, fractured in the rear-view mirror. They are being followed. The man at the wheel is certain now – now that they have taken this remote road that climbs higher and higher, narrower and narrower, going nowhere.

The lights come closer and the man drives faster, then swerves. There are rocks on the road, suddenly vivid and jagged in the headlights. The car skids and, as if in slow motion, careers over the edge and down the bank towards the dark lake.

The woman cranes her neck round to look at her terrified

children for the last time, her mouth fixed in a horrified "O".
The twins' mouths mimic their mother's, but opening and shut-
ting like those of baby birds about to be torn from their nest;
their howls drowned out by the scream of rock on metal and
the shattering of glass.

The car turns on its side, then on to its roof, the front wing
hitting a huge boulder, and the vehicle flips nose to tail into
the blackness of the water, making barely a splash. Beneath
the surface, the mother's screams fall silent; her voice no more
than bubbles. In the darkness, lit only by the car's headlamps,
strands of hair swirl across her face like seaweed. Blood streams
from the man's head: mushrooming red clouds in the water.
Four small fists pummel silently against the back windows,
desperate to live.

Flying high above, Rachel sees the silver shape of the car as
it slips into the depths like a slow and heavy fish. Two bubbles
burst through the water like globes of mercury, and she sees
two small bodies kicking and thrashing, floating to the surface,
spotlit by the headlights of the black car that waits on the road
above.

Rachel sat bolt upright.

She was soaking wet and shaking as she ran her fingers
through her hair, which was thick and sweaty. She must
have drifted off. She had felt so sleepy after that bellyful of
food, and the room was so warm.

Laura had told her she must rest, that it would take her

a few days to get back to normal. Normal? Rachel wondered
if she would ever feel normal again. She looked round the
familiar bedroom with its unfamiliar feeling, searching in
vain for something that might control the temperature. She
realized that, although she still couldn't hear her brother's
thoughts, she had started dreaming again.

It was nothing to be grateful for.

The dream, with its nightmarish images of drowning in dark
water, had left her with a cold, sickening feeling of panic.

Who were the twins in the car?

They certainly hadn't been her and Adam; they had
never been in a crash, and the man and woman in the car
hadn't been their parents. Maybe the twins *represented* her
and Adam? Rachel thought. Maybe it was just a nightmare
about being torn from your parents? She screwed her eyes
shut and strained to recall the images from the dream. She
had felt as though she'd been in the car *and* high above it,
watching each terrible moment like the slow-motion replay
of a film. She recalled the faces, the inside of the car, with its
scuffed leather seats and the green lights on the dashboard.
She could smell the damp. She could see purple flowers
sprouting among the rocks.

Then she remembered a curious detail. The little girl on
the back seat had been wrapped in a plaid blanket, held
together by a large, gold brooch.

A brooch in the shape of a Triskellion.

* * *

Laura Sullivan sat in her office, staring at the screen of her laptop and wrestling with her conscience.

She had never questioned her own motives before, but it was becoming increasingly difficult not to. Surely she had done the right thing in bringing the kids here? They wouldn't have been safe in Triskellion after all, and going back to the States would certainly have been dangerous for them. Laura instinctively felt that something was wrong in the US. Van der Zee was certainly under pressure from his bosses to send Rachel and Adam over for more "invasive" testing, but so far he had backed Laura by keeping the twins in the UK. Laura had argued that they needed to be observed at close quarters, to be allowed to relax and develop in this safe environment with their mother near by. But was it right to be medicating them?

Laura shook her head, annoyed that she was not being honest with herself. They may not have run *surgical* tests on the twins, as she was sure was the intention of the Flight Trust hawks in the States, but they were *drugging* them. It couldn't be right.

She had bonded with Rachel and Adam and was sure that they felt the same way. She wanted to protect them, but there was no denying that they were the most important scientific find of the century. Maybe the most important scientific find *ever*. The project needed to keep the kids under control, she accepted that, but they had insisted on keeping them sedated for *four* days already while they did the scans. Today had been the twins' first day awake, and Laura could see that Rachel and Adam were disorientated and not quite up to speed. Laura had protested but the project was still tranquilizing their food. At least they had agreed to reduce the dose.

She slammed the lid of her laptop closed and stared at the wall. This wasn't archaeology; this was a violation of the kids' rights. Their childhoods had been hijacked, and she knew that she was one of the hijackers.

She'd thought her life would be very different...

She remembered the sun-bleached days of her own childhood in Perth. While her sister had played with dolls, Laura had walked around the yard in Subiaco, giving the rocks names and memorizing every dinosaur from the Triassic Period to the Cretaceous.

Even then, she had known that her future would revolve around her obsession with the past.

She remembered hunting for fossils, and how that had got her interested in the Aboriginal sites, the Songlines and the Dreaming stories. Invisible maps of the ancient landscape that the tribesmen kept alive in their heads or in songs and stories. They held the past, the present and the future in their *minds*. In time she had become intrigued by sacred sites in other parts of the world: in caves and long-forgotten tombs, in Bronze Age burial-grounds.

And one day, some odd pieces of information had started to add up.

That had been when the American guy at the University of Western Australia had approached her to work for the Hope Project. He'd read a few of her papers and had said that they were working along the same lines. In return for open access to her work, the Hope Project had offered Laura complete freedom to continue her research wherever she chose, saying it would open doors for her where necessary.

As someone who hated the red tape involved in gaining permission to dig foreign sites, Laura had welcomed the access-all-areas ticket that the Hope Project had seemed to offer. And while it had never been a priority, it had to be said that the large sums of money which appeared in her bank account overnight had made a big difference to someone who had lived on educational grants for ten years. Looking back, it had seemed like a golden opportunity.

And now she was complicit in the drugging of children.

Laura opened her computer again. She checked her email and then clicked on to her webcam. She was glad to see Rachel up and about and pacing her room, rather than lying dormant as she had been for the past six hours.

Laura watched for a few minutes. She slurped at the coffee she'd made earlier, but it was stone cold.

Rachel appeared to be looking for something, waving her hand in front of light bulbs and the air-conditioning vent. She looked as if she was searching for a bug ... or a camera. No sooner had Laura thought it, than Rachel spun round and looked up to the corner of the room and stared straight into the hidden lens of Laura's webcam.

Laura Sullivan felt herself flush hot, exposed, as Rachel climbed on a chair, then, waving a single finger in front of the camera lens as if to say "caught you", plugged up the spy hole with a wad of chewing gum.

Laura let out a sigh of annoyance as the picture on her screen went black; at the same time, she felt a sneaking admiration for Rachel that was stronger than the irritation. There was no keeping a good girl down, she thought. Maybe she *did* need sedating a little longer.

Like the others had.

7

R achel slammed the door behind her, furious at having discovered the spy camera, and angry at herself for not having discovered it sooner. She had felt for a while that she was being watched. It was no less than she had expected really, but still, to have it confirmed enraged her beyond belief. Could she trust no one? She was surprised to find that her room hadn't been locked.

She stormed down the corridor, rapped on her brother's door and threw it open without waiting for an answer.

"They're spying on us, Adam!" she shouted, knowing full well that Adam's room would be wired too. "Adam...?" She stepped into the room, but her brother was missing – his messy bed the only evidence that he had ever been there at all. Rachel slammed the door closed again and stamped off along the hallway that Laura had taken them down when they'd gone for breakfast.

Turning right towards the older part of the building, Rachel suddenly found herself face to face with a woman in a white lab coat. The woman, who was no taller than Rachel, looked shocked and backed against the wall, fumbling in her pockets for a set of small earphones and trying to avoid eye contact.

Rachel glanced at the double doors that led through to the kitchen and which could only be opened with a passkey.

Her anger made her bold.

"Open that door for me, please," she said to the woman. The woman looked frightened. She tried to avoid Rachel and slip round her, but Rachel cut off her escape with her own body. "I said, open the door! I'm not a prisoner; I'm a free person!"

The woman looked up briefly, her eyes darting left and right, trying frantically to avoid Rachel's gaze. "We're not… We're not meant to talk to you."

She tried again to escape, but Rachel dropped her shoulder and barged the woman back against the wall.

"Where's Adam? Where's my brother?" Rachel grabbed the back of the woman's short, bobbed hair, pulled her head back and glared straight into her face.

"Please! We're not even meant to *look* at you," the woman said.

Rachel gave the short hair a good yank. "Open it. *Now!*" She pulled the hair again for good measure, talking close; looking hard into the woman's eyes. Suddenly the resistance went from the woman's body. She ceased struggling and turned calmly back towards the door, swiping her passkey in the slot on the wall.

"There you go," she said, pushing open one of the doors, before smiling weakly at Rachel and continuing on her original path as if nothing had happened.

Rachel stood in the open doorway and watched her go. She was astonished at the sudden capitulation and felt guilty for the violence she'd used to make it happen.

"Sorry!" she shouted. But the woman didn't look back.

Rachel walked on down the corridor and into the empty kitchen. Mr Cheung's head appeared from behind the plastic curtains of the walk-in larder.

"Hi, Rachel. Hungry?"

"No, thank you," Rachel said briskly. "I'm looking for my brother." She continued past the breakfast bar and headed for the swing doors that led out of the kitchen on the other side.

Mr Cheung tensed, and stepped towards her. "Rachel, I'm sorry … I don't think…"

Rachel held up her hand imperiously, silencing the chef, then pushed through the double doors.

They led through to another part of the building, clearly older, with a thickly carpeted floor and pictures on the wall. Rachel could smell woodsmoke and hear faint classical music coming from somewhere at the end of the passage.

She followed the sound to an open doorway. Inside, the room was large and comfortable, with a roaring log fire and huge, over-stuffed armchairs and sofas. On the mantlepiece over the fire sat several antique-looking clocks, their workings exposed beneath glass domes. Glancing around the room, Rachel could see contraptions and mechanical figures of varying shapes and sizes perched on shelves in alcoves on either side of the fireplace. Sitting in one of the big chairs, behind a coffee table in front of the fire, was a middle-aged black man. He raised his head to look at her and smiled.

"Hello, Rachel," he said. His voice was a comforting, low rumble: a reassuring voice, an *American* voice. The man stood up and gestured for her to join him at the fireside. "Shut the door, would you?"

Rachel did as she was asked and stepped forward tentatively.

"Hi, Rachel," her brother said, his head popping over the back of the chair that had been concealing him.

"Come and sit down," the man said. "I've just been getting to know Adam a little. I'm Dr Clay Van der Zee." He held out his hand. "I guess I'm what you would call Head of Research here at Hope. Welcome."

Rachel shook his hand, noticing that it was smooth and dry and that his fingernails were very clean.

He ushered her into a richly upholstered chair next to Adam. "Well, your brother's got me well and truly beat," he said. He pointed to a board game set out on the table in front of him.

Adam grinned.

"It usually takes smart people at least eight attempts to

figure this game out," Van der Zee said. He shook his head in mock amazement. "Adam's getting it in two."

Rachel recognized the game, or at least the *type* of game. There had been a version of it at the holiday house they used to stay in at Cape Cod. The board had had ten rows of four small holes. In one row, a player would set up a code of four colours using pegs concealed behind a small shield. Then his opponent would try to guess the hidden combination by placing coloured pegs into the remaining holes on the board. The colour code could be worked out logically, by a process of elimination. But this game looked more difficult. There were six colours to choose from, which meant that there were virtually endless permutations. To get it in two would be sheer luck ... or something else.

"Adam's always been good at that kind of thing," Rachel said. Adam nodded, not about to contradict evidence of his own genius.

"How about you, Rachel?" Van der Zee said. "Fancy a game?" He turned the board towards her. "Hide your eyes, I'll set one for you."

Rachel felt childish covering her eyes while the man shielded the coloured pegs with his hand. When he was ready, he tapped her on the knee enthusiastically and nodded. Rachel looked up into Van der Zee's dark eyes. He reminded her of a spaniel: a little sadness dragging at the corners of his eyelids, but warm, friendly and eager to please.

"Ready when you are, Rachel," he said.

She stared at the empty peg holes on the board. No clues. She closed her eyes. She thought for a moment, then, as her pupils adjusted to the darkness behind her eyelids, colours began to glow: pulsating and forming sequences like traffic lights. As Rachel concentrated, the colours settled into a row: red, green, blue, yellow, red again and purple.

Rachel opened her eyes and looked at the board.

"Go on," Adam said. "I think I know it already."

Rachel picked up some coloured pegs from the box in front of her and placed them in order: red, green, blue, yellow, red, purple.

Van der Zee smiled to himself as Rachel's pegs went into the holes. Nodding, he lifted the small screen, revealing the same order of pegs that Rachel had placed on the board. Adam looked at his sister, a little disappointed that he had been bettered.

"In one," Van der Zee said. "Fantastic guesswork, or should I say, intuition?"

"Whatever," Rachel said, shrugging. Her gaze darted around the room, trying to disengage from the insistent eye contact of Van der Zee, who seemed forensically interested in her every breath and blink. "Why do you have so many clocks?" she said, trying to change the subject.

Van der Zee beamed. "They just fascinate me," he said. He stood up and gestured at the mantelpiece. "Each one is different. Their shapes, their sizes. But no matter how different they are, all those cogs work in harmony together to keep things regular, to keep the world on track. Individually, each cog is useless, but put them together and they become something else." Van der Zee meshed his fingers, making a nest of his hands and looked from Adam to Rachel. "Some clocks may have painted faces, disguising what goes on underneath; a blank exterior that gives no idea of the cogs tirelessly working away. But I particularly like these ones, because I can see how they work."

"I bet you're never late," Adam said, attempting one of his feeble jokes. Rachel winced.

Van der Zee laughed indulgently. "It's not so much the timekeeping I'm interested in; it's mechanical things synchronizing. Every little component is as important as the big wheels in making the whole thing tick. Look at these…" He directed them to the shelves on the left of the fireplace, to what looked like a collection of old dolls and mechanical toys.

"This one's real old, about two hundred years," he said. He pointed to the figure of a small stuffed monkey in a silk waistcoat sitting on a stool and holding cymbals in its paws.

"Is it a *real* monkey?" Adam asked.

"No sir," Van der Zee said. "It's what we call an automaton. Man-made. Like a little robot. I guess the fur might be real; most likely from a rabbit. It's French, I think. Look." Van der Zee pressed a lever in its base and something began to whirr and click. The monkey's head jerked sideways as if looking at them through black, glass eyes.

"It's creepy," Rachel said.

"Cool," contradicted Adam.

The body under the brocade waistcoat began to twist as if alive and, sounding like a musical box, it began to play a tinkling melody from an old nursery rhyme. Rachel shuddered and Van der Zee grinned at her. The monkey's head jerked forward again and thin leather lips drew back across its face in silent laughter, revealing a row of tiny, yellow teeth. The twins jumped as the monkey's arms suddenly sprang together, making tiny crashing sounds with the cymbals, its head flipping from side to side and its body twisting.

Van der Zee turned it off. "Great, isn't it?"

He showed them a few others: a tiny canary in a gilded cage that let out a breathy whistle and flapped its wings; a rubber-faced chef who flipped tin eggs in a pan; a clockwork clown in tartan pants who rotated and drank non-existent beer from a bottle. Rachel and Adam were most fascinated by the mechanical bee that flew on a wire round a small, metal honeypot, its wings whirring as they flapped.

"That one's *my* favourite too," Van der Zee said.

Rachel suddenly pictured their friend Jacob Honeyman and wondered what the old beekeeper would make of a mechanical bee. "Yeah, it's pretty neat," she said.

Finally, Van der Zee drew the twins' attention to a wooden box on top of his desk. It was about the size of a shoebox, but made from heavy, dark wood. Inlaid on the lid, in something that looked like bone, was a Triskellion. Rachel and Adam exchanged a look. Their fascination with the automata replaced by a stab of apprehension.

"I was wondering if you guys could give me any clues about this?" Van der Zee unlocked the box and lifted the lid. Rachel felt a throb of power, like a vibration, as the dull gold of the Triskellion was revealed, shining against a plush red lining. Van der Zee picked up the amulet and instantly the throb seemed to fade away.

"It's a Bronze Age artefact, as far as we know," Rachel said.

Adam could sense that she wanted to keep their answers simple; to give nothing away. "Most people think the design is of Celtic origin," he added.

Van der Zee looked from one twin to the other, as if he were trying to size them up. Apparently changing his mind, he casually put the Triskellion back in the box, locked it, and grinned.

"Here's a good one for you guys," he said. He guided them to an old-fashioned fruit machine in the corner of the room. "The one-armed bandit." He picked up a stack of worn brown coins and handed one to Rachel. "Put a penny in the slot," he said. "See if you can guess what you'll get."

Rachel dropped in the coin, pulled the handle and momentarily shut her eyes. Small red blotches immediately began dancing again in the darkness behind her eyelids.

"Cherries. Four cherries," she said. The wheels clunked into place. Four cherries lined up. Coins spewed from the metal mouth of the machine and bounced across the floor.

Van der Zee smiled. "A winner every time. Now that's what I call intuition."

"I'd call it *super*-intuition," said an Australian voice from behind them. Rachel and Adam twisted round to see Laura Sullivan standing in the doorway. Holding her hands, one on either side of her, were a small boy and a small girl, each wrapped in a bright, tartan shawl.

Twins.

8

I'm Morag, the little girl said.

Rachel was about to introduce herself, then realized that the girl had not opened her mouth. She watched the girl smile and straight away she could feel the connection between them, like a deep vibration moving along an unseen wire. It was a comforting feeling. Familiar…

Laura Sullivan cleared her throat as though prompting someone who had forgotten their cue.

"I'm Morag." This time it was spoken out loud. A high-pitched, sing-song accent. "And this is Duncan. We're twins, like you."

Like you.

Rachel stepped across and introduced herself and Adam. The younger children were both redheaded, their hair neat and shining, with co-ordinating clothes: trousers and skirt in green and black tartan. Adam thought they looked like the drawing on a biscuit tin he'd seen at his grandmother's house.

"You're Scotch, right?" he asked.

Morag giggled and shook her head. "Nooo! Scottish."

"Oh. Sorry," Adam said, not quite sure what he had done wrong. "You from Glasgow? Or…?" He knew Edinburgh was the capital, but hesitated as he had never been quite sure how to pronounce it.

"We're from Orkney," Morag said. "It's a tiny island. Have you heard of it?"

Adam hadn't. He leant down towards the boy who was staring at the floor as if studying the grain in the bare, polished boards. "Hello," he said. He waited for a reply, but the boy did not even look up. Adam glanced at Rachel and shrugged.

Rachel reached out to her brother. Adam seemed livelier than he had for days. Perhaps something had worn off? She could feel channels reopening…

He's shy, she said with her mind.

Or dumb, Adam replied with his.

"He's not dumb," Morag said out loud, shocking Rachel and Adam, pulling them up short. "Duncan just doesn't speak much."

"Doesn't he say *anything*?" Adam asked aloud, trying to cover his embarrassment.

Morag shook her head. "Nope, not really." She put an arm round her brother. He tensed, tapping the sole of his shiny black shoe against the floorboards.

Morag's stare was intense, and Rachel found it hard to drag her eyes away from those of the younger girl. The vibration that Rachel had felt moving between them was suddenly intensified – the gentle buzz becoming jagged and almost deafening.

"Rachel?"

Her brother's voice was all but lost beneath the noise in Rachel's head, as she struggled to break free from whatever was passing between her and the young girl: to disconnect herself.

And then it was over.

Rachel blinked and tried to clear her head. When she focused again, she saw that Morag was already skipping past her and throwing herself on to the lap of Clay Van der Zee. He welcomed her warmly, smiling happily at Duncan, who calmly followed his sister across the room and settled into a small armchair to the side of the doctor's desk. Morag stared at Rachel with big eyes, fixing her in their beam, calling out, trying to say something that Rachel could not read.

"Morag and Duncan have been here a long time," Van der Zee said. He pulled the girl close and squeezed her. "Ever since they lost their parents, more or less."

"Four years, eight months and twenty-three days," Morag said.

"They're part of the family."

Morag smiled widely at Van der Zee, but it was the kind of stiff smile a little girl puts on for a photograph: not quite real. She then turned the smile on Rachel, fixing her again with her eyes as if trying to tell her something. "Have you done the tests yet?" she said aloud.

Rachel dragged her gaze away from the strange little girl and looked across at Laura Sullivan. "Er, tomorrow, I think." Sullivan nodded.

Morag had obviously heard the apprehension in Rachel's voice. "It's really nothing to worry about," she said. Rachel guessed that Morag and her brother were eight or so, but suddenly the girl sounded mature beyond her years. "They're a lot of fun actually. Just like games."

"Speaking of which" – Van der Zee nodded towards the board lined with coloured pegs – "Rachel here is pretty good at this one. Almost as good as you in fact."

Rachel blushed and felt foolish. "Beginner's luck."

"Can I play her?" Morag squeaked. "Please?"

Van der Zee chuckled. "Maybe later," he said.

Morag looked sulky for just a second or two until Van der Zee muttered something to her and quickly the two of them were whispering and laughing, as if there were no one else in the room at all. Behind the desk a large wooden wall clock ticked loudly, and logs spat and crackled on the fire.

It was all very cosy, and horribly strange.

Rachel wandered across to join Adam. They exchanged nervous smiles with Laura Sullivan, who moved past them and began clearing away Van der Zee's board game.

Rachel kept her voice low. "Did you feel it?"

"What?" Adam asked.

"With the girl? Just after she told us about her brother not speaking."

"I felt something. I didn't know if it was coming from you."

"It was definitely *not* coming from me," Rachel said. "It felt like someone was drilling inside my skull. I don't know what was going on inside her head, but they weren't happy thoughts."

Morag laughed loudly at something Van der Zee whispered. "She looks happy enough," Adam said.

"Then it was like she just ... released me." Rachel remembered the vibrations surging through her. It had been like an arcade game at the fairground their mother took them to every summer. For a dollar, you could grip a plastic handle as an electric current passed through it – the voltage increasing every few seconds – while you tried to cling on, until the shocks became too painful and you had to let go.

Adam read her thoughts. "I was always good at that game," he said.

"Then she switched the power off, or something."

"They're the same as us, aren't they?" Adam said.

"Better than us. *Way* better..."

They stared at the Scottish twins for a few seconds. Morag was listening intently to something Van der Zee was telling her as she played with the buttons on her cardigan, while her brother sat a few metres away, staring into space, his face screwed up as he concentrated on something they could not begin to guess at.

Adam shrugged. "Maybe they've just been doing this for a lot longer than we have." His voice was certainly not loud enough to have carried across to where Duncan was sitting, but suddenly the boy looked over at them and gave Adam the hint of a smile.

Rachel looked across at Van der Zee. "Why does everyone around here wear those weird headphones?"

"Yeah," Adam said. "I thought they were listening to music, but—"

Van der Zee smiled. "Not music. And not everyone. I don't need to wear them."

Adam looked at Rachel. "Neither does Laura. Or Mr Cheung."

"They're inhibitors," Van der Zee said. "They protect the wearer from having their thoughts ... interfered with. That's one of the things kids like you can do." He gave Morag a squeeze and nodded at Duncan. "These two used to have quite a lot of fun with the staff until we kitted everyone out with the inhibitor kits."

"You're such a big spoilsport," Morag said, grinning.

"So how come you don't need them?" Adam asked.

"I used to work with the military," Van der Zee said. "We were taught certain ... techniques."

"Like anti-interrogation stuff? I saw that in a movie once."

"Right, and Dr Sullivan has learnt some of the same techniques." Van der Zee pulled a face at Morag. "Ways of handling troublemakers like these."

Like us, Rachel thought.

"What about Mr Cheung?" Adam said.

"Ah, now Mr Cheung is a special case. He used to be a Shaolin monk, did you know that? He has a very powerful mind; it's one of the reasons we hired him." Dr Van der Zee smiled. "That, and the fact that he makes the finest hot and sour soup outside Shanghai."

"I've got a surprise for you…"

Rachel turned at the voice, to see Laura Sullivan at her shoulder. "Another one?"

"Life's been pretty full of them lately," Adam said.

Laura nodded a little sadly, but then her features softened and broadened into a smile. "OK, but this is one I think you'll like." Adam and Rachel looked at each other. "Promise."

Rachel started to wonder how much Laura Sullivan's promises were actually worth, but, before the thought could take real shape, she was startled by a knock at the door. From the corner of her eye she saw Van der Zee ease Morag from his knee, as though something were about to happen that he did not want to miss.

"It's OK, Kate," Laura said. "You can come in."

Kate?

Before the name was out of Laura's mouth, Adam and Rachel were moving quickly towards the door and throwing themselves into their mother's arms as she stepped into the room.

"That's something special to see," Van der Zee said, patting Morag on the top of her head. "Very special…"

The phone on the desk across the room bleeped, and, grinning all over his face, Van der Zee dragged himself away to answer it.

Rachel hugged her mother close. "I was so worried," she said.

Adam rubbed his mother's arm. "We both were."

"We didn't know where you were."

"Or if you knew where *we* were."

"I'm fine," Kate Newman said.

Laura Sullivan stood near by. "I *told* them you were OK."

Wonderful as it was to see her mother again, Rachel knew that something was wrong. Insisting on seeing her had paid off, and Laura had obviously caved in. But now Rachel realized that Laura may have been protecting them: worried about the twins seeing their mother in this … state. Rachel clung to her, but there was no urgency in the embrace she received in return. Her mother's arms had been slow to move round her and there was no pressure from them against her back, no hand stroking her hair.

"Where's your room?" Adam asked. "Is it exactly the same as your room at home? Mine is, and Rachel's. And there's this amazing kitchen where you can get anything you want. This Chinese guy made me a BLT that was the best I've ever had. We could go there now. He'll make you a steak, or do you sushi, or whatever. Shall we go get something to eat? Are you hungry?"

Rachel wished that her brother would stop jabbering. There were other things she wanted to say to her mother; other questions she needed to ask.

Have they told you about us? About where we come from?

"I think your mum's tired," Laura said, moving towards them. "Maybe she should get some sleep. You can catch up properly later."

"Yes … tired," Kate Newman said. She spoke slowly, and her voice was a little slurred, as if she were having difficulty getting her mouth round even these simple words. "Later."

Rachel broke the embrace and stepped back. She tried and failed to look her mother in the eye. "Mom…?" She turned to look at Adam and caught a glimpse of Van der Zee putting down the phone and trying to communicate something to Laura Sullivan.

"What is it?" Rachel asked.

Kate sat down heavily on the sofa and Rachel looked from Laura to Van der Zee. There was an awkward pause, and fear fluttered in her stomach. Van der Zee coughed and broke the silence.

"I'm afraid I've got some rather bad news."

9

The coffin appeared to be in soft focus as it was lowered into the wet, black earth.

Looking up, Rachel realized that everything else seemed softened and blurred by the chilly blanket of mist that hung in the air. It shrouded the surrounding gravestones and dampened the sparse collection of mourners around her grandmother's grave. Rachel looked down again at the wet fans of fern leaves that brushed at her feet like skeletal fingers beckoning the living to join them underground.

The undertakers lowered the small coffin into the hole and tears sprang unexpectedly to Rachel's eyes. When Van der Zee had told her and Adam that Granny Root had died, both twins had felt curiously little reaction. Kate had shown no emotion beyond the fragile state she was already in. Rachel knew that her mother had not been close to Celia Root, and had left both her and England behind at the earliest opportunity. Perhaps because of this, neither Rachel nor Adam had felt that they had ever really connected with their grandmother. But now she was about to be put in the ground, Rachel felt a sudden pang of regret that she would never have the chance to really get to know her grandmother. For the first time in her life, someone she had known was never coming back.

An important link to her past had been severed.

Earlier, inside the church, with the Triskellion on the stained glass window glowing behind his head, the vicar had said a few kind words. He was a chubby, fresh-faced young man who had been seconded from a nearby parish following the unfortunate death of Reverend Stone. Although he hadn't really known Celia Root, he had clearly been well briefed. He had described her as a unique woman. A very private woman, but brave, loyal and stoic: one of a dying breed. He had talked about her career as a pilot both at home and in the United States, delivering aircraft from one air-force base to another. He had told them all how brave she had been after a terrible accident and how she had put up with constant pain for many years. He'd said she had been the backbone of the village.

Rachel had glanced at her brother. As far as they knew, their grandmother had been terrified of flying, incapable of boarding a plane to the US, let alone being able to fly one. Neither Granny Root nor their mother had ever mentioned it.

One of many things that had not been mentioned.

On the coffin, a black and white photograph in a silver frame had been propped up in front of a bunch of white lilies. It was an image Rachel was familiar with. A smart young woman with wavy hair and distinctive lipstick leaning against an old car, a cigarette between her fingers. She had once been so alive, so brave, so good-looking.

Rachel had felt her chest tighten and a sob rise in her throat. Standing in the front row of the church and feeling the eyes of the rest of the village burning into the back of her neck, she had reached out tentatively for her mother's hand. Her mother had taken it and squeezed, but the gesture had felt half-hearted. Automatic.

They had spoken little on the drive down, which had taken most of the night. The big silver people-carrier had left the Hope Project sometime in the small hours of the morning, and Rachel had tried, in vain, to see where on earth they were in the darkness. Once or twice, through the tinted windows, she'd seen a road sign caught in the headlights and had committed it to memory, just in case...

Rachel and Adam had spent most of the time sleeping, reading or listening to music. Any occasional bursts of conversation had quickly faltered and they had fallen into silence again. The twins had felt understandably nervous about returning to the village and had been inhibited talking to their mother with Laura in the car with them. Even when the others had been asleep, or Laura had been plugged into her laptop with headphones on, they'd still felt that somehow they would be overheard. Besides, their mother had also slept for much of the journey, and when she had been awake, the twins had been reluctant to press her. Ever since they had been reunited two days before, she had seemed distant: responding to most questions with a small, down-turned smile.

Rachel couldn't remember the last time her mother had seemed "normal". Not for months, certainly, but Rachel guessed – hoped – that depression, divorce and the death of her own mother had been largely responsible.

Rachel had returned her mother's feeble squeeze as the pall-bearers had stepped forward and lifted the coffin. Watched, unblinking, as they'd begun the slow march down the aisle, past the "Crusader's" tomb and out into the grey morning.

Now, as the modest assembly began to disperse from the graveside, Rachel and Adam could see who had come to pay their respects. One or two stepped forward to throw a handful of earth in after the coffin or to lay flowers: Hatcham, the landlord of The Star; the woman from the post office; a doctor who Rachel vaguely recognized. Of all the villagers present, the only one to make eye contact was Jacob Honeyman, the beekeeper. He shuffled forward, cap in hand, to sprinkle earth into the hole and lay a small handful of sweet peas, wrapped in kitchen roll, at the graveside.

Honeyman looked across at Rachel and Adam. He smiled grimly, winking and nodding as though desperate to communicate in the way he knew the twins could but lacking the facility himself.

Rachel and Adam nodded back.

We're fine, they said in their minds. In the cold morning away from the Hope building, they could clearly hear each other again. That they were fine was far from the truth and they said it mainly for their own benefit, knowing that Honeyman couldn't hear them. He nodded again, pulled his woolly hat on, waved, turned and walked away.

Standing away from the rest of the mourners, still and grey as if carved from the same stone as the graves, stood Commodore Wing. He had sat alone in the church, in the front row across the aisle from Rachel, Adam and Kate Newman, and had acknowledged neither his daughter nor his grandchildren. He had stared impassively ahead as the vicar had spoken, and later he had gazed blankly into the middle distance, barely noting the deference paid to him by the villagers as they had passed him on the way out.

"Why doesn't he talk to us?" Adam half whispered to his sister.

Rachel shrugged. "He's lost his son and ... well, I guess the woman he loved, more or less at the same time," she said.

"And somehow that's our fault?" Adam asked.

Rachel looked around the pretty graveyard and saw two other freshly filled-in graves, each covered in flowers and awaiting tombstones.

Hilary Wing's, perhaps? Reverend Stone's?

Rachel knew that she and Adam had not been directly responsible for either death, but she couldn't help wondering if Stone, Hilary or even their grandmother might still be alive if they had never arrived in Triskellion. Then again, perhaps what had happened had been unavoidable. The village had been brewing up to this for centuries and maybe their arrival had merely been the catalyst that had been needed to make it happen.

The mist turned to drizzle, and Rachel saw her mother begin to shiver, her teeth chattering audibly. The twins hugged her close, and saw Laura step forward from where she had been standing discreetly under a tree, next to the driver in dark glasses.

"We should think about getting back," Laura said, putting a black shawl round Kate's shoulders and opening an umbrella.

Adam looked around the near-empty graveyard and across towards the moor: two places where he had been more frightened than at any other time in his life. "Yeah, we should go," he said. "I'm looking forward to getting back."

Rachel looked at her brother, realizing for the first time that, despite the initial strangeness, she also felt oddly secure at the Hope Project. Not happy, not yet, but happier. Life had been chaotic and frightening until they had been taken from the village, but within a few days they had settled into a safe routine. Tucked away, insulated from the outside world.

Then the noise started.

At first Rachel thought it was a bee, circling somewhere

in the autumn chill. But then she realized that the buzzing was inside her head, louder now and more urgent, like a signal tuning into her frequency.

She looked into her brother's eyes. He wasn't getting it.

Then the voice came, a faint whisper, just audible through the buzz. Calling her name…

"Right, let's go," Laura Sullivan said, touching Rachel on the arm, and breaking the moment, before walking on.

Rachel felt giddy, as if she were about to fall over or throw up. She closed her eyes and rolled her neck, attempting to clear her head. Then the voice came through loud and clear, shouting out for her as though the speaker was lost: searching.

Rachel…

And when she opened her eyes, she saw him. Or at least she could have sworn she had. A strange, dark-haired boy, standing on the other side of the graveyard, shadowed and half hidden by a large memorial surmounted by a carved stone angel.

Rachel blinked, and he was gone again.

"You OK, Rach?" Adam asked.

Rachel said nothing. She stared across at the stone angel, to the spot where the boy had been standing.

"You look as though you've seen a ghost," Adam said.

Laura took Rachel's arm and began to lead her back towards the car. "Well, you're in the right place for it," she said.

* * *

There was a hot meal waiting for them when they got back to the Hope Project. They ate in silence in Mr Cheung's kitchen before being escorted back to their rooms.

Just before bedtime, Laura Sullivan knocked on Rachel's door. "Just wanted to see how you were doing," she said.

Rachel was exhausted. She couldn't think of much to say. "Thanks."

"You've had quite a day."

"I can't remember the last ... *ordinary* day." Laura nodded, like she understood.

Rachel sat, then lay down on the bed. She knew that, tough as the funeral had been for her and Adam, it would have been harder for their mother. She and Granny Root had not seen much of each other for many years, but Rachel knew how she and Adam felt about *their* mom; knew how strong the bond was. "How's Mom holding up?" she asked.

Laura took a few seconds. "That's actually what I came to tell you."

Rachel sat up quickly. "She OK?"

"She's fine." Laura couldn't quite meet Rachel's eye. "But she needs some time on her own. She's heading back to New York. She's—"

Rachel was off the bed and reaching for her dressing gown. "I want to talk to her," she said.

"You can't," Laura said. "She's already on her way to the airport."

Rachel felt her fingers curling into fists. She marched past Laura Sullivan and yanked the door open. "Well I want to talk to Adam then."

She marched along the corridor and barged into her brother's room, slamming the door behind her. He was sitting, hunched over, on the bed and when he looked up, it was clear that he had already been told. He looked like he was trying hard to keep it together. It was an expression Rachel had seen a lot since they'd arrived in England. Since the nightmare had begun.

"She's going to call us tomorrow," Adam said, sniffing. "When she gets home."

Rachel's mind was racing. Why hadn't she said goodbye? Wouldn't she have preferred to stay with them? Why had Laura seemed so ... shifty about it?

"Rach—?"

"I saw Gabriel," she said, under her breath.

"When?"

"Today, in the churchyard. At least I *think* I did."

"Did he say anything?"

"Just my name." Rachel stared out of the window at the fake New York skyline: the lights in the skyscrapers, the blur of neon against a manufactured night sky. She thought about her mother on the way back to the real thing. "It was like he was waiting... He had this look on his face."

"What sort of look?"

Rachel shrugged. "You know what he's like. It's hard to tell."

"Come on!" Adam leant forward. "Happy? Sad? What?"

Rachel turned from the window and stared hard at her brother. "It seemed like a warning," she said.

10

Over the next few days, Rachel and Adam settled into their own, very separate routines. There were things they did together – the two hours each morning spent studying with a Hope Project tutor, mealtimes in Mr Cheung's kitchen – but increasingly, and without really discussing how or why, they spent less and less time together.

When they weren't eating and studying, the tests continued in Dr Van der Zee's testing suite: Adam doing exercises to gauge the speed of his reflexes, while Rachel was put through her paces doing increasingly complex memory tests and guessing games with Laura Sullivan. Between sessions they were free to enjoy what Van der Zee called "down" time. Adam would spend most of his listening to music or perfecting his already considerable skills on a variety of high-tech computer games, while Rachel preferred to sit in her room. She told Laura Sullivan that she was happier on her own, that she wanted some time to think about things, to sit quietly and read. But her mind quickly lurched into places that were dark and disturbing and it was hard to concentrate on any of the books that Laura provided for more than a few sentences at a time.

Impossible to concentrate on reading once she began to hear Gabriel again.

Each evening at ten o'clock – five p.m. New York time – they would arrive at Laura Sullivan's office and wait impatiently for the telephone call from their mother. Laura would leave them alone, as most of the time there would be tears. Then, once it was over, Adam and Rachel would head back to their own rooms.

To their own, very different thoughts.

It had been a week or so since the funeral in Triskellion but as Rachel sat on her bed, she was still disturbed by the memories of that day. The damp, grey headstones, the mist that hovered around them like the breath of the dead. The face of Commodore Wing – her grandfather – statue-still and desolate and that of the boy who watched from the other side of the graveyard.

Rachel, what are you doing?

Gabriel's voice had been clear for days now, and determined. It woke her in the middle of the night with that same question, the tone harsh and exasperated. It nagged at her during the day: desperate … adamant.

Rachel, don't believe them.

The voice – demanding, questioning, urging her to doubt – had changed her mood utterly, and while Adam had seemed to grow happier, content even, with their situation, Rachel had retreated into herself. She had all but stopped eating. She had become surly and uncommunicative, prone to tantrums. She had barely fought off an overwhelming urge to lash out at Laura Sullivan or Clay Van der Zee; to scratch and bite until she drew blood, until she could feel her own blood rushing through her veins like a powerful, gorgeous current.

Rachel ... Rachel!

And the voice was growing stronger...

She tried to focus on something else, thinking back over that evening's long-distance phone conversation. Her mother was a long way away, but the distance between them could no longer be measured in miles alone.

"Mom, is everything OK?"

Her mother had sounded weak and worn out. Even something as simple as crying seemed to exhaust her. "It's the stuff with your dad, that's all."

"Divorce stuff?"

"Nasty stuff, baby. Letters from lawyers, seeing a different side to someone you love, you know..."

"When can we come home?"

Static had crackled through the silence. "I don't know. I think you're probably ... better off where you are right now."

"How long?"

"New York's still the same you'll be glad to hear. Still noisy and crowded. Still a million miles an hour—"

"How *long*, Mom?"

Rachel had pictured her mother closing her eyes; covering her mouth to stop her breath from catching.

"I don't know. I don't know anything. Listen I need to go…"

"Mom."

Rachel! Don't believe them.

"I'm fine, though, baby. I promise."

And Rachel had heard the lie, like a bad attempt at a foreign language. And she had known that her mother was suffering and that she could not say anything that might make her feel worse than she already did.

And so Rachel had lied too.

"I'm fine as well," she had said. "We both are…"

Rachel was startled by the knocking at the door, but couldn't bring herself to get up from the bed and answer it. She stared at the door, her head still swimming with the image of her mother, alone and unhappy, in an empty apartment.

Whoever was at the door knocked again.

"Rach? It's me."

Adam.

"I'm tired, Adam. I just want to go to sleep."

The door opened and Adam strolled in, as though he hadn't heard what she'd said or was choosing to ignore it.

He moved around the room for half a minute, looking through Rachel's CD collection, picking up a magazine and flicking idly through it.

"What do you *want*, Adam?"

Her brother looked across at her. Blinked and shrugged. "I'm worried about you, that's all."

"About *me*?"

"Yeah, course. You're not eating, you don't really talk to anyone…"

"You're the one who's behaving like a freak. As though all this is … *normal*."

Adam looked back down at the magazine. "I'm just trying to make the best of it."

"Best?" Rachel was suddenly buzzing with anger. "This place is a prison." Adam pulled a face, like she was being stupid. Rachel raised her voice. "We're being tested like lab-rats, we're not allowed to go anywhere—"

"They're trying to keep us safe."

"We're prisoners, and you're acting like it's some kind of high-class hotel."

"Right. How many prisoners get to eat whatever they like? Have this much fun?"

"*Fun?* You think this is OK? Just because you can play computer games and eat cheeseburgers all day? What about our *lives*, Adam? What about our friends? What about Mom?"

Adam flicked through the pages more furiously. The skin

tightened round his mouth. "We don't have to go to school. That's a good thing, right? And we're … special in here. It's like we're stars or something."

"What have they been telling you, Adam? What have they done to you?"

Adam tossed the magazine back on to the bedside table and stood staring at the floor. His fists were clenched at his sides. "Nobody's done anything. We're just different, OK?"

Rachel lay back on the bed and turned away from her brother. Closed her eyes. "Yeah, different," she said.

They stayed as they were for another minute, the silence only broken by the artificial, ambient sound of night-time New York and the distant hum of machinery from somewhere far beneath them. Finally, Adam marched across to the door and opened it.

He turned in the doorway. "So this is the way it's going to be? You're going to be … difficult?"

Rachel didn't bother to open her eyes. "One of us has to be."

"Yeah, and it's always you."

"Can't you hear him?" Rachel asked.

"Hear who?"

"Gabriel."

Adam's voice was thick with derision. "That's another good thing about this place. I haven't heard from *him* since we got here. If you ask me, we're better off protected from him."

"You're not *listening*."

"I'm not *interested!*"

Rachel's fingers tightened round the edge of her duvet. She wanted to jump up and slap her brother hard. She held her breath and lay still until she heard the door close.

Adam was still angry when he walked into Laura's office a few minutes later. Laura was at her computer. She turned to look at him, taking off the wire-rimmed glasses she wore to read.

"Any luck?"

Adam shook his head, feeling himself blush. He thought Laura looked beautiful without her glasses. "I did my best."

"Don't worry."

"She's just being stupid."

Laura summoned a smile. "It's going to take her a little longer than you to settle, that's all."

"She's the stubborn one, always has been."

"She's very bright," Laura said. "Kids like you usually are. She'll figure out what's best eventually."

Adam grunted; he wasn't sure. His eyes drifted towards Laura's computer screen. There were lines of data down one side, some kind of map on the other. Laura cleared her throat and quickly hit a button which replaced the desktop with a screensaver image of an arid Australian landscape: the vast, flat-topped mountain known as Uluru.

"I think you should go and get some sleep."

Adam nodded. The argument with Rachel had left him feeling wrung out and ready to drop. "I'll try again tomorrow," he said. "See if I can bring her round."

"Probably best to leave it a day or two," Laura said. "But thanks. And thanks for trying…"

When Adam had gone, Laura switched on a monitor mounted on the wall of her office. She stared at the CCTV image fed from the new, hidden camera in Rachel's room: the picture of a girl curled up on her bed, legs pulled up, turned in on herself. Laura adjusted the volume and listened to the slow, steady sound of Rachel's breathing.

After a minute, Laura went back to her laptop; back to the work which had occupied the best part of her life for almost ten years. She stared at the maps and the graphs, the analysis of a hundred sacred archaeological sites. The results of the tests on Rachel and Adam, Morag and Duncan, and others. She tried to concentrate, but she wouldn't get any more useful work done tonight.

She hoped more than anything that what she'd told Adam was true. She prayed that Rachel would become … easier to deal with.

She did not like to think about what might happen otherwise.

Rachel lay in her room and thought about the fight with Adam. They had always fought, same as any other brother and sister, but not like this. Not about anything this important.

More than anything, she wished her mother was there to sort things out, but Rachel knew she was going to have do it on her own.

She opened her mind and waited for Gabriel's voice. She needed his guidance now more than ever: his reassurance.

When the voice came, it was no more than a whisper, from lips that she could almost feel pressed close to her ear.

It told her to sleep.

11

Rachel falls down, down, down through the night sky, tumbling through the air and falling silently into the inky water. Neither cold, nor warm, but somewhere near her own body temperature, it feels painless as the water invades her ears and nostrils, pours into her throat: becomes part of her. She is pleased to find that she does not panic as she drowns, that she is almost comforted as the peaty water suffocates her. Yet she is not dying, she is becoming one with the soft water which pulls her, like a returning mermaid, towards the two pale orbs of light that shimmer deep in the lake.

Rachel kicks and swims, moving effortlessly deeper and deeper, closer to the twin lights and to the silvery shape from which they shine. A car balances on an underwater ledge, teetering over a deep abyss that falls away into a cold, bottomless dark.

Closer now, green ribbons of frilly weed dance slowly in front of her eyes, part concealing the rubbery shape of the diver, his legs kicking behind him, frog-like, as he struggles to *pull something through the car's open window. Then, hand in hand, two small bodies wriggle free like fish from a net, and float upwards, coaxed and guided towards the surface by the beam of the diver's torch.*

Closer still, and the torchbeam searches for something else…

A woman's face, her hair swirling about her cheeks; the water inside the car, pink with her husband's blood; her white palms banging helplessly at the window of the locked door.

Don't worry, Rachel thinks, swimming close to the window and pressing her hands to the glass, signing to the woman. I am here. Help is here.

Then the horror: the terrible lurch as the car pitches forward, is levered forward by the two, glass-faced frogmen who push it over the edge. Rachel holds on tight to the door handle as the car suddenly slips. She is pulled down with it, unable to do anything but watch as the woman's face smashes into the glass. The woman's eyes open wide in terror, then she falls back as though resigned to her watery death.

And Rachel lets go; the sleek, silver flank of the car slipping past her. She floats up, watching the pale lights become paler still as they go down, down, down…

The bed was soaking wet.

Rachel kicked off the soggy blanket and felt her pyjama bottoms and T-shirt. They were soaked as well, as though she really had been swimming. She could not go back to sleep like this, could not stay in bed at all. She would need to sleep somewhere else, get herself a hot bath and change her clothes.

Rachel climbed out of bed and immediately felt shivery. She was coming down with something, that was it. That was what the horrible dreams and the night sweats were about. That was why she could not gather her thoughts. She was feverish.

She tried to switch on a light, but nothing seemed to be working. Perhaps the electricity supply was switched off at a certain time. She wrapped a towelling bathrobe round her damp shoulders and sat in the armchair, wondering what to do with herself. She drew her knees up but was unable to get comfortable, so she got up again and began wandering aimlessly around the room, bumping into things.

Rachel stood in front of the window and drew back the curtain. She stared out at the night sky. Fresh air would help, she thought. Being a city kid she was no great fan of open windows. In her experience, the air they let in was dirtier than the air they let out but, staring at the starry blue-black sky, she craved a lungful of crisp night air, to clear her head of this fuzzy feeling. To clear it of the horrifying images from her dream. She fiddled with the catch and slid the window open, but found no change in air temperature at all, nor any hint of a breeze.

God, she was stupid!

She knew that it was all just an illusion. That the city,

the skyline, the night sky were nothing more than a projection on a continuous loop that changed according to the time of day. It might not even be night-time at all. Delirious, Rachel began to speculate. Maybe they were just being told that it was night-time, so that they would be more disorientated; so that they could be more easily controlled and observed, like specimens in a laboratory.

Rachel felt a sudden fury at the deception. She needed to get out. She would get past the screen and see exactly what was on the other side of the window and out in the world beyond.

She would breathe fresh air.

She stood on a chair and wrenched the blocked-up webcam out by its roots. Its red eye died instantly. Climbing down, Rachel grabbed a shoe and smashed the heel hard into the centre of the plasma screen, which flashed and went black. Her hands felt round the edge of the screen and she tried to wrench it from the wall. She found a wooden coat-hanger and wedged it into the top corner of the screen and levered the box forward. There was a sudden *"crunch"* as the screws gave and the screen was left dangling from the wall, wires curling from its back. Rachel pulled it to the floor, revealing a wall of solid breezeblocks.

She punched the wall, hurting her hand. She stamped on the already dead screen, cursing her own stupidity: why had she even thought there *might* be a window behind the screen? For all she knew, she might be fifty feet underground.

She was suffocating. She needed to get out. Now.

Rachel stumbled into the corridor, which was lit by dim night-lights that threw yellowish puddles of light every few metres. She paused outside her brother's door. Their argument had been brewing for days. Ever since she'd mentioned Gabriel, every time she'd tried to connect with his mind, she'd felt him resist; mentally, he was turning his back on her, putting up a barrier.

She reached for the door handle and stopped. He would almost certainly be asleep. Even if she woke him up, he would try to talk her out of any action.

Rachel continued on alone, padding along the corridor, turning left then right, towards Laura Sullivan's office. As she approached, she hugged the wall, seeing the glow of Laura's laptop casting shadows on the open door. Laura must be working late. Rachel sidled along to the door as quietly as she could, not really sure whether she was trying to evade Laura, or if she needed to talk to her. She peered in and saw that Laura was not in her office anyway. The familiar image of Uluru on Laura's screensaver glowed like a red beacon in the darkened room.

Rachel stepped in, instinctively closing the door behind her. She glanced up at the webcam monitor but saw only interference on the screen. It was not surprising, considering the damage she'd done to the camera. Perhaps Laura had gone to investigate, Rachel thought. She could be back at any moment...

Rachel walked over to the desk and touched the keypad. Uluru evaporated, revealing an open document. Rachel stared at the map, at the images of mummified bodies.

A heading: TRISKELLION SITES

This she had to read.

Take the key, a voice said. *Take the key.*

Rachel started, turned round and saw nobody there, realizing simultaneously that the voice had come from inside her own head.

Take the key, Gabriel said again. Rachel looked around the room, her eye finally settling on Laura's white lab coat on the back of the door.

Hanging next to it was a plastic passkey.

Rachel ran down corridor after corridor, doors sliding open as she swiped the key in the slot at the side of each one. She knew that she would only have a short amount of time to find her way out before someone realized she was missing. She reached the end of another passage and turned left.

A man. With a torch.

Rachel stopped dead, silent in her bare feet, and turned back, moving quickly down another corridor, lit at the end by a single night-light. She ran towards the light and, as she approached, saw that she was coming to a dead end. She looked to her right and saw the steel doors of a lift.

The only way out.

She swiped the key through the electronic reader. A tiny

light turned from red to green and the doors slid open. Rachel jumped in and the doors closed behind her.

The lift juddered and began its descent. Rachel caught a glimpse of herself in the grubby mirror that made up the back wall of the lift. She looked like a bag lady: her towelling robe was patchy with brick dust and her damp hair was matted round her white, sickly face. Suddenly the lift lurched to a halt and the doors opened again.

This corridor was different. It was as if she had descended to the bowels of the building. While the upper storeys were shiny, and clad in glass and laminate, this level was concrete and industrial and wet underfoot. Huge pipes and ducts ran overhead and warning symbols on yellow triangles and red plaques were screwed to every surface.

Rachel walked slowly, the hiss of steam and the clanking of a distant pump echoing in her ears. Thick, plastic curtains barred her way, and Rachel pushed them apart. She found herself at the entrance to another room and *another* pair of plastic curtains, through which a milky light was visible.

She stepped through and the strong smell of disinfectant assaulted her nostrils. As Rachel looked around, she realized she was in some kind of laboratory. Surgical instruments were laid out along stainless-steel work surfaces and, in the centre of the lab, a heavy-duty hospital gurney dominated the room. Rachel's mouth fell open, the scream frozen in her throat. Her knees began to shake uncontrollably as her guts turned to water.

On the gurney was the naked body of her grandmother.

Rachel took in the white, withered legs, the face still made-up but shrunken now and bony, like a mummified Egyptian queen. The once-perfect hair had been scraped back and flattened against the tiny head, and Rachel gasped at the jagged Y-shaped cut that ran from her grandmother's throat to below her navel and at the ribs that lay splayed against the cold steel.

Rachel took a step forward. She pressed her hand against her mouth to stem the flow of bile that rose up in her throat. She saw that, like her Bronze Age ancestors three thousand years before, Celia Root had been disembowelled.

12

Mr Cheung had outdone himself. It was a five-course Chinese banquet with all the children's favourites: hot and sour soup; crispy duck with pancakes and plum sauce; Singapore noodles; slow-cooked pork with water chestnuts.

"You must have been cooking for days," Adam said.

Mr Cheung bowed, accepting the compliment, but then shrugged it off, reddening slightly and straightening his chef's hat. "Just something I knocked up," he said.

They were gathered round the large wooden table in Mr Cheung's kitchen. Dr Van der Zee and Laura Sullivan sat, one at either end, with Adam and Rachel on one side, and Morag and Duncan on the other – the younger children boosted by small, tartan cushions.

"Delicious as always," Van der Zee said, biting into an over-stuffed pancake. He held up a wine glass and swallowed quickly. "Can I propose a toast?" He waited while the others held up their own glasses, the children's filled with

Mr Cheung's special gingery punch. "To Mr Cheung obviously, and to the Hope Project. To us!"

"To us," squeaked Morag.

Duncan nodded and took a mouthful.

Laura echoed the toast, but Rachel sensed that her enthusiasm was a little forced. Rachel herself clinked glasses with her brother, and they both beamed at Van der Zee, who returned their smiles with interest.

"To us!"

Rachel cleared her throat before anyone else could say anything, and raised her voice. "And I just wanted to say … thank you."

"Please," Laura said. "There's no need."

"Yes, there is," Rachel said. "I've been a nightmare and I've made everyone's lives hell." She looked at Laura, then at Van der Zee. "And I'm sorry. No excuses, I've been a royal pain in the butt, so thanks for … sticking with me, OK?"

Next to her, Adam smiled and shook his head. "I think I deserve some kind of medal. I've had to put up with you for fourteen years!"

"Why were you a *royal* pain in the butt?" Morag asked innocently. "Are you some kind of princess or something?"

There was a good deal of laughter round the table and Rachel blushed. Laura leant across and squeezed her hand, and Adam pretended he was going to be sick when Rachel kissed him on the cheek. Once the laughter had died down, everyone went back to tucking in, while Mr Cheung brought out extra plates of crispy seaweed and steaming tureens of soup. The room was filled with the sounds of spoons and chopsticks flying across the crockery – each plate and bowl decorated with a single word, glazed in blue:

HOPE

"I'm so pleased that you've turned the corner, Rachel," Van der Zee said. "I always knew you would."

"Even when I was behaving like a brat and smashing my room up?"

"Well, I *hoped* you would, anyway." He grinned. "And obviously, I'll be sending you a bill for the camera."

Rachel laughed and turned to Laura. "I'm OK now, though, *really*. It's taken a bit of getting used to, but I think I'm going to be happy here."

"Course you will," Morag said. "It's brilliant here. It's fit for a princess even."

"Princess Pain-in-the-Butt," Adam said.

Laura leant close to Rachel as the conversation grew more animated round the table. "I'm over the moon," she said. "I couldn't stand you being so miserable."

Rachel apologized again. Laura certainly looked as though she meant it. She seemed genuinely pleased, but more than that, she seemed relieved, as though some disaster had been averted.

Mr Cheung brought out fresh lychees and banana frit-
ters for dessert and the kids piled them on to their plates.
Van der Zee leant back in his chair and watched them eat.
When Rachel caught his eye he winked at her. He was like
the head of a family, she thought, enjoying the contentment
of a happy brood.

"I couldn't eat another thing," he announced. "What
about you, Dr Sullivan?"

Laura shook her head. "Stuffed."

"Not even one little fritter?" Mr Cheung asked. "Very
good."

"Sorry," Laura said. "I don't think I'll be eating for the rest
of the week."

Van der Zee pushed back his chair. "Perhaps we should
leave the children to it then," he said. "It's time you and I
had a chat anyway." He stood up and moved away from the
table, leaning down as he passed to ruffle Duncan's hair, to
kiss the top of Morag's head. "Enjoy the rest of your evening,
everyone, and don't make yourselves sick…"

Rachel caught the nervousness in Laura Sullivan's eyes as
she stood up to follow Van der Zee, who had left the room
without looking back, as though knowing she would follow.

"I've *never* been sick," Morag announced proudly. "She
tossed a fritter across the table to get Adam's attention.
"Have *you* ever been sick?"

When the adults had left and the table manners had de-
teriorated still further, Rachel and Adam spent half an hour

talking nonsense with Morag, while the ever-silent Duncan nodded and occasionally half smiled beside her.

Rachel caught Adam's eye, heard his voice inside her head. *Well done*, he said. *I never knew you were such a great actress.*

You were pretty good yourself, she said back, and watched him smile. Actually, she was almost enjoying herself, enjoying the fact that, once again, her brother was communicating with her, though the pretence was proving to be even more of an effort than she'd imagined.

It wasn't *all* an act, of course. She *was* happy…

Happy that she had a plan. Happy that she knew the truth, that she was only hours away from seeing her mother. Pulling her close and telling her everything, hard as it was going to be.

Happy that she and Adam would soon be free.

"Fortune cookie?"

Rachel looked up to see Mr Cheung standing over her, brandishing a small basket. She leant across and took a cookie, cracked open the shell and pulled out the message.

"Well? Good fortune or bad?" Cheung grinned.

Rachel unwrapped the slip of paper and read: HOPE IS NO GOOD WITHOUT LUCK. She looked up at Mr Cheung, searching for something in his eyes.

But they were as dead as beads. Blank as the black eyes of the mechanical monkey.

13

"Look, I'm glad the girl seems to have come around," Van der Zee said. "But we don't seem any closer to getting results. *Real* results."

Laura Sullivan stood a little nervously in front of Van der Zee's desk. He had called her into his den, which, despite the cosy surroundings, usually meant that there was something serious to be discussed. His tone was friendly enough, but he was a man who rarely raised his voice. Laura had come to learn that the more relaxed Clay Van der Zee sounded, the more trouble she and everyone else were likely to be in.

That smile – wide and welcoming – was usually a very ominous sign.

"Research takes as long as it takes," Laura said. "You can't rush it. Not if you want results that *mean* anything."

"There are ways to … speed things up."

Laura took a step towards the desk, shaking her head, trying to keep the tremor from her voice and sound as though she was fully in control. Maintaining a scientific detachment.

"We can't do that. There's so much we can learn from these kids."

"Taking the other route will teach us a great many things."

"It's short-term thinking," Laura said. "It's ... stupid." The detachment was quickly falling away.

"It's merely a suggestion."

"Surgery should only ever be used to *benefit* those it's performed on!" Laura was shouting now.

"It might be of enormous benefit to millions of others. It's a last resort, of course."

"More like a final solution." Laura could feel her face reddening, her fists clenching inside her pockets. "It's what the Nazis did."

Van der Zee raised a hand, nodded slowly: a signal for Laura to keep calm. "Relax, Dr Sullivan. I'm merely trying to remind you that there *is* another option, how ever distasteful you and I may find it. You know very well that there are those to whom I'm answerable, and many of them favour a swifter resolution to this research. The Hope Project is far from being poverty-stricken, but the funds for this research will not last for ever. Do you understand what I'm saying?"

Laura could do little but nod. She understood well enough. She had seen what had been done to the body of Celia Root in the project's autopsy suite a few days before.

"Obviously, we are focusing on the children and what they know," Van der Zee said. "What they are capable of, but—"

"They're capable of extraordinary things," Laura said. "And it's going to take time because even *they* don't know what those things are yet. We'll learn when *they* learn."

The hand was raised once again, held in the air for a few seconds before it drifted across to the wooden box in the corner of Van der Zee's desk, turned the key and lifted out the highly polished lid. "But … we still do not know what *this* does." Van der Zee reached into the box. "What the Triskellion *is*." He gently lifted the three-bladed amulet from the plush red interior.

Laura held her breath. She studied Van der Zee's face as he laid the Triskellion in his palm. He stared at it, lifeless in his hand, and there was something desperate in his eyes. As though he were urging it to *do* something.

Laura remembered the rush of excitement when she had first seen one of its golden blades clutched between the entwined skeletal fingers of the two bodies uncovered in the village that bore its name. The blade had seemed to glow, to give off something … *more* than light. That light had died quickly, and the Triskellion – the amulet made up of all three blades – had seemed no more than a simple artefact when she had taken it from Rachel after she'd been drugged; when Laura had handed it over to Van der Zee for testing.

Those tests – metallurgical studies, X-ray fluorescence spectrometer analysis – had revealed next to nothing of the object's properties or origins, and since then it had been under lock and key in Van der Zee's den, in the hope that the children themselves would provide a way to unlock its secrets.

"I want to know why this is so important, Dr Sullivan," Van der Zee said. "I want *this* to be the focus of your work with the Newman children."

"I'll do my best."

"I know you will." Van der Zee carefully laid the Triskellion back in its box. When he twisted the key in the lock, it sounded like a small bone snapping. "I know you want what's best for the children."

"Same as you, right?"

"Of course." He was placing the key in the top pocket of his waistcoat when a buzzer sounded on his desk. He picked up the phone and listened, then placed a hand over the mouthpiece. "I'll let you get on then," he said. "I've got a transatlantic phone call being patched through. I'm sure you can figure out who that will be from."

Laura did not know the name, but from the look on the director's face, she knew it would be one of those to whom he was answerable. One of those who favoured Dr Van der Zee's other option.

Clay Van der Zee waited until Laura had left before taking a deep breath, flicking a switch and greeting his caller. The man on the other end told him that it was a very hot day in New Mexico, but that, then again, it was always a hot day. Van der Zee tried describing the weather where he was, but was cut short. The caller had limited time for such small talk.

"We've seen the data and there doesn't seem much to get excited about."

"Actually, I was just saying the same thing." Van der Zee hit the speakerphone button, got up and moved round his desk. "Passing that very message on to Dr Sullivan."

"That's good."

"We've had some trouble with the Newman girl. It's held things up a little."

"Trouble?"

"Just high spirits. I'm sure you know what fourteen-year-old girls can be like. Do you have children?"

The question was ignored; dismissed as irrelevant. "*Had* trouble, you said?"

"I think we're over the worst."

"Let's hope so. Did she get the message?"

Van der Zee was momentarily confused. "Sorry…?"

"Dr Sullivan? Loud and clear, I hope."

"Definitely." Van der Zee began to pace the floorboards in front of the fireplace. "She's very bright. The best there is in her field. We're lucky to have her."

There was a pause, a few seconds over and above the delay on the line. "I think *she* is the lucky one, doctor. To be given this opportunity."

"Oh, she understands that."

"And does she understand that we will not wait for ever?"

"I made it very clear. I'm every bit as keen as you—"

"We are happy to go down the … enlightened route,

as long as the results prove to be significant. Failing that, we will learn what we can from a more straightforward examination of these children. We have the Scottish kids…"

"Morag and Duncan."

"Right. We can continue testing them and they don't seem to be giving you the trouble you're getting from the newer arrivals. These Newman kids are older, adolescents almost. Maybe we need to cut our losses and get what we can from more … mature specimens. You see what I'm saying?"

"I do. And so does Dr Sullivan."

"OK, then. We're singing from the same hymn sheet."

Van der Zee stared into the fire, jumping slightly as it spat a spark on to the rug. He stamped it out.

"We're not monsters," the caller said. "She needs to understand that."

"Of course not."

"To answer your previous question… Yes, I do have children."

Van der Zee slipped off his jacket and dropped down into the armchair next to the fire. "How many? Boys or girls?"

But the line was already dead.

14

Adam's door opened, and one look at his pale face told Rachel that her brother was now one hundred per cent on message; the terrible images she had recounted were still horribly fresh in his mind. He did not want to stay a minute longer.

Adam hoisted his backpack over his shoulders and braced himself, adjusting the straps like a soldier about to go into action. Rachel put out a hand and squeezed his shoulder reassuringly. Hearing him swallow loudly, she pulled him towards her and held him in a tight embrace.

"Let's roll," she said in a hoarse whisper.

"One thing," Adam said. Rachel released him from her grip.

"How are we going to get out?"

Rachel fished inside her sweatshirt and pulled out the passkey she had stolen from Laura's office the night before.

"That'll do nicely," Adam said. He switched off the light to his room and closed the door behind him.

They passed the first three doors without any problem, and without seeing anyone, but this part of the complex – the more domesticated zone – was always quiet at night. They turned into the carpeted area that led towards Clay Van der Zee's den.

"Why are we going this way, Rach? If anyone's around, it's most likely to be Clay."

"Because we need to take the Triskellion, don't we?" It was more of a statement than a question.

Adam stopped dead in his tracks and looked deflated. "Oh, man. That piece of metal got us into this mess. Can't we leave it here, where it's safe?"

"It's not safe here, Adam. This place is dangerous. Anyway, we need it to keep *us* safe." Rachel said. "It's saved our lives once already. It's the one thing we know will protect us."

"But Clay is looking after it. He's protecting it."

"He keeps it in that spooky wooden box, Adam. Not exactly keeping it under strict scientific supervision, is he? I think he's pretty obsessed by it. Remember the effect it can have on people; what it did to Dalton? We're better off with it in our hands than in theirs."

Adam sighed in resignation. "C'mon then," he said.

The door to the den was locked with a big, old-fashioned mortise lock, a reflection of Van der Zee's fascination with ancient mechanisms, cogs and wheels. Adam knelt down and put his eye to the keyhole, but it was too dark to see anything.

"That's blown it," he said.

"Try this," Rachel said. She knelt beside him and held a pocket torch to the keyhole. Adam dug out a small penknife from his backpack and began to fiddle with the lock, in the hope that something might spring open.

"What are you doing?" a small voice piped behind them.

"Oh my God," Rachel gasped. "You nearly scared us to death."

She looked into the smiling face of Morag. Duncan, by her side as always, looked from Rachel to Adam and back again, his face fixed in its customary expression of bemused seriousness.

"We're just trying to get into Uncle Clay's room," whispered Adam, trying his best to make it sound like a cosy adventure. "We left something in there and we need it back."

"And Uncle Clay's gone to bed," Rachel said, attempting to endorse Adam's weak story.

"No, he hasn't. He's in a meeting," Morag said, with a decisive nod of the head. Rachel and Adam looked at each other. This was good news.

Rachel knew it was a long shot, but asked anyway, "Do you know where he keeps the key, Morag?"

"We don't need a key. Duncan can open it for you, can't you, Duncan?" Morag pointed towards her brother in case anyone was in doubt as to who he was. Duncan thought for a few seconds, then nodded once.

"Would you open it for us, Duncan?" Adam asked.

The small boy stepped forward and placed his hand over the lock. He shut his eyes for a moment and breathed in deeply, then, taking his hand a few centimetres away from the lock, he rotated his palm anticlockwise, quickly flicked it through ninety degrees and took his hand away. Rachel and Adam almost laughed at the boy's expression of concentration: his little pink tongue poking from the corner of his mouth. They heard a *"click"* followed by a deep, metallic *"clunk"* and Adam's smirk of amusement switched to an expression of wonder as the door creaked open.

"Neat trick," he said.

Adam stole into the room first and Rachel followed, the ticking of the many clocks sounding extra loud in the dark stillness. The beady eyes of the various automata stared down at the two of them as they crept across to Van der Zee's leather-topped desk. Suddenly, a mechanical whirring noise caused Rachel to freeze and grab Adam's arm. The whirring was quickly followed by a ratcheting sound as, high up on the wall, a cuckoo sprang out of its clock and piped the hour. Other clocks on shelves around the room began to chime one by one, all slightly out of synch. Eleven o'clock.

Rachel let out her breath and Adam switched on the desk lamp. He leant across and pulled Van der Zee's wooden box towards him. "Locked," he said. He grabbed a letter opener from the desktop and attempted to force the box open. "Come on!" After a few, frustrating seconds, he moaned as the flimsy knife bent against the hard wood of the lid.

Rachel looked round at the younger twins, who had again crept up behind her without a sound, their faces lit eerily by the desk lamp.

"You'll break it!" Morag chirped. "Duncan?" She pointed at the box.

Moments later, the small boy was pressing his hand against the box's keyhole, the same look of intense concentration etched across his face. After a few seconds, the lock clicked and he calmly lifted the lid. Adam looked at him in amazement.

"Thanks, Duncan. Awesome. You're a pretty useful guy to have around."

Duncan almost smiled. Adam reached into the box, took out the Triskellion and placed it down carefully on the desktop. The amulet immediately began to glow, golden against the glossy green leather.

"It knows you're here," Morag said. She watched, open-mouthed, as the Triskellion began to oscillate, vibrating and rotating, picking up speed and rising from the box. It spun above their heads and cast rays of golden light around the room. "It knows we're here too," she added, smiling, her wide blue eyes and red hair catching the dancing fingers of light.

The children watched in silent awe as the Triskellion spun around the room, setting the clocks chiming and every one of Van der Zee's automata whirring and jiggling. The tiny metal chef flipped his tin eggs over and over. The mechanical monkey grimaced and clashed his cymbals together as if in celebration of the magic unfolding in front of his glass eyes. The Triskellion finally came to rest, spinning slowly down and landing in Rachel's palm like a giant golden butterfly.

"Let's get out of here," Adam said.

Rachel nodded, stuffing the Triskellion into her backpack, and the four children filed quickly into the corridor as the clocks ceased chiming and the room became silent once again.

15

Rachel and Adam moved along narrow, darkened corridors that ran through the old part of the Hope Building. They emerged after a few minutes into the new, high-tech research area and moved towards where they knew the main entrance to be. All the while, creeping through the shadows, Morag and Duncan were tripping along behind them.

"You guys should be in bed," Rachel said. "It's pretty late." She and Adam would never have got this far without the little twins, she admitted to herself, but now it was time to shake them off.

"Oh no," Morag said. "We're coming with you." She nodded to her little brother and, in perfect unison, they each held up a small, tartan suitcase.

"Why? You can't—"

"Please," Morag begged. "We don't want to disappear like the others."

"Others?"

"There were … other twins before you came."

Before Rachel had a chance to learn any more, she became aware of a light in the small office to their right. As they approached it, a security guard stepped out, his protective glasses perched on his head and his inhibitor earplugs dangling on their wires round his neck. Rachel and Adam instantly hit the wall, disappearing into shadow, leaving Morag and Duncan standing squarely in the middle of the corridor, suitcases in hand. Just as Rachel realized that there was no time to pull the twins to safety, the guard turned and froze: caught in the twin headlight stare of Morag and Duncan's bright blue eyes.

Rachel watched, aware suddenly of a distant buzzing; aware that it was growing less distant. A sound she hoped meant help was coming.

"Hello, Martin," Morag said.

The guard fumbled quickly for his glasses and struggled to plug in his inhibitors, but he was forced to flap his hands at the bee which had appeared from nowhere and had begun buzzing angrily around his head. Suddenly, the panic died in his eyes and his hands dropped, hanging uselessly at his sides as the bee landed and began to crawl lazily across his shoulder. The man could do no more than stand, like a waxwork, transfixed by Morag and Duncan.

"Now. You're going to escort us, and our friends, to the main entrance," Morag continued. The guard stared, his mouth opening and closing slowly. "Dr Van der Zee's instructions."

"OK," the guard said. Though it was clearly too late, he plugged in his earphones, pulled down his dark glasses and walked slowly away down the corridor.

Morag grabbed her brother's hand and grinned at Rachel and Adam as they emerged from the shadows. "Don't dawdle," she said.

Rachel began to move, pulling Adam with her, while watching the bee rise from the guard's shoulder and drift away ahead of them.

"We haven't got long," she said.

The guard, whom Morag called Martin, dutifully took them down corridors, through sliding doors and past other security guards, punching in key codes, giving passwords and swiping keys as he went.

"Martin's a nice man," Morag explained to Rachel as they trotted along behind him. "Me and Duncan caught him out once before. We made him think he was a cat. It was really funny, he kept purring and licking milk off the floor. We got in trouble when Dr Van der Zee caught us and Martin rubbed himself against his leg." Rachel grinned. "Not as much trouble as Martin, mind you," Morag added.

Not as much trouble as he'll be in this time, Rachel thought.

They passed another security office near the main entrance and Martin spoke to the duty officer. He filled in his name and number in the log and assured the officer that he was escorting all four twins on the explicit instructions of Dr Van der Zee.

"That's all right then," the duty officer said, before going back to his crossword.

As the guard slammed the steel doors behind them and the chilly night air filled their lungs, Rachel and Adam could not quite believe how easily they had got outside.

In front of them, the wide gravel driveway snaked off past the near-empty car park towards the security hut. Rachel looked at the field of long, wet grass that stretched out to the right and saw the tops of the dark trees in the woodland beyond. She didn't want to hang around in front of the building a moment longer.

"Let's head that way," she said, pointing towards the trees. All four jogged off through the wet grass, keeping their heads low. The trees appeared to be around thirty metres ahead of them. Adam led the way, Duncan trotted behind him with Rachel following, holding Morag by the hand. The tops of the trees, now distinguishable as tall pines, loomed closer and closer, and Rachel began to allow a mounting sense of relief to take hold of her, now that they were clear of the building.

Then Adam tripped and fell.

A few steps ahead of the others and only a few metres shy of the trees, Adam had been caught by a low-level tripwire concealed in the long grass. Instantly the whole area was lit by strong halogen spotlights and the two sets of twins could do little but stare at one another in horror, their faces bleached out and bewildered in the harsh white light.

The *"whoop-whoop"* of an alarm sounded from the Hope complex and Adam struggled to his feet. Bells rang and lights flashed as he joined the others, staring back towards the main building, rigid with panic. Turning to the woods, lit now by the powerful spotlights, they could clearly see the fence that ran the whole perimeter of the grounds. A high fence topped with razor wire and marked with warning signs of lightning flashes and skulls. A fence that was crackling with the thousands of volts of current that ran through it.

A fence that Duncan, in his panic, was running towards…

Adam threw himself after the boy, his feet slipping on the wet grass. "Duncan! *Duncan…!*"

But the boy was too far ahead, and Rachel, Adam and Morag could only watch in silent horror as the small figure jumped up and grabbed at the wire, as a jagged blue flash delineated his body, then scream as his limp form was thrown back several metres and delivered lifeless at their feet.

An unearthly, terrifying howl came from Morag as she dropped to the ground in front of her brother. A noise that sounded as if her lungs were being torn from her by unseen hands: an ear-splitting pitch that wailed above the sounds of the alarm. Rachel fell to the ground and clasped the girl's shaking body to her own, feeling the sharp sting of guilt that told her she was responsible for this tragedy.

Adam gently touched Duncan's chalk-white face, placed a finger under his nose to feel for breath, but there was none. He put his hand on the shallow chest, feeling for movement beneath clothes that were still smouldering. Nothing. He grabbed at the limp wrist and felt for a pulse. Not a flicker. Adam looked at Rachel and his lip began to quiver as hot tears spilled from his eyes and splashed on to the body of the dead boy.

The three living figures huddled together in the wet field and howled, their escape attempt clearly over as guards began to pour from the building out into the grounds. Rachel and Adam pressed their heads together in anguish.

Suddenly, Morag's sobs subsided and she pulled away from Rachel and Adam, as if to look at Duncan again, to confirm that the worst had actually happened.

"Michael?" she said, suddenly calm: "What are you doing here?"

Rachel and Adam looked up, expecting to see another security guard, but instead they saw somebody they already knew.

Gabriel.

Speechless, they watched as Gabriel crouched down and put one hand to the chest and the other to the smooth forehead of the dead boy. Rachel's jaw dropped as Gabriel took his hand away from Duncan's head, keeping his left hand on the boy's chest, and her tears came even harder as she saw Duncan's eyelids flicker, and then open.

"That was amazing," Duncan said.

All four twins looked up at Gabriel with expressions of wonder.

"Duncan spoke!" Morag said.

"Wouldn't you?" Gabriel replied, helping Duncan up on to wobbly feet. "Now come on, or they'll catch us."

Gabriel nodded in the direction of the main building, where guards with flashlights were beginning to swarm towards them.

Gabriel took the ten steps towards the perimeter fence and calmly lifted the wire up from the bottom, creating a gap for the others to crawl under. The children looked stunned as sparks fizzed and cracked around him, but Gabriel suffered no ill effect from the electricity that was obviously surging through his body.

"Hurry up!" he said. "I can't stand here all night."

Quickly, the four twins scrabbled underneath the fence and into the woods. Gabriel followed them, leaving the fence as he had found it and melting into the blackness.

Kate Newman was woken by the alarm.

The siren had snaked into her nightmare, pulling her from it, clammy and breathless, and as she sat up in bed there was only one thought in her head.

The children.

She flung back the blankets and rushed for the door, slammed her palm against the panic button and waited for a guard to arrive. She tried to shout, but the words would not come clearly: the drug she was given at night was far too strong.

Waiting for the guard, the dream came back to her in flashes. Home. Walking in the park. The three of them safe, somewhere bright and familiar. She hammered on the door, then clapped her hands tight against her ears, the siren deafening, making her feel as though her brain was bleeding.

Finally, the door opened and one of the nurses stepped in. She shouted above the relentless wail of the siren, ordering Kate back against the wall a second before she raised the needle.

Kate knew it was useless to fight – if she wanted the children to stay safe. Nothing was her choice any more, least of all the bogus calls from America every evening.

The siren continued to scream and suddenly the lights flickered, just the once. She wondered what was happening. It had to be something to do with the children.

Held as she was, deep underground in the Hope Project's sick bay, she could only pray that Rachel and Adam were all right. Could only wonder when any of them would see one another again.

part two:
flight

16

They hid in the woods until the search was abandoned.

Gathered beneath an enormous pine tree, they watched as the lights of those looking for them moved through the woods like giant fireflies. At times the guards passed within a few metres of them, and on several occasions they heard the voice of Clay Van der Zee close by, marshalling his troops, and then later telling them that they would begin searching again at first light.

Rachel knew that it was Gabriel keeping them hidden; that when it suited him he could make himself, and those close to him, all but invisible in plain sight. At one point Gabriel had leant across and whispered to her, the shouts of the search party echoing in the darkness around her, "They can't see the wood for the trees."

Once the searchlights had been switched off, they broke cover and began to move cautiously through the forest. The darkness was almost impenetrable and the noises of unseen animals caused the little ones to clutch each other as they followed Gabriel on a path that wound through the columns of tall trees. Rachel knew she would have been every bit as frightened as they were, had her head not been buzzing with a thousand questions. She could see the fear clearly enough on Adam's face.

"We need to move faster," Gabriel said.

After half an hour or so there was a break in the blackness ahead of them, a momentary sweep of passing headlights and eventually they stumbled on to a narrow country road.

"Where to now?" Adam asked.

Gabriel thought for a few moments, staring along the road in both directions. "Away," he said.

Adam nodded. "Sounds good."

Rachel was about to ask one of her many questions, but was distracted by the crying behind her. She turned to see Morag and Duncan sitting on the side of the road, the girl being comforted by her brother. Rachel asked if she was OK.

"I'm cold," Morag said.

Rachel realized that it was only adrenalin keeping the chill from her own bones and that the temperature would continue to drop: none of them would be able to spend the night outdoors.

"There's a car coming!" Adam shouted suddenly. Morag and Duncan climbed excitedly to their feet and the children gathered together as Adam stuck out his thumb in preparation.

"It's not going to stop!" Morag shouted.

The headlights grew bigger and the growl of what was clearly a large truck got louder as it rumbled towards them.

"Course it will," Adam said. "Who wouldn't pick up a bunch of kids out here in the middle of the night?" He stretched his arm out, the hope tight round his mouth as the lights moved across his face.

"Come on, come on," Rachel muttered to herself as the truck got closer, but could only watch in alarm when, at the very last second, Gabriel moved past her and stepped calmly out into the middle of the road: the screams of the younger children were lost in the roar of the truck's engine as it bore down on him.

"Michael!" Morag shouted.

Rachel stared. Why did they keep calling him that?

"Michael" raised his hand and the light seemed to bounce off his splayed fingers, reflecting back into the truck driver's face in a tangle of thin beams.

The truck driver *knew* he was in big trouble.

He knew too that he shouldn't have been driving while he was tired, that he shouldn't have been going as fast and that he *certainly* shouldn't have had that pint of beer with his dinner. Still, running into a random police check on a road he'd driven down a hundred times before was unlucky. When he'd seen the policeman step out into the road and start waving him down, he could only curse his bad luck and wonder what he'd done to deserve it.

The policeman had looked deadly serious. The truck's headlights had reflected off the badge on his cap and the buttons on his blue uniform. Big, *big* trouble…

The truck driver had slammed on the brakes, realizing that the policeman was closer to him than he'd first thought. Why didn't the stupid idiot get out of the way? He'd closed his eyes, praying that he'd be able to stop in time and that, if he did, he'd manage to hold on to his driving licence.

As it was, he got away with it.

He sat there in the cab, holding his breath, and when he finally pulled away again he couldn't help wondering why he'd been stopped in the first place. The policeman – and they were *definitely* looking a lot younger these days – had done nothing but give him a good telling off and kicked his tyres a couple of times before sending him on his way. What had been the point of that? It bothered him as he drove on, pointing the big truck east, towards the coast, wide awake now and watching his speed this time.

Didn't the police force have better things to do?

Within a few minutes of the truck starting up again and rumbling away down the road, Morag and Duncan were fast asleep in the back. In the half-light from the driver's cab, Rachel watched them curled up among the sacks of turnips and potatoes as though it was the most ordinary thing in the world, and envied their innocence.

She lay back against the side of the truck, Adam next

to her and Gabriel sitting opposite them. Gabriel smiled, pleased with himself, but Rachel resisted the temptation to ask how he'd talked the driver into taking them. There didn't seem much point. She knew Gabriel could get people to do almost anything and besides there were other, far more important, questions she wanted answers to.

"Why didn't you come and get us?" she asked. Gabriel said nothing. "When we were in there. I know you could have done it. You could have just come in and got us out of there. Why—?"

"I couldn't just walk in there. I'm sure that's what they would have wanted and … I was waiting for you."

"What?"

"Biding my time until you made a move. Until you took the initiative. I can't do this all by myself, you know. I need your help. I needed *you* to get the Triskellion. It's stronger in your hands."

Rachel thought about it. She remembered Gabriel's face when she'd seen him – or *thought* she'd seen him – in the churchyard, the faraway look in his eyes. Waiting.

"So it's like some kind of battery that needs us to charge it up?" Adam asked.

"It's all sorts of things," Gabriel said. "All sorts." He looked far away again, closing his eyes and letting his head drop. When he looked up again, he was smiling. "You have *got* it, haven't you?"

Rachel reached over and laid a hand on her backpack.

"In there," she said. "I couldn't leave it behind. Something told me we had to bring it with us."

Gabriel nodded, satisfied. "Good. Now we can get out of here. Get the others."

The last few words had been mumbled and Rachel couldn't be sure she had heard correctly.

"What others?"

Adam leant forward. "Other *Triskellions*?"

Gabriel closed his eyes again and leant back as though going to sleep. After a minute or so he said, "You didn't think there was just one, did you?"

The truck drove on through the night. Lights passed across the children's faces as they moved on to bigger, better-lit roads. Rachel pulled an empty sack round herself when it got colder but, though it warmed her a little, she was still unable to sleep.

"Why do they call you Michael?" she asked. She nodded towards Morag and Duncan. The young boy moaned softly in his sleep and threw out an arm.

Gabriel shrugged, his eyes closed. "I've got a few names," he said.

"What, like aliases?" Adam asked.

"Yeah, I suppose. Comes in useful, keeps people guessing."

"Are you hiding your real identity then?"

"We all are," Gabriel said.

Gabriel's face was in shadow. His voice sounded no more

than a whisper, although they were shouting above the noise of the engine. The sacks piled all around them were dark, hulking lumps, and loose vegetables rolled and rattled on the bare metal floor as the truck swayed on the bumpy road.

"So where are we going?" Adam asked.

"I thought you were happy enough with 'away'," Gabriel said.

Rachel turned to her brother and looked at him like he'd gone mad. "We're going home, *obviously*. We're going to see Mom." She turned back and stared at Gabriel, who was now sitting up, eyes wide open. "That's right, isn't it?" The look that passed across Gabriel's face was like ice pressed against her skin.

"Your mother isn't at home."

"We've spoken to her," Adam said. "She called every night from New York."

"She's not in New York," Gabriel said. He glanced towards the road. "She's back there."

Adam moved across the floor of the truck. "Don't be stupid!" he shouted. "She's at home. We *spoke* to her."

"She never left," Gabriel said simply. "It was a trick, that's all."

Rachel got to her feet, almost falling as the truck lurched. She grabbed on to the metal rail that ran round the inside of the trailer.

"Turn the truck round."

"It's not me driving it," Gabriel said.

Now, suddenly, Rachel was shouting too. "Do whatever you did before then. Get the driver to stop and turn round. We have to go back."

Gabriel shook his head.

"You don't understand," Rachel said. "We can't leave her. She's our mother … she's in danger. We *have* to go back."

By now Adam was on his feet next to her. They stared down at Gabriel, urging him to move, to do something, but the boy looked calmly back at them as though unable to comprehend their panic.

Rachel glanced across to make sure that Morag and Duncan were still asleep, then lowered her voice. "Their parents were killed. I saw the whole thing in a dream. I guess I must have tapped into their thoughts, or memories, or whatever." She was aware of Adam's look. She hadn't told him: had not wanted to frighten him. "Their car was driven off the road and there were frogmen waiting under the water. They took the children out and left their mother and father to drown." She waited for a reaction from Gabriel, but did not get one. "I *saw* it. Those people back there are murderers." She looked across at Morag and Duncan again. "They orphaned those kids…"

"Take us back," Adam said. "Now!" His fists were clenched, as though he was a split second from falling on Gabriel and beating him into submission.

"I know exactly what they're capable of," Gabriel said, "and they won't hurt your mother. I promise. She's safe as long as they're still trying to find you." Now he was the one who seemed desperate, and there was something like a plea in his voice. "We've got to keep moving; we've got to stay ahead of them." He held out a hand to each of the twins but let them drop when neither Rachel nor Adam responded. "I know how you feel, really, but you'll have to trust me."

Rachel and Adam looked at each other, then finally, after a few long seconds, they moved back to their own side of the truck and dropped down among the heavy sacks of vegetables.

There was nothing else they could do.

Rachel thought about the argument she'd had with Adam the night she'd discovered their grandmother's body. She remembered what he had said about Gabriel: how their lives were easier where they were; how they were better off without him. At the time Rachel had been furious, but now she could see what her brother meant.

She pulled the sack back round her, lay down and cried quietly.

She'd wanted to get away so badly, had been certain it was the right thing to do, had talked Adam into it. But now, within a few short hours of being reunited with Gabriel, she felt as though their lives were no longer their own.

She felt uncertain and terrified and out of control. As though anything might happen.

None of it good.

17

Rachel was not sure how long she had been asleep when she was woken by Gabriel; how long since the truck had stopped. This time she took his hand and let him pull her to her feet. Adam was already awake, and Morag and Duncan stood next to each other at the back of the trailer, suitcases in hand, ready to go.

The driver had already left by the time they jumped down from the back of the truck and looked around.

"What's that smell?" Morag asked.

"Gasoline," Adam said.

Rachel could smell something else. They had pulled up in a vast lorry park, the huge wagons lined up side by side. In the distance, she could see a ragged line of lights moving slowly across an expanse of blackness. She stared until she saw the blackness heave and shift and realized that the line of lights was actually a huge boat.

"It's the sea," she said.

A high chain-link fence ran along three sides of the lorry

park with a long, low building making up the fourth. A cafe. Through the steamy windows Rachel could see groups of men gathered at tables inside, eating or reading newspapers. She read the sign: MY OLD DUTCH. "I don't get it," she said.

Adam pointed to a far bigger sign high above them: HARWICH FERRY TERMINAL. CROSSINGS TO THE HOOK OF HOLLAND.

"That's where they wear clogs," Morag said. "Where the tulips come from." Adam nodded and Morag looked pleased with herself.

Rachel looked at Gabriel. "Why are we going to Holland?"

"It's the quickest way out of the country."

"Why do we have to leave the country?" she asked. Gabriel said nothing. "Why this way though? Why not just catch a plane to Africa or Australia or whatever?" Rachel continued.

Gabriel began walking towards the exit and shouted back over his shoulder. "Come on, you heard what Morag said. Don't you want to try on some clogs?"

Rachel and Adam heaved up their backpacks and started to follow. After a couple of steps, Adam looked back and saw that the younger twins had not moved. He trudged back.

"Come on, I know you're tired, but—"

"We're hungry," Morag said.

Adam nodded, immediately aware of his own stomach grumbling. It seemed a long time since dinner the evening before at the Hope Project. He shouted to Gabriel and

Rachel, who walked back to join him. "The little ones are starving," he said. "*I'm* starving." He nodded towards the cafe.

"There isn't time," Gabriel said.

Rachel was already walking towards the steamy windows, drawn by the inviting smell that had begun to waft across the car park. "We have to eat," she said.

The place was far smaller than it had looked from the outside; no more than a dozen small, Formica-topped tables lined up around a serving hatch. While two fat men worked at an enormous, sizzling griddle, an equally large woman, with her grey hair pulled back and wearing a dirty apron, bustled between the diners with steaming mugs clutched between her fingers, or carrying plates, three at a time.

"It's not like Mr Cheung's kitchen," Morag said.

Adam stared as a plate piled high with bacon, eggs and baked beans passed within a few centimetres of his face. "It'll do."

They crowded round a table in the window and Rachel waved the waitress over. A badge on her apron said "Dawn". If she was curious as to what five unaccompanied children were doing ordering breakfast at two o'clock in the morning, she didn't show it.

Gabriel said he wasn't hungry. Morag and Duncan each ordered beans on toast, while Rachel and Adam plumped for what the menu described as the "Hungry Trucker's Breakfast Special". Dawn looked blank when Adam asked for eggs over easy and even blanker when he asked if there was any maple syrup. She pointed him towards the plastic container on the table, brimming with sachets of ketchup, vinegar and brown sauce.

"Brown?!" Adam said, when she'd gone. "That's just the colour of it, right?"

The portions were enormous, but they each cleared their plates easily enough. Nobody spoke, and Gabriel stared out of the window as he waited for them to finish.

"Are we done?" he asked, as the last knife and fork clattered on to an empty plate.

"Duncan needs the toilet," Morag whispered.

Gabriel nodded and watched as the girl led her brother away. He had emptied a sachet of sugar on to the table-top and was absent-mindedly tracing a pattern with his finger. Rachel looked across, instantly recognizing the familiar shape: the three interlocking blades.

"You mentioned others?" she said. Gabriel looked up. "When we were in the truck."

Gabriel went back to tracing the shape of the Triskellion with his finger. A quick, smooth motion: his fingertip squeaking against the plastic table.

"You never really answered Adam's question," Rachel continued.

Gabriel glanced to his right and saw the waitress coming back to clear the table. He looked into Rachel's eyes and casually scraped the grains of sugar over the edge of the table.

"There are three of them," he said quietly. "Three Triskellions."

When Morag returned with Duncan, the waitress came back to the table and handed over the bill. Gabriel picked it up and looked at her as if he was confused.

"We've paid this already."

"You what?"

Gabriel kept looking, spoke a little more slowly. "We've paid this already, Dawn."

The waitress shook her head for a few seconds as if trying to clear it, then rolled her eyes. "Sorry, I think I must be going mad. Course you've paid it. Course you have…"

They watched her walk back towards the counter, muttering, and began to gather their things together.

"I wish I could do that," Adam said.

"You can," Morag said. "We *all* can. You just need to get the hang of it."

"Come on," Gabriel said. "There's a ferry leaving in five minutes."

Outside, it had begun to rain gently. The children gathered undercover and Gabriel urged them to hurry. On the other side of the fence, the sea had begun to roll and swell, slapping against the dockside.

Gabriel stepped out, eager to get down to the ferry. Rachel reached out to stop him. "This is the quickest way out, you said?"

"Right. So can we—?"

"The quickest ... and the most obvious."

Gabriel looked at her. "What are you thinking?"

It had struck her in the cafe; just an idle thought at first, but now she was certain of it. "It's the way they'll be expecting us to go," she said. "They're probably watching the port already."

Gabriel nodded, stared out towards the North Sea for a few seconds, then turned back, resigned to it. "Any bright ideas?"

Rachel could see by the look in Gabriel's eye that this was some kind of test. "Where were you planning to take us?" she asked.

"Across to Rotterdam, then down through Belgium and into France."

"What's in France?"

"Just a stop we need to make." He flashed Rachel half a smile. "Maybe a little bit of sightseeing."

Adam had been distracted by Morag and Duncan and had only half caught the conversation. Now he stepped across. "What's going on?"

"Ask your sister," Gabriel said.

Adam looked at Rachel. "There must be other ways to get to France," she said.

They stood discussing the options, and when it had been decided, they waited a few minutes longer, until a likely looking candidate emerged from inside the cafe.

He wore jeans and a padded waistcoat over a red

lumberjack shirt. He turned to say his goodbyes to Dawn, his blonde mullet highlighted by the glare from the sign above his head.

"Dutch," Gabriel whispered. "Probably just got here on his way to London."

"He's perfect," Rachel said. She watched as Gabriel followed the Dutchman across the car park towards a huge lorry with a foreign number plate.

"What's happening?" Morag asked.

Adam and Rachel watched. Gabriel was deep in conversation with the lorry driver. He pointed back towards the children still gathered under the awning outside the cafe and the lorry driver stared and nodded enthusiastically, waving his arms around and smiling.

"Whatever he's saying, it seems to be working," Adam said.

When Gabriel beckoned them across, they ran through the drizzle and huddled together by the side of the Dutchman's lorry. Rachel raised an eyebrow at Gabriel. He gave her a small nod: sorted.

The driver opened his arms wide and beamed at them. "Hi, you lot. I'm Ronald. You're welcome aboard."

"Thanks," Rachel said.

"No, no. My pleasure," Ronald said. "Now climb into the cabin and you can ride up front with me."

The children did as they were told and moved around to the far door while Ronald climbed into his seat. He patted the seat next to him and beckoned Adam across. "Come on, sit over here next to me."

"OK…"

Rachel helped Morag and Duncan up, then climbed in herself, waited for Gabriel to join them and shut the door. It was a tight squeeze, so Rachel lifted Duncan on to her lap.

"There we are," the driver said. "All set?" He turned the engine over and the lorry juddered into life. "Hold tight…"

They pulled out of the car park on to a rain-swept road that curled slowly around the terminal before joining traffic filtering on to a main road and, finally, a motorway. Rachel stared straight ahead, listening to the squeak of the wind-screen-wipers and the driver's constant, sing-song chatter as he told them all about his journey across from Holland.

He had been delighted to offer them a lift and seemed friendly enough.

But people seemed to be a great many things, and Rachel was learning a lot of lessons, fast.

Number one: trust nobody.

18

The blue sign at the side of the motorway announced that London was just another twelve miles away. Rachel had counted them down from nearly a hundred and now the city loomed, an orange glow on the horizon.

Duncan and Morag were still asleep, as they had been for the last hour or so, in the poky bunk positioned above the cab. Rachel was squeezed between Adam and Gabriel on the seat behind the driver, and every now and again, Ronald would turn and wink at them, offering them gum, before continuing to hum a tune that sounded like the theme from a kids' TV show.

Twenty minutes later, with the sky getting lighter, a vast, silvery city of skyscrapers and massive glass towers seemed to grow in front of their eyes. Lights sparkled in thousands of windows and multicoloured neon signs shouted corporate names from the rooftops: Citibank, HSBC, Barclays.

"Welcome to London Town," Ronald said cheerily. The

lorry driver's accent was thick, even though his English was excellent. He opened his mouth in a wide yawn that made Rachel realize how tired she was herself. She yawned in sympathy and saw that Adam was doing the same.

It was not the London they had expected to see. Where was St. Paul's? Where were Big Ben and the Tower of London? This was something far more modern, newer than New York.

"I don't recognize *any* of this," Rachel said. "Where are we exactly?"

"The Docklands," Ronald said. "This is the new bit, where the old East End and the docks used to be. It's fantastic."

Ronald swung the huge, refrigerated juggernaut round a roundabout and down a slip road towards an industrial area below them, where many more white trucks were parked, lit up by banks of floodlights. Rachel felt uneasy, having spent half the night blinded by spotlights, outside in the cold. She felt queasy and her tongue tasted bitter in her mouth. In the dark, Adam squeezed her hand and, seconds later, Gabriel squeezed the other one, reassuring her.

"This is where we stop," Ronald said. He swung the truck through a barrier and under a vast yellow canopy with a sign that said: BILLINGSGATE MARKET

Adam and Gabriel helped the weary younger twins down from the bunk and out into the air, where they shivered and blinked in the white light. The smell of fish hit them all like a powerful gust of sea air. Ronald handed down their bags and then jumped from the cabin.

"Thanks for the ride, Ronald," Rachel said, holding out her hand and shaking the Dutchman's firmly.

"No worries," Ronald said. He took a chewed ballpoint from the pocket of his shirt and scribbled down a number on a scrap of paper from the dashboard. "And if you ladies are ever in Rotterdam, give me a call. I'll show you around; we'll have a good time!"

"You bet!" Rachel said, dragging the twins away, waving. Adam and Gabriel waved too as Ronald began to open the tailgate of his truck.

"Ladies?" Adam said, affronted.

"Let him see what he wants to see," Gabriel said. "I convinced him that we were American air stewardesses on our way to the airport." Gabriel winked at Adam as Ronald had winked at them, then laughed.

The source of the fish smell became evident as the five children walked across the lorry park towards a steel shed the size of an aircraft hangar. They saw hundreds of men in wet, white coats stacking polystyrene crates which rattled with overflowing ice. The plastic sides of refrigerated trucks advertised their countries of origin: France, Spain, Holland. Smaller vans, with pictures of fat-lipped dolphins, mermaids and scallop shells painted on their doors, displayed addresses in Devon, Cornwall, Lowestoft and Hull. All were either disgorging or loading up with fish. There were big, silver fish with dead bug eyes; smaller red-skinned fish with spiny fins; slimy, long ones; flat, black ones; crabs and lobsters, their claws shackled with rubber bands; and tangles of squid and octopus, their suckered tentacles curling and trailing over the edges of the crates, as if in a failed attempt to escape.

Rachel did not like fish at the best of times – not to eat, at least. She found them alien somehow, mysterious and scary, and was more than happy for them to remain undisturbed at the bottom of the sea. Now, the stench of thousands and thousands of dead ones, catching at the back of her throat after a greasy cooked breakfast, was making her nauseous. As they approached the hangar, she saw men in plastic aprons gutting massive cod from throat to tail with long knives and watched as wet, red guts spilled into big plastic vats at their feet.

Rachel was suddenly, and violently, sick.

Adam rubbed her back as she wiped her mouth with a tissue and spat on the wet asphalt. Gabriel looked at her with an expression of sympathy and curiosity.

"Are you OK, Rachel?" Morag said. She joined Adam in stroking her back. Rachel nodded.

"We've got to move on," Adam said.

Gabriel pointed to a track several metres above them. Against the pink, dawn sky a red train with brightly lit windows was slowly coming to a halt at a station somewhere over their heads.

The train did not appear to have a driver. A robotic voice advised them to mind the closing doors as they sat in seats looking out of the front, where the driver's cabin ought to be. Their few fellow passengers, wearily texting or reading papers, completely ignored the children and the unfolding cityscape that developed around them. The train followed a narrow electrical track and burrowed into the undersides of the skyscrapers, revealing a stainless steel and glass under-world of supermarkets and coffee shops, each getting ready to open for business.

"It's like *The Matrix*," Adam said.

"Like what?" Gabriel asked.

"It's a film," Adam said.

"About the future," Rachel added. She lifted her pale face from the window and gave Gabriel a sickly smile.

Gabriel looked out of the window as the train hummed to a halt at a station signposted CANARY WHARF. He looked at a pair of men sweeping the platform, their heads down, brushing in opposite directions without acknowledging each other. He looked around the carriage at the weary workers and waved his hand at the labyrinth of offices that towered way above them.

"If this is your future," he said, "I don't think I like it. Let's get off. We have to change here…"

19

Brakes squealed as the black London cab pulled into the cobbled bay at the side of St Pancras station.

"Enjoy your holiday," the cabbie said cheerily. He pocketed the wad of crumpled paper Gabriel had just handed him, believing it not only to be the fare from Bank Underground station, where they had got in, but also a handsome tip. "Nice to meet you all!" He grinned at what he perceived to be a pleasant young family with two small children and a nanny, clambering out of his cab on their way to France. He switched on his "For Hire" light, pleased that his day had got off to such a good start, and pulled away to look for his next fare.

"We're looking for the Eurostar," Gabriel said. "It goes to Paris." He led them into a vast, airy concourse, now bustling and crowded with morning commuters.

"Paris?" Adam said, impressed.

"I have … friends there. I'll check on the departure board to see when—"

"The next one leaves in twenty minutes," Duncan said in a monotone. "07.28 hours. The journey takes approximately two hours and thirty-five minutes. Platform 14A."

The others stopped and looked at him in astonishment. It was only the second time that Rachel and Adam had heard Duncan speak at all, and the first time, it had taken several thousand volts to get him going.

"Duncan remembers things like that," Morag said. "He only has to read something once."

They walked towards the ticket office, weaving through crowds of people dressed for work and others pulling suitcases on wheels, all of whom seemed intent on running over their toes at every possible opportunity. They squeezed past a statue of a small, fat man in a hat who appeared to be looking up at the glass-domed roof high above their heads. The long queue for the Paris train trailed back from the platform entrance, slowly passing through a ticket barrier and the arch of a metal detector.

"We'll never get on," Rachel said, walking towards the queue. "We haven't even got tickets yet."

A jogger wearing wraparound sunglasses, apparently oblivious to the outside world – earphones plugged in and determined in his trajectory – clipped Rachel's shoulder as he ran by. Rachel spun round, holding her shoulder more in shock than in pain.

"Hey!" Adam called after the jogger, instinctively leaping to his sister's defence. But the man was already gone. Rachel watched the lycra-clad figure disappear and was about to move on when someone else caught her eye. It was a man in a black biker jacket, putting in his own earphones as the jogger passed. He glanced at Rachel, then, quickly breaking the eye contact, fumbled in his pocket and put on a pair of glasses. Rachel was relieved to see him pull out an MP3 player and apparently adjust the volume.

She let out a long sigh of relief. She was tired, she had been sick, and now she was feeling paranoid.

"Here are our tickets," Gabriel said. He tore up what looked like the back of a cereal packet and handed them a piece each. "Let's get on the train."

At the barrier, the guard, having spoken to Gabriel, seemed happy to let them through. Those at the front of the queue smiled indulgently at the young people pushing past who appeared to be helping their ancient grandmother through the turnstile and on to the train for her ninetieth birthday treat in Paris.

"I still don't know how you do it," Rachel said to Gabriel as they climbed aboard the train. "It's like they look at us and see something else."

"It's just a knack," he said. "You'll pick it up."

The train was almost full as it pulled out of St Pancras and shot across London, through tunnels and underpasses, emerging five minutes later into the sprawling suburbs. Rows of identical Edwardian houses became a blur in the window as the train sped past. Within another few minutes, the houses had been replaced by trees as they moved on into the countryside.

Rachel breathed deeply, and allowed herself the luxury of shutting her eyes and relaxing back into the velvety seat of the train.

"I want a wee," a voice piped up from the seat next to her. Rachel opened an eye and saw Morag's cheeky face, refreshed by a few hours' sleep, beaming at her. This is what it must be like to be a mother, Rachel thought to herself. She winced as thoughts of her own mother flooded back. She prayed that Gabriel was right; that their mum would remain safe.

"I said, I want a—"

Rachel got to her feet and ushered the little girl back along the carriage.

Walking towards the toilet, she glanced to her left and felt a fierce jolt of panic. Sitting two seats behind them was the man in the biker jacket. His eyes were closed beneath his glasses and he was still wearing his earphones. Rachel told herself to stay calm. He was just a traveller; another passenger going to Paris. He did not stir as Rachel guided Morag past him and pressed the button on the curved, automatic door of the toilet. It slid open.

"You OK by yourself?" Rachel asked. Morag nodded and the door closed behind her. "Don't lock it!" Rachel shouted.

She waited and looked back down the carriage, just able

to make out Adam's tousled head, above the seat opposite hers, lolling with the movement of the train as if he were asleep. Rachel felt conspicuous standing outside the lavatory and walked a few steps, through the sliding door at the end of the carriage, and looked out of the window. Fields rolled by and the train passed without stopping through an old red-brick station, not unlike the one in Triskellion.

That seemed like a very long time ago.

Mesmerized by the passing landscape, Rachel was only vaguely aware of the hiss as the toilet door opened, but reality came flooding back in an instant, with a shrill scream.

"Help!" Morag squealed.

Rachel spun round to see the jogger who had barged her on the platform. He held Morag round the waist with one arm, his other gloved hand clasped across her mouth. He wrestled the child forward towards Rachel as one or two other passengers craned their necks to see the source of the commotion. Unable to see clearly, they quickly returned to their laptops and papers, not wanting to become involved; sure that someone else would deal with whoever, *whatever*, was making the noise.

Rachel stepped through the doorway into the path of the man. He barged her with his shoulder for the second time that day, and this one was far from accidental.

Rachel fell back against the window, banging her head. The door to the next carriage slid shut, leaving them in a muffled airlock and giving Rachel a second to swing back her leg and deliver a hard kick to the man's shin. He grunted in pain and slammed his body into Rachel again, with Morag still writhing in his arms.

Rachel knew that if she made too much noise, the train would be stopped. The police would be called and they'd be delivered back to where they started. Every fibre in Rachel's body screamed out for Gabriel, but Morag's panic alerted her own brother first. The doors slid open again and, like a small dog, Duncan flew through the opening and sunk his teeth into the back of the jogger's leg.

The man yelled and dropped Morag.

Then, as if appearing from nowhere, Gabriel was on him. The long index and middle fingers of his left hand pushed under the jogger's dark glasses and into his eye sockets, his thumb pressed deep into the soft flesh under the man's jaw, keeping his mouth shut. With his other hand flat, Gabriel delivered a stiff-fingered jab hard underneath the man's ribs. The door of the toilet hissed open again, and Gabriel pushed the jogger back into it, releasing his fingers from the man's face. The man's eyes were clenched shut in agony and his mouth flapped open and shut, gasping for air like a dying fish. As he writhed on the toilet floor, the door closed and Duncan, reaching up to the electric lock, made sure that it would not open again.

A few people had gathered at the end of the carriage and, with Adam helping a tearful Morag back to her seat, Rachel reassured the gawping passengers, telling them the little girl had become stuck in the bathroom and was upset. The guard gave Morag a pack of chocolate buttons as she sat back in her seat.

"Told you that you could do it," Gabriel said, wiping his hands on a napkin.

"Do what?" Rachel asked, her own hands still trembling on the tabletop.

"Convince people," he said. "Make them think what you *want* them to think. Make them see what you *want* them to see, by suggesting it to them."

"Like hypnosis?" Adam said.

"Call it what you like: suggestion, hypnotism, programming. It's probably the most useful tool we have. *Practise* it," Gabriel said. "*Use* it—"

He was cut off as an automated voice came over the speaker in English, then in French: "The next station is Ashford International…"

Gabriel stood up. "Change of plan," he said. "We're getting off here."

The five kids were the only passengers to leave the train at Ashford and, as it pulled away from the station, the man in the biker jacket opened his eyes. He watched the children cross the platform and climb the footbridge.

He removed his earphones, took the phone from his pocket and dialled.

20

The ferry was the size of a small town, with gift shops, restaurants, bars and even a cinema. Rachel's eyes darted about. She checked out her fellow passengers, fixing on any person wearing earphones, of which there were many. She and Adam had become hypersensitive to any movement, any stray glances that were cast their way.

Gabriel, on the other hand, seemed relaxed and settled back in the big plush seat, whistling through his teeth and watching through a panoramic window as the white cliffs of the English Coast receded into the distance and finally melted into the grey-brown sea.

The slow train from Ashford had taken an hour or so to arrive at Dover. On reaching the docks, they had quickly assimilated themselves into a group of returning French students. They had disappeared easily among the high-spirited jostling school party; the stressed teacher somehow failing to register them every time she'd attempted a head count. They had been treated as school-fellows by the other kids as they had sat on the coach and been driven on to the cavernous car deck of the ferry.

At first the gabble of the French schoolchildren had sounded like gobbledygook to Rachel, then gradually the odd disconnected word in English had sounded familiar to her ear: "weekend ... super ... rock..."

As she had concentrated, Rachel had begun to comprehend more and more of their chatter.

"Can you understand what they're saying?" she had asked, turning to her brother.

"Oui, un peu," Adam had said, his eyes widening in surprise at the words that had come from his mouth. "I ... I mean, yeah ... a bit."

Rachel insisted that they all stay close together on the ferry. Morag and Duncan were restless, but Rachel knew that they were safest among the gaggle of French kids. She watched them as they sat playing an elaborate game of cards.

It was the first time that they had really had a chance to talk to Gabriel, and Rachel and Adam sat on either side of him in an attempt to pin him down.

"How did they know we were on that train?" Adam asked.

Gabriel shrugged.

"Listen," Rachel said. "We doubled back from Harwich. No one could have known we got a ride on that fish truck. No one saw us, I swear."

"Unless, for some reason, *you* told them?" Adam said, trying to provoke a reaction.

"You think I'd tell them?" Gabriel asked. He turned to Adam and stared at him with such an intensity that Adam had to turn away. "With everything you know about me, with everything you know about *us*."

"I'm just saying…"

"Listen, Adam, there's part of you that is very … human. Part of you that still hasn't seen the bigger picture. It's like you only see this in terms of yourself."

"You think I've got an ego problem?"

"Whatever you want to call it. It's not something I really understand. You need to see where you fit in the bigger scheme of things, like the bees in one of Honeyman's hives. We're all part of that whole. Bees in a hive do not let each other down; *we* do not let each other down. Understand?"

Adam was not really sure he did, but knew he'd been given a harsh lecture and nodded.

"We still have no idea how they knew we were on that train," Rachel said.

"'How' doesn't really matter," Gabriel said. "These are powerful people, and there are a lot of them. We know how to evade them up to a point, but in the long term, there's nowhere to hide. We've got to keep moving, got to keep one step ahead of them."

It was a little over twelve hours since their breakout from

Hope, but it seemed to Rachel that they hadn't stopped moving in that time.

"Can me and Duncan go to the shops now?" Morag piped. "We're bored."

"No, we're nearly there," Rachel said, sounding like her mother. "Stay close to us."

You could lose someone on a ferry this size, she thought, and the English Channel that rose and fell behind them looked very cold and deep...

Clay Van der Zee turned away from the huge map of Europe on a screen above the fireplace and looked again at the message on his PDA. The report from their agent in the field. He grunted and shook his head. "Strange."

Laura Sullivan studied Van der Zee's expression. There was annoyance there, of course, but also a degree of amusement, as though he was relishing the challenge that Adam and Rachel Newman had set him. She'd seen it too the night before, when the sirens had been ringing through the building and the guards had been sent out to search the surrounding countryside.

A search that had never been meant to succeed.

"These kids are good," he'd said to her. He'd walked in from the woods, where the guards were still searching, taking off his thick coat and rubbing his hands together, relieved to be back in the warmth of the research facility.

Laura had stared out of her office window into the

blackness of the pine forest, the torchbeams dancing in the darkness. "I told you they were special."

"Still, it's impressive, and they do keep surprising me." Van der Zee had nodded, almost pleased. "I certainly hadn't expected them to escape quite this quickly. Almost caught me off guard…"

Laura had been learning a lot about Clay Van der Zee, and those he worked for, in the hours since the children had escaped from the Hope Project. She had known that the escape had been expected; that it had been allowed to happen. She had argued that they could learn more by setting the kids free, to see where they went, how they behaved. The long arms of the Hope organization could keep track of them. She had argued passionately against the surgical "intervention" that Van der Zee and his superiors favoured a little further down the line.

There were other … interests that could be served first.

She had not known that Van der Zee had *allowed* the children to take the Triskellion. He had guessed, correctly – thanks to the research that Laura herself had helped conduct – that Rachel and Adam would never leave without it. Now Laura was beginning to understand that Van der Zee saw its loss as a small sacrifice. He was confident that he would get the Triskellion back. That, and plenty more besides…

"What is it?" Laura asked now.

Van der Zee looked up from his PDA. "It's … interesting.

They're heading for France, but they got off the train before it went into the Tunnel."

Laura felt a wave of relief pass over her but tried not to let it show. The children were being clever; they were not making it easy.

"And something else," Van der Zee said. "A couple more surprises."

"Yeah?"

Van der Zee was almost smiling again. Laura felt the temperature in his den drop a couple of degrees. "Our operative swears there were five of them."

"Five?"

"The Newman twins, Morag and Duncan, and a boy. About the same age as Rachel and Adam. Foreign looking, according to the report."

Something clicked in Laura's brain; a memory she couldn't quite get hold of. Slippery and half-remembered. Had Rachel and Adam mentioned a boy they'd known back in the village? The idea twisted away as she tried to bring it into focus. "A *couple* of surprises, you said."

Van der Zee looked at her. "When the train arrived in Paris, they found a man locked in the train toilet. He was half dead by all accounts; blinded in one eye with three broken ribs." The doctor leant back in his chair and stared up at the map. "And he wasn't one of ours…"

21

After the ferry had docked at Calais, they spent a few hours tramping around the grey streets, weaving among the afternoon shoppers intent on their business in spite of the drizzle. "Probably best to keep moving for a while, after what happened on the train," Gabriel said. "It's easier to disappear in a town."

They walked past bakeries and butcher's shops, past windows filled with hanging sausages, and cafes with old men gathered smoking outside. There was plenty to look at, and in the market square, where stalls were packing up for the day, the tempting smell from a caravan dispensing steaming paper cones of "frites" caused Adam to hang back for a moment. But Gabriel would let no one dawdle. He told them that this was what the future held for the time being. That theirs were now the lives of fugitives; they needed to think fast, stay alert and be ready to leave wherever they were at a minute's notice.

"It's harder to hit a moving target," Rachel said.

Morag inched closer to Adam. "Target?"

Adam threw Rachel a look, then laid a hand on the young girl's shoulder. "It's just an expression."

"Right," Gabriel said, "we need supplies."

They walked out of the town centre towards a huge, spiky bell tower with a yellow clock face that loomed over the otherwise featureless horizon like a reject from Disneyland. They headed out on a busy ring road and found a hypermarket – a vast store the size of three football pitches – that sold everything from marshmallows to motorbikes.

"We can get everything we want in here," Gabriel said. "Let's be as quick as we can though." He watched as Morag eyed up the children's clothes and Duncan began edging towards the section of the shop that sold toys and games. "And try not to get lost."

Rachel pushed a trolley up and down the wide aisles, while the others stacked it high with those urgent supplies they would be able to carry: bottled water, fruit, chocolate bars, crisps and peanuts. Adam grumbled when Rachel told him there would be no room for fizzy drinks, then stared at her as she dropped in gloves and woolly hats and finally, a multi-pack of toilet roll.

"Somebody's got to be practical," she said. "We might have to spend the night outdoors."

Adam pulled a face. "I thought we were fugitives," he said. "Not Boy Scouts."

Approaching the checkout, Adam noticed that most of

the other trolleys were piled high with alcohol: cases of wine, boxes of beer, bottle after bottle of lethal-looking spirits. "Do people in France have, you know … some kind of problem?"

"English tourists, I think," Rachel said. "I guess shopping must be cheaper on this side of the Channel."

"Not as cheap as this," Gabriel said. He smiled as he took control of the trolley and wheeled it straight through the line of tills, past the checkout staff who looked but saw nothing, and out into the car park.

They quickly loaded their purchases into cases and back-packs. Rachel saw Morag whispering to her brother and asked her what the matter was. "It's wrong," Morag said. "Not paying for things."

Adam moved across and helped her load the things faster. "We haven't got a lot of choice," he said. "And it's not like we've really paid for anything since we escaped."

"I know, but this feels like … stealing."

Adam looked at Rachel and shrugged. She glanced across at Gabriel and knew at once what he was thinking. They hadn't talked about what he had done to the man on the train; it had just been accepted. It had been necessary, Rachel knew that, but it did not mean she was completely comfortable with it.

Gabriel scanned the horizon, as he had done every few minutes since they'd been reunited with him, as though he knew something was coming. "We might have to do a lot worse than steal, before this is over," he said.

It was getting dark quickly and, although the rain had stopped, it was starting to get very cold. Toilet roll or not, Rachel decided that they needed to get the younger twins indoors and, after walking back towards town for a few minutes, they turned into a quiet side street and stopped in front of a small hotel.

Morag read the name aloud. *"L'Etoile..."*

Adam looked up at the tatty neon sign above the entrance, a blue star with white beams radiating from it.

"The Star," he said. "Same as the pub in the village."

Rachel led the way inside, hoping that it was a good sign and not a bad omen.

The man at reception looked up from his newspaper as the children dumped their bags in front of the desk.

"Do you speak English?" Rachel asked.

The man ignored her.

"Guess that's a no then," Rachel muttered. She'd studied a bit of French at school, but couldn't remember much beyond a few useless phrases: "I have lost my exercise book" and "Is this the way to the railway station?" She looked to Gabriel for help.

"Ask him if he's got a room," Gabriel said. "I'm sure you can make him understand."

Rachel cleared her throat and the man glanced up at her. He was stick-thin and balding, though he had tried to disguise the fact by combing over what little hair he had left. "I wondered if you might have a room available for us?" Rachel's mouth dropped open in amazement as soon as she'd finished speaking. Though the thought had formed in her head in English, by the time the words had come out of her mouth they were in flawless and perfectly accented French.

Gabriel grinned. "I knew you could do it."

The man behind the desk shook his head then spoke. Rachel knew very well that he was speaking French, but his answer came to her in English. "Sorry, we are completely full."

Rachel was still too stunned to say anything, so Adam stepped forward and took over. "Excuse me," he said. Once again, the thought had been translated – somewhere between brain and mouth – into perfect French. "I'm sure you can find room for *us*." The man looked up. Adam found eye contact, and held it. "If you look hard enough…"

The Frenchman's eyes widened and then he shook himself as though trying to wake up. He glanced down at his register and raised his arms, and when he looked at the children again he was beaming. "I'm sorry, I am being very stupid. Of *course* I have room for you. *Plenty* of room."

Adam leant close to Rachel and whispered, "This is awesome!"

The Frenchman stepped from behind his desk and struggled to pick up all their bags. "Yes, plenty of room, no problem. Will the four of you be requiring dinner?"

"Sorry? *Four* of us…?"

Adam and Rachel turned, but saw only the shining faces of Morag and Duncan staring up at them expectantly.

Gabriel had gone.

The Englishman took a small sip of dark, red wine and looked back across the table. He could not help but enjoy the look of fear on the face of the man sitting opposite him. How much greater that fear would be if he could only see the Englishman's face…

The bar was not crowded, but the Englishman had taken a table in a quiet corner, with a view of the door and the busy Paris street beyond. He'd sat and watched the world go by while he'd waited, rolling cigarettes with dark, pungent tobacco and studying the faces of the men and women hurrying past on the pavement. They were all so very busy, with such full lives, but each remained ignorant of the real world around them – of its power. Much of the time this amused the Englishman, but when a black mood descended, when he thought of all those things he had been denied, he wanted nothing more than to wipe them all out.

All he needed was the instrument.

"Are you sure you don't want some wine?" he asked.

The man on the other side of the table shook his head, grimacing. "I … can't," he stammered. "The … medication."

The Englishman nodded. "Of course. You must still be

in very great pain." He smiled. "I'm not exactly a stranger to that myself."

The man, who had been disguised as a jogger a few hours before, was indeed in agony. He wore a bloodied patch over his damaged eye and he could barely breathe. To the horror of the doctors, he had discharged himself from hospital – more afraid of the man he was answerable to than of the damage he might be doing to himself. He swallowed hard. He could still feel the hands of the boy on him, the power in those delicate fingers.

"It wasn't my fault," he said. "The boy was so strong."

"The *boy*." The Englishman winced, as though the word tasted vile in his mouth.

"Next time I'll be ready for him; I'll…"

The Englishman smiled. Ignoring the NO SMOKING signs, he blew a plume of blue smoke across the table. "Don't worry about next time. You're not really in any fit state to do any more."

The man peered desperately into the shadow under the Englishman's hood, where his face should have been. The jogger's voice was high and cracked. "Please. I didn't mean to let you down."

"You let all of us down. Now, get out of my sight."

Out on the street, the Englishman pulled his hood a little further forward. He swallowed a handful of painkillers and began to walk back towards his small, rented room. There would be a good deal to do when he got back. He would have to put the word out across the network; formulate a new plan of action. It was annoying, but really it was no more than a minor setback.

There were countless others he could turn to, who believed as he did. Others who would follow him. He had no doubt at all that he would find Rachel and Adam Newman eventually and that the Triskellion would be his.

They were only two children, a long way from home.

And he had an army to call on.

It was no more than a trickle – cold one minute and scalding the next – but it was the best shower Rachel could ever remember having.

In the end, the hotel owner – seemingly convinced that they were VIPs of some sort – had given them two large rooms next to one another with French windows overlooking the street. The two sets of twins had decided to split up. Morag had been keen to share with Rachel, who she was starting to treat as an older sister, while Adam and Duncan had been happy enough to share the room next door.

Either would have room to squeeze Gabriel in, if he ever decided to come back.

Rachel scrubbed at her body with the soap and stiff brush she'd found in the soap-dish; scrubbing until her skin was red and sore. She was desperate to wash away the dirt and the exhaustion, but she was also trying to wash away what for anyone else would have been a lifetime's worth of bad memories.

The Hope Project.

The village.

Her grandmother's body…

She stood and let the water run over her, closed her eyes and thought about her mother back there. Was she really as safe as Gabriel had promised? She and Adam had put so much faith in him, had entrusted their lives to him, but perhaps they had been foolish. She was starting to suspect that there were other things he considered more important than their safety.

She stepped out of the shower and rubbed at her wet hair with a towel.

Where *was* he?

Gabriel – or whatever his real name was – had been disappearing, for days at a stretch sometimes, ever since that night she had first set eyes on him, marching around the chalk circle in the rain. She had learnt early on that there was little point in asking for an explanation. His answers were always annoyingly vague or just plain meaningless. There was a part of him, Rachel knew, that would always be hidden, but she would have given anything to know why.

"Rachel! Come and look."

She wrapped the towel round her chest and walked out of the bathroom. Morag was beaming proudly, pointing to the clothes which she'd taken from Rachel's backpack and laid out neatly at the end of her bed, as if she had been arranging her dolls.

"Just trying to make it feel a bit more like home," Morag said.

"Thanks. That's great. But..." Rachel quickly scanned the room and began rummaging in the pockets of her empty backpack. She could not find the Triskellion.

She sat on the bed.

"Can I brush your hair?" Morag said, kneeling behind her, already dragging at the wet curls with a brush.

"Sure," Rachel said distractedly, panic rising over the missing Triskellion. Morag's brush tugged at her hair then slipped, causing a sharp pain between Rachel's shoulder blades.

"Ow!"

"Sorry— What's that?" Morag squealed, prodding Rachel's back. "You've hurt yourself. I'll get a wee mirror."

Rachel craned her neck as the younger girl held the mirror up to her. She began reaching round, trying to touch whatever it was that had made Morag so alarmed.

"Between your shoulders. It's a scar or a boil or something..."

Rachel manoeuvred the mirror until she was able to see her back. She could just glimpse a small, angry bump sitting beneath the skin. It was the size of a kidney bean, raised and red. Rachel froze, thinking about those first few days at the Hope Project, about the way time had passed in a slow haze or a crazy rush. She'd been convinced they were drugging her in some way; disorientating her.

She began to wonder what else they might have done.

Rachel flung open the door and tore down the corridor, Morag a step or two behind her. When she burst into Adam's room, he and Duncan were lying on their beds, giggling over some TV show. Adam glanced up.

"I think you forgot to get dressed."

"Take your T-shirt off," Rachel said.

Adam and Duncan were already laughing again. Adam pointed at the small TV set. "This is fantastic. *The Simpsons*, in French. *Les Simpsons*, right?"

"Shut up and take your T-shirt off, Adam."

Seeing the look on his sister's face, Adam got off the bed and did as he was told.

"He's got one too," Morag said. "What is it?"

"Got one what?" Adam began to reach round, as Rachel had done.

"That's how they know where we are," Rachel said. "We're being tracked."

22

Gabriel marched slowly up and down between the lines of standing stones.

He was some way down the coast and, although the air was clearer, a strong wind buffeted him and blew his hair over his face. The sound of the waves crashing on the nearby coastline added to the roaring inside his head as he tried to focus; tried to home in on a signal that he was sure was there.

He knew he was in the right place. The symbol carved into the rock in front of him told him so. These two lines of stone had stood in the remote French countryside for as long as the chalk circle had been carved into the moor at Triskellion. They had been planted by similar people. To mark a similar event. Now, Gabriel needed to find the descendants of the villagers who had marked this spot, who had lived here, isolated for many centuries. People who had stayed close to home in an effort to protect their bloodline.

People who, at some point, had produced twins.

As the dusk deepened into darkness, the stones appeared blacker and more jagged. They were like two rows of teeth about to snap shut and devour anyone who ventured too close. To swallow the boy who paced their length, holding out a gold, three-bladed instrument in front of him as if it were a compass.

Gabriel sat on a stone in the darkness. Rounded and flattened on top, it was like a stool, worn smooth by more than a millennium of use. Instantly, he became aware of the thousands and thousands of people who had sat on this same stone over the many centuries; he began to feel the microscopic imprint each of them had made. His fingers tingled, as though a low-voltage current was passing through them; as if he was in touch with every one of their souls. He could feel the vibrations that pulsed through every molecule of the rock gradually seeping up into his limbs. Then, one by one, he felt the pulsation from the other stones, each one a slightly different pitch from the last. He felt the vibrations build until he was in tune with every last stone; the frequencies growing and layering, like a monolithic orchestra conducted by his hands, and creating a harmony that surged through his body.

And then the Triskellion glowed, rocking from side to side in Gabriel's hand, then slowly spinning, hovering, in the air and glinting with the pale blue beams of the reflected moon.

Somewhere across the field, in the sparsely populated

village, dogs began to bark and a light went on in a cottage window. Then another, and another, until the ten or so cottages that made up the entire community were all lit up. Gabriel smiled, as if he had given the village a wake-up call it had long been expecting.

Hello...? The voice in Gabriel's head was no more than a whisper at first, but it quickly grew louder. *Hello? Ariel?*

"I'm here," Gabriel said aloud. As he spoke, he felt a powerful surge of excitement rush through him from somewhere deep underground, his mind fizzing with the energy that he had harnessed from the rocks. "I'll be with you very soon. I promise."

Rachel lay face down on the thin mattress and cushioned her face on her arms. Morag and Duncan sat together on the other bed, silent, impassive, afraid of what was about to happen.

"Do it," Rachel said.

Adam was tentatively probing the bean-sized bump on her back. The nerves were all too clear in his voice. "OK, OK. I'm ... doing it."

Rachel could feel the movement under her skin, as Adam prodded and pushed at whatever had been implanted in her back, and in his own. The skin was inflamed where he had tried to squeeze the lump to the surface, and a minuscule scar, where the incision had originally been made, had begun to pucker angrily.

Adam carefully adjusted the bedside light, as if getting more light to shine on the bump might suddenly make it disappear. His hand shook. He did not need telling that whatever Rachel was about to go through would soon be his to endure in turn.

"I can't, Rach," Adam said, finally. "It's too deep. The pain would kill you."

"I don't care about the pain," Rachel said, sounding braver than she felt. "Unless we cut these things out, they're going to be on our tails all the time. Just do it!"

Adam shook his head. "I can't believe Laura would just let them microchip us like dogs." He sighed deeply and took out the disposable razor.

On the other side of the room, Morag reached for her brother's hand.

Adam snapped open the body of the cheap plastic razor and removed the blade. He waved it through the flame of a candle to sterilize it, then laid it on the pillowcase next to a teaspoon, a pair of tweezers from Rachel's wash-bag and a complimentary sewing kit from the hotel. He'd seen enough hospital dramas to know the procedure, but had no idea whether he could actually carry it out. He hesitated.

"Get on with it!" Rachel said.

Adam leant over his sister's back. He wiped the reddened area with the damp tissue.

"Get ready…"

Rachel's body tensed and her back arched instinctively

as she felt the first touch of the razor blade.

"You OK?" Adam said, pulling back his arm. Rachel nodded and gripped the pillow.

Adam took the flimsy blade between his fingers again and drew it across the raised bump on his sister's back. A thin red line of bright blood flowered on the surface of her skin.

Rachel screamed before gritting her teeth and trying to suck back the coppery-tasting spit flooding her mouth. She forced her face hard into the pillow, muffling her cries. "It hurts, it hurts…"

Adam examined the wound. He had only just broken the surface and knew he would need to cut much deeper. The line of blood thickened along the incision and a trickle of deep red began to run down on to Rachel's ribs. Feeling his sister's pain, Adam began to cry.

"I can't," he said.

"You've got to." Rachel's voice was muffled by the pillow. "Come on!" She grabbed at the corner of the sheet and stuffed it into her mouth. She bit down hard to stifle her cries, then nodded for Adam to continue the torture.

Adam's hand trembled and tears blurred his vision as the thin blade cut once again into the bloody mess smeared across Rachel's back. Rachel bucked and snorted with the pain as more blood pulsed to the surface.

"Stop!" Morag squealed, jumping up from the bed, tears streaking her face. "I want to do something…"

Adam wiped the tears from his eyes with the back of his

hand, leaving a bloody stripe on his cheek. He looked at the little Scottish girl. He was willing to listen to anyone, to do anything that might get him out of this nightmare.

"I might be able to help," Morag said. "Sometimes when Duncan's poorly or has a sore knee, I talk to him and it makes it better."

Rachel raised her tear-stained face from the pillow and looked at the little girl's round face. She tried to summon a smile. "Talk to me," she said.

Morag knelt at the head of the bed and took Rachel's wet face between her chubby hands. Rachel was transfixed by the huge, ice-blue eyes and the halo of curls that glowed in the bedside light.

"I'm going to tell you a story." Morag's voice was soft and sweet-sounding. "We are going to a beautiful place far away where the sun is always shining and the sky is always blue and the sea is as green as the grass. We are flying there now, up through the air into the clear, blue sky..."

Rachel felt calmer suddenly as the sing-song voice lulled her, and her mind became full of the deep-blue sky.

"We are flying higher and higher until the earth is way down below, like a ping-pong ball ... and we're getting closer to the beautiful place where the sand is hot and the sea is as warm as a bath ... and now we're there, lying on that sand, feeling the sun warm our bodies, and as each wave laps over us, it washes it away the pain, and we go deeper ... and deeper."

Rachel sighed and felt the warmth creep through her bones, closing her eyes as the warm sea washed it all away.

As she went deeper … and deeper…

Adam removed the blade from the wound.

He held back the thin layer of flesh and fat with the tea-spoon and inserted the tweezers. As Morag's sing-song voice continued and Rachel's body relaxed, he was himself lulled into an altered state; he felt a strength that guided his hand and focused his mind as the metal dug deep into his sister's back.

"Got it!" he said. He pulled out a small, metal cylinder, the size of a headache capsule, and dropped it with a *"clink"* into the glass that Duncan held out for him. "It's so *small…*"

Duncan looked away suddenly and smiled. "Michael!" he said.

Adam turned to see that Gabriel was standing silently in the doorway. Morag looked up too, taking her eyes from Rachel's face and dragging her thoughts from her story.

From somewhere a million miles away, where she had been floating on a calm sea, Rachel came racing back to reality. The vision of the beach and the warm ocean was torn away from her subconscious, vanishing as she came hurtling back towards earth: down, down towards the planet, the continents coming closer, now countries, towns, streets…

Rachel hit the bed with a crash.

She opened her eyes and cried out in agony, instantly

able to feel the open gash in her back, the air moving against her exposed, raw flesh. As she tried to raise her head from the pillow a jagged stab of pain tore through her like a hot knife. She turned her head to one side and was violently sick.

Then she passed out.

23

"Where *were* you?" Rachel asked.

Gabriel said nothing, continuing to stare off into space, deep in thought, as he had been for most of the time since he'd returned, since he'd been told about the tracking devices that had been implanted back at the Hope Project.

Morag finished applying the makeshift bandage to Adam's back and nodded as she gazed down at her handiwork. "There," she said. "All nice and neat. Rachel made a nice job of it. Like a proper surgeon."

Adam shrugged, wincing a little as the wad of tissue tightened against his skin. "Yeah, well, it was more difficult for me. I had to go first."

Rachel had cut out the tracking device from her brother's back as soon as she had been able to stand. Morag once again provided the necessary pain relief with the soothing power of her voice. Now, the two microtransmitters lay on the bedside table; tiny capsules spattered with red, next to the blood-stained razor blade.

Rachel had recovered quickly from her operation and the pain had eased almost as soon as Gabriel had returned. As soon as he'd handed the Triskellion back to her. She'd shoved the amulet deep into her backpack, surprised and concerned at the enormous wave of relief she had felt flooding through her. She had felt jittery without it – vulnerable – and now the realization that she was so connected to this ancient piece of metal, so *dependent* upon it, was starting to scare her.

She'd seen what it had done to others.

"Gabriel?" Rachel waited until she had eye contact. "I asked where you were."

"I had something to do," he said. "I'm sorry if I *forgot* to ask permission."

"Yeah, well, we really could have done with you here, you know?"

"It was important."

"Why did you take the Triskellion?"

Gabriel's eyes narrowed to bright filaments of green. "It doesn't belong to you. You do *know* that?"

"I just asked."

"I needed to … get a signal."

"Like a cellphone?" Adam asked.

Gabriel smiled, the anger seemingly gone as quickly as it had arrived.

"Maybe you *should* have a mobile phone," Morag said.

"Then we could get hold of you when you're not around."

The smile broadened. "Never really seen the need for one."

"It's not a bad idea," Adam said. "We should all get them, in case we're ever split up."

Adam and Rachel's own phones had been taken away from them when they'd first arrived at the Hope Project. When Adam had asked, Laura had explained that they could interfere with the delicate equipment in the labs. He'd believed her, of course. They had both believed all sorts of things back then.

He glanced across at Rachel and she read his thoughts. "One of the *smaller* lies," she said.

"No phones," Gabriel said. He pointed to where the twin transmitters were lying. "If they can do *that*, don't you think they'd be able to track us through our phone calls?"

Morag and Duncan nodded thoughtfully.

"I guess so," Adam said.

"Besides," Gabriel said, "we have our own way of keeping in touch."

"I *tried*," Rachel said. "I … reached out, tried to make contact, but you weren't there." Gabriel looked awkward, as though he were searching for the words to explain things in a way that Rachel would understand. "Because you were using the Triskellion, right?" she continued.

"I was … somewhere else."

"I guess the line was busy," Adam said.

Gabriel nodded. "Kind of."

Rachel flopped down on to the bed, exasperated. She knew it was as much of an explanation as she was likely to get. She pointed at the bedside table. "What are we going to do with those?"

"I presume they're still transmitting," Adam said.

"Oh yes." Gabriel walked across and looked down at the tracking devices, grinning like a naughty schoolboy who's just come up with a great idea for a prank. "I'm sure they are." He looked up as a foghorn sounded somewhere out in the Channel, then turned round, suddenly serious. "Right, we need to get moving."

"What?" Rachel sat up. "It's the middle of the night."

"We haven't had any sleep," Morag said.

Gabriel picked up the two tiny capsules, held them out towards Rachel. "They know we're here. We have to go now!"

Morag and Duncan immediately began to pack, throwing their belongings into their suitcases. Grudgingly, Adam did the same, but Rachel did not move. She sat where she was, staring at the transmitters between Gabriel's fingers.

"Maybe they're not really after us," she said. Gabriel said nothing, waiting. "Maybe they just want to see where we're going."

Gabriel stared at Rachel for a moment. Her suggestion had clearly hit home. "I think you might be right," he said.

"I mean ... don't you think we escaped a bit *too* easily?"

she asked. "What if they *let* us walk out of there?"

For half a minute Gabriel said nothing, but Rachel could see his mind was racing, as if he was reconsidering their options. And whatever conclusion he was reaching was not one he had entirely bargained for.

Adam looked up from his packing. "Where *are* we going anyway?"

"It doesn't matter," Gabriel said. "Either way we need to go."

Rachel began to pack away her things, but kept one eye on Gabriel, as frightened by his uncertainty as anything else. Whatever her doubts had been, he had always seemed so … sure of everything. Now he looked disturbed. There was a sadness too that she was reluctant to acknowledge, but which gnawed at her as she thought about where he had disappeared to. Whatever it was that had been so important.

She looked across at Adam and sensed that he felt the same: they had both, finally, realized that Gabriel was not *theirs*.

Mr Cheung's kitchen was crowded, but remarkably quiet. There had been a different atmosphere throughout the Hope Project complex since the children had escaped. There was still plenty to do, of course, but it was as though everyone was waiting for something to happen. For the next stage of the operation to begin.

Laura Sullivan carried her plate across to a corner table and sat down opposite Kate Newman. For five minutes they sat in virtual silence, while all around them lab technicians, security staff and archaeological assistants ate their breakfasts and murmured to one another. Conversations were now a little easier, since there was no longer a need for dark glasses or inhibitors.

Mr Cheung bustled across to the table and stood at Kate's shoulder. He pointed down to the plate of untouched scrambled eggs in front of her. "Something you don't like?"

Kate Newman said nothing, waiting for Mr Cheung to go away.

"You should eat something," Laura said. "You'll feel better."

"Will I?"

"The drugs were for your own good, Kate. To help with the depression, to keep you calm."

Kate looked straight past Laura; her eyes everywhere. Anything but calm.

Laura pushed cereal around her bowl. "Why don't you want to talk to me?" She waited, but got no reaction. "I understand how you feel, you know."

Kate looked up. "*Really?* Have you lost any children?"

"They're not lost."

"So where are they?"

Laura took a second or two. She had been given no instructions to keep it secret. "They're in France."

"*France?* What the hell are they doing in…?" Kate gave up before she'd finished the question; her head dropped as though the hopelessness of her situation was more than she could bear.

Given the shocking things that Kate had learned about her own children from Laura since she'd been in England, the idea of them now being in France did not come as so much of a surprise. It just meant that they were further away from her. Again.

"We don't know," Laura said. "*Really*, we don't. We're guessing they're headed for another site. You know, something like the one we found in Triskellion. Not that we know why…" She let out a heavy sigh. "Like I said, we're *guessing*."

Another long minute passed. Laura winced at the sound of cutlery being scraped across a plate on the adjacent table. When Kate finally spoke, her voice was no more than a whisper, but there was steel in it.

"I trusted you."

"I know."

"I know why you are interested in them, but you swore that they wouldn't come to any harm."

"I meant it. I still mean it. They may even be safer there." Laura took a deep breath.

"So you *really* have no idea why they went to France? Where they might be headed?" Kate raised her head, enough menace in her smile to make Laura draw back a little from the table. "You're sitting there telling me you know how I feel, like you're on our side. Making out like you care about Rachel and Adam—"

"I *do* care."

"And all the time you're just after information."

"I'm trying to help, Kate."

Kate stared hard across the table, unblinking. Her eyes never left those of the woman opposite her, even as her hand was reaching for the knife and tightening round it. "There's not much I can do, stuck in here, I know that. But I can be honest with you. Would you like that?"

Laura nodded, said that she would.

"Good. Because if anything happens to my children, anything at all, I promise I will kill you. You understand *that*?"

Laura mumbled a "yes", but her eyes never left the knife. Kate smiled again and let the blade drop on to the table as she pushed back her chair and stood up. She saw the relief in Laura's eyes and used that second of relaxation to grab the coffee cup and hurl the liquid into the archaeologist's face.

Laura screamed.

Mr Cheung came dashing across to help, but Laura raised a hand to let him know it was OK. That *she* was OK. She sat and watched Kate Newman walk out of the room, feeling the tears come.

Pathetically grateful that they were hotter than the coffee had been.

24

They had just about warmed up by the time the train rumbled through the Paris suburbs into the Gare du Nord.

They had spent the early hours of the dawn on a cold, flat beach in Calais, huddled together in front of a small row of beach huts which had protected them from the worst of the wind. Gabriel and Adam had lit a fire and Rachel had wrapped the little twins in the blankets that they had taken from the hotel. They had all fuelled themselves on a slab of dark chocolate and the last of a bottle of milk. As the two sets of twins had become increasingly cold, Gabriel had strolled up and down the dark beach, apparently impervious to the chill, staring out to sea, as if looking for something.

Looking for someone.

As soon as it had become light, they had walked the half kilometre to the train station. They had been glad of the exercise. Happy that it had restored feeling to their feet and hands, and happier still to see the orange lights of the station platform glowing ahead of them, promising escape.

"What time's the train?" Adam had asked, not really expecting anyone to have had an answer.

"First one's 05.48," Duncan had said. "Arriving in Paris at 09.23."

Rachel and Adam had laughed, despite the cold and lack of sleep, and Adam had ruffled Duncan's hair. "The boy's a genius," he'd said.

"He's got a good memory," Morag had agreed.

"But the 06.29 is better." Duncan had continued, getting into his stride. "It takes forty-four minutes less, stops at fewer stations and arrives three minutes earlier at 09.20." Then he had become silent again.

"Perfect timing," Gabriel had said.

They had trudged on towards the station, happy enough, though Rachel was still unsure as to just what the timing was perfect for.

Now, after a three-hour train journey, they walked out between the columns of the Gare du Nord into a chilly Paris morning. This was France as Rachel had imagined it: less like grey, industrial Calais and more like the pictures she had seen at school. She smiled as a man walked past, holding a long stick of bread under his arm. Small motorbikes and mopeds raced down the street, missing oncoming taxis and cars by millimetres. Horns honked and the mopeds buzzed away from them like angry bees. Past the queue of taxis and across the street, a cafe was already busily serving customers at small, round tables. Rachel, Adam, Morag and Duncan wove through the traffic, following Gabriel, who seemed oblivious to the congestion that surrounded him.

They sat at a table while a waiter, smart in a black waistcoat and white apron, took their order for breakfast: coffee, hot chocolate, croissants.

Rachel cradled the bowl-sized cup of milky coffee in her hands, enjoying its warmth as much as its comforting smell.

Opposite, the rows of statues that decorated the classical front of the station gazed impassively over the city. Some metres beneath them, under the station awning, several street entertainers were beginning to set up for the day. One was painted from head to toe in gold: hair, hands, face, clothes, shoes, hat, umbrella. He moved slowly and deliberately, setting up a wooden plinth, also painted gold. He put his hat on the pavement, ready for contributions, then mounted the plinth.

He struck a pose, held it statue-like and began to stare out across the street.

A dozen Métro stops away, the Englishman shuffled painfully into the Cafe Meteor for his usual breakfast. He placed his stick on the bench beside him and took out a laptop computer from his shoulder bag. He sat down and booted it up.

"*Un café, m'sieur ... et un calvados.*" The waiter laid down black coffee and the small glass of strong, apple brandy that the man always ordered. The Englishman grunted his approval, then, with a shaky hand, pushed back the front of his hood, before draining the brandy in a single gulp.

The email browser appeared on his screen and, once the laptop had found the cafe's Wi-Fi connection, he watched as mail began to stack up in his in box. He deleted the usual spam with a few lazy clicks, then began to read the messages that really interested him.

The messages from those who were pledging their help.

The croissants and coffee had not long been finished before Gabriel began to seem agitated. He walked back through the traffic to the station, pacing back and forth underneath the awning and looking up and down the street.

Rachel watched him as the others chattered around her.

When Gabriel arrived back to the table, the waiter was clearing away the cups and plates and seemed happy with the handful of Calais pebbles that Adam gave him in payment.

"Who were you looking for?" Rachel asked.

"Something's gone wrong," Gabriel said. "They're late."

"Who's late?" Rachel persisted.

"Some friends. People we need to hook up with." Gabriel craned his neck to look back across the street. "I can't … hear them."

"Hear *who*?"

Gabriel shook his head, impatient. "We're going to have to go and meet them later."

"Go?" Adam said. "Go where?"

Gabriel stood up and gestured around him. "We're in Paris. It's a big city. Let's go and see some of the sights. At least we know we're not being tracked." He led them back towards the Gare du Nord. "We can get the Underground here and go into the centre of town." Rachel was still asking questions as he ushered the group towards a flight of steps leading down off the street, beneath a sign saying "Métro".

As they walked towards the entrance, Morag was transfixed by the "living" statue. The golden figure nodded suddenly, making Morag jump, then gave her a robotic wave. Morag's mouth opened wide. Rachel waited patiently, remembering how and where the little girl had grown up and guessing that she had never seen such a thing in her life.

"I don't like that man," Morag said, pointing at the statue. Rachel laughed and dragged her along after the others down into the Métro.

As the five of them disappeared underground, the statue watched them go with jerky head movements. Then, as soon as they were out of sight, he took a gold-painted phone from his coat and began sending a text.

25

They got off the Métro at a stop called Saint-Michel and walked to the Cathedral of Notre-Dame. The church loomed over them, massive and dark against the grey sky, as a crowd of tourists and worshippers filed through its doors, a bell clanging a doleful note high above them.

Gabriel seemed keen for them to see inside. Rachel and Adam's only experience of a European church had been in the village of Triskellion. This cathedral was almost as old as the tiny parish church but inside it couldn't have been more different: the unfamiliar smell of incense hit them as soon as they walked in and the high-vaulted ceilings, which soared up into space, way above their heads, made them feel dizzy. The huge, circular stained glass window twinkled ahead of them like a giant, antiquated roulette wheel.

Adam was familiar with the name Notre-Dame from the Disney film and the legend of the hunchbacked bellringer.

"What was he called again?" Rachel asked.

"Quasimodo," Adam told her. He started to gurn and perform a very poor impression of a hunchback, until a smartly dressed French lady put a finger to her lips and told him to "*shhh*".

"I don't remember the name, but the face rings a bell!" Adam whispered to his sister, who thumped his arm, acknowledging the bad joke. Adam was encouraged both by her playful punch and also by his feeling of relief: the safety that they felt being anonymous in a big city, almost as if they were home in New York.

He tried his other hunchback joke: "Hey, where does Quasimodo keep his sandwiches?" he said, smirking at Morag. "In the *lunch*-pack of Notre-Dame!" Rachel groaned and Morag looked confused, but suddenly Duncan began to gurgle with laughter. Gabriel looked at them all blankly. This time they were told to be quiet by several, stern middle-aged French people, and the gargoyles that peered down from every pillar and buttress watched their exit with fixed snarls and stony stares.

They crossed a bridge over the river and stopped to eat crêpes from a stall on the riverbank.

Rachel sighed and looked across the sluggish brown river. For a few hours it had been possible to feel almost normal, and the water flowing slowly by, through the heart of the city, had begun to make her feel relaxed.

She chewed the last of her lemony pancake, licking granules of sugar from the corners of her mouth. She screwed up the paper plate. "Where next?" she asked Gabriel. "When are your ... friends arriving?"

"Still no sign," he said. "Let's keep walking. They'll be in touch."

They walked away from the riverbank into an area that became busier, passing shops with smart window displays of glamorous mannequins and modern furniture. A few streets further on, the shops gave way to a vast, open square. On the far side, looking like a giant aircraft hangar, covered in coloured, oversized scaffolding and snaking walkways, stood the Centre Georges Pompidou.

"Pompidou Centre," Rachel said, reading a street sign in English. "It's some kind of art space."

"Awesome!" Adam said. He instinctively preferred this sleek, modern architecture to that of Notre-Dame, and liked the look of the fashionable young crowd thronging through its doors. "Can we go in?"

They walked across the square, past small groups of people gathered around the many street performers that juggled, tumbled and mimed in front of the building. As they drew closer, they could see that the transparent tubes zigzagging diagonally across the outside of the building carried people to the upper floors. Rachel was looking up to the roof when Morag tugged at her sleeve.

"There's the nasty man, Rachel," she said, drawing Rachel's attention to another gold-painted "living statue", who was waving mechanically at tourists across the cobbled square.

"Oh, I think there's more than one of those guys in Paris," Rachel said, laughing as they moved through the automatic sliding doors into the airy foyer of the building.

The Englishman shook the bottle and emptied a dozen pills into his reddened palm. He tossed them into his mouth and crunched them, swilling them down with his last gulp of beer. He waved his glass, signalling to the bar for another. The chime from his laptop computer alerted him to the arrival of an email. He studied it, replied quickly, then, with shaky fingers, launched an internet search engine and typed in some words. Within seconds he had skipped the home page and the list of forthcoming exhibitions, and the live webcam from the forum of the Pompidou Centre appeared on his computer screen. Small figures moved jerkily across the screen, updating every five seconds.

The Englishman clicked his keypad and zoomed in...

The two sets of twins and Gabriel wandered around the floor of a gallery and past the re-creation of an artist's studio. The bronze sculptures of elongated, skeletal figures reminded Rachel of twisted and mummified bodies: images buried deep in her psyche. When the younger twins became bored, they decided to ride the escalator in the tubes they had seen from the outside and go up to the cafe on the roof.

The square grew smaller below them, the clusters of people, scuttling around the central giant sculpture of a gilded flowerpot, becoming progressively more ant-like.

None of them had noticed that the golden figure had left his plinth and was entering the building.

The children arrived at the top floor and went outside to look out over the zinc roofs of Paris: the Eiffel Tower on one side and the white dome of the Sacré-Coeur on the other. Very few others had ventured out as it was cold and windy so high up. Gabriel disappeared off with Adam to find them some drinks.

"You can see everything from up here," Rachel said, holding hands with each of the small twins. A maternal nervousness made her keep them back from the edge, even though it was protected by the thick, white struts of the building's external structure.

"I can see the nasty goldy man again," Morag said, gripping Rachel's hand tight.

"What from all the way up here?" Rachel leant over to try and see the square below.

"No, he's *there*," Morag said, pointing to the top of the escalator where it arrived at roof level.

Rachel turned in time to see a golden hat before the man wearing it rose into view and walked briskly off the escalator towards them. Rachel instinctively felt that he shouldn't be here – and that if he was, they *definitely* shouldn't be.

"Quick!" she said. "Come with me." She dragged Morag and Duncan across the roof towards a pair of

ventilator ducts that ended in big white trumpets, like those
on a ship's deck. She looked around wildly for Gabriel and
her brother, catching a glimpse of the golden man talking on
his phone and scanning the roof terrace for them.

Rachel pushed the younger twins behind the ducts, allowing herself a view across the roof through a gap between the
outlets. She could see the top of the escalator and watched
as another performer from the square joined the gold-
painted man on the roof.

This one was dressed as a robot: painted in silver and
black, his arms covered in extra-long sections of corrugated
tubing that waved about as he danced. A metal funnel was
pushed on top of his head, which made him look like the
Tin Man from *The Wizard of Oz*. Rachel edged herself out a
little to see the pair better. Perhaps she was being paranoid,
maybe they were on a tea break. These thoughts quickly
evaporated, though, when the gold man caught her eye.

"Là-bas!" he shouted, running quickly towards the ventilator ducts, the robot a few steps behind him.

Rachel pushed Morag and Duncan along the roof.
"Through there," she hissed, pointing towards a mesh fence.
A small gate led through to a caged inspection area under a
red metal box that housed the workings of a lift. The whole
caged area hung over the edge of the building and was supported by thick, steel girders. Rachel threw herself into it
after the little twins.

The two street performers had split up in an attempt to

corner the children on the roof, and within seconds a golden face appeared at the gate that Rachel and the twins had just squeezed through. There was just room for him to stand in the opening.

"Here you are!" he said. "I've got you now."

"Leave us alone!" Rachel pressed herself and the twins back against the wall of the cage. She looked down at the mesh decking. Through the gaps, she could see the square, some thirty metres below.

The golden man grinned as he pushed into the cage after them, his gold lips pressed against his yellow teeth. Seconds later, the robot followed him, long arms flailing and clanking against the steel cables of the lifting gear. Rachel caught sight of a pair of vicious-looking pliers protruding from the end of one tube-covered arm and from the other, a length of wire.

Rachel struggled as the golden man grabbed her arms and twisted them up behind her. The wound on her back made her shriek with pain, and the man slapped her face.

Huddled in the corner of the steel cage, Morag and Duncan began to squeal too, like trapped mice, their high-pitched voices drowned by the whistle of the wind through the steel.

The man was so close Rachel could smell cigarettes on his breath, which came hard and fast as they struggled in the confined space. Suddenly another, deeper scream joined that of the twins. From nowhere, Gabriel had appeared in the cage and grabbing the robot's coil of wire, he looped it up and hooked it round the robot's neck. The golden man turned to see his friend strung up, his own wire round his throat and looped over one of the crossbars and then pulled taut from behind.

Rachel saw Gabriel tying the wire to a huge metal cog and, seizing her moment, she kicked out, her foot crashing into the golden man's stomach and winding him.

The robot continued to thrash around, his arms flailing, desperate to loosen the wire from his neck. But his efforts only made it cut deeper into his throat.

"Aidez-moi!" he gurgled.

Somewhere below, somebody pushed a lift button.

There was a metallic *"clank"*, a *"whirr"* and the cables began to move, and the dancing robot was lifted into the air, up into the workings of the lift.

The golden man scrabbled around, eager to escape the cage in which he had trapped Rachel and the twins, but where he was now trapped himself: the strange boy with the cold eyes blocking his way.

"Let him go, Gabriel!"

Gabriel turned to see Adam coming towards them. There was a look of horror spreading across Adam's face as he watched the robot's feet kicking from beneath the red box. He beckoned to his sister and the twins. Rachel pushed Duncan and Morag out past Gabriel and the gold man before following them herself.

"He might say how he found us, Gabriel," she said, gesturing at the gold man as if pleading for his life.

"*Oui!* Yes, I will tell you." The man began crawling towards Rachel and Adam on his hands and knees, begging. "Only please, don't—"

But they could see that Gabriel had already decided.

He knelt down and grasped the man's forearms, staring directly into his face, the watery gold-painted eyes darting desperately around until Gabriel fixed them with his own. Suddenly, the man's body was trembling uncontrollably and his hands began to smoke as the steel mesh beneath him turned red hot. Gabriel's eyes bore into him and flakes of gold started to peel from his face. His mouth opened in a silent scream as the floor melted away underneath him. Then Gabriel casually let go of his arms, allowing him to fall the six floors on to the square below.

Nobody noticed the five children hurrying away across the square a few minutes later. A crowd had gathered round the groaning, golden figure who had fallen from the top of the Pompidou Centre and miraculously survived. A broken gold-painted statue who now hung limply over the rim of the giant flowerpot.

A few wondered if his fall had been part of some strange performance.

In a caravan park, just outside a pretty sailing port in Normandy, Mr Alfred Brunt, from Stoke-on-Trent, treated himself to the first glass of French wine of his holiday. He congratulated himself on his careful route planning, delighted that he had made the journey along the coast in under four hours.

He was glad to be away from Calais, where they had parked the camper van overnight in the station car park, only to be disturbed early that morning by a gang of youths on their way to the station.

He was sure that one had fiddled with his petrol cap.

But now, Mr Brunt was on holiday proper and looking forward to his lunch: a steak and kidney ready meal that his wife, Glenda, had brought with them from England and was popping cheerfully into the microwave.

Glenda screamed as the first boot crashed through the skylight above her head, and her husband bellowed in fear as the side window was smashed in, leaving a riot baton tangled in the net curtain. Both of them shouted for help as the door of the camper van was blown off its hinges and meekly raised their hands as two men, wearing dark glasses and headphones, burst in and levelled automatic weapons at them.

26

The Métro thundered into Les Halles and the doors hissed open, allowing the five children on to the crowded train.

Rachel's knees still felt weak and it was all she could do to support herself by grabbing desperately at the overhead strap. Adam helped Morag and Duncan on board and made for the three available seats, only to be beaten to it by an elderly nun, her face smiling primly from behind a wimple. Adam nodded and gestured for her to sit down, the younger twins taking the two seats beside her.

Morag and Duncan had maintained a traumatized silence since they had escaped from the roof. Gabriel had not said a word, and neither Rachel nor Adam had dared say one to him. In truth, at that moment, they were terrified of him – and what he was capable of.

Rachel decided to break the silence.

"Those men back on the roof – how could they *still* be tracking us? We took those transmitter things out."

Gabriel was clutching on to the metal handrail above his head. The motion of the crowded train took him close to Rachel as he swayed and fought to keep his balance. "I don't think they were working for the Hope Project."

Adam was pressed closely against his sister, one arm stretched out to clutch Morag's hand. She, in turn, was holding tightly on to Duncan. Adam stared at Gabriel, his eyes wide with confusion.

"Well, did they *look* like they worked for the Hope Project?" Gabriel said.

"They were French," Rachel said. "We heard them speak."

"Doesn't matter where they're from," Gabriel said. "There are people like that in every country. People with … extreme beliefs. They keep themselves well hidden, so we'll need to be careful."

"So who were they?" Adam asked. He raised his voice just enough to be heard above the rumble of the train as it roared beneath the Paris streets. He did not want to alarm Morag or Duncan. "Who the hell else is after us?"

Gabriel looked from Adam to Rachel. He laid a hand on Adam's shoulder, reached round to pull Rachel close and spoke to them both without saying a word.

Are you ready to fight?

Rachel's fingers tightened round the rail. She leant her head against her arm and closed her eyes, wishing that she could open them and find herself back at home, instead of running for her life through foreign countries, trying to keep one step ahead of people out to hurt her for reasons she did not understand.

She opened her eyes and stared out into the blackness of the tunnel.

Duncan's eyes were fixed on the adverts above the heads of the passengers sitting opposite him. His lips moved as he mouthed the words and, next to him, Morag knew that he was memorizing every line, every piece of information, how ever trivial. Her brother could remember everything he'd ever read; every picture he'd ever seen. They'd never talked about it, not properly, but she knew that he could remember far more than she could about what had happened all those years before in the loch. The car and the lights and the dark water.

She'd heard him crying out in the night often enough.

Feeling a hand on her knee, Morag looked up to see the nun smiling at her. The old woman had a kind face, Morag thought, even though the clothes she wore were strange and her free hand was furiously twisting the necklace of wooden beads snaked between her thin fingers.

The nun mumbled something and Morag leant closer to hear.

"N'aie pas du peur, mon enfant."

Morag heard the whispered words in perfect English. *Don't be afraid, my child.* She nodded, feeling warm suddenly and safe, as though a thick coat were being wrapped round her shoulders.

"Tu es vraiment speciale."

Morag nodded, then watched as the nun glanced up and the blood left her sunken cheeks. Morag followed the old woman's gaze and saw a tall man in a long brown robe standing directly behind Gabriel and the others. Next to her, the nun crossed herself and lowered her head, clutching at her beads for all she was worth.

"Michael!" Morag shouted.

Gabriel, Rachel and Adam turned and found themselves staring into blackness; into the shadow beneath the thick hood, where the figure's face should have been.

He towered above them, his cloak giving him the look of a monk. There was nothing kindly about the figure, though, nothing *benevolent*, and Rachel and Adam began backing away immediately, only to find their escape route blocked by the crush of passengers behind them.

"It's OK," Gabriel said, but he didn't sound as though he meant it.

The man in the robe did not move. One hand, the skin livid and blistered, was wrapped round the handle of a black stick. The other was slowly raised, reaching out towards the children.

"Give it to me."

The man's voice was broken and whispery, but there was no mistaking the insistence in his request. He waited a few moments, the shadow beneath the hood growing deeper as Rachel and the others stared into it. Then he spoke again, calmer this time and more dangerous, "Give it to me."

"No," Gabriel said.

Rachel knew straight away what the man was asking for. She pushed back harder against the crowd, reaching round to take hold of her backpack; to get as close as possible to the thing she knew was nestled at the bottom of it, among her T-shirts and dirty socks.

Although the man's face remained hidden, unreachable, Rachel could sense a smile growing within the blackness for the second or two before he lowered his hand.

"Your choice," he said.

Gabriel stepped forward, putting himself between the older twins and the robed figure, then spoke to them over his shoulder. "Go," he said. "Move out of the way."

They did not need telling twice. They turned and pushed their way through the crowd, grabbing Morag and Duncan as they went, pulling them along through a tangle of angry passengers who shouted and cursed as they were barged out of the way. Once they had reached the door at the end of the carriage, Rachel turned. She reached for Adam's hand and together they peered back through the sea of heads at Gabriel and the hooded figure, straining to hear what was being said.

"I know what you are," Gabriel said.

The hood quivered slightly, as the man in the robe cocked his head. "And I know what *you* are."

"So you'll know that I'm not afraid then," Gabriel said.

"That I'll do whatever it takes to protect what's mine."

The hooded figure turned his head towards the window. Were it not for the impatient tapping of his stick against the floor of the carriage, it might have been the most casual conversation in the world.

"I *will* have it," he said. "You need to know that. And if you insist on protecting it … protecting those who carry it, people will die."

"They already have, and even if I gave it to you right now, it would not be yours." Gabriel was sounding more confident now, inching closer to the man in the robe as he spoke. "Whatever you think it will give you, you're wrong. You and the idiots who follow you like sheep."

The man's head snapped forward. "Until now, you were just an obstacle, but I'm really going to enjoy … clearing you out of the way." He glanced over to where Rachel and the others were huddled. "All of you. I'll know where to find you."

The train was slowing for a station. "I think we'll be getting off here," Gabriel said. "Keep in touch."

The man in the robe gave a small shrug. "Like I said, your choice. We could have done this the simple way. The painless way."

Gabriel was already moving away from him, squeezing between the passengers, gathering up Rachel, Adam, Morag and Duncan as the train pulled into the Métro station and urging them out the instant the doors opened.

"He didn't have a *face*," Morag said.

"Yes, he did," Gabriel said. "He's just choosing not to show it to us yet."

They stood on the platform as the train pulled away, watching as the carriages rushed by them. The man in the robe was nowhere to be seen, but Rachel caught a glimpse of the nun, the black and white habit flashing past her, before the train disappeared.

She was still frantically crossing herself.

27

Laura Sullivan would not normally have been watching an early evening discussion show, but she'd been flicking through the channels on the set in her office and come across a face she'd recognized.

Chris Dalton.

The man with whom she'd been working just a month or so earlier, on the dig at Triskellion, had changed. It was as though he'd aged ten years in a few weeks. He was ranting at the cameras, red-faced and raving, while the programme's host struggled to get a word in and the studio audience laughed and squirmed in their seats.

"... they've been coming here for centuries! Coming here and breeding with us. I saw the bodies with my own eyes. You all saw them ... it was on TV, for heaven's sake. And they're still here, and the children are here—"

The host cut across him. "Come on, Chris, are you seriously asking us to believe that—?"

"I'm *telling* you!"

"Well, thanks for—"

"It's in their DNA, don't you see? They look like ordinary kids, but they're dangerous. They need to be stopped."

The camera panned quickly away from him, settling back on the perma-tanned host. Looking somewhat relieved, he tried to wind things up while Dalton continued to burble on in the background until his microphone was cut.

"So, there we are. Chris Dalton. Once a trusted archaeologist, and now? Visionary? Nutcase? You decide…"

Laura switched the TV off, then jumped slightly when the door opened. The image of Dalton's face in her mind, wild-eyed and haunted, was wiped away as Clay Van der Zee marched into her office. He looked a lot calmer than Dalton had, but when he spoke, it was clear he was every bit as worked up.

"We've lost them!" he said.

"What?" Laura remembered her conversation with Kate Newman that morning. She felt something lurch in her stomach.

"We knew they were clever," Van der Zee said. "But even so…"

"Tell me."

Van der Zee paced up and down Laura's small office as he spoke, waving his arms around, more passionate than she had ever seen him. "Our equipment tracked them to a town called Honfleur. A small sailing port on the Normandy Coast."

"Sounds like a nice part of the world."

"Very nice part of the world, if you're a tourist. Say a middle-aged couple on a caravanning holiday."

Laura got it. "They found the transmitters."

Van der Zee nodded. "Six hours ago our agents kicked in the door of a small camper van. Now we have two very frightened and angry tourists, and a lot of egg on our face."

Laura failed to suppress a smile at the absurdity of what had happened, and at the ingenuity of the children. Van der Zee caught her expression. He smiled himself, but there was no joy in it.

"So, now it's down to you, Dr Sullivan."

"What can I do?"

"You can do something useful with all those years of research. You can get on your damn computer and call up all the data you've amassed on these sacred sites. I want you running location programs around every one of them. Every stone circle, every burial mound, everywhere anyone has so much as dug up an old coin, until you work out where those kids are headed. Is that clear?"

Laura's eyes dropped, but only for a second or two. What was clear to her, and becoming more so with every hour that passed, was that she was starting to root for Rachel and Adam Newman.

"I'm not sure I want to."

"Excuse me?"

"I don't think I'm what you'd call 'on message' any more, OK?"

"I thought we'd been through this, Dr Sullivan. I'd hoped I'd put your mind at rest."

Laura shook her head. "I'm sorry. You'll have to get someone else to find the children for you."

Van der Zee nodded, as though he were seeing her point of view. "I did mention the other … mystery, didn't I?"

"What mystery?"

Van der Zee strolled across to Laura's computer, began tapping at the keys. "I think this might rekindle your interest." An image appeared on Laura's screen: grainy black and white. Four figures standing on a train platform. "This is CCTV footage from Ashford station, just after they jumped off the Eurostar."

Laura looked hard at the picture. The children were huddled close together. They looked lost. She wondered if they'd been cold. Van der Zee leant across her, jabbing his finger at the screen, at the image of each child in turn.

"Rachel, Adam, Morag, Duncan."

It took a few seconds. "I thought there were supposed to be five of them?"

"There were," Van der Zee said. "Our agent saw another boy, got a good look at him. Quite the artist too…" He took out a sheet of paper from his pocket, unfolded it and handed it to Laura.

She stared down at the picture of a dark-haired boy with

green, almond-shaped eyes. Had she seen him before? He looked familiar…

"So, we have a child who seems to be leading the others. A child who, for whatever reason, fails to register on CCTV cameras. I thought, you know, that might be … of interest."

Laura tried not to let her excitement show, but her heart was thumping against her ribs. "Can I keep this?"

Van der Zee was already at the door. He knew he had her; that she was firmly back "on message". "Sure," he said. "We'll need your initial findings on the route as soon as possible, OK?"

Laura nodded as she heard the door close. She took a pin from her drawer and fixed the picture of Gabriel above her desk. She stared at it for a few seconds longer before opening the file she needed on her computer and getting down to work.

"Who are these two?"

The boys had been waiting at the gate when Rachel and the others had arrived at the Gare d'Austerlitz in the southeast of the city. They were sixteen, maybe older, and Rachel had disliked them on sight. They had long, greasy hair and wispy moustaches and wore matching nylon anoraks. A dirty, red beanie hat was the only thing distinguishing one from the other.

Identical twins.

The boys sneered at Rachel, and the one wearing the hat turned to Gabriel. "Ariel?"

"Who?" Rachel asked.

Gabriel looked flustered and began ushering everyone towards the platforms. "No time for introductions now," he said. "We've got a train to catch."

As if on cue, Duncan rushed up and began tugging excitedly at Gabriel's sleeve. "Platform seven, the Francisco de Goya express. Non-stop, overnight service. Departs 19.43. Arrives 09.17 tomorrow morning."

"Arrives where?" Adam asked.

Duncan cleared his throat. "Chamartín station, Madrid."

28

It had been a long time since Rachel and Adam had slept in bunk beds. Rachel guessed it would have been when they were five or six, in the tiny apartment their parents had moved into when they'd first got married. She could remember green curtains at the window and brightly coloured posters on the wall and the furious race to get to the ladder each night at bedtime and claim the top bunk.

They'd fought about almost everything back then.

Neither she nor Adam had been able to summon the energy for any such competition when they'd eventually found their way to the tiny sleeper compartment on the overnight train. Once he'd kicked off his jeans and trainers, Adam had wearily hitched himself up on to the top bunk, giving his sister a little privacy to undress, and as soon as she was ready, Rachel had settled down on the bunk underneath without a word.

Both were hoping that sleep would come quickly.

Thirteen-and-a-half hours, Paris to Madrid; it was far and away the longest train journey that either of them had ever taken. They'd made the four-hour trip to Washington DC a few times – traipsed round the Smithsonian and had pictures taken outside the White House – but that was about it. A train journey through the night was a marathon by comparison, and, if there hadn't been so many other things to think about – so many worries – they would both have been pretty excited.

Rachel lay back and listened to the sound of the train, letting its gentle, rhythmic rocking carry her away. She knew that Morag and Duncan were in the compartment across the corridor and that the French boys were somewhere further along, towards the restaurant car. She had no idea where Gabriel was. She imagined him striding up and down the length of the train, his mind racing faster than the engine, unable to sleep.

If he ever slept at all.

The French boys…

Jean-Luc and Jean-Bernard. It had taken over an hour of surly looks and inaudible grunting to get so much as their names out of them, and even then they had been given grudgingly. They'd sat huddled at a table with Gabriel, while Rachel, Adam and the younger twins had sat across from them, trying and failing to make conversation.

"So where are you from?"

"You speak English?"

"You speak *at all*…?"

The new boys had insisted on calling Gabriel "Ariel", talking in whispers and tossing dirty looks across at Rachel and the others if anyone had so much as offered one of them a stick of gum.

"Maybe they just don't like us because we're American," Adam had said.

"Maybe," Rachel had answered.

"Didn't we fall out over Iraq or something a few years back? Remember, we weren't allowed to call them 'French' fries…?"

"*We're* not American," Morag had said. "And I don't think they like us either."

Duncan had glared across at the two French boys. Jean-Luc, the one with the hat, had turned and stared right back, picking at something stuck between his dirty teeth.

"Just ignore them." But even as Rachel had said so, she had known she would find it difficult. She had been desperate to find out who they were and where they lived; not because she was genuinely interested in them, but because she wanted to know what their connection was to Gabriel. How long had they known him? What had he told them about himself? Why on earth had he invited them along?

The guard had come by an hour or so into the journey, and, after a few words from Gabriel, had happily taken the children's non-existent tickets. Everyone had ordered food from the buffet – sandwiches and cold drinks – and once they were eating, Jean-Luc and Jean-Bernard had begun talking to Gabriel in French but neither Rachel nor Adam had been able to understand what was said. The boys were obviously capable of understanding English and could translate a foreign language into their own as easily as Rachel and Adam, but it seemed they were also able to *block* the translation powers of others when they felt like it.

"I can just hear … *noise*," Adam had said. "Like some kind of interference."

"Me too." Morag had pulled a face. "It's not fair."

Furious, Rachel had sworn under her breath. She'd seen the look from Jean-Bernard. "They can still understand *us*, though."

"I bet we can do it too." Adam had glanced across and seen a slight smile from Gabriel, who had looked as though he was enjoying himself, and Adam had known he was right. "Come on … *concentrate*."

Rachel had closed her eyes and tried to focus. After a minute or so, she'd begun to picture a barrier forming, layer upon layer inside her mind.

Adam's words had come into her head as the wall took shape. *That's it*, he'd said. *Keep going*. It had been delicate yet powerful; a latticework of light that had hummed with energy and strength, and had twisted around every phrase and sentence, darting between the letters like an insect in flight, until each had been bound up tight.

Protected.

Opening her eyes again, Rachel had looked at Adam and spoken with her mind. *You want to try first?*

Adam had smiled. *Chicken.* He'd cleared his throat and turned to look at the two French boys. "Hey, you ... doofus!" When he'd caught Jean-Luc's eye, he leant across. "You two look like monkeys, you know that?"

Rachel, flashing the pair her nicest smile, had added, "Smell like them too."

It had been clear from the shrugs that neither boy had understood a word, and Rachel and Adam had settled back in their seats, mentally congratulating each other. On the other table, Gabriel had only stopped laughing when Jean-Bernard had banged a fist on the table, like a small boy who was not getting enough attention.

The conversation between the tables had become rather more animated after that, though every bit as unfriendly; Gabriel – the only one able to understand both sides – had done his best to keep the peace until darkness fell outside, and all three sets of twins had wandered off in search of their beds.

Rachel lay listening to Adam shifting his position on the bunk above her. She knew that he was not asleep; that he was finding it as difficult as she was.

"Adam, are you OK?"

"I'm fine."

"You sure?"

"Positive. G'night."

Then, ten minutes later, Rachel heard her brother say, "You ever think about Dad?"

"Course I do."

"Lately, though? I mean, it's all been about Mom, hasn't it? I know she's the one who stuck by us, the one who's in trouble, but it's not like he's … dead or anything, is it?"

"No."

"So, *do* you?"

Rachel realized that, although her father popped into her mind many times every day, she could not remember the last time she had really sat down and *thought* about him: how he might be feeling; if he was missing them. If she was missing him. He had been the one who'd walked out, who had decided that the marriage was not working, but still… She felt guilty for taking her mother's side quite so easily. If it took two people to make a marriage work, didn't it take two people to wreck it?

She knew that Adam had found it much harder to decide where his sympathies lay.

"When everything's … back to normal, or as back to normal as it's ever going to be, I'm sure we'll get to spend time with him, you know?"

"Yeah…"

"He could hate Mom's guts," Rachel said. "But that wouldn't change the way he felt about us."

"I know that. I was just asking, that's all."

Rachel heard him swallow and turn over again. "We

should try and get some sleep."

There were a few more murmured words after that, but soon Rachel heard her brother's steady breathing and she knew he was asleep, and almost as soon as she'd had the thought, she was asleep herself. She woke once in the middle of the night and reached down to the floor for a T-shirt to wipe the tears away. When she opened her eyes again it was light outside.

Adam was still dead to the world as Rachel crept out of bed and across to the small window. Mist lay low across brown fields strewn with vast boulders, and, craning her neck, she could see a walled city ahead: towers and turrets rose up on the summit of a rocky hill, where the tracks swept round in a wide curve to the left-hand side.

She pulled on her clothes and stepped out into the corridor. The guard was on his way past her door. "Are we coming into Madrid?" she asked.

"No, miss; Madrid's still a couple of hours away." He led Rachel to the small area between carriages and pointed out of the window. "That's Avila. It's medieval, matter of fact. An amazing place … if you like churches all over the place, that sort of thing. You should go and visit."

Rachel saw Gabriel step through the door at the far end of the carriage. "Maybe next time," she said. The guard shrugged and wandered away. From the look on Gabriel's face, Rachel knew that there would not be a great deal of time for any sightseeing.

Adam was out of bed when she walked back into the compartment, and Rachel gasped when she saw him turn to pull his T-shirt over his head.

"What?" Adam said. "What's the matter with my back *now*?"

Rachel just shook her head and pointed. It had been a little over twenty-four hours since she'd dug into her brother's flesh with a razor blade.

"It's completely … healed," she said. "There isn't a mark on you."

29

Laura Sullivan rubbed her knuckles into her tired eyes. She took a gulp of strong black coffee and tried again, without success, to focus on the screen of her computer. She looked up, as she had done periodically throughout the night, at the coloured pencil sketch of the narrow-eyed boy pinned above her desk. It felt as if he was guiding her, telling her where to look next.

She had been working feverishly since the previous evening, putting all her data together. She had eliminated a network of false leads and had gone down a dozen blind alleys. She had re-examined significant findings and now, as a new day dawned over the Hope building, she felt she may have finally made a breakthrough.

Laura knew she had to produce a result, or enough of one to placate Clay Van der Zee. Something to convince him that her preferred course of action was the correct one to follow: to let the children's powers develop in the wild. To allow Rachel and Adam free access to roam across Europe and lead them to...

Laura didn't know *where* they would lead her. Her greatest hope was that it might be to another site like the chalk circle at Triskellion. A site that might yield more important remains and ancient treasures. Anything that would throw light on the meaning or the function of the Triskellion.

She hoped too that they would lead her somewhere that might reveal the identity of this mysterious fifth child. The boy in the picture. Just the *possibility* of meeting him was more exciting than anything in all her years of research.

Above all, she hoped that wherever the trail led, whatever happened at the end of their journey, would liberate the twins: would leave them free to get back into society. Laura was convinced that any lessons they might learn from Adam and Rachel would benefit mankind in some way. She felt instinctively that their way of thinking, their communication and their mind skills could be learned by others; could even be bred into future generations.

She believed that kids like Rachel and Adam Newman might *be* the next manifestation of humanity. The New Man.

A new breed...

Homo erectus: the caveman. *Homo neandertalensis*: Neanderthal man. *Homo sapiens*: us.

Then what?

Homo triskelliensis? Triskellion man?

Laura laughed to herself. Now her mind really *was* racing: buzzing with too much coffee and too little sleep. What she *did* know was that anything less than a plan of action and a convincing route would have Van der Zee marshalling a sweep of agents across Europe to bring the kids back in.

She couldn't let that happen.

Most of Van der Zee's superiors in America considered these children a "threat to humanity" and would insist on continuing with what they worryingly called "invasive research". If they could tag kids without a thought for their civil liberties, then heaven knew what else would be considered valid research.

Research that might well be terminal.

Throughout the night, Laura had eliminated dozens of Bronze Age sites from her inquiry. Since discovering that the twins were in France, she had hoped that they were heading for the ancient standing stones at Carnac on the Brittany Coast. That would have made sense. The village was geographically and geologically similar to Triskellion. It had a very static population and a high occurrence of twins. Even the ancient symbol used on flags and monuments to represent the region of Brittany was a Triskellion.

She had fed in some of the data from the Triskellion site: metal analysis from bronze beakers, fabric samples, carvings, symbols and signs found in the area. A bewildering array of matching burial sites dotted right across Europe had appeared on her screen. It was only when she had factored in some genetic information about the inhabitants – the incidence of twins, the age of the population – that a definite pattern had begun to emerge.

A line could be drawn directly between certain sites. Starting from Orkney in the north of Scotland, where Morag and Duncan were from, it ran all the way down the West Coast of England and Wales, to Triskellion in the West Country. Then it jumped across the Channel to Brittany and continued south-west through France. From the Dordogne area, the line went south again, across into Spain and continued further down, still in a clear, unbroken line…

Laura stared at the map and tried to keep the mounting excitement under control. Looked at in reverse, it was the same line that tracked the development of Bronze Age man across Europe and into the British Isles.

A theory was taking shape and her meeting with Clay Van der Zee was in two hours.

She needed more coffee.

"Je déteste les Espagnols," Jean-Luc grumbled to his brother. He shambled ahead along the tree-lined avenue that led from the station. He'd been honked at aggressively by a car as he had wandered aimlessly into the road.

"I think I got the meaning of that," Rachel said to Gabriel, some steps behind. "He hates the Spanish."

Gabriel smiled at her and, fixed by his green eyes, she

felt a brief, but powerful, surge of the warmth that had once existed between them. It was something she missed hugely; that she had not felt since they had left Triskellion. The day was bright and a little chilly and Rachel pushed her hands deep into the pockets of her fleece. She took the opportunity to probe a little.

"I think Jean-Luc and Jean-Bernard hate everything, don't they?"

Gabriel shrugged. "They've had a tough time. They come from a village in Brittany, a small place like Triskellion. People have treated them badly since they were born."

Several metres ahead Jean-Bernard spat on the pavement.

"I thought you said they were friends. *Our* friends."

Gabriel let out a sigh and stared at the French boys. They were fighting with one another, landing playful kung-fu kicks with scuffed trainers and bumping into people on the street. "They are," he said. "They're like you. Like us. I didn't say you had to *love* them. Can't you see them for what they are?"

Rachel said nothing.

She had felt it when they'd escaped from Hope, when they'd gone many hours without sleep and when her brother had carved a microtransmitter from her back. Rachel looked at Gabriel and felt yet again that he was testing her.

They turned down a smaller street with shops on either side. Dawdling some way behind Rachel and Gabriel, Adam was struggling to keep Morag and Duncan moving. They moaned that they were still tired, stopped each time something new arrested their attention and now Morag was hungry. Adam ducked into a greengrocer's, then emerged a few seconds later with a bunch of bananas. He handed one to each of the younger twins and watched as Morag greedily peeled and chewed, as if she hadn't eaten for a week.

Then he became aware that someone was following them.

Adam grabbed Morag's hand. "C'mon, we're getting left behind." He could see Rachel, Gabriel and the French boys up ahead, but they were a good distance away and Morag whined as her little legs tried to keep up.

"Quick as you can," Adam said. He glanced behind him, trying not to alarm the youngsters.

A man was coming up fast behind them. He caught Adam's eye and quickened his pace. Adam looked frantically around but saw nowhere to run, nowhere to hide. Before he could move, a car pulled up hard alongside them and Adam watched its driver, a big man with a black moustache, jump from the driver's seat and step out in front of them.

Adam took a defensive stance, but the man just looked at him quizzically before snatching a parcel from the passenger seat and carrying it into a nearby shop. Adam let out the breath he had been holding and looked behind him again. The first man was closer now.

The driver had left the engine running…

"Get in!" Adam pushed Duncan into the front of the car and helped Morag clamber over into the back. He slammed the door behind him and locked it. In the rear-view mirror, Adam could see their pursuer trying to work out where they had gone and then the realization on his face that they had got into the car.

Adam began to panic, cursing himself for locking them into what was effectively a cage. He was sitting in the passenger seat. Duncan was next to him, his hands clamped tightly round the steering wheel. They weren't going to get far like this, Adam thought. Not that *either* of them knew how to drive.

"I do," Duncan squeaked, tapping into the scramble of thoughts going through Adam's mind. "I know how to drive."

"*What?*"

"Are you sure?" Morag asked.

"I read a book," Duncan said.

In the short time he had known Duncan, Adam had been amazed time and again by the little boy's abilities. Now, as the man bashed his fist on the roof of the car, there was no time to question them.

"Go!" he shouted.

The engine screamed as Duncan stretched one leg to depress the accelerator and the other to operate the clutch. He let off the handbrake and his body twisted with the effort of turning the steering wheel as the car took off down the street, its tyres squealing.

Adam looked behind as their pursuer was thrown into the

gutter. He caught a glimpse of the man with the moustache come tearing out of the shop. Adam watched him help up the first man, and they both started running after them.

Adam stared across at Duncan, who was leaning forward, his head barely higher than the wheel.

"Fast as you like," he said.

However carefully Duncan had read and memorized the manual, knowing *how* to drive and actually *driving* on a busy Spanish street were two completely different things.

Rachel, Gabriel and the French boys were astonished, then horrified, as the red Seat screeched past in second gear, driven by an eight-year-old boy who could not steer. The car was smashing off the kerb and knocking over rubbish bins. Rachel saw her brother's terrified face through the window – his body was being thrown from side to side and his arms were braced against the dashboard. She saw Morag flying around on the back seat, and she saw two angry men running down the centre of the street after the car, each one waving fists and shouting curses.

"Adam!"

"Whoa!" Jean-Luc jeered after the car in French-accented English, while his brother whistled and jumped in the air as the car snaked off out of sight.

"Supercool!"

The two of them immediately began sprinting after the car, with Rachel and Gabriel doing their best to keep up, while a few streets away, a police siren began to wail.

"Stop!" Adam shouted, grabbing at the steering wheel, but Duncan's foot was jammed down on the accelerator. Adam pulled the wheel clockwise and the car turned into another street, missing a news-stand on the corner by a whisker. Adam tried to straighten up, but the car was going too fast, revving too high. Every yank he made on the wheel needed a push in the opposite direction to compensate, sending the car crashing into the kerb and squealing against the body-work of vehicles parked on either side of the street.

"Look out!" Morag screamed as a taxi came up the street towards them. A white wall, painted with the bulbous, waving figure of the Michelin Man, stretched between the parked cars, announcing the entrance to a garage.

The taxi was still coming.

Adam saw the gap and pulled the wheel clockwise again, heading straight for the garage's entrance. Duncan took his hands off the wheel and closed his eyes. Adam wrenched the handbrake and the car spun sideways, bounced over the high kerb and smashed into the long, white wall.

For a few seconds there was silence. Then…

"Quick! *Ven aquí!* Come here; get out!"

Adam heard a kindly voice above the hiss of the burst radiator as the car door was wrenched open. The smiling face of the Michelin Man peered through the shattered windscreen as Adam and the twins clambered out of the wreckage, dazed but unhurt.

"You will be all right."

The voice belonged to a small, neat man in a white warehouse coat. He ushered Adam, Morag and Duncan across the street to a shop, above which, on a sign spelled out in gold letters, was a single word:

A few minutes later, the policeman examining the written-off car wondered why there were so few witnesses about. Two surly French boys seemed to be the only people who had seen the accident and they simply smirked and shrugged incomprehension whenever he spoke to them.

Then two, out-of-breath Spanish men came charging round the corner.

"They took my car," said one. "I was just making a delivery."

The other nodded. "I was serving a customer," he said. "And this little tearaway stole some bananas."

Jean-Luc and Jean-Bernard were already walking away, their absence going unnoticed. They were relieved that the explanation was a simple one, that the events had not been more sinister, and they were already looking forward to the fun they would have at the American boy's expense.

The idiot had simply forgotten to convince the shop-keeper that he had paid.

30

Rachel and Gabriel arrived to find Jean-Luc and Jean-Bernard walking away from the scene of the accident. Jean-Luc grinned and smashed his right fist into the palm of his left hand. Jean-Bernard supplied sound effects and mimed a crash with screeching tyres, explosive noises, police sirens and, for reasons best known to himself, machine-gun fire.

"Cool!" they said as one, grinning.

"Where's my brother?" Rachel demanded. "And the little ones?"

Jean-Luc studied her for a moment, then nodded across the street to a row of small shops. They walked over the road, towards one selling straw baskets, and another whose window was full of smoked hams. In between the two was a smaller shop: its window crammed with jars of various shapes and sizes, their contents catching the light in a hundred shades of gold. Etched into the glass door of the shop was an elaborately detailed picture of a bee and above were the words "Abeja" and "Miel" in old-fashioned script.

"Miel … honey, right?" Rachel asked.

Jean-Luc nodded. "It's the same in French."

"This is the place," Gabriel said. He pushed open the door and walked in.

A man in a white coat was waiting for them. He was standing to attention in the middle of the shop and his face lit up as the boy with green eyes walked through the door. He marched up to Gabriel, his hands trembling, as if he were summoning the courage to touch his face. Then, as though thinking better of the idea, he lightly patted the boy's arms and spoke, a little nervously.

"I am Señor Abeja."

The man was in early middle age, nearing fifty perhaps, but his olive skin was so free from wrinkles and the cheeks around his goatee beard so cleanly shaven that the general effect was one of an ageing little boy. His shoulders sloped away from his small head, and the legs of his sharply creased trousers ended in small, black shoes, like those of a dancer.

"I knew you were coming," he said. Rachel had no need for translation, as the man spoke in good, if slightly tentative, English. "I had a dream about the car crashing across the road. I saw the American boy and the little ones…"

"Where are they?" Rachel asked. She still did not know if anyone had been injured.

Señor Abeja looked at Rachel for the first time. "I'm sorry," he said. "They're in the back. They're fine. A little shaken, perhaps."

The shop was packed, floor to ceiling, with jars of honey; some clear, some solidified, some with honeycomb suspended in pale golden liquid. Señor Abeja's elaborate bee picture was printed on each jar, along with a handwritten label bearing the names of the flowers that had produced the pollen: thyme, orange blossom, rosemary. Screens, smokers and other beekeeping equipment were piled up against the walls, from which hung nets of all sizes and an assortment of beekeeper's hats and gloves.

"Come through," Señor Abeja said. He opened a rickety door at the back of the shop that led through to a tiny kitchen. Adam, Duncan and Morag were sitting at a table, sipping from small glasses. "I gave them lemon juice with brandy and honey. It's good for shock."

"Hi, sis," Adam said.

Rachel moved quickly towards her brother. He was very pale and she could see blood on his chin. "You OK?" She looked across at Morag and Duncan. "You guys OK?" They nodded.

Gabriel turned to Adam. "What happened?"

"We were being followed," Adam said. "I don't know if it was someone from the Hope Project, or one of the ... others." He saw that the French boys were smiling. "What?"

"Bananas," Jean-Luc said.

"Bananas," Jean-Bernard echoed. They no longer seemed

bothered about blocking the translation. "You forgot to 'pay' for the bananas."

"Oh," Adam said, reddening.

Gabriel walked across and laid a hand on Adam's shoulder. "No harm in being careful," he said.

"Yeah, well…" Adam rubbed at the small cut on his chin, then rubbed the bump on his head and looked down at the table to hide his embarrassment.

Rachel stepped towards him and knocked playfully on the top of his head with her knuckles. "That's what happens when you let an eight-year-old loose in a car."

"He just needs practice," Morag said, and everyone laughed.

Señor Abeja's house was a few streets away. Having watched from his window as the battered Seat was towed away, he shut up shop for the day and led them through the narrow back streets.

"I don't think anyone knows we're in Madrid," Gabriel told him.

"*I* know you are in Madrid. And if I know, someone else may know. But you will be safe in my house for a while."

As the French boys kicked an empty plastic bottle across the cobbles of the deserted road, Señor Abeja stopped in front of a green gate, took out a key and opened a little door within it. Rachel looked up at the tightly shuttered windows, joined together by a cobweb of telephone wires, that stretched high above her on either side of the street. The buildings looked as if they had their eyes shut: giving no sign of life to anyone on the outside.

Rachel gasped when the shopkeeper opened the little door and ushered them through into a fabulous, tiled courtyard. She guided Morag and Duncan through, then followed after him. Exposed staircases – their ornate metal banisters twisted like roots and branches – climbed up from the courtyard to whitewashed balconies on each floor. Palms, creepers and trailing plants gave the space a lushness, as though it was a secret jungle, hidden away, just a few metres off the busy street.

In the centre of the yard, quietly buzzing in the afternoon calm, stood nine beehives.

"My bees," Señor Abeja said, proudly stating the obvious, as Gabriel and the three sets of twins stared around the fantastic courtyard. "Now, you must meet my mother. Afterwards you can get some rest, and later we will eat something together."

"Sounds good," Adam said. And as he and Rachel climbed the staircase up to the first floor, they noticed that, fired into the little tiles on either side, was the sign of the Triskellion.

Laura Sullivan walked towards Van der Zee's office like a schoolgirl on her way to face the music. Worst of all, *she* was the one who would be expected to do the talking.

Word had come through that the children had been

spotted in Madrid. News of an incident involving a car –
apparently being driven by a small boy – had been picked
up from police radio by Hope agents in Spain and quickly
filed back. As soon as Laura had heard the report and the
location, she had felt certain about where the children were
headed. She'd rushed back to her computer to look at that
line again, snaking down from Scotland and out across several countries, and she had been as sure as she could be.
It wasn't their final destination – that was still debatable
– but it was definitely the next stop on their journey.

She'd have bet her life on it.

Van der Zee had called her almost immediately. He had
been excited; insistent that now Laura had been handed
another piece of the jigsaw, he was expecting a much clearer
picture.

Expecting answers.

She slowed as she approached the door of his den and
took a good long breath. She thought about Rachel and
Adam and the boy with green eyes. Now she had to decide.

It wasn't so much *what* she should tell Van der Zee,
as *if*…

31

Señora Abeja was a round, bustling woman dressed head to toe in black. She would probably have appeared stern and somewhat frightening had her hair not been dyed an improbable shade of orange. Rachel guessed she was around the same age as her own grandmother had been and smiled to herself as she watched the old lady issue instructions to her son in machine-gun Spanish, gesturing with arthritic fingers as she fired out her orders.

"Salvador, fetch a clean tablecloth. The *good* linen, Salvador, and bring up some wine while you're about it. The good Rioja ... the Reserva! Salvador, slice some ham. The Ibérico, Salvador ... we must have the best, and not too thick; you always slice it too thick..."

Sitting round the table in Señora Abeja's salon, the twins watched, amused as the middle-aged man did his mother's bidding. He had changed into a smart grey suit with a bow tie, and he tugged at his goatee beard or twisted the ends of his moustache as he went about his errands.

He glanced nervously at Gabriel, winked at Rachel and pinched Morag and Duncan's cheeks as he filled the table with ham, wine, olives and bread until, finally, they were ready to eat. The French boys had been watching a loud game show on Señora Abeja's old TV, but the food, beautifully laid out on large wooden platters, lured them to the table.

Only Gabriel stood away from the table, deep in thought on the balcony outside the room. Señora Abeja sheepishly beckoned him in, making "eating" gestures, then, gaining confidence, waving a variety of incoherent blessings over him. Finally, she grabbed him, pressed his face to her bosom and kissed the top of his head repeatedly. Gabriel looked more than a little relieved once he had sat down and everyone had started eating.

Rachel asked Señor Abeja about his bees, explaining that their friend in England, Jacob Honeyman, was a beekeeper. Abeja did not seem surprised, as if everyone had beekeeping friends. He told them excitedly that Spain had the biggest bee herd in Europe: about seven hundred billion strong. "That is about eighteen thousand bees for every person in the country."

Morag gasped. "Where does everyone keep them?"

Abeja laughed. "Did you know that the earliest recorded beekeeping and honey gathering was here in Spain?" Everyone shook their heads, hanging on his every word. "It's true. It is recorded in eight-thousand-year-old cave paintings."

"Paintings of bees?" Morag asked.

Abeja nodded and turned to Gabriel, his enthusiastic demeanour changing in a moment. He looked sad suddenly; beaten down. "In the last few years, though, the bees have been dying..."

"Why?" Rachel asked.

Abeja shrugged and explained that entire colonies had been struck by a mystery disease he called *desabejacion*: de-beeing. Some claimed it was pesticides, he said; some that it was caused by mobile phone waves. Others claimed that the ecosystem had been irreparably damaged by modern man.

"No big surprise," Gabriel said.

Abeja shook his head sadly and told them that forty per cent of all Spain's bees had been wiped out. "It is destroying my livelihood, and if it gets worse it will destroy *everything*."

Adam looked unconvinced. "Everything?"

Jean-Luc looked at his brother, equally sceptical. *"Je ne comprends pas..."*

"There's not much to understand: without bees there is no pollination," Abeja said simply. "The bee makes food for us. The only animal that works so that we can eat. If bees die out, within four years, life on this planet will come to an end."

It was conversation that came to an end; silence descended like a shadow across the table, until Señora Abeja finally spoke up: telling her son that he was a miserable doom-monger and eagerly encouraging the children to carry on with their dinner.

Adam leant across to Rachel and whispered, "We could still eat meat, though, right? If all the bees … you know?"

"I guess so," Rachel said.

"Except, what would the *animals* eat?"

"Looks like we should stop using mobile phones."

The second glass of good, red wine that Señor Abeja had poured made Rachel feel warm inside. She felt her cheeks flush as she ate more of the delicious food that had been placed in front of her: a huge clay dish of yellow rice, tiny roasted peppers, meatballs and crisp legs of chicken. The French twins gobbled their food noisily and with enjoyment, as did Adam. Thanks to the wine, he was becoming even more chatty than usual.

"Best food I've ever eaten," he said.

"Gracias," Señora Abeja said.

"Delicious," Morag chirped. Next to her, Duncan nodded, his mouth full.

"Better than anything in France," Adam said. Jean-Luc looked up briefly from his chicken leg and made a gesture with his finger that Adam chose to ignore. "A toast!" Adam raised his glass in the air theatrically. "To Spain!"

Morag raised a glass too, though hers was only filled with water. "My favourite country in the world," she said. "So far."

Everyone raised their glasses, even Jean-Luc and Jean-Bernard, who grudgingly expressed their liking for the country. "Better than England anyway," Jean-Bernard muttered to his brother in French.

"Or America," Jean-Luc replied.

Señor Abeja and his mother beamed, delighted that their honoured guests were so clearly enjoying their hospitality. Señora Abeja blushed to the roots of her orange hair and her son told them all that they were very welcome.

He looked at Gabriel. "Especially you," he said.

Gabriel appeared to pay no real attention. To have no interest in celebrating anything. Rachel thought that perhaps the wine had affected him too. He appeared distracted suddenly, his green eyes wandering as he stood up and spoke, more to himself than to anyone else.

"Listen to us all … *chattering* happily," he said. "Getting on like a house on fire, aren't we?"

Rachel could hear the anger creeping into his voice. She leant across and put a hand on his arm, but he did not seem to notice.

"This is what we exist for, what we *should* exist for anyway. The kindness of strangers. People who do not think just of themselves, but who think of individuals as part of a whole."

On the other side of the table, the French boys exchanged a look. Rachel caught their thoughts; sensed their confusion as Gabriel ploughed on.

"People like Señor and Señora Abeja here, who behave like the bees they keep and care about so much. Working so that others can survive. Acting for the good of the hive, *always*."

Rachel thought she saw tears brimming in Gabriel's eyes – just in that second before his voice dropped to a whisper and he looked down at the table.

"Hurt one of them and you hurt them all," he said. "Hurt one of us … and you hurt us all."

Señor Abeja's face was serious once again. He cleared his throat and opened his mouth to speak, but a look from Gabriel made it clear that he should wait.

"You hurt us *all*…"

The old lady went to bed, after kissing them all on both cheeks twice and calling out a croaky *"Buenas noches!"* as she climbed the stairs.

Señor Abeja showed the children to their rooms. Rachel settled the younger twins down in a pair of small beds off the landing and, while Adam and the French boys ran noisily up to the top floor, Señor Abeja ushered her graciously into the room next door. "I hope you will be comfortable here, Raquel," he said. "This was my grandmother's room."

Rachel stared at the carved wooden bed, thick with blankets and covered in lace. "I'm sure I will," she said, trying to look like she meant it.

Abeja pointed to a pile of blankets and clothes on a wooden chest in the corner. "Those are for you all to take with you when you go. You must take care of the little ones; you are like their mother. And you must take care of Gabriel too. You have a great … responsibility."

Rachel nodded, thinking, that isn't fair. I don't *want* it.

Señor Abeja wished Rachel goodnight, kissing her lightly on both cheeks, his moustache tickling her face. Then he opened a cupboard, took out two books and handed them to her. One looked almost new: *All About Bees*, by Salvador Francisco Ortiz Abeja. The other was far older, leather-bound and falling apart, a Triskellion stamped in gold on its spine: *The Ancient Churches of Seville*.

"Thank you," Rachel said, a little confused.

A few minutes later, propped up against the feathery pillows, Rachel opened the newer book and began to leaf through the diagrams of bees. The drawings were delicate, done with great care, and she thought about how much Jacob Honeyman would have loved it. She found herself able to read in Spanish about the bees' flight patterns, their rituals and inexplicable "dances". She looked at a passage about how the hive worked for the good of all, just as Gabriel had described, and soon she found herself drifting into a deep sleep.

32

The beat of the drum gets louder as the procession makes its way slowly across the square. It is Sunday, so that everyone can be here. They have been told to attend by the king himself. It is compulsory. It is an act of faith. Absence will be a sign of guilt, to be punished as these poor people are to be punished.

It is not cold, but the little girl shivers as the parade comes closer. A twisting, terrible serpent: its body black with the sweating pelts of horses and the cloaks of men, its nostrils streaming plumes of smoke and its glittering eyes the flames of burning torches.

The approaching footsteps shake the girl's body in time with her pulse. She thinks her heart will burst as the bugles sound and the first of the black horses approaches. She hears its urgent whinny, sees the flash of its wild eyes and teeth. She feels the flecks of frothy spittle on her face as it tosses its head.

The man on the horse has had his shirt torn away and his

upper body is naked. His hands are tied behind him and he writhes in pain as soldiers on either side tear into his back with whips. He is followed by another man, then a woman, then three others – their faces all masks of pain as the soldiers lay on vicious strokes without mercy.

This is what comes of helping the Traveller, for believing his words. For being his friend.

She presses her face into the coarse material of her mother's skirts. Her twin brother does the same. They feel the warmth of her legs and try to breathe in the scent of her body, in the hope that it will take them away from this dreadful place.

The little girl hears a roar from the crowd, and she cannot help but look.

Here is the man himself, held high and strapped into a wooden chair. A gnarled green candle has been forced into one hand and a string of beads has been woven between the fingers of the other. A pointed hat has been pushed on to his head. It is decorated with suns and moons and stars, giving him the appearance of a terrible, tragic clown.

A steel collar attached to the back of the seat holds the man's head upright and his mouth is gagged with a red cloth. The others can speak; can cry out in pain. They can stop the whipping by yelling out their admissions of guilt and save themselves from the flames.

But no one wants to hear what the Traveller has to say.

The king and the priests have heard enough of his ridiculous and wicked ideas. They do not want to hear that the universe is endless; that this earth is neither flat nor unique. They have seen enough of his sorcery and his so-called "healing" powers.

The little girl looks up. She sees the tears rolling down her mother's face as the Traveller passes and she sees that his eyes are unafraid, calm and green. She hears her mother sobbing and muttering blessings. She knows that her mother is remembering the stranger's kindness; remembering how a few years before, he had healed her and had eventually become anything but a stranger.

The little girl remembers how, after she and her brother had been born, her own grandfather had been among the first to denounce the very man who had given him grandchildren. Had accused him of sorcery and heresy: of witchcraft. The same grandfather who now walked with the grim procession and helped to carry the chair up the few wooden steps to the stake, before adding his own flaming torch to the bonfire.

The little girl and her brother cry as the heat from the flames scorches their faces and the terrible smell catches in their throats.

As the Traveller burns, he reaches out a hand to those who have condemned him and to his own children, who have been condemned to watch him die. The little girl sees her father, sees the love in his eyes; she looks around and sees the bloodlust in the eyes of everyone else.

She takes her brother's hand and runs...

* * *

It was clear that Salvador Abeja would have been happy to see his guests stay a lot longer. He certainly seemed in no hurry to get back to his shop. The next day, when Gabriel announced, after a late breakfast of milky coffee, pastries and freshly squeezed orange juice, that it was time to be moving on, the Spaniard's face fell.

"Are you sure?"

"Yes, I'm sure," Gabriel said. "We have a lot to do."

While the children gathered up their things, Abeja led Gabriel to a quiet corner of the courtyard. "Seville is over five hundred kilometres from here," he said. "How will you travel?"

"We can get the train, or it's only an hour's flight…"

Abeja shook his head and whispered conspiratorially, "There are people who are looking for you, yes?" Gabriel nodded. "Well, they can always get on the same train as you. The same flight. You would be trapped, like sitting ducks."

"We are not helpless," Gabriel said.

"All the same…"

Gabriel saw the concern on the man's face. "What have you got in mind?"

Once the others were packed, they all followed Abeja down to an old wooden garage at the back of his house. It was filled with ancient beekeeping equipment and crates of honey, ready to be shipped. In the middle sat a large vehicle of some sort under a dusty, black tarpaulin.

"This is the best way," Abeja said. He whipped away the sheet to reveal a grubby, blue camper van. "I have had this since I was a young man," he said. "I used to make lots of deliveries."

"That would explain the ... decoration." Adam pointed to the large, flaking painting of a beehive on the side of the van and at the huge plastic bee on the roof, just above the windscreen.

Abeja nodded. "The engine is still good. It will get you to Seville. I have no real use for it any more."

Rachel saw the sadness in his eyes as he spoke and remembered what he had told them the night before about the bees dying out. She wondered how much he had suffered financially; how much longer he would be able to stay in business. She walked across and slipped an arm through his. "Thank you," she said.

He seemed to brighten up suddenly. "You are more than welcome." He pointed at the van. "It's not exactly inconspicuous ... but it's the best way."

"Who's going to drive?" Adam asked.

Duncan's arm shot into the air. "I don't think so," Gabriel said.

The French boys were muttering to each other, and after a few moments Jean-Luc spoke up. "We can drive," he said. "We can take it in turns."

"What are you? Sixteen?" Adam asked. "That the legal age in France?"

Jean-Luc shrugged. "Legal, illegal, what's the difference? We are good drivers."

Gabriel nodded and the children started loading up their stuff and clambering into the camper van. As they bickered about who was going to sit where, Abeja hurried back to the house, insisting that his mother would want to see them off. When the two of them returned, there were tearful goodbyes: Morag sobbing her heart out as the old woman hugged her and stroked her hair; Rachel fighting to control the quiver in her lip as she thanked Abeja once again. Even Adam had a lump in his throat as the camper van pulled out on to the side street that led back to the main road, and everyone craned their necks to wave goodbye to the beekeeper and his mother.

"Which way?" Jean-Luc asked. He was taking first turn at the wheel.

Gabriel began unfolding the large map that Señor Abeja had given him, then stopped when Duncan cleared his throat in the seat behind him.

Morag leant forward and tapped Gabriel on the shoulder. "We don't need a map."

"Head for the Paseo de Santa María de la Cabeza," Duncan said. "After half a kilometre, take the exit towards Toledo, then two kilometres after that, turn on to the A-42. Exactly the same distance later, turn on to the service road and take exit six towards the M-40, then…"

Adam, Rachel and Morag were starting to giggle.

Jean-Luc held up a hand. He waited for Duncan to stop, then leant towards the dashboard and began fiddling with the old radio to try and find some music.

"Just tell me where to turn," he said.

Two hours later, they were making good progress along the main motorway that twisted through Andalucia. The road was busy, and the landscape grew greener and more hilly as they went, becoming warmer and bathed in honey-coloured light as the sun began to drop in the late afternoon sky. On the back seat, Rachel gazed out of the window and let her mind wander; her thoughts dancing to the rhythm of the engine's incessant sputter. Voices echoed in her head, blending into one another like a twisted tape-loop.

Her mother. Abeja. Gabriel.

I'm fine, though, baby. I promise.

You have a great responsibility.

Are you ready to fight?

It was quiet in the van. Bar the odd snippet of conversation, nobody had said much once they had negotiated their way out of Madrid and into open country. Rachel had been especially struck by how quiet Morag was. She sensed enormous apprehension radiating from the two youngest, and wondered if this was the longest time they had spent in any vehicle since that fateful journey with their parents five years before. Rachel knew that, if she looked hard enough, she would be able to see the pictures in the minds of Morag and Duncan, but it would have felt invasive, somehow. If she was right, she knew what they would be thinking.

Dark water and green weed, and the lights of a car tumbling down into the depths. The silent screams for help.

Adam had tried to generate a little enjoyment. He'd told them about the games that he and Rachel had played during long drives with their parents. The silly quizzes and competitions on road trips from New York to Connecticut or down the East Coast. "See who can spot the most cars of a particular colour, like blue and red. First one to get ten red and ten blue cars is the winner, OK?"

"What do we win?" Morag had asked unenthusiastically.

"It's just for fun," Adam had said. "Remember, fun?"

Adam had started counting the cars out loud, but had given up when nobody had seemed willing to join in and Morag had lain down across the seat. Half an hour later, when Adam had been dropping off himself, Duncan had suddenly begun talking. "We've passed seventeen blue cars and fourteen red ones, and that includes lorries and coaches. There were thirty-six other vehicles of assorted colours – the most common of which was white." It had been when he had began reciting the individual number plates that Adam had announced he was the winner and undisputed champion. That had been the last time anyone had spoken.

Rachel must have drifted off to sleep. When she opened her eyes she was cold and the sky was full of stars. They were driving along an unlit, deserted road. Jean-Bernard was now at the wheel, and with the van's interior in virtual darkness, she could not be sure if anyone else was awake. Then she heard Adam sigh, and up front, Jean-Luc whispered something to his brother.

"Where are we?" Rachel asked sleepily. "Are we lost?"

In front of her, Gabriel raised an arm and pointed. "Follow that," he said.

"Follow *what*?" Jean-Bernard asked.

"The star…"

Jean-Bernard peered up through the windscreen and Rachel leant forward to do the same. One star was far brighter than the rest and, as she watched it, it seemed to drift a little. She closed her eyes for a few seconds and looked again. Jean-Bernard began shaking his head and muttering in French.

Adam nudged her. "Bit early for Christmas, isn't it?"

"*Follow* it!" Gabriel said. "It's not far now."

Rachel looked out of the window but could see nothing. Not far to *what*? she thought.

The Englishman stared at the screen on his laptop. He reread the email from one of his followers, followed the link to El Telegrafo website and studied the news story from the local paper. The picture showed that the car involved in the accident had been badly damaged, but the report made it clear that nobody had been hurt.

A shame. That would have saved him a lot of trouble.

The sender went on to detail the children's movements for the rest of their stay in the city, such as he had been able to piece together. It was all a little late now, of course, but the Englishman had not expected it to be easy.

He remembered how close he had been on the Métro in Paris. The look on the face of the boy with the green eyes. The *defiance*, even after he had been warned…

He glanced at the bottle of painkillers on the desk. The agony was almost unbearable in the evenings, but he left the bottle unopened. There were times when the pain was useful. It reminded him of what *had* been done and it helped take his mind off minor disappointments.

So he had missed the Newmans in Madrid; he would pick up their trail quickly enough. His followers were growing in numbers and the more there were, the harder they would be to avoid. Once he had put the word out, they would deal with the interfering Spaniard.

There would always be those who tried to help these children; to offer them protection. They were foolish, of course, and the Englishman would make it his mission to put them right. They would be made to pay.

An hour and a half later, the camper van began rattling across a track that felt as though no vehicle had travelled on it for a long time. The wheels tossed stones up against the underside of the van as it bumped and lurched. Staring out of the windows, Rachel could still see nothing beyond a sea of blackness, a jagged line of mountains silhouetted against a dark grey sky and the solitary star.

They hadn't seen a single sign of life for many kilometres.

It was getting colder inside the van. Morag and Duncan were huddling together and Adam had wrapped a jacket round his shoulders. Rachel could see Jean-Bernard shiver as he leant forward, straining to see past the camper van's headlights, to catch a glimpse of what lay ahead of the weak, milky beams.

On Gabriel's instruction, he had slowed the van to a crawl. The engine spluttered, as though it might die any second. Rachel was on the verge of asking where the hell they were going, when Gabriel turned round and smiled, reading her thoughts.

"We're here," he said.

He jumped from the van as soon as Jean-Bernard had killed the engine, slid back the doors and helped the others out. Nobody seemed in much of a hurry, but Gabriel was very patient: unusually relaxed, Rachel thought. The change in his mood had been almost instantaneous. A calm had taken hold of him the second his feet had touched the ground.

Rachel felt her own mood change just as quickly, but not for the better. It was almost pitch-black and freezing. Huge boulders loomed out of the darkness and it was hard to take so much as a step without tripping on the uneven ground.

Were it not for the fact that they were breathing clear and ice-cold air, they might have stepped out on to the surface of the moon.

"Where are we?" she asked.

Gabriel bent to pick up a stone, rubbed off the dirt and rolled it over in his palm. "We're among the dead," he said.

33

"But … I thought Seville was a big city," Morag said.

Gabriel walked round to the back door of the camper van. He produced torches and handed one each to Morag, Adam and Jean-Bernard. "It is. We're still an hour or so away from Seville."

"It's cold," Morag said. "Can I get back in the van?"

"Course you can. Stay warm."

"What do you *mean*?" Rachel said.

"Mean by what?"

"Where on earth *are* we?" Adam asked.

Rachel took the torch from Morag and shone it in Gabriel's face. "'Among the dead'?"

"One question at a time would be good," Gabriel said. He turned his face away from the glare and Rachel let the torch drop. The children waited. By now all the torches were shining in Gabriel's direction. "This place is called Sierra Norte," he said. "It's a protected site. It's … very special." He turned and pointed, though for the life of her

Rachel couldn't understand how he could see anything. She could barely make out a thing. "There's a Bronze Age necropolis a kilometre or so in that direction. A city of the dead."

"Perfect," Adam said. "You know, with it being so dark and spooky and everything…"

Gabriel turned again and lifted his face up, like he was trying to catch the scent of something. "There are caves too," he said. "With prehistoric remains. Neolithic paintings. Like I said, it's a special place."

Rachel took a step towards him. "So why are we here?" She looked into his green eyes, shining in the torchlight, and knew the answer. "You'll be needing the Triskellion then."

"I won't be very long," Gabriel said.

As soon as Rachel had retrieved the amulet from her backpack and handed it over, Gabriel began to walk away. Adam waved the torch around and shouted after him. "Hey, what are we supposed to do?"

"Make a fire," Gabriel shouted back. "Weren't you in the, what d'you call them, Boy Scouts?"

"Cub Scouts," Adam said. "And I never got as far as making fires."

"So rub some sticks together." Gabriel's voice was growing fainter. "Or maybe some old *bones*…"

Adam couldn't see Gabriel any more. He raised the torch anyway and shouted into the darkness. "Very funny."

* * *

Laura Sullivan watched as Kate Newman turned on to the corridor that led to her room. Laura saw her avoid all eye contact with the security personnel and scientific staff she passed as she moved through the building. Watched her keeping her head down.

Though Kate was not at liberty to leave the premises, she was no longer held under lock and key in her room, and the drugs had been withdrawn. Clay Van der Zee had made it clear, however, that the dosage could be reinstated at any time. Especially if there were other incidents like the one in Mr Cheung's kitchen, or like the hour she had spent hammering on his office door in the middle of the night, kicking and screaming, until she'd had to be forcibly restrained by guards.

"I cannot have you endangering yourself," Van der Zee had said. "Or any member of my staff."

Kate had assured him, and Laura, that there would be no further episodes of that sort.

Now, as Laura Sullivan watched this woman walk, slowly but surely, towards her room, she felt that she would still be unwilling to get too close, if Kate Newman was holding anything hot ... or sharp.

Laura had to time it carefully. She needed to reach Kate just as she was going into her bedroom. Laura knew that, given the chance, Kate would not let her in the room at all.

God knows, Laura would not have blamed her.

She put on a burst of speed over the last few metres of floor space and got there just as Kate was opening her bedroom door.

"What the *hell*—?" Kate said.

Laura all but shoved her through the door and closed it behind them both. She held up a hand when Kate turned and raised her arms, ready to fight. "Please, stop and listen, Kate. You've got to *listen*." Laura tossed a canvas bag down on the bed.

Kate glanced across at the bag, unwilling to take her eyes off Laura for longer than she had to. "What's in there?"

"A change of clothes; some essentials." Laura took a second to control her breathing. Her heart was pounding. "Your passport."

Kate's eyes narrowed. "What's going on?"

"You need to trust me, OK?" Laura waved away the objection, the abuse she knew would be forthcoming. "Please … you need to do *exactly* what I tell you, or this won't work. I'm taking you out of here."

Kate swallowed hard. Her voice dropped to a whisper. "How? How can you?"

"I've got security clearance," Laura said. "Highest level. I can get us out of here. But I need to take you out now. *Tonight*."

"Take me where?"

"To your children."

* * *

Jean-Luc and Jean-Bernard spent ten minutes watching Adam gather twigs and leaves. Then spent five more sniggering as he cursed in frustration and rubbed uselessly at stones and sticks before Jean-Luc casually tossed across the lighter that had been in his pocket all the while.

"Whoops," Jean-Bernard said. "Forgot we had one of those."

Adam looked like he was about to explode.

Rachel laughed, until she remembered that she also had a lighter tucked in a pocket of her backpack; she'd bought one during their trip to the hypermarket back in Calais. She and Adam watched as Jean-Bernard and his brother got the fire going.

"I guess we're not very good at this," she said.

Morag and Duncan had crawled off to sleep under blankets in the camper van. Once the fire was well established, Adam, Rachel and the French boys sat around it and began to relax a little. They drank coffee from old-fashioned flasks that Señor Abeja had given them and dipped into some of the supplies he had sent with them. Tinned fish and biscuits. Strong cheese and huge, juicy oranges.

Jean-Bernard and his brother spoke about their lives: a sequence of unhappy foster homes and years spent in care or in trouble with the police.

"There was nobody else around to look after us," Jean-Luc said. "So we had to do it ourselves."

Jean-Bernard shrugged and spat an orange pip into the fire. "But we always had each other. Always." He gestured towards Rachel and Adam. "Same as you two, yes?"

Adam and Rachel nodded. "We've got our mom, too," Adam said. "And our dad… Wherever he is." He stared across the flames at Rachel.

They told Jean-Luc and Jean-Bernard about their visit to Triskellion and about the time they had spent at the Hope Project. They explained that they may have been allowed to escape so that their movements could be tracked, describing all those who had been on their trail ever since. The French boys listened, showing no emotion, even when Adam described what Gabriel had done to the gold-painted statue or when Rachel spoke – unable to keep the tremor from her voice – about the sinister monk they had run into on the underground train in Paris.

"These people," Jean-Luc said, "whoever they are, will find things a lot harder from now on."

"Right." Jean-Bernard stuck a cigarette between his lips and leant forward to light it directly from the flames. "Because now they are up against all of us."

"You understand?" Jean-Luc said.

Rachel and Adam said that they did and they both shook the proffered hand when it was stretched out towards them. It was a strangely formal gesture, a little awkward perhaps, but the French boys' hands felt strong and warm against their own, and the handshake was only broken at the sound of something howling in the darkness.

Adam tried to look unconcerned. "Wild dog?"

Jean-Luc shook his head. "A big cat, I think."

His brother agreed. "A lynx, maybe."

"*Maybe?*" Adam turned to Rachel. "I don't suppose you remembered to pick up any silver bullets…?"

There was a lot more laughter around the fire after that, but Rachel no longer found the notion of monsters as ridiculous as she might once have done. After all she had seen, all that she now knew existed, was it really any more ludicrous to believe in werewolves or vampires or three-headed, blood-sucking zombies?

Even if it was, Rachel knew very well that there were plenty of ordinary monsters at large in the real world. Far more dangerous and a lot harder to spot.

Nobody could say for sure how long Gabriel had been gone, but suddenly he was back with them again, sitting around the fire and drinking coffee as though he'd never been away.

"I know you're good at coming and going real quiet and sneaky," Rachel said, "but sometimes I think you do it just to try and make me jump."

"I think you're right," Gabriel said. He grinned, seeming delighted to see the two sets of twins getting on so well.

"We bonded over making the fire," Adam said. He winked at Jean-Luc and was pleased to get a wink in return. "So, you … made contact or whatever?"

Gabriel nodded. "We will meet two more friends tomorrow in Seville."

"Spaniards?" Jean-Luc shook his head, grimaced at his brother.

"I'm afraid so." Gabriel smiled and closed his eyes, beginning to make himself comfortable.

"We are going to Seville tonight, though?" Rachel said. "Right?"

"No need," Gabriel said. "Everyone's eaten, haven't they? We've got a good fire going." He raised a hand and began to wave it around. "It's nice here. It's…"

"'Special', I know," Rachel said. "Only you kind of forgot to mention the big cats."

Gabriel sat up and looked at her. "We'll be safe here, I promise."

She believed him. There had been a time when believing him would have been automatic but now it required more of an effort.

Safe for one night, perhaps. For a few hours in the middle of nowhere. But as far as the rest of their lives went, how ever long or short they might prove to be, Rachel would need some convincing that any of them could ever really be safe again.

Señor Abeja tucked his mother in for the night. He sat with her while she prayed, just as he always did, then leant forward to kiss her goodnight.

"It was nice to have visitors, Salvador," she said.

"I know," Abeja said.

"I prayed for them." The old woman turned on to her side. "I prayed that they stay safe."

Abeja turned the light off in his mother's room and walked slowly down the stairs towards the courtyard. He liked to check on his bees last thing; to sit outside if it was warm enough and enjoy half a glass of red wine and perhaps a piece of dark chocolate before going to bed.

It was a lovely evening, and from the balcony on the first floor, he could see the lights of Madrid stretched out below him. At the bottom of the stairs, he reached up to take a lemon from the tree that was growing in a large pot. It was perfectly ripe. He would have it with the fish he was planning to cook for dinner the next evening.

Halfway across the courtyard, he stopped. He never bothered to switch on any lights – he knew every inch of the place – but even in the semi-darkness he could see that something was wrong.

It was the shape of the hives.

They had been pushed to the ground … trampled. Abeja rushed across and dropped to his knees. He scooped up the fractured pieces of each honeycomb; the muddy print of a large boot clearly visible against the delicate skein of honey. He gently laid each piece to one side and began using the edge of his hand to brush away the bodies of the crushed bees, while those that were still alive crawled across his arms and legs.

"Abeja."

The voice came from behind him. He stood and turned, frozen in terror, as the figure moved out of the shadows. "What … what do you want?"

The man wore a wide-brimmed black hat, and his eyes were obscured by a carnival mask. His voice was slightly muffled by the red silk scarf tied across his nose and mouth. "You should have stuck to putting honey in jars," he said. "Then there would have been no need for this."

Abeja recognized the man's long, yellow jacket, embroidered with flames and dancing devils. He knew what it meant and his knees began to buckle beneath him.

"Then no harm would have come to your bees."

There was nowhere for Abeja to go. His back was pressed hard against the courtyard wall and he knew that the man coming towards him was a lot bigger and stronger than he was.

"No harm would have come to *you*…"

Salvador Abeja saw the moonlight dance on the blade in the man's hand. He crossed himself and hoped that his mother had remembered to include her own son in her prayers.

34

On the edge of Seville's ring road, near the river, stands a tower some forty-five metres high. It was once an ammunition factory, built for the manufacture of lead bullets. The blobs of molten lead were dropped from a cauldron at the top – cooling on the long drop – into a tank of water at the bottom. In more recent times it was converted into a camera obscura, or magic box: a type of periscope, combined with a projector, that allows the viewer a live overview of the whole city from inside the darkened tower.

The Englishman pushed back his hood and leant over the milky image that was projected on to the large white dish from the mirrors above. Seville moved in front of his eyes: people scurried, ant-like, across the square below, ladies walked dogs in the park and a solitary boat chugged along the river.

He had been watching the town from this vantage point since dawn and would stay watching until dusk, if he had to. As he cranked the handle to focus the image

and trained the lens on to the road that led into the city,
he smiled, realizing that such a long wait would not be
necessary. An ancient VW camper van spluttered along the
ring road, sticking to the inside lane. It was a vehicle he
was familiar with. Loved by surfers and hippies alike, a
VW camper had been the transport of choice for his own
travels across Europe nearly thirty years before. But this
one was blue, painted with a beehive and had a large bee
attached to its roof.

The Englishman watched as it drew alongside the park,
directly underneath his viewpoint and, as if working to his
instructions, came to a halt in a parking bay. He nodded to
himself as the van door slid back and revealed its contents.

Seven children of varying ages. Six of them twins.

The Englishman took out his phone and began to type a
text with a scarred finger.

The first thing that struck Rachel about Seville was the
orange trees that lined the streets and surrounded the park.
After the cold air of the Sierra Norte, the city was warm and
bathed in sunlight, almost as if spring were in the air.

They had all slept fitfully. The French boys had slept
out in the open air, not just because they were the
hardiest of the group but because the rest of the van had
voted them out on account of their smelly socks and trainers. Rachel had slept uncomfortably, stretched out on a
bunk with Morag and Duncan curled against her like small

cats, while Adam had sprawled across the front seat of the van. She was not sure where Gabriel had slept, if indeed he had slept at all. Sleep never seemed to matter to him.

As she stepped out of the camper, Rachel felt a tingle, a sense of anticipation and excitement about the town that seemed to be carried on the breeze. She instantly liked the place. Gabriel seemed distracted, standing away to one side and staring into the distance at a tower on the far side of the park.

"Gabriel?" Rachel said. "The little ones are hungry again."

He looked round slowly. Eating seemed to matter to him about as much as sleep did, and he sometimes became impatient with the constant demands for food. Now, Morag and Duncan looked up at him imploringly, clearly reading his thoughts.

"Please, Michael; we're hungry."

Gabriel realized he'd been caught out and laughed. "OK. But we can't hang about here. We're a bit conspicuous in the bee-bus. We need a change of transport." He looked at Jean-Luc and Jean-Bernard, who were jumping up and snatching oranges from a tree, then throwing them at passing cars. "Can you two drive around the place a couple of times, get yourselves noticed, then head out of town to the east for a few hours, then get some new transport and come back and meet us tonight?"

"Sure," Jean-Bernard said.

"What do we do with the camper?" his brother asked.

"Be imaginative," Gabriel answered.

The French boys looked at each other. The prospect of racing a van round a ring road, then heading out of town to wreck it clearly appealed enormously. And finding a change of transport would be a breeze for two boys who had been hot-wiring cars since they could walk. They grinned at Gabriel and gave him a thumbs up.

"Cool," Jean-Luc said. "Where do you want to meet?"

"We meet back here; beneath the tower. 12.15. That's *fifteen minutes past midnight*, OK? It's really important that you're here on time."

"Not a problem," Jean-Luc said.

"Good," Gabriel said. "Because we have a boat to catch."

Rachel sighed as the French twins jumped back into the van. She had thought they might sit tight for a few days in this warm city. "A boat? Do we *have* to leave tonight? We're so tired. And what's with the time being so … specific?"

"When you see what happens at midnight, you'll see why we need to be out of here by twelve-fifteen. Believe me."

Rachel's stomach sank as she realized she *did* believe him.

As the French boys gunned the engine of the VW and waved through the dirty window at Rachel and Adam, Gabriel smiled across at the little twins.

"How about ice cream?" he asked.

Duncan and Morag nodded enthusiastically and, as the camper van roared away down the ring road, the remaining

five of them set off across the park, away from the long, thin
shadow of the tower.

Laura Sullivan and Kate Newman's flight had arrived in Seville
early that morning. Laura had picked up a hire car and, armed
with a map on which she had drawn lines, cross-references
and calculations, they headed north out of the city.

Kate sat in the passenger seat with the map spread out on
her lap while Laura steered the hatchback out of the airport,
on to the motorway and away from Seville.

Kate had said very little to the Australian since they had
left Hope behind and Laura had seemed comfortable enough
with the silence, as if it was no more than she had expected.
But now, with the sun rising over the red earth of the Spanish countryside and her own feeling that they were following
a trail that would lead to her kids, Kate felt a little more dis-
posed to talk.

"Why are we heading out of the city?" she asked, unable
to conceal the deep suspicion in her voice. "I thought you
said they were in Seville."

Laura cast her a glance, eager to regain Kate's confidence.
"I'm following a hunch," she said. "More than a hunch. A
theory. All the work I've done suggests a spot an hour or so
outside the city. All the grid references point to a Bronze Age
site in a national park called Sierra Norte. It's so similar to
Triskellion … it just stacks up that if they're heading this
way, Sierra Norte will be the first port of call."

"Why?" Kate asked flatly, not looking at her.

"I don't know," Laura said honestly. "I just think … my research shows it's the most likely place. It's a Bronze Age site; there are caves, there are paintings. It sits on a line of sites I've traced across Europe. There's a necropolis too…"

"A what?" Kate said, half recognizing the word.

"A burial place. A city of the dead."

"You don't think…" Kate's voice went up in pitch.

"No, no, no … a place of *ancient* dead. And if I'm right, a place of … not entirely human dead."

Kate sat silently for the rest of the drive, trying not to think about the implications of Laura Sullivan's words.

They arrived at Sierra Norte about an hour later and followed the obvious track across the plain into a more mountainous area, covered with pines and thick banks of oaks. The track became bumpier as they climbed higher and Laura saw an old wooden sign on which someone had daubed CUEVAS in white paint.

"Caves," she said. "I think we're on the right track."

They came to an area where the track flattened out into a wide clearing and boulders gathered around a large crack in a stony outcrop. Sweet chestnut and oak trees dotted the immediate surroundings. Laura stopped the car and both women got out.

"I can smell rosemary," Kate said, sniffing the air and looking up at the bright blue sky. For the first time in weeks, a smile crept across her face.

Laura Sullivan rooted around, kicking at small stones, clambering up on to rocky ledges and looking at the savage land that stretched out before her; the same landscape that had remained unchanged for many generations. Then she saw something and jumped from the rocks and ran off, returning moments later.

"Over here, Kate," she panted.

Laura beckoned Kate over to a spot where there were tyre tracks in the damp earth. Kate followed as Laura pursued the tracks for several metres into a clump of bushes, then through into a clearing that was protected from behind by the opening of a cave and from the sides by trees and tangles of thorns. On the ground were the remains of a campfire. Save for the tyre tracks, the scene could have been left by a caveman thousands of years before.

"They've been here," Laura said. "Not long ago, either. The ashes are still warm."

"How d'you know it was them?"

Laura took Kate by the wrist and led her to a spot several metres away where the clearing fell into an incline. There, in the flat, red earth, as if designed to be seen from above, someone had drawn the sign of the Triskellion with a stick. It was three paces across and bounded by a circle. A stone had been carefully placed on the point which faced south, back towards the city.

Laura Sullivan looked Kate squarely in the eye and smiled triumphantly. "*That's* how I know."

35

The ice-cream parlour was on a side street that ran between the river and one of the many small plazas or squares dotted along the banks. Like every other open space in the city, the square was decked with brightly painted flags and bunting, and the trunks of the orange trees were wrapped with necklaces of coloured lights, their bulbs as big as the fruit that hung from the branches above.

There was more decoration in the parlour itself; tiny lights had been strung across the ceiling above the booths and along the length of the polished metal counter. There was uptempo trumpet music blaring from a speaker on the wall and everyone in the place seemed to be in a good mood.

Adam watched a waitress hugging two of her colleagues and heard a group of customers cheering and clapping in the corner. Like others Adam had seen on the streets, many were carrying bright yellow jackets and had what looked like red scarves draped across their arms. "What are they all celebrating?" he asked.

Gabriel casually dragged one of the menus towards him. "It's a saint's day," he said. "There's a big fiesta later on." He leant across to Morag and Duncan, who had already been studying the menus for five minutes. "Made your minds up?"

Rachel lowered the book she had been reading – the one Abeja had given her in Madrid about the churches of Seville. "That's why we're here today, isn't it?"

Gabriel smiled.

"What?" Adam asked.

Rachel went back to her book and read aloud. "It's the celebration of San Rafael. He was a traveller who came here in around 1500 and worked as some kind of healer, or shaman. Apparently he performed miracles, but the religious authorities didn't like it, so he was hunted down, then burned alive five hundred years ago, along with anyone who followed him or refused to denounce him."

"Nice," Adam said.

"They made him a saint in 1850 because the Pope at the time felt guilty that he had been killed in the name of the church. But there are still some here who celebrate his death like it was a good thing."

"At least they made him a saint, I guess," Adam said.

"A bit late for Rafael," Rachel said, reading on. "He was burned on the site of that church, where we parked the van." She leant across and showed Adam a picture from the book.

Adam grimaced at the grisly image. "Is that all that was left of him?"

"Yeah, and we're going to steal it," Rachel said with sudden certainty. "Aren't we?"

Gabriel shrugged. "It's not really stealing if you're just taking back what belongs to you."

Rachel closed her book, starting to see it all clearly. "Like the hearts in the church," she said. "Back in Triskellion."

"Like the hearts," Gabriel said.

Suddenly, Morag slapped her menu down on the table. "I want chocolate chip," she announced.

"Sounds good," Adam said. He was far happier talking about ice cream than discussing stolen body parts.

Gabriel asked Rachel what she wanted, telling her there were forty-eight flavours to choose from.

"Forty-nine, actually," Duncan said solemnly. "Almond, apricot, banana, blackcurrant, blueberry, butterscotch…"

Rachel smiled. "Vanilla will do fine."

Gabriel called a waitress over and everyone placed their orders. Adam watched her go, then gave Gabriel a nudge in the ribs. He nodded across to a table on the far side, to the two heads just visible above the back of the booth; the manes of black hair tied into ponytails with red ribbons. The twin sets of dark eyes had been glancing in their direction ever since they'd walked in.

"Those girls are looking at us," Adam said.

"You wish," Rachel said.

Gabriel sneaked a look back over his shoulder. "Well, I don't know how you're going to choose between them."

Adam sniggered conspiratorially, but the laugh froze on his lips as he watched the girls stand up and start walking towards their table. "They're coming *over*…"

The girls were the same sort of age as the French boys. Both had dark hair and dark eyes, flawless complexions and broad smiles.

Twins.

They stopped, one either side of Gabriel's chair. *"Hola, Rafael."*

Gabriel saw the look from Rachel. "Like I said, lots of names…" He introduced the girls as Inez and Carmen, and, within moments, the group had expanded to include them. The girls sat and talked happily, as though they had known everyone for a long time; the Spanish they spoke instantly understandable to everyone round the table.

"I thought there were two others," Carmen said.

"Jean-Luc and Jean-Bernard will join us later," Gabriel said. "They'll be sorry they missed you."

Rachel grinned. "I bet they will."

The Spanish girls seemed especially struck by Morag and Duncan, fussing over the youngest twins and sharing their ice creams once the waitress had delivered them. Morag clearly enjoyed the attention and chatted happily to the newcomers, while Duncan was forced to hide behind a menu, struggling to conceal his blushes each time he was spoken to, or had his hair ruffled.

Once the first round of ice creams had been eaten, they

ordered more, and for a while, with their laughter rising above the music, it was almost possible to relax and forget the journey that had brought them here; the dangers that they still faced.

Rachel watched Gabriel, though, and she could see that he *never* forgot. Not for one second. She saw his eyes drift lazily around, even as he chatted and laughed, and she knew that he was keenly drinking in every detail, sizing up every stranger, each murmured conversation or casual glance in their direction.

He leant across the table and spoke to the Spanish girls, "Do you two mind looking after Morag and Duncan for a few hours tonight? You can meet us later."

"Not at all," Carmen said. "We will show them the sights."

"You must keep them close."

"I understand." Carmen ruffled Duncan's hair again. "We will have fun." Duncan giggled and Morag beamed, excited.

"Did you talk to your uncle? Will the boat be ready?"

Inez nodded. "Everything will be ready," she said. "But he thinks the middle of the night is a funny time to be going fishing."

Morag's ears pricked up. "We're going fishing?"

Inez and Carmen laughed.

"We'll have made our catch well before then," Gabriel said.

He looked across at Rachel and Adam and the message was clear enough. Rachel knew that their final destination was not far away; they were getting close. And she knew that

until they got there, *they* were the ones who would continue
to be hunted, who would be struggling every moment to stay
away from the fishermen's hooks.

Laura Sullivan studied her guidebook as she hurried across
the street, narrowly avoiding an oncoming motorbike.

The Church of San Rafael was just off the main square
in Seville. It was a tiny building, long overshadowed by the
Giralda, the bell tower of the city's massive cathedral. But
the Church of San Rafael had its own loyal band of devoted
followers. The original Saint Rafael had been imprisoned
during the Spanish Inquisition – for some real or imagined
heresy – and had been burned alive in the Plaza de la
Constitución, the very square that Laura and Kate were now
crossing. All that had remained, so the guidebook said, was
the saint's right hand which, legend said, had been held out
in forgiveness to his killers and had not been so much as
scorched by the flames. The church had been founded on the
spot where he'd died and the hand remained mummified in
a glass casket in front of the altar in a side chapel.

"Why would they keep it?" Kate asked.

"If I'm right," Laura said, "it's more valuable than they
know."

Laura and Kate were struck by the smell of frankincense
as they opened the door. The little church glittered like a
jewel; the rays of the afternoon sun filtering through its
many coloured windows.

It was unusually busy and the priest seemed a little annoyed that tourists had found their way in on his special day. It was, after all, the high point of his year. Women scrubbed the floor and polished the pews. Others arranged flowers, lit candles and adorned a wooden statue of the saint with garlands. Carved, gilded flames licked at the bottom of San Rafael's robe, and his blank, almond-shaped eyes stared skywards as he held out his unscathed hand.

The priest bustled over to head the two women off at the top of the aisle. He was dressed in a white shift, tied at the waist and knotted with gold cord. His ceremonial yellow robe, richly decorated with embroidered red flames and gold-braided crosses, was draped across the altar.

"Can I help you?" he said in heavily accented English. "You are tourist? 'Merican?"

"Er, yes ... no. I mean, we're students," Laura said. "We're doing research."

The priest nodded. He forced a tight-lipped smile and smoothed a hand across his slick, black hair. "Is better if you come back tomorrow. You can see we're very busy today." He waved his hand at the general activity.

Laura strained to remain civil. "Oh, I'm sorry," she said. "I kind of knew that, but you see we are only in Seville for the day."

"Such a shame."

Laura's temper began to fray a little. "OK. So you're telling me we can't enter a public place of worship that we've flown thousands of miles to see?"

"You can see it now. There," he said, waving behind him and not letting them past.

"We're English actually and we would like to see the relic." Kate Newman found herself speaking in an authoritative tone that had long lain dormant; her English accent reasserting itself after years of living in New York.

The priest stood his ground. "I am sorry, señora. The fiesta of San Rafael is our most important holiday."

"Why?" Laura asked.

He smiled tightly again but there was no humour in his eyes. "The king decreed many years ago that this day should always be remembered as the day Seville was rid of a dangerous heretic."

Laura had done her homework. "But I thought the Pope had made him a saint? Surely *that's* why the day is celebrated?"

The remains of the smile disappeared from the priest's face. "It depends on your viewpoint. This city has a very long memory. Now, if you'll excuse me, señora."

Laura peered past him and, straining to see into the side chapel where the relic was held, caught sight of a little stained glass window decorated with the sign of the Triskellion.

"So which side are you on? Heretic or saint?" she said.

The priest glared at her. "I'm sorry. I am too busy to chit-chat…"

And then Laura saw the Triskellion everywhere: on the roof beams, cast into brass chalices, embroidered on the hem of the priest's ceremonial robes, dangling from the end of his rosary. And then she knew she was right. Laura took a potshot. "This *saint* was a man perhaps who came from far away, *too* far away? A man who challenged the way people thought and who frightened them?"

The priest clutched at his rosary beads. "You need to leave now. It is none of your business."

Laura scoffed; she clearly felt that it was very much her business. "A *foreign* man who had children with local women and had to die for being different?" She had hit her stride.

"Enough!" The priest's voice echoed around the church. He ushered Laura and Kate forcefully back towards the entrance. "I do not have time for this. You have to get out."

Laura suddenly dodged away, pushing past the priest and heading towards the side chapel. "I want to see the relic."

Suddenly, a group of five or six women, who had been going about their work, formed a line in front of the side chapel. Armed with mops and brushes, their arms beefy from years of polishing, they looked quite formidable.

Kate Newman, shocked by Laura's passion, grabbed her arm and pulled her back. "Come on, Laura; we'll come back another time." She looked at the line of ferocious women, the mask of hatred on the priest's face. "These people obviously have something to hide."

36

The man behind the counter laid down a small dish of spinach and chickpeas and poured out another measure of sherry. He turned round to cut two fresh slices from the huge leg of ham hanging behind him, then chalked another mark on the counter; another few Euros on the customer's tab.

Standing at the bar, the Englishman devoured the food hungrily, then used the sherry to wash down a fistful of painkillers. Around him, the tiny tapas bar was filling up with revellers. They would be keen to line their stomachs for a night of drinking and dancing ahead.

A night of ... *celebration*.

The Englishman ignored them as they milled around him; ignored the odd looks thrown in his direction. He would be celebrating something very different. Not least, if all went well, the moment when the two children he sought would stand at his mercy. When he would once again possess what was his by right.

The barman held up the bottle. *"Un otro, señor?"*

The Englishman shook his head, tossed a handful of notes on to the counter and marched out into the street. Outside, a man in a decorated, yellow jacket was waiting to meet him. He fell obediently into step as the Englishman walked past, then pointed the way through a maze of narrow streets, each growing more crowded as the hours passed and the huge, red sun sank lower in the sky.

"How was the honey-seller?" the Englishman asked.

The man in the yellow jacket smiled. "He was ... surprised."

"Good. It will send out a message to anyone else who is stupid enough to try and help these children."

They walked round a corner into a blind alley where music drifted through air that was thick with woodsmoke. His companion led the Englishman to a pair of heavy, wooden doors. "We are here," he said.

A tall, thick-set doorman stepped out in front of them and raised a hand that looked as lethal as a sledgehammer.

"Is there a problem?" the Englishman asked.

The man in the yellow jacket stepped forward, ready to argue their cause, but as soon as the man guarding the doors had stared into the blackness beneath the Englishman's hood, he stepped meekly to one side, his gaze fixed firmly on the cobbles at his feet.

The Englishman nodded. "I thought not."

The music grew louder as they pushed through the doors

and followed a winding staircase down into a vast hall. Its walls were lined with timber and wreathed in smoke from an enormous open fire at one end. A musician sat beating out a rhythm on the strings of a guitar and two women in flamenco costumes stamped their heels against the floor, crying out and clapping their hands as they danced. There were antlers and bull horns mounted on shields above a wooden stage, and a long trestle table ran down the centre of the room, round which were gathered perhaps fifty men.

As the tempo of the music increased and the dancers whirled faster and faster, the men dug into the piles of yellow jackets and red scarves that were heaped on the tabletop. They tried on the jackets, admiring themselves in full-length mirrors and striking poses as they tied the thin, blood-coloured scarves across their faces. Some jackets were brightly decorated with garish devils, while others had images of bones or fearsome-looking beasts or grinning skeletons that danced across the wearer's chest and along his arms.

"This is not a fancy-dress party," the Englishman muttered. "They must be made to understand."

"Once you tell them…"

But the Englishman was already marching across the floor towards the musician. He snatched away the guitar before slowly climbing the small staircase up on to the stage.

Catcalls and boos began to ring around the hall. The men were still howling out their displeasure when the robed figure reached the centre of the stage and turned to face them. But once he had banged his black stick against the floor and slowly removed his hood, a silence descended on the crowd like a shadow, until only the hiss and spit of the fire could be heard echoing around the hall.

When the signal was given, a man hurried to the side of the stage. Even as he translated, he could see nothing but the Englishman's face and feel nothing but the fear jumping in his guts. The scarf round his neck felt like a noose, as though the embroidered devils on his jacket were digging their nails deep into his skin.

"Tonight the streets will fill with those keen to remember a man they call a saint." The Englishman's voice was low, but it reached the back of the room easily. "A man who was hunted and who died in terrible agony. Why was he hunted?" He waited, let the question hang, then drift away on the woodsmoke. "They would have us believe that he had a different faith; a faith that would not be tolerated. They would have us believe that he died for freedom, or for truth, or so that others could follow and not be hunted as he had been. These are *lies*." He paused again, letting the man finish translating.

"The people on the streets tonight will celebrate this man's memory, but I will be celebrating for an altogether more noble reason. I will be celebrating his death. Yes, he was different. Yes, he had different beliefs. And your ancestors were right to hunt him down and destroy him before those beliefs could spread. Because they were not *Earthly* beliefs…

"Do we welcome poison? Do we embrace a deadly virus?" The Englishman stared from face to face, his passion intensifying as he saw the reaction he was looking for begin to spread throughout the room. "No. We isolate it and we wipe it out. It is not wrong to protect yourself, to protect what is yours and what you wish to leave behind for generations yet to come. That was the right thing to do five hundred years ago, when the outsider they now call Saint Rafael came to your city, and it is the right thing to do now.

"And as the descendants of those who acted as they did all those centuries ago, you must do the same thing now, the *right* thing, because *his* descendants are among us. *Here. Tonight*…"

Voices began to speak up in the crowd, *encouraging* voices, and the Englishman's voice rose up above them. "I don't need to tell you what you have to do. Your ancestors felt it in their blood and so will you. It is an instinct for survival, plain and simple, and it has been bred into all of us. Believe what I tell you and you will be safe. Your city will be safe. Your children will be safe. I have only one question to ask you…

"Are you ready to follow your blood?" He stared out, turning his face – such as it was – towards every other and asked the question again.

"Are you ready to follow your blood?"

It was as though a switch had been thrown suddenly and a current passed between the men in the crowd. The Englishman watched, smiling as best he could, as they came towards him. A mass of bright yellow streaked with crimson; the bones and beasts and devils dancing as they surged forward.

He watched as each man stooped down at the foot of the stage to collect a firebrand wrapped in petrol-soaked rags. Each man walked past him with a look of understanding and gratitude for the valuable guidance they had been given.

He saw ferocity and commitment in every step of every soldier in his perfect little army.

He saw the blood beating in every face – every one lit up as each man passed his torch through the flames of the open fire.

37

The night buzzed with the chatter of thousands of voices as the population of Seville poured out of restaurants, bars and cafes and into the square. Ropes of decorative lights were lit up like a million fireflies and strands of fringed paper-chains rustled in the breeze.

The procession was forming on the far side, near the church. The parade would take its course round the plaza and through the surrounding streets, ending up where a huge bonfire had been set, at the very point in the square where the saint was thought to have been burned.

Horsemen in tight-fitting suits adjusted their wide, black sombreros and tugged at reins, bringing their dappled, grey stallions into line. Behind them, gypsy ladies in frothy flamenco dresses sat side-saddle on less thoroughbred horses, their manes braided and their coats polished and glossy. Fifty or more flamenco guitarists strummed and tuned their instruments, while a marching band of bugles and drums formed into ranks behind the religious element of the parade: the priests, monks, altar boys and the choir.

Behind the organized part of the procession, clubs, societies, religious groups and members of the general public turned up in traditional costume. Boys were decked out as bullfighters, little girls marched in gypsy costumes, or in white lace, like tiny brides. Marshalling the parade, the members of Los Hermanos de las Llamas, the Brotherhood of the Flames, were out in force, their yellow and red embroidered jackets bright yet sinister in the light of their flaming torches.

Rachel checked her watch. 11.35. "I thought the parade started at 11.30?"

"The Spanish are not robots." Inez chuckled, clacking the castanets she held in her hand.

"Nothing runs on time here," Carmen confirmed, fanning herself.

As if to contradict the Spanish girls, a bugle sounded a fanfare and Rachel felt her stomach fizz with the collective excitement of the square as it rose to fever pitch. Rachel looked at Carmen and Inez. She thought they looked wonderful with their jet-black hair scraped back from their faces into tight buns. The tortoiseshell combs that held their hair in place stuck up from their heads like ornamental crests and the figure-hugging, polka-dot dresses fell in cascades and ruffles to their high-heeled black tap shoes.

Then Rachel looked down at herself. The girls had done their best to pour her into a blue version of the red dresses they wore, but her athletic, American figure had fought against it; angular and awkward. Her chestnut curls were rebelling against being tied back. She thought she looked a mess, and she had never worn high heels in her life! At least the little twins look cute, Rachel thought. She looked down at Duncan in his devil costume, his red-painted face unrecognizable, and Morag, sweet in an angel outfit, with silvery wings and a little halo.

Gabriel had told them to keep close but to blend in with the crowd. Inez and Carmen had done a good job. If only Gabriel had told her where he and Adam were going. But he wouldn't, and it was making her anxious.

The procession started to move. Bugles and drums squawked and thundered, whistles blew, and people started to cheer as horses clattered and whinnied. Dotted along the line, the Brotherhood of the Flames, their red kerchiefs now concealing their faces and their refuelled torches burning brightly, started a slow chant in an ancient tongue.

Rachel felt a force moving through her; a chill from across the ages. She began to get a sense of how the saint must have felt...

At the front, the priest had blessed the wooden effigy from the church. It now stood, garlanded with flowers, on a wooden platform carried shoulder high by a group of monks in white robes. On a satin cushion, inside a glass case at the saint's feet, sat what at first looked like a gnarled and blackened piece of wood. Those close enough to get a better look could see that the twigs which twisted from the stump were topped by brown fingernails.

It was the hand of San Rafael.

The priest chanted an incantation, sprinkled the group with holy water and led the line forward. An altar boy swung a perforated brass ball full of burning incense, shrouding them in wreaths of fragrant smoke. The drums kept a slow marching beat, and the guitars strummed in unison, joined by straining voices, bugles, castanets and the rhythm of hundreds of dancing shoes clacking across the cobbles.

The people watching on either side of the parade sang, shouted blessings and crossed themselves. They threw handfuls of petals at the participants as they crossed the square towards the symbolic pyre of wood that would be set alight at midnight in memory of the saint.

And then the procession stopped.

As the parade was about to peel off into the street running out of the square, a boy stepped in front of the priest. The priest stopped dead and the procession juddered to a halt behind him, the music dying as bugler bumped into drummer into guitarist. As the music stopped, the chanting faded too, then the chatter, until the square fell silent.

The priest looked into the boy's eyes and shuddered. This was no youth trying to disrupt a tradition as an act of casual vandalism. This was a boy with a mission. The priest looked into the slanting green eyes and recognized something.

"Move, will you? What do you want?"

The boy held out a hand in front of him.

"What do you want?" the priest repeated. Members of the Brotherhood began to move forward and form a semicircle round the boy, the flames from their torches glittering in his eyes.

"What is my name?" Gabriel said.

"I don't know!" the priest shouted back. "Now get out of the way." He waved his arm, but it was clear that something was preventing him from actually moving forward.

"Tell. Me. My. Name!" Gabriel yelled.

The yellow-shirted men began to close in on him and a murmur went up from the crowd as a sense that something was about to happen filtered back through the ranks: the kind of murmur that could infect a crowd and turn it into a mob.

Gabriel opened his mouth. A noise came from him, high pitched at first – audible – but then growing higher and higher until it was not a noise but a searing vibration that hurt people's ears. They could feel it in their hearts; it shook their lungs and made it hard to breathe. It gnawed at their stomachs. People held their heads, put their fingers in their ears or clutched their ribs. Light bulbs in the garlands above began to pop and shower the crowd with sparks and puffs of powdered glass.

"Tell me my name!" Gabriel's voice boomed across the square, hitting the priest like a hurricane, blowing his smooth hair across his face and forcing him to his knees.

The priest clutched his head and his voice came out as a dry croak that only Gabriel could hear.

"Are … you … *Rafael*?"

It was the same question the priest's ancestor had asked centuries before, as he had ordered the executioner to light the pyre.

Gabriel nodded.

As one, all the lights in the square exploded. Women wailed and children screamed as the frequency Gabriel was creating became unbearable. Then the cortège from the church began to cry out as the wooden saint started to smoulder.

Smoke poured from the artificial, gilded fire carved into his robe, and then the saint burst into flames. The pall-bearers struggled to keep the statue upright, the heat of the flames scorching their hair and faces. Gabriel ran forwards and, as he did so, the case holding the relic shattered, sending shards of glass, glittering with the golden light of the fire, into the night sky. The priest screamed as Gabriel grabbed the relic from the box, barging into and unbalancing the pall-bearers, who, finally giving in to the heat, allowed the flaming wooden saint to tumble to the ground.

A gasp went up from the crowd, now released from the agony Gabriel had created to subdue them. The pall-bearers tried to rescue the statue, covering it with their robes. Riders struggled to get horses back under control and mothers tried to calm crying children. At the head of the procession – while most of the crowd were frightened of going near him – the men in yellow closed in on Gabriel, fire in their eyes and hatred in their hearts.

Out of the shadows, another boy suddenly appeared. He ran, leaping across the street, and burst through the Brotherhood's line, pushing past Gabriel, before tearing across the square in the opposite direction and off into the darkness.

Adam had played his part well. The ancient relic was tucked safely beneath his jacket.

The men in yellow dived on Gabriel, throwing heavy punches and flashing blades before realizing, seconds later, that the strange boy had slipped from their grasp. From ten metres away, near the entrance to the church, Gabriel gave them a shrill whistle and waved to get their attention, and moments later they were after him again.

Immune from the noise that Gabriel had used to control the crowd, Rachel, the Spanish girls, Duncan and Morag had only been vaguely aware of what was going on. But whatever the commotion, Rachel had been sure it was Gabriel's doing. Whenever they were supposed to be keeping a low profile, something like this happened. It was as if he had no concern for their safety. They had seen and heard the screams and pandemonium and were aware of the fire at the front of the parade, some thirty metres ahead of them, through the crowds.

Now, another sound in her head was bothering Rachel. She was getting a terrible feeling of rising panic from Adam; a feeling she knew she could not ignore.

"I need to find my brother," she said to Inez and Carmen. She looked at her watch. 11.50. They had twenty-five minutes. "Listen," she said. "Could you guys take Duncan and Morag to the tower? I'll meet you there in twenty-five minutes."

The Spanish girls nodded, sensing Rachel's concern, and ushered the little twins away, blending instantly into the scattering crowd.

Rachel looked around her, eyes closed, feeling for the direction her brother's thoughts were coming from. She opened her eyes and began to walk diagonally across the square towards the little streets of bars and restaurants. Ahead, she saw two men in yellow jackets and red scarves moving fast towards her. Rachel made a stupid slip by looking at one of the men and making eye contact with the black eyes behind his mask. She saw him size her up in a millisecond. A millisecond was long enough for him to realize that she was different: ill at ease in her Spanish costume and hobbling on her high-heeled flamenco shoes.

Long enough to see the panic on her face.

Rachel quickened her step past the men and heard the scrape of their heavy boots as they turned on their heels to follow her. She made it across the square, feeling safer where people were drinking late or drifting back to the bars and discussing the bizarre events that had taken place minutes before. She crossed the street. Rachel caught her reflection in the window of a restaurant and could see, several paces behind, *three* yellow shirts now following her.

Rachel kicked off her shoes and ran. She darted into a little side street behind a restaurant.

A dead end.

Rachel backed into the shadows, trying to make herself invisible, but her fear prevented her from finding the state of mind to allow her to blend into the background. She held her breath and pressed herself tight against the wall, hoping for the best.

It was at that moment that the sky exploded.

38

G abriel kept running, glancing up at the dazzling showers of red, green and gold as the fireworks exploded high above him, the bangs rattling around the square like machine-gun fire. The crowds parted ahead of him: mothers, seeing the figures in yellow that were hot on the boy's heels and sensing the danger, pulled their children out of his way as he ran at them.

Behind him, Gabriel could hear shouts and screams. He knew that there would be others pursuing Rachel, but felt fairly sure that Adam had made it away unseen. That had always been the plan: create enough chaos and confusion to give Adam the time and space to get away with the relic.

Gabriel could hear the men gaining on him, but he did nothing to quicken his pace. He knew where he was going and was happy to let them think they had him trapped.

He took the stone steps up to the church three at a time, stumbling at the top and quickly picking himself up.

He could hear them panting, their firebrands crackling just a few steps behind.

"*Diablo!*" he heard one shout. "*Monstruo.*"

Devil. Monster.

Gabriel crashed through the heavy, wooden doors and turned, waiting. He watched the four of them as they stepped inside after him, the cascades of fireworks lighting up the night sky behind them.

The tallest smiled beneath his black mask. "*Sangre envenenada,*" he said.

Poisoned blood.

More poisonous than you know, Gabriel thought, as he slowly backed away down the central aisle of the church.

The three men in yellow coats moved slowly through the pools of shadow, spreading themselves out across the alleyway, leaving no space for escape. They seemed in no great hurry; seemed rather to be enjoying their moment of triumph, now that they had the girl trapped and at their mercy.

Mercy which they had no intention of showing...

Rachel watched them moving towards her, with their dark masks and the slashes of red round their necks, and felt goose flesh prickle along her bare arms. She reached out with her mind for Gabriel and knew straight away that he was in no position to help her. That he was in as much danger as she was.

She was on her own.

The abilities that she and Adam had inherited, that were in their bones and their blood, had been developing quickly since they'd escaped from Hope, but now she needed to call on powers of a very different sort. This was not convincing someone that she'd paid for something, or talking someone into giving her a hotel room. Now she had to save her own life, and she had no idea at all how to go about it.

If she was going to fight, it would have to be as the girl she had been before. She would use the only weapons she had and, if it came down to it, she would fly at them with her nails and with her teeth. She would do whatever she had to, but she would not surrender to these men.

The thought must have shown on her face, or in the stance she took, ready for them. She heard one of them snigger behind his mask and mutter something to his friends.

They started to come faster.

Rachel backed hard up against the wall, feeling the jagged edge of the bricks pressing through the material of her dress. She clenched her teeth and balled her fists.

She watched them drop their torches and reach into their pockets. She saw the blades appear in their hands and knew for certain that she had no more than moments to live.

"*Es tu ultimo momento,*" one of them said.

The end.

The three men turned at the growl of an engine and watched the huge, dark van roar past the end of the alley. They turned back to Rachel, smiling, then froze at the vicious scream of brakes and the pounding footsteps that grew louder, until two figures ran round the corner towards them.

Jean-Luc and Jean-Bernard.

Rachel felt the blood start to rush through her veins, the tension ticking in her, thumping in time with her heart. She still felt as though she was about to die, but guessed that now it might take a little while longer.

Gabriel stood with his back to the altar. The stained glass windows behind him were lit by flashes from the fireworks which continued to crash and fizz outside.

He could hear screams and the mounting tide of aggression, like building drums, coming from the mob that still milled around the square. He hoped more than anything that Rachel was all right.

The four men who had been sent after him moved a few steps closer...

Their eyes glowed in the torchlight behind the masks they wore and as Gabriel watched, he could see their dark intention flickering against coal-black pupils that were otherwise flat and dead.

He saw what they were there to do; they carried their weapons blazing in their fists. Considering where they were, and what the crowds had come to commemorate, these men would probably consider it fitting.

Gabriel gave them a small nod. *He* thought it would be fitting too.

He raised his arms and in the second before he closed his eyes, he saw the confusion on the men that were there to murder him. He sensed their bewilderment.

What was this boy doing? This *monster*. Why wasn't he running for his life?

With his eyes shut tight, Gabriel could feel the power surging through him, building to the point where it could not be stopped, even if that was what he wanted. He could hear the boom and the crackle of the fireworks outside and the shattering of glass as the crowd began throwing stones through the windows of the church.

And then the other sounds; the ones from only a metre away.

The gasps, as the first, tiny flames began to lick at their bright yellow jackets. Then the screams as they began to burn.

Adam looked at his watch. Five minutes after midnight. He had ten minutes to make the rendezvous with the others in the shadow of the tower. He had to keep moving.

The plan had worked out exactly as Gabriel had wanted and as Adam pushed through the crowds, unhurried, unseen, he could feel the package, beneath his jacket, bouncing against his chest as he picked up the pace.

The remains of someone who, like the man whose body they had found back in Triskellion, was his own ancestor…

The traffic was at a standstill. It would have been busy

enough anyway, but now, after what had happened back in the square, chaos had created panic and virtual gridlock in every street for miles around. Cars sat nose to tail, the drivers leaning on their horns or hanging out of the windows screaming at one another. Adam moved round or between them, pushing through the crowds, trying to keep one eye on street names, checking the landmarks and his own position relative to the river to make sure he was moving in the right direction. He began to feel another fear growing in his mind and gnawing at his guts. Rachel. Something was not right.

He jumped as a rocket exploded above him, clutched the package a little tighter to his chest and began to run.

The fighting was not clean or elegant, and as Rachel watched, she guessed that this was the way Jean-Luc and Jean-Bernard had learned to survive on the dirtier streets of Paris.

Within a few seconds of the French boys rushing at the men, the knives had clattered to the cobbles and kicks and punches were being thrown with frightening speed and ferocity. She heard the Spaniards gasp as the breath was kicked from their lungs and saw their eyes bulge as the red scarves were torn from their necks.

The boys moved with incredible power and speed; talents – if they could be called that – conferred on them by the unique DNA they had inherited. They were unstoppable and their opponents were no match for them.

"Enough!" Rachel shouted.

The blows continued to rain down on the three men, who by now were crawling along the cobbles, desperate to escape with their lives.

Fists, feet, foreheads. Fingers jabbing at eyes and tearing at ears.

Rachel rushed across and yanked Jean-Luc back by his hair. He turned on her and she saw the cold, hard determination in his face, heard it in the growl that came from somewhere deep in his throat.

"We need to go," Rachel said. She took hold of Jean-Bernard's collar and pulled him away from a lifeless body on the ground. "We've only got a few minutes." She placed a hand flat against his cheek, left it there until she could see he was calm.

"Are you OK?" he asked.

Rachel nodded. "Thank you."

He dropped a hand on to his brother's shoulder and took a deep breath. He began to walk away, then turned to deliver one final kick to the man on the pavement before joining the other two and running back out of the alley.

39

Gabriel heard the doors of the church crash inwards and opened his eyes. He watched as the local priest staggered towards him, shouting, waving his arms in horror at the sight and the dreadful *sound* of the three burning men. One for each of the innocents who had died for Rafael.

"Give it to me!" the priest shouted.

"Why?" Gabriel asked. "Are you worried you won't get quite so many tourists?"

"Give it to me!"

Gabriel stood his ground. "I don't have it."

"Liar!"

"Don't worry; it will be taken back where it belongs."

The priest's face was white with fury and his voice was high and cracked as he screamed out curses in Spanish. He ran to the side wall and pulled one of the ornamental axes from its mount, swinging it awkwardly in front of him as he moved past the men on the floor and advanced on Gabriel.

"All this, for a dead man's hand," Gabriel said.

The priest ran at him…

Gabriel closed his eyes a second time until he heard the buzzing begin. Then he opened them, keen to see the look on the priest's face when *he* heard it; when he dropped the axe and began trying to fend off the bees.

"The truth stings," Gabriel said. "Doesn't it?"

The priest flailed and spun, waving his arms helplessly at insects that he could not see; that existed only in his mind. The pain was real enough, though – sting upon sting on every exposed inch of flesh, until it felt as though his body was on fire.

Gabriel read the man's mind and made it happen.

The priest turned and ran, as his body was engulfed by the flames. Tearing out of the church, down the steps and out into the square he followed the same route his ancestor had taken half a millennium before on his way to light the pyre. From the doorway, Gabriel watched as the burning figure carved its way through the crowd, its scream echoing as shrill as any firework.

Gabriel watched as the priest finally collapsed on to the pyre that he had helped to build, and Gabriel saw the fire begin to rise. He watched the horrified crowd move back from the searing heat, turning their eyes away, then he turned and hurried out of the square in the opposite direction.

* * *

Jean-Luc drove the van, that he and his brother had stolen, as fast as he could, but the traffic was snarled up and many roads had been closed off altogether.

Rachel looked at her watch. "We've got two minutes," she said.

They pulled up hard at a line of stationary vehicles. Jean-Luc sounded the horn but nobody moved. Jean-Bernard pointed across the cars to a narrow street beyond that was all but empty.

"We need to go down there," he said. "Look…"

Rachel leant forward and peered up the street. She could see the top of the tower a few streets south of them. She looked at her watch again. "Why don't we just get out and run?"

"No need," Jean-Luc said. He slammed the van into reverse and backed it up twenty metres.

"You're kidding, right?" Rachel said.

Jean-Luc shook his head, then gunned the van forward and smashed straight through the two cars that were blocking the route across the road.

Jean-Bernard cheered and banged his hands on the dashboard as his brother put his foot to the floor and accelerated hard down the empty street towards the rendezvous point.

Adam could see the tower and knew he was going to make it. He wondered if the others were already there. He knew that

Inez and Carmen would die before they let any harm come to Morag and Duncan and that the French boys would not let anybody down. He was sure that Rachel and Gabriel had been chased, but knew equally that both would have taken some catching.

He wondered where they would be heading next, what this boat trip was that Gabriel had been talking about.

He stepped out into the slow-moving traffic and wove his way between cars until he reached the pavement on the other side. The tower was no more than a minute away.

He checked his watch.

"Adam!"

He turned, stared across a sea of heads on the pavement, but could see nothing. But that voice. It had sounded like...

"Adam ... over here."

He looked again and saw Laura Sullivan, the red hair unmistakable. She was waving him over, pointing to the woman standing next to her. Adam's breath caught in his throat.

His mother.

He pushed pedestrians aside and began running towards her, flinging himself into her arms, forgetting the package beneath his jacket.

"Mom..."

"Baby, are you OK?"

Adam couldn't speak, unable to disentangle the mess of

thoughts in his head. He clung on, vaguely aware that his mother was asking him where his sister was when he felt other hands on him, pulling him away...

"Adam ... no!"

And pushing him through the door of the silver van that had drawn up silently alongside them and down on to a long, low bench inside. Held fast, he could only watch as Clay Van der Zee stepped out to where Laura Sullivan stood, to where his mother was being held back.

"Thank you, Dr Sullivan; we'll take it from here."

"But you said ... you promised you wouldn't take them."

"You bitch! You lied to me!" His mother was shouting and struggling to get at Laura; to hurt her. "You set us up."

"No, Kate. I swear..."

Adam cried out for his mother as the door of the van slammed shut. He was still crying out as it pulled away into the traffic.

As soon as Rachel arrived, she could see that something was wrong, could *feel* that something was very wrong. Inez and Carmen were both in tears, clinging for dear life on to the hands of Morag and Duncan, who stared around helplessly. Lost.

She felt excitement flood through her as she glimpsed her mother slumped against the wall, but seeing her face and the way she looked at Laura Sullivan, who stood stock-still a metre or so away, froze her to the spot.

She turned back to the Spanish girls. Asked the question with her mind.

"They took Adam," Inez said.

Carmen stepped across, took hold of Rachel's hand. "We saw it as we arrived. A van pulled up, men got out…"

Rachel threw her arms round her mother, holding her close as Kate's body began to shake with sobs. Rachel stared at Laura, who looked beaten and bloodless, and began to get some sense of what had happened.

Adam…

Just then, Gabriel came strolling round the corner. He looked pleased with himself. "Perfect timing," he said. "Now we need to leave." He looked at Rachel holding her mother. "What's happened?"

Rachel shook her head. Between the explosions of the fireworks, the sound of her mother crying was like a hand getting tighter round her throat.

"What's happened?" Gabriel said again. He looked from face to face, counting them, and then he knew.

The technician moved forward and leant across the front seats to speak to Van der Zee as the Hope Project's Mobile Experimentation Unit accelerated away from the city.

"Just to let you know, sir. The thing he was carrying" – the man pulled a face – "it's a hand. A mummified hand…"

Van der Zee nodded. "Run all the usual tests. Complete medical analysis, and rush the DNA results through."

The technician said he'd get straight on to it.

Van der Zee asked the driver to find some nice, sooth-ing music and settled back in his seat. He glanced round and saw that the technician was still there, awaiting further instructions. "Oh, and give the boy something to help him sleep, would you?"

Twenty minutes after the fireworks had finished, when people had begun to gather over supper to talk about what had happened in the Plaza de la Constitución, a man in a bright yellow jacket walked up on to a narrow bridge over the river.

The Englishman was waiting.

"They got away from us."

The Englishman did not bother turning round. "I'm well aware of that," he said.

The man in the yellow jacket with the embroidered dancing devils held out a package towards the Englishman. "I brought you this," he said. "I thought it might cheer you up a little."

The Englishman took the parcel and began to unwrap the stained strip of sheet that bound it.

"From the honey-seller."

The Englishman nodded his understanding and took out his gift. He turned it over between his fingers. The hand was cold and waxy, its perfectly manicured fingernails already starting to come away from the flesh. "This is good," he said.

"I'm sure you can still harvest honey with one hand."

The other man looked pleased that his "present" had been so well received. "Don't worry," he said. "The children won't be so lucky next time."

"I'm not worried."

"Of course not. I just meant…"

The Englishman held Salvador Abeja's hand up to the light. "This will show what happens if anyone is foolish enough to lend those children a helping *hand*."

The other man laughed, then stopped when he realized that the Englishman was not making a joke. He watched him pull the hood of his robe up a little, before casually dropping the severed hand into the water and turning to walk away across the bridge into the darkness.

part three:
trust

40

Waves crash against the jagged grey rocks, throwing explosions of spume into the evening sky. The roar of the sea never stops. Incessant and eternal: background music to the life of the cave dwellers.

Every day the small boats go out, whatever the weather. Every day as the sun the fishermen worship lowers in the sky, the boats return with what they have lured from the unforgiving sea.

The girl stands on the beach, as she does most days, watching the boats come in to provide her family with food. She watches with more interest than usual, because she knows that today, something is different. She saw the blinding flash of light far out to sea just after the sun came up, and now, as the boats come back, she can see that the fishermen are waving their arms and shouting.

She watches as the men run the boat up on to the beach and drag the body on to the sand, pale and apparently lifeless. Her eyes run over the body, curious, fascinated by its whiteness.

How smooth and hairless it is compared to the dark, squat men of her tribe; how long and slender. She watches as the body jolts suddenly and as thick, green water pours from its mouth. She watches as spasms of chest and limb bring it back to life.

As the narrow eyes blink open. Deep and green.

She stares as the chief pulls away a golden object clutched tight in the newcomer's fist, and holds it up high, its three blades glinting in the evening sun…

And now, several seasons later, the girl watches as the stranger works within the caves. She watches, astonished as he paints, then channels light through fissures in the rock on to his strange and wonderful creations: visions of the past, present and future. She sees him mould metal and stone into elaborate and beautiful vessels; she is aware that the men in her tribe are gathering, and talking secretly. She knows that they are frightened, afraid of what he can do, threatened by its complexity. She watches as they drag the stranger deeper into the caves and order him to build to their instructions, to work his magic for their own purpose. She sees the look of acceptance on the stranger's face as he realizes he is being made to build his own tomb: a place where his bones and relics will be locked away for ever so they are no longer a threat.

Later, the girl cries out as the sun goes down and the men come; as they drag the stranger away from her. She hides her infant twins' eyes as the men take their father away; as the cave dwellers hold him down on a flat rock and bring the huge stone smashing down on to his skull.

Hides her eyes as the body is pegged out; as the gulls swoop down across the roaring sea to peck the bones clean...

Rachel was dragged from the depths of the dream by a wailing sound, robotic and metallic, cutting deep into the silence of a chilly dawn.

She had had dreams or visions like this before. They had come to her back in Triskellion and had only really made sense when the bodies of Gabriel's ancestors, of *her* ancestors, had been discovered.

Dreams and visions.

The arrival of a stranger. A young girl, curious and unafraid. Twin children.

Dreams and visions that always ended the same way. In terror. In murder.

Rachel had not really slept. She had been up late, talking with Laura, her mother, the French twins and the Spanish girls. They had been going over and over the circumstances of Adam's disappearance and how, since he'd been taken, she had not been able to communicate with him. She had not had a word. It was as if he had been insulated from her so that she could not tune in. What she *was* receiving, and had been for the last three days, was a terrible sensation of dread in the pit of her stomach.

The other twins had been hugely sympathetic, each knowing the importance of being able to communicate with one another. Each knowing that to lose that channel of communication would be like losing a limb. Rachel's mother was in a numb state of grief. Having developed a grudging trust of Laura Sullivan, she was now back to where she had started. To resentment and suspicion. For Kate, losing her son felt worse than losing a limb.

It felt more like a death.

"Allahu akbar... Allahu akbar... Haya ala as-sala... Haya ala as-sala..."

God is the greatest... Come to prayer. The recorded, robotic voice droned again, calling to the faithful from a loudspeaker on top of a nearby mosque. Rachel lay back in bed, the arches and decorative patterns in the room just becoming visible in the half-light. She felt the lurch in her guts, at the realization that, for the fourth morning in a row, Adam was still not there. Lulled by her mother's steady breathing from the bed on the other side of the room, Rachel tried to gather her thoughts and dampen the panic.

To face another day in Marrakesh.

From Seville they had driven in the stolen van to a small port on the Spanish Coast, but when they had arrived at the harbour, Rachel's idea of the boat they were supposed to be picking up had quickly dissolved.

In her mind's eye, she had seen a small fishing vessel, white or blue, bobbing at a berth, with a clean, crisp sail and a jolly name like *Salty Sue* or *Seaspray*. A boat like the well-polished craft of the fair-weather sailors she had seen back in Cape Cod.

By contrast, the *San Miguel* was a workhorse. Squat and stubby, its rusting hulk lurked, black and heavy, in the greasy water of the fishing port. As it approached, the boat had slapped its sturdy side against the quay, like a truculent sea monster straining to be free of its ropes. As they had climbed aboard, helped by Inez and Carmen's Uncle Pepe, Rachel had been winded by the stench of old fish and diesel oil.

Eight of them had bundled into the cabin behind the wheelhouse, while Pepe had started up the engine; the milky bulkhead lights flickering on their pale faces as the generator powered up. Pepe had shouted instructions in Spanish to Jean-Luc and Jean-Bernard, who had stayed on deck, to let the ropes go from the quayside bollards. The boat had juddered out of the harbour into a black night and beyond into a bumpy sea, headed for the coast of North Africa.

The combined smells of fish, oil and Pepe's strong black cigarettes, coupled with the lumpy motion of the boat, had been too much for Rachel and her mother. They had staggered from the cabin and, helped on deck by the French boys, had thrown up over the side: retching their discomfort, their grief and the remains of their last meal into the Atlantic.

They had stayed out in the air, huddled together for comfort and staring up at the bright stars that were the only signs lighting their way.

As dawn had broken the following morning, they had all

gone out on deck. A sliver of coastline had just been visible
a few kilometres to the left of them and Laura Sullivan had
shouted above the roar of the engine. "Where are we?"

Pepe had pointed at the coastline. "Casablanca."

Rachel had recognized the name from an old film. It had
sounded incredibly foreign and exotic.

"We're docking at a smaller town further up the coast,"
Carmen had said. "Uncle Pepe has friends there. We have
friends there."

They had arrived at a harbour that looked as if it had come
from a different era: from hundreds of years before. Primitive, wooden boats had been bobbing about, and fishermen
in ragged clothes had been stacking crates of sardines and
laying out still-twitching eels on the dockside slabs.

They had stepped across tangled nets and wooden crates,
walked past hulks of old ships and out through a gate to an
area where ancient cars and taxis were haphazardly parked.
Pepe had hugged and kissed his nieces. Then he had wiped
the tears from his eyes, before squeezing them all into two
battered old Mercedes, handing bundles of notes to the very
grateful drivers and sending them on their way to Marrakesh.

Three hours later, the taxis had arrived at the red walls
of the old town, which the driver had called the medina,
before announcing that they could go no further. Men,
dressed in skullcaps and long, hooded garments, had filled
narrow streets. Mopeds had weaved dangerously around
carts pulled by sad-looking donkeys.

Rachel had never seen anything like it…

Before visiting England and Triskellion, Rachel had only really seen New York City and a couple of places upstate. Aside from the cars and bikes everywhere, this place had seemed like something out of the Middle Ages: beggars dressed in rags; street sellers pushing carts full of mint and oranges; craftsmen hammering out ornate pieces of metalwork on the pavement; the smells of manure and perfume, woodsmoke and drains…

From nowhere, an old man pulling a wooden barrow had appeared. After a gabbled exchange with the taxi drivers, he had grabbed the few backpacks and bags that the group still possessed and had piled them into his cart. Before anyone could question him, he had barked a command for them to follow and had pushed the barrow through the gate into the old town.

"Wait!" Rachel had shouted. "Where are we going?" She'd seen that Laura, her mother and the others were all as bewildered as she had been by the sudden chaos that surrounded them. The old man had stopped as Rachel caught up with him.

"Don't worry," Gabriel had said. He'd stepped through the gate and rested a hand gently on her shoulder. "He knows this place like the back of his hand."

The man had grinned at Rachel and placed his left hand on his chest, bowing his head to her. That had been when Rachel had noticed the tattoo. It was faded but still distinct, etched on to the web of skin between his thumb and forefinger: a smudgy blue symbol against the leathery brown flesh.

A Triskellion.

They had reached the Riad Magi after a seemingly endless trek that had taken them down alleys and across small squares, past shops festooned with conical red pots, copper basins and carpets of every colour and size. They'd followed the cart past men mending piles of worn-out shoes, past holes in the wall stacked with flat loaves of bread and past tiled shopfronts displaying a single, skinned rabbit or a hook draped with the innards of a recently butchered animal.

With no street names and precious few signs, the whole group – with the exception of Gabriel, who had seemed to know every sudden turn and each hidden alleyway – had collectively lost its sense of direction. Morag and Duncan had looked terrified. They'd stuck close to Kate and Laura, as bicycles and carts had ploughed past them with no apparent concern for their safety, or acknowledgement of their existence.

Finally, they'd turned down a narrow passage, ducked under a low arch and stopped outside a weathered brown door; its polished brass plate was engraved in Arabic. The old man had stepped away from his barrow and knocked. Rachel had taken a deep breath and shuddered as a three-legged black cat had brushed its matted and emaciated body against her leg. Then the bolts on the other side of the door had been thrown back.

The tranquil interior of the riad had been a complete contrast to the filthy, bustling alleyways outside. Guided through a dark entrance hall by a boy dressed in white, the group had shuffled into an open courtyard. A small pool bubbled in the middle and the courtyard walls had been bleached white by the sunlight pouring in through the open roof. Stairs twisted up and away to rooms on each side, their entrances concealed by thin curtains that had danced on the gentle breeze.

"You are welcome! Most welcome."

A man had poked his head over the balcony and had called down from the first floor. He'd grinned widely then disappeared, clattering down some stone stairs before reappearing next to the pool.

"Welcome, welcome. I am Mahmoud." The man, though clearly Moroccan, had spoken with an almost flawless English accent, like the people Rachel had seen reading the news back in Triskellion. "Have you had a good journey?"

Before anyone had been able to answer, he'd moved quickly from one member of the group to another, shaking hands, bowing, blinking through heavy-framed glasses and beaming through his close-clipped grey beard. He wore a fez and a long, hooded garment – white with orange stripes – like most of the men they had seen.

Rachel had stared down at his yellow slippers. He reminded her of a character from a *Star Wars* movie.

"You must be hungry," he had said. He'd instructed the

boy in white to take their bags upstairs, then led them into a beautiful room where, on a table strewn with rose petals, a fantastic breakfast had been laid out.

Since their arrival, Mahmoud had catered to their every whim. They had eaten well and slept in the afternoon, or sat in the sun on the roof terrace, or read books in the peace by the side of the pool. There had been no reason to venture outside into the mayhem of the city, but suddenly, today, everyone had started to get itchy feet. Unwilling to let them go alone, Mahmoud had taken Laura, Kate and the little twins for a look around the souk: the network of market stalls that packed every inch around the main square.

With the French boys up on the roof terrace – showing off to Inez and Carmen, who were sunbathing, reading magazines and pretending not to notice them – Rachel found herself alone with Gabriel.

They were sitting on cushions by the pool. Rachel could not remember when they had last spent time together, just the two of them. Gabriel had been spreading himself thinly among all of them and, at first, sitting with her feet in the cool water, Rachel could hear nothing in her mind.

Gabriel did not seem uncomfortable with the silence, but Rachel pushed.

Talk to me, she said, with her thoughts. *Tell me where we're going.*

We're close, Gabriel's mind spoke back. *Our journey is near its end.*

There was something about his words that gave Rachel a great sense of relief, a feeling that this might all soon be over. But there was also something sad in his tone; something ... final that suggested the ending might not be a completely happy one. She was about to push him further when a clatter of noise in the corridor told her that her mother and the others had returned. The little twins ran across the courtyard to Rachel and Gabriel.

"Look at us!" Morag shouted. She pointed at her and Duncan's identical outfits of hooded djellabas and brightly coloured slippers.

"Same as mine," Mahmoud said proudly.

Laura Sullivan grinned. "We thought they should blend in a bit."

"We saw snake-charmers," Morag said excitedly. "And monkeys in the square."

Duncan did not need prompting. "King cobra, green mamba, corn snake..."

"That's good," Rachel said.

Duncan ignored the interruption and continued reeling off a list of everything they had seen. "Barbary ape, monitor lizard, chameleon, tortoise..."

"I bought you a few things, Rach," Kate said. Her lip was trembling as she handed Rachel a parcel of clothes: a thick white cardigan to wear in the evening, a woollen hat and some furry boots. "I thought you could do with a change from those filthy jeans and sweats."

Rachel looked down at her stained and torn sweatshirt. Clothes were the last thing she had been thinking about for the past few days.

"I got some stuff for Adam too…" Kate's face contorted as she hugged another bundle of clothes to her chest. Laura tried to put an arm round Kate's shoulder, but was firmly shrugged off; the polite level of communication that had grown between them in the past days shrugged off with it. "Find him," Kate said. "Find my son, you…"

Her words tailed off as the tears came and she ran upstairs. Laura quickly bustled Morag and Duncan away to their room and Mahmoud made himself scarce.

Rachel found herself alone with Gabriel again, but the moment of quiet intimacy had gone. She felt some of her mother's anger. "Why did you let them take Adam?"

Gabriel turned and looked at her. "I didn't *let* them. They just did. You haven't got it yet, have you? I don't control everything; I can't manage *every* event. People like me have been overpowered and destroyed before. I can do some things, but there are times when I need help. From you. From the others."

Gabriel looked deep into her eyes and Rachel became a little frightened at the ruthlessness she glimpsed beneath the green. He paused, as if considering whether or not to say what was on his mind, but Rachel could already read it.

The thought was out in the open.

I told you there might be sacrifices.

Anger flashed and burned deep inside her. Adam had been silent since they'd been here. She'd tried, and failed, to make contact. The notion that her brother was a "sacrifice" was more than she could take. Her fist lashed out, hard and fast, at Gabriel's face. But in the fraction of a second before it smashed into his nose, Gabriel's hand had taken hold of Rachel's fist, gripping it tight, pulling her close.

For a split second, Rachel thought he might be going to kiss her.

"Why are we here?" Rachel shouted into his face, recovering herself and wrestling her fist away. "Where the hell are we going?"

She saw a rare look of uncertainty slide across Gabriel's features. He broke eye contact. "I don't know exactly," he said. He stared down into the pool. "I'm waiting for guidance."

41

Adam was dreaming about home…

He'd been walking, somewhere near their apartment, and he had seen Rachel and his mom on the other side of the street. He'd shouted, but they hadn't been able to hear him above the noise of the traffic, and each time he'd tried to get close to them the street had just got wider, or a car had moved to block his way.

Now, back in the apartment, he was making popcorn in the microwave and waiting for Rachel and his mom to get back. He looked out of the kitchen window and saw them just a few metres away … in a different apartment. They were standing in an identical kitchen. Rachel was saying something, waving her arms while she talked and their mother was laughing … *really* laughing.

Adam hammered on the glass, but got no reaction.

He tried to open the window, but there were bees swarming across it and he couldn't find the latch.

The beeper on the microwave began to go off, and he started to wake up…

Adam could hear the beeping of medical equipment all around him. The smell of popcorn drifted away, overpowered by the stink of bleach and rubber and the disinfectant they had dabbed on his arm before they'd slipped the needle in. He felt the thin mattress beneath him. The metal bars on either side of the bed. The wide, black straps across his chest and legs.

Adam opened his eyes and blinked slowly as the dream slipped away from him. The face of his mother – her *happy* face – began to disappear, like a picture fading to black at the end of a movie. Now, he could only see her face as it had been back on that pavement in Seville; the tears and the twisted mouth as she'd watched them drag him away. He'd still been able to hear her screaming, even after they had slammed the doors and started to tie him down. She'd sounded like a wounded animal.

"Good afternoon, Adam."

Adam turned his head. Watched Clay Van der Zee close the door behind him and move into the room.

Was it a room? There were no windows and the walls were made of metal. Had they stopped somewhere? He guessed that he was in some kind of mobile lab or hospital. He remembered a lot of driving. He'd felt the movement as he'd drifted in and out of consciousness, the drugs pulling him back under before he'd had the chance to get his bearings. Before he'd had the chance to try and communicate with Rachel.

It had been several days since he'd been snatched, he was sure of that, and he had all but given up trying to contact her. Even when he'd been fully conscious, he had been unable to reach her. Unable to receive the messages he knew she would be trying to send him.

The drugs – it had to be.

"I said 'Good afternoon.'"

Adam saw Van der Zee smile, as though this was a perfectly normal conversation. As though he did not go around kidnapping children. As though Adam was not strapped to a gurney or pumped full of God only knew what…

"All depends on your definition of 'good'," Adam said.

Van der Zee pulled a small metal stool across and sat down next to the bed. "Well, it would be good for *you* … if you answered my questions. One question in particular…"

"I've told you; I don't know."

Van der Zee nodded, a tightness round his mouth. "This *boy* … whose name you refuse to tell me—"

"Like I said, he's got lots of names."

"This boy is clearly … leading you all somewhere, and you insist he hasn't told you where that is?"

"Not a clue," Adam said.

"Or why?"

"It's kind of a … magical mystery tour." Adam looked up

at Van der Zee, enjoying the barely concealed anger on the man's face. "What's the matter, don't you like surprises?"

Van der Zee stood up and moved round to the foot of the bed. He stared at Adam for a few seconds, as though trying to reach a difficult decision, then he leant down and took hold of Adam's hands.

"I thought we were friends," he said. "I thought that, unlike your sister, you could see that the Hope Project had your best interests at heart. Now, I'm in a … tricky situation." He leant in further, his grip strengthening round Adam's hands. "You see, I very much *need* to know where your sister and all your friends are headed. I really need your help on this one, Adam, and I think we could both save ourselves a lot of trouble if you just told me. You understand? Get us both out of … a difficult situation. What do you say?"

Adam tried not to cry out as Van der Zee's huge hands tightened round his own.

"Do we have a deal?"

He wasn't even sure if Van der Zee was aware just how hard he was squeezing. Not that it mattered: the pain was the same either way. Adam gritted his teeth, feeling the knuckles in his hands grinding against one another as the pressure increased, convinced that any second the bones would be crushed.

"Adam…?"

He screamed out in pain. Suddenly someone was knocking at the door and Van der Zee released his grip. Adam heard a mumbled conversation; something about a call from New York. He heard Van der Zee leave.

His hands trembled, weak and useless. Even without the restraints he doubted he could have lifted them to wipe away the tears. The fight against the pain had taken away every ounce of strength and Adam was grateful when a figure appeared at the side of his bed, when he saw the plastic tip taken off the syringe.

The Hope Project's mobile unit had been Clay Van der Zee's idea. It comprised a fleet of high-spec vehicles which remained permanently on stand-by and could be transported to almost anywhere in the world at short notice. There were offices and living quarters for a small crew of technicians and security staff. There were fully equipped laboratories and hospital facilities. There was a state-of-the-art communications centre.

And there was an autopsy suite.

Van der Zee tried not to think about this last ... *vehicle*, as he walked into the office and took one more look at the DNA results from the mummified hand that Adam Newman had been carrying when they'd snatched him.

It was not human DNA. Instead, it shared characteristics with samples taken from the bodies in Triskellion, from bodies found at other sacred sites throughout the world and with samples that had been kept on file in the US for nearly fifty years.

Not human…

It was little wonder that Van der Zee's superiors were getting so worked up, so impatient. They were counting on him, he'd been told in no uncertain terms. It was with some trepidation that he laid the file to one side to take the call he had been dreading for the last few days.

"So where's our target?"

"I'm still … working on it."

"You've had three days."

"It's a matter of building up trust," Van der Zee said. "Of gaining the boy's confidence."

The man on the other end of the phone took a drink of something. It was early morning in New York so Van der Zee guessed it was coffee.

"Confidence," the caller said, "is something *I'm* rapidly losing."

"There's no need," Van der Zee said quickly. "I *will* get the information." The few seconds' delay on the line turned into fifteen. Van der Zee wondered if his caller was alone in the room or if he was conferring with anyone else. "Are you still there?"

"Tell me about Dr Sullivan."

"She's gone," Van der Zee said. "She's gone with … them. But I don't see that as a problem. We presume she'll be travelling with them to the … final destination. We'll pick her up there."

"Do we know where *there* is?"

"We know where they are now," Van der Zee said. "We'll follow them when they leave."

"No good," the caller said. "Not if we want to be waiting when they arrive."

Van der Zee studied the map above his desk. A hand-drawn line ran from the Hope Project, through London, Paris, Madrid, Seville and stopped abruptly in Marrakesh. "I will get the answer," he said.

"How are you … asking the question?"

"Excuse me?"

"OK … let me try and make this nice and clear. I'm asking you *this* question … *simply*. Are you with me, doctor?"

"I think so…"

"So, how are you asking the boy?"

"I don't … understand," Van der Zee said. "I'm just … *asking*."

Another slurp of coffee. "So, find a different way to ask."

"There's no need for that, just give me time and—"

"You have lots of nice, shiny equipment in that fancy mobile unit of yours, right?"

Van der Zee tried to swallow, but his mouth was dry. His voice sounded hoarse when he spoke. "Right."

The caller was having no such problems. "So, use it!"

42

Mahmoud drew the curtains and lit candles while his houseboy poured everyone glasses of mint tea. For the three days since the group's arrival he had treated them like royalty, and there had never been any suggestion of payment.

Rachel had asked Gabriel about the Triskellion tattoo that she had also seen on Mahmoud's hand. Gabriel had explained that Mahmoud's people were Berbers: one of the ancient tribes believed to have been the original inhabitants of North Africa. He'd explained that the symbol was a charm to ward off evil and that the tattoo was worn by all members of Mahmoud's tribe; a tribe that could be considered friends.

"Friends who believe that they have a sacred duty to look after the needs of travellers," Gabriel had said, smiling. "Which is exactly what we are."

They sat round a long, low table in a small salon off the central courtyard. The walls were tiled with elaborate mosaics and colourful rugs lay in piles, two and three thick, across the stone floors. Lanterns swung from the ceiling and cast shadows across the faces of Jean-Bernard and Jean-Luc as they leant close together, whispering about the others: Carmen and Inez, who chatted about the food; Duncan, who sat delightedly between the two girls; Gabriel and Rachel, who watched and waited; and Kate and Laura, who said nothing.

Morag stared across at the log fire that crackled in one corner. "It's like that fire Dr Van der Zee had," she said.

Rachel had only half heard. "What?"

"In his den, remember? With all those wind-up toys above it."

Rachel could hear the anxiety in the young girl's voice; the fear that the memory had triggered. "You don't know some of the things we had to go through," Morag whispered.

"Don't worry about him," Rachel said. "He's a very long way away."

While the children sat, Mahmoud supervised the comings and goings as three or four staff brought a variety of dishes to the table. Rachel watched the food arriving and reddened when her stomach growled noisily.

Her mother leant across and put a hand on her arm. "Me too," she said.

When all the dishes had been delivered, Mahmoud stood, grinning at the head of the table. He placed his hands together and nodded. "Please enjoy…"

"Thank you for this," Gabriel said. "For everything."

It was Mahmoud's turn to redden, smiling and nodding as he backed away from the table. "You are more than welcome."

They all tucked in hungrily without needing to be asked twice, piling their plates high and, when they were almost empty, mopping up the rich sauces with large pieces of flat bread.

When Rachel had finished, she looked across at Gabriel. As usual he hadn't seemed interested in eating. Mind you, she had been concentrating so hard on stuffing her own face that he could have eaten three plates' worth and she would not have noticed.

"That was good," she said.

"Better than Seville?" Gabriel asked. "The food we had at Abeja's…"

It was a close call. "That was great too," Rachel said. "I think any food tastes good when you've got time to enjoy it."

"When you don't feel like you're being hunted, you mean?"

"Right."

Gabriel nodded, as if he agreed, then said, "Oh, we're being hunted all right. But sometimes the hunter stops for a while, you know? While he figures out his next move."

Rachel was about to speak, to tell Gabriel that he could always be relied upon to bring her down, when her eye was caught by a movement at the end of the room. She looked up to see Mahmoud standing in the doorway, his eyes darting around anxiously.

"Mahmoud?" He looked at her and began walking slowly towards the table. He was wearing stained camouflage trousers and a dusty, brown leather jacket. Rachel watched him as he got closer, seeing something in his eyes that made her uncomfortable, and remembering the immaculate striped robe and slippers he had been wearing just a minute or two before. "Why did you change?"

He would not meet her eyes. "I did not change."

"But…" Then Rachel glanced up and saw another Mahmoud – the original Mahmoud – in the striped robe and slippers, at the far end of the room. He looked across at the man in the leather jacket and nodded a little nervously.

"Oh, right," Rachel said. "Sorry."

Twins? Why she was even the tiniest bit surprised?

The man in the leather jacket squeezed in next to her without waiting to be asked and began grabbing at the leftover food. Rachel tried to inch away from him without making it too obvious.

"This is Mahmoud's brother," Gabriel said. "Ali."

Ali glanced up at her, then went back to his food, attacking it as though he had not eaten for a week. Rachel moved a little further away. There was a smell coming off him, from his clothes or his skin. Sweat and oil. She noticed the tattoo on his hand.

Gabriel stood up. "Ali is the man we've been waiting for," he said.

"What?"

"He'll be our guide from now on." He turned and spoke to the whole table. "You all need to get a good night's sleep. We have to make an early start in the morning."

Rachel stared at the newcomer and was embarrassed when he looked up quickly and caught her. She tried to summon up a smile. She felt a small shiver pass through her when a slimy string of gristle fell from the corner of his mouth and he snapped at it, quick and vicious, like a wild dog.

Laura Sullivan had watched Gabriel's every move since Seville. She had studied every expression on his face, hung on every word he had uttered, trying to find out what made him tick. Having got so close, she was now terrified that she would scare him away; that he would leave before she could ask the questions which had been burning in her mind for years.

Now, with everyone else in bed, Laura knew where she would find him. She climbed the stone stairs up on to the roof.

He stood on the far side of the roof terrace, silhouetted against the night sky. Laura's knees felt weak as she crossed the tiles to meet him.

"Gabriel?"

He looked over his shoulder at her without saying

anything. He smiled. Laura stood nervously beside him, looking out across the satellite dishes that flowered from the roofs, at odds with the ancient houses below.

"Hi. I didn't want to disturb you, but…"

"There are questions you want to ask me. I know."

Laura laughed. He was way ahead of her.

"So, ask," Gabriel said.

Laura had dreamed about this moment, but now she had been given the go-ahead to ask whatever she wanted, she did not know where to begin. She took a deep breath and followed Gabriel's gaze up into the sky, to the bright star on which he seemed to be focused.

"What's that star?" she asked. "Is it … home?"

Gabriel spoke without looking at her. "It's not quite as simple as that. It's more of a beacon, or a satellite. I use it to get information, to get guidance. I use all the stars like that; to work out where I am, where I'm going. The sun too. It gives us energy; it gives us power."

"When you say us?" Laura probed.

"People like me. People like you too…"

"Yeah, people on earth worshipped the sun for thousands of years … and got information from the stars. They set up big clocks, stone circles…" Laura realized she was gabbling, excited that his thoughts chimed with things she knew so much about. But she wanted him to do the talking. "I guess we just lost the skill over the years."

Gabriel nodded. "That's kind of why I'm here," he said.

"Have you been here before?"

He nodded again, then fell silent.

Laura felt he was switching off. She tried another angle. "Listen, I have this … theory."

"I know about your theory. You're on the right track."

Laura had no idea how he knew about her work, but could not contain a grin.

"Who else knows about it?" Gabriel asked. He fixed her with a stare. "How much do the people you work for know?"

"Only as much as I've told them," Laura said. "But they're not dumb; they can work stuff out."

Gabriel was still.

"Who are you?" Laura asked. "No, wait, that sounds stupid. Are there any more of you … any more coming, I mean?"

Gabriel smiled. "We have to get away early tomorrow. We'll talk some more, but for now…"

Laura realized that the conversation was over for the time being. She could not push too hard and risk blowing everything. She held out her hand to Gabriel, who shook it gently.

Then she went to bed.

When he was as sure as he could be that the guests were in their rooms, the Moroccan slipped into a passageway at the back of the building and made the phone call.

He cleared his throat before the call was answered. He did not want to sound unsure of himself.

"Tomorrow morning, first thing," he said.

There was no response.

"But I will try and delay them. To give you time to get here."

43

The old man pushed the barrow that contained their bags across the main square. Mahmoud and his brother led the party. Mahmoud pointed out items of interest, while Ali looked suspiciously left and right.

The Djemaa el-Fna was a vast, open area at the centre of the city which only a hundred years before had been used for the trading of slaves. Although you could no longer buy people there, Rachel thought that it looked as though you could buy almost anything else. Smoke and steam from a hundred food stalls hung in the air, offering everything from boiled snails to devilish-looking roasted goats' heads. The square was bordered by market stalls which branched out in every direction into the alleys of the souk.

In front of the stalls, herbalists and witch doctors set out their wares on carpets. They offered cures and charms and curses in the form of ostrich feet, hedgehog skins and live chameleons locked in bamboo cages. Lagging behind at the rear of the group, Rachel and the Spanish girls stopped to look at snake-charmers with cobras in baskets and monkeys tethered by chains.

"Photo! Monkey!" An unshaven man in a filthy djellaba stepped out in front of Rachel, Inez and Carmen. "English? *Françaises?*" he asked. The Spanish girls tried to wave him away, but Rachel was simultaneously fascinated and horrified by the monkey chained to the man's umbrella and wearing a nappy in an attempt to make it look cute.

"You like snake? Photo?" Grinning a toothless smile, the man pulled a long green snake from inside a sack and tried to drape it round Carmen's neck. Both Spanish girls squealed.

"Get it off!" Inez screamed. "We hate snakes!"

"Leave us alone!" Rachel shouted at the man. He held up a hand and backed away as Gabriel turned to look at him. The girls thanked Rachel and they hurried off after the rest of the group across the square.

By the time the girls reached the battered old coach that was parked on the far side of the Djemaa el-Fna, Mahmoud and Ali were already arguing. The vehicle which Ali had procured had obviously been used, many years before, as a tour bus for a holiday company. Spelled out on the side of the bus in ornate red script was the word:

Casablanca

Faded palm trees, along with some words in Arabic, flanked the lettering. Some of the rear windows were broken and patched up with packing tape. Others were hung with scraps of towel to ward off the sun, and none of the coach's wheels looked as if they matched.

"It was working last night when I parked it, I swear," Ali shouted at his brother, casting nervous glances at the rest of the group, who were already gathered around the open bonnet of the coach. "I drove it here."

Mahmoud looked ready to explode with rage. "I said to get something reliable, you idiot. Where did you get this heap of junk? I gave you money! This is really bad. We need to get them away quickly. Time is against us!"

Mahmoud and his brother continued to argue loudly in Arabic, pushing and shoving each other and waving their arms in the air.

Jean-Bernard removed his head from under the bonnet, where he and his twin had been fiddling, and pulled out a fistful of wires.

"Kaput," Jean-Luc said.

Mahmoud and Ali stopped squabbling. Ali looked puzzled.

"This is terrible," Mahmoud said despairingly. "What can we do?"

"It's OK; we can fix it," Jean-Bernard said.

Jean-Luc nodded. "One hour, perhaps."

Mahmoud apologized profusely for his brother's stupidity and inefficiency. Gabriel just nodded, watching Ali out of the corner of his eye as the Moroccan ducked beneath the bonnet and attempted to help the French boys. Mahmoud offered to take the rest of the group to the terrace of a nearby cafe. Kate accepted and said she would take care of Duncan and Morag. Seeing the steely look on Kate's face, Laura hesitated, but then she decided to grasp the nettle and tag along.

Rachel, Inez and Carmen asked if they could go and look at some of the stalls on the other side of the square instead, promising they would be back within the hour.

Carmen and Inez laughed as Rachel haggled for the orange pointed slippers that were already on her feet. She was running rings around the trader who was happy to be doing business with what he believed to be a very special customer.

"One hundred fifty dirhams. Good price."

"Two hundred!" Rachel said, confounding his expectations.

"Take them ... *please*," the man said. "I would be honoured, Your Majesty!" He watched the girls turn away with the slippers and immediately began telling the stallholder next to him about the gift he believed he had just given the Queen of England. Inez and Carmen giggled and clapped at Rachel's developing powers of suggestion.

The girls walked into an alley where all the stalls were selling brightly coloured blankets. They turned into another where everything seemed to be made of tanned leather and then a third where ornate lamps twinkled at the front of every stall.

Inez and Carmen stopped to look at some silver jewellery. Rachel tried to look interested, but it was not really her thing. She wandered on a few paces, then turned into a small square. Looking around, she was lured by the intensely coloured spices stacked in barrels and intrigued by the skins of pythons and leopards that hung from the shopfronts.

She was a long way from the Mall of America.

On the terrace in front of the cafe, Laura and Kate sat sipping mint tea while Mahmoud joked with Morag and Duncan. Laura decided to break the silence. To try again.

"Listen, how many times can I say 'I'm sorry', Kate?"

Kate shrugged.

"I just want to say … you know, everything you think about me is probably true. I *was* working solely for the project, yes. I *did* only have my own research and my own interests at heart. But, in my defence – if I *have* one – this time they spun me a line. They double-crossed *me* too. I didn't know they'd take Adam."

Laura took a deep breath. She was telling the truth, but Kate wasn't buying it. "Look, Kate, if I hadn't bargained with them to let your kids 'escape' from Hope in the first place, I think they'd be in a worse situation than they are now."

Kate's curiosity was momentarily piqued. "Worse? How much worse exactly? OK, Rachel's with us, but we're all on a one-way ticket to God knows where. Oh and if you remember, my son has been abducted. Does it *get* any worse?"

Laura couldn't tell Kate what she really thought: that if she had left Rachel and Adam at the Hope Project, they might be dead now, like specimens in a jar. Or that if Kate had stayed, she might be dead too; things might have been a whole lot worse.

"I will get Adam back," Laura said. She looked Kate straight in the eye, hoping that she could actually deliver. "I promise I will do my very best to get him released. The only problem is … I might have to make contact with the big boys at Hope."

"Whatever it takes," Kate said.

Laura looked up and realized that Mahmoud was hanging on her every word. He looked flustered.

"What is it, Mahmoud?" Laura said. "You look worried."

"I was just thinking, we must get back soon. We really need to get going."

Kate thanked Mahmoud for the tea and they all set off back towards the coach.

Inez looked at her watch. "We'd better head back."

The time had flown, and both sisters were now laden with shopping bags. They drew every eye as they strolled through the souk, heads held high, dressed in identical silk djellebas and rattling with bangles and rows of coloured beads.

"Where's Rachel?" Carmen looked around. They were

somewhere inside a maze packed with booths, dead ends and dark corners, and both realized that they hadn't seen Rachel for the last quarter of an hour.

"We should head for the square. That's where she'll go if she's lost us." Inez looked around too. She had no idea which way the central square was.

A young Moroccan boy who had obviously overheard their conversation grinned at them. "Djemaa el-Fna? Main square? I take you." He winked, and the girls, grateful for a little guidance, followed him. Five minutes later, having pressed a few coins into the boy's hand, they found themselves back in the hubbub of the square.

They walked briskly back in the direction they had taken an hour earlier, worried that they were going to be late. They hurried past the cages of reptiles and walked diagonally towards the spot where the coach was parked.

"Hey! Photo! Monkey?"

A familiar man stepped out in front of them, grinning his toothless smile and holding the monkey on a chain. Other men were starting to surround them, some with monkeys, and others – they saw to their horror – with snakes.

A circle began to form as other hawkers saw their opportunity. Sunglasses, toy serpents, wooden drums, fake watches were all thrust under the girls' noses. Suddenly, the crowd was three deep around them, and Inez and Carmen began to panic; their fear bouncing from one to the other and escalating by the second.

"Photo! Monkey!" The first man shouted in Carmen's face, holding the Barbary ape so close to her that the scabby animal was able to put a long arm round her neck and tug at her beads.

"I don't want your ... monkey!" Carmen shouted. "It's wrong; it's cruel," she bawled, adding a very rude phrase which she only knew in English, but which was universally recognized.

Suddenly the crowd went quiet. The toothless man in the filthy djellaba looked offended by Carmen's words and, spitting on the ground at her feet, he uttered a curse of his own.

Somewhere in the crowd a huge dog began to bark. The monkey grabbed hold of Carmen again, looking straight into her face and baring his yellow teeth.

Inez reached into her handbag. "We'll give you money," she said. "Just let us go."

Carmen shrieked as the monkey pulled her hair, but Inez screamed louder when she saw several long black snakes slithering from their baskets and moving quickly across the ground towards her feet...

44

Rachel made her way slowly through the crowded, narrow alleyways. Many of the stalls that pressed in on her from either side sold almost identical goods, so it took longer than it might normally have done for her to realize that she had walked past the same ones several times: she was lost.

And she had no idea where Carmen and Inez had got to.

She had heard a few different languages as she'd moved through the lattice of small streets and alleys: Arabic, French, a smattering of Spanish. She'd been able to understand them all, so decided to ask for directions. She stopped at a stall selling leather goods. The stallholder moved quickly across to her and began pointing at bags.

"These are top quality. Finest leather. You English? American?"

Rachel told him that she was American, that she did not need a new handbag, then asked, in perfect Arabic, for directions back to the main square. The stallholder looked taken aback. He raised an arm and pointed, seeming eager to be rid of her.

Rachel smiled and thanked him, *"Shukran bezzaf."*

Walking back across the main square, Rachel tried to reach out to Carmen and Inez with her mind. She knew straight away that something was terribly wrong. She could sense their panic and confusion; the ragged pattern of distorted thoughts could only mean one thing.

Fear.

She turned at the scream coming from somewhere behind her and began pushing people aside, hurrying towards the far corner of the square where a small crowd had gathered.

Now, through the white noise of dread and helplessness, a simple message was coming through. Two words battering at the sides of Rachel's skull as she picked up speed.

Help us…

She smelled the animals before she saw them; something pungent came from each one that made her very afraid. They were ready to attack; to kill. It was in every creature's eyes too: a naked aggression that Rachel saw as the last onlooker stepped to one side, revealing the terrible trouble that Carmen and Inez were in.

The girls caught sight of Rachel and began to shout for help, their voices all but drowned out by the barking of the dogs, the terrible shrieking of the apes and the noise of the crowd.

I'm here, Rachel said with her mind. *Try not to be afraid.*

It was easy enough to say, but there were two big dogs,

straining at leashes that looked set to snap at any moment. The apes had bared their fangs, and one was pinning Carmen to the ground while two others dragged their owners across the cobbles in their desperation to reach the girls. Snakes had begun to coil round the girls' ankles and there were plenty more wriggling towards them, along with the lizards and scorpions which were starting to slip free from bags and wicker baskets at the edge of the crowd.

Please, help us...

Rachel closed her eyes, emptied her mind and focused. She pictured a thin beam of light: created it in her mind and sent it out. She moved it across the square and wove it around the animals that were surrounding Carmen and Inez. She called them away; called them to her.

The barking and the snarling stopped immediately, then, one by one, each animal turned and started to move. The apes yanked their owners in the opposite direction, as did the dogs. The snakes and lizards slithered and skittered, turning towards the girl standing at the edge of the crowd with her eyes closed.

Rachel drew the circle of light in tighter.

And, as each animal got to within a metre or so of her, it dropped to the floor, as though waiting to be told what to do next. Gasps went up from the crowd as dogs settled on their bellies and began to whimper, as snakes curled up at her feet and as each vicious Barbary ape lay prostrate, its head down and its long arms outstretched.

Rachel waited a few seconds before stepping slowly
through the crowd of animals and hurrying across to
Carmen and Inez.

"Thank ... you," Carmen stammered.

Rachel nodded. "We need to go."

She took each girl by the hand and began to back away.
They made slow progress. Every face in the square was
trained on them and Rachel watched as onlookers stepped
aside, lowering their heads and muttering oaths: terrified.

They had almost reached the coach when an old man
appeared in front of them and began to shout in Arabic.
Rachel heard and understood and, without knowing why,
began to slowly raise her hand and turn her palm towards
him as he continued to shout.

"The evil eye! She has the evil eye."

She did not know exactly what was happening. She felt
the pain of it, saw the thin ribbon of smoke rising from her
hand, but it did not seem to matter. She felt powerful suddenly, enjoying the look of terror on the old man's face when
he saw her palm, then he turned and scuttled away.

Inez grabbed her by the wrist. "Your hand..."

Rachel turned her hand over and stared down at it. The
shape had risen up through the skin, burned its way into her
flesh: bright red and livid, and still smoking against her pale
palm.

"*Triskela,*" Carmen said.

Some words did not need to be translated.

* * *

In the mobile unit's office, Clay Van der Zee rummaged in the back of a drawer until he finally brought out the bottle of whisky he'd hidden away. He sat down and poured himself a glass.

Hadn't he always known it would come to this? After all, he knew what the people who funded the Hope Project were like; what they were capable of.

So why did he need a drink – *several* drinks – so badly?

He felt the warmth of the whisky spreading through him as it went down, and thought about the conversation with the man from New York. He remembered a day when he would never even have considered … *this*. When he had been an eager young scientist ready to change the world, every bit as full of fire and optimism as Laura Sullivan.

That eager young scientist would have hated the man he had become.

He took another drink.

You have lots of nice, shiny equipment in that fancy mobile unit of yours, right?

Science could be a ruthless business, he accepted that. He knew very well that sometimes, if you wanted to get anywhere – to make *real* breakthroughs – then normal rules did not apply. Hadn't he said more or less the same thing to Laura Sullivan? With an end as … monumental as this in sight, then all means could be justified.

Even hurting children.

Van der Zee looked down at the whisky and realized that he'd finished it. He returned the empty bottle to the back of the drawer and slammed it shut.

The phone rang and he snatched it up.

"Yes?"

"Doctor? Your visitor from HQ has just arrived. Shall I bring him across?"

Van der Zee blinked and wondered what that younger, more innocent version of himself would say.

"Yes, that's fine. Can you just give me a few minutes first…?"

When he put down the phone, Van der Zee noticed that his hands were shaking.

45

Rachel, Carmen and Inez hurried back towards the coach. As inexplicably as it had appeared, the mark on Rachel's palm had vanished.

"Has that happened before?" Carmen asked.

Rachel shook her head. She told them that it had made her feel … powerful. She thought about the group that Gabriel had gathered together, about some of the things she had witnessed, and began to wonder why they all seemed to have different capabilities.

"Why didn't you do something yourselves?" she asked. "Back there, with the animals? Why couldn't you make them stop?"

Inez looked a little embarrassed. "I did it once, years ago to a dog that was trying to bite me. But this was different. I was so … scared that I couldn't do anything. It was like the fear took away the power, you know?"

"It was the same for me," Carmen said.

Rachel nodded, understanding. It was a lesson she'd need

to remember, although fear was not normally something she, or anyone else, could control.

"There is something else you must not forget," Inez said. "We are not the same as you. None of us are."

"I don't understand."

"We are older, yes, but you are stronger. You and your brother."

They reached the part of the square where the coach was parked. Carmen squeezed Rachel's hand. "There is so much more *you* are able to do…"

Jean-Luc and Jean-Bernard were still busy beneath the bonnet of the coach. Jean-Luc looked up when the girls approached, winked and wiped an oil-stained sleeve across his face.

"More or less fixed," he said.

"What was the problem?" Rachel asked.

Jean-Bernard raised his head. "Well, that's the funny thing, because—"

There was a sudden shout from the alleyway behind them. Everyone turned and began running towards it. Rachel led the way. She had recognized her mother's voice.

She turned into the alleyway and stopped, as shocked as her mother had clearly been to see Mahmoud pressed up against the wall, a knife against his throat.

"Ali, stop!" Rachel shouted.

Ali did not bother to turn round. "Stay out of this."

"Help me!" Mahmoud said.

Rachel knew that she'd been right to take such an instant dislike to Ali. She remembered what Carmen had said: she was obviously sensitive to such things.

"I'm going to kill him," Ali said calmly.

Mahmoud pleaded for help again, but Ali only pushed the tip of the knife harder against his neck, drawing blood.

Rachel took half a step towards the brothers, then stopped when she saw Mahmoud knock the knife away and wrestle his brother to the ground. They began to exchange vicious blows, screaming at each other in Arabic, until they reached a deadlock, each with an arm wrapped tight round the other's neck, their heads pressed together as though they were Siamese twins.

Rachel moved a little closer. "Ali, you need to let go of your brother."

He shook his head.

"He's gone mad!" Mahmoud shouted. "He just attacked me for no reason."

"He's lying."

"No, *he's* lying…"

Ali turned slowly and looked at Rachel, wincing as Mahmoud's arm squeezed his neck. "He has betrayed you."

"He is insane," Mahmoud said.

"No. *He* is the one who has lost his mind." Ali's face was twisted with rage and hatred. "He has been trying to keep you here—"

"Don't listen!" Mahmoud screamed. "He is the one who cannot be trusted. You *know* me!"

"He is taking money from someone, I am not sure who. He has taken money in exchange for you. For your lives."

"No…"

"*He* sabotaged the coach."

"It's not true."

Ali nodded towards Jean-Bernard and Jean-Luc. "Ask them."

Jean-Luc turned to Rachel. "It's what I was trying to say before. Someone removed the distributor cap. We had to find a new one, rewire it—"

"Please don't listen to him," Mahmoud said. "Haven't I taken good care of you? I *welcomed* you—"

Mahmoud was cut off as he was swung across Ali's back and thrown to the floor. Ali quickly knelt down and grabbed Mahmoud's wrist, ignoring the squeals of pain.

"There!" Ali nodded towards the tattoo between Mahmoud's thumb and forefinger. The same tattoo that he had. Ali leant down and spat on his brother's hand, then rubbed hard at the blue lines of the Triskellion until they disappeared.

Rachel gasped. She had been wrong about Ali.

"You see?" He looked up at Rachel. "You do not have much time. You have been betrayed."

"Why?" Rachel asked. "Who is it that's paying him?"

"It doesn't matter…"

Rachel turned at the voice behind her and saw Gabriel.

His expression was blank, but there was something dangerous flashing in his eyes.

"You heard Ali," he said. "We need to go. *Now!*"

Half an hour later, the old coach was rattling out of
Marrakesh. Ali steered it expertly past the airport and the
cluster of tall hotels and through an area of olive groves
and small farms that gradually died away until there was
nothing but scrub and sky and a long dirt road.

Rachel sat at the front with Gabriel. "Where are we
going?"

"It's a small town on the coast," Gabriel said. "Mogador…"

"That is its ancient name," Ali announced. "The name
many of us still know it by. We should be there before it gets
dark."

Gabriel stared out of the window. "From there, it's on
foot. Ali knows the way."

"Trust me," Ali said. "I'll get you to the Rocher des Tueurs."

Rachel understood what the words meant and felt a shudder pass through her.

The Killing Stone.

Ali glanced at Gabriel. "What about Mahmoud?"

Gabriel shrugged and turned away. "He will have to live
with himself," he said. "Provided he *does* live."

Rachel looked across at Ali and saw him slowly nod. If
there was any sadness on his brother's behalf, he showed no
sign of it.

"I think I know the man he's working for," Gabriel said. "And he doesn't like to leave a mess behind…"

Mahmoud was still shaking from the fight with his brother, though he would have been shaking anyway as he reached for the phone and dialled the mobile number he had been given.

"I couldn't keep them here," he said. "I'm sorry."

"It doesn't matter."

Mahmoud sat back in his chair and let out a long breath. He could have wept with joy and relief. "I'm pleased that it hasn't caused you a problem."

"Change of plan, that's all. I prefer being one step ahead of them. I'm already here."

"That's good," Mahmoud said. "That's very clever."

"Thank you. Now, you look after yourself, OK?"

Mahmoud nodded, saying he would be happy to help if there was anything else he could do.

He looked up when a shadow fell across the table and wondered what the noise was behind him.

It was his last thought.

46

Adam could hear voices outside the door. When it swung open, he raised his head from the gurney and was pleased to see a friendly face.

Mr Cheung.

"Hi, Adam," he said.

"Hi." Adam's voice sounded strained and weak.

Mr Cheung smiled. "You've been one busy guy."

"You could say that."

"You OK?" Mr Cheung asked, a look of concern passing over his face.

"I've been better," Adam said, forcing a pained smile.

"OK," Mr Cheung said. He swung a heavy metal suitcase up on to the steel worktop and opened it. "Let's try and get this over with as quickly as possible."

He took a pair of cables and electrodes from the case and attached a couple of clips to the wires. Adam strained his neck round to try and see what the Chinese man was doing. He remembered the sensation from trying to watch the dentist fix the needle and felt the same flutters of panic spread though his stomach and into his bladder.

He remembered what Morag had taught him, when he was having the tracking device cut out. He would need to be brave. To avoid the pain, he would need to go elsewhere in his mind, to create a personal space away from whatever was about to happen.

Mr Cheung took a long pair of forceps and clamps from the case and swabbed them with antiseptic wipes. Adam's legs began to tremble.

"What are you doing?" His voice was high-pitched and cracked.

Mr Cheung looked at him, the smile gone from his eyes. He pulled on a pair of rubber gloves and switched on a CD player. Light, classical music began to fill the room.

"I'm sorry, Adam," he said. "I'm afraid I'm not just here to cook."

The old coach bumped along the narrow, pitted road. The journey was punctuated only by the occasional lorry roaring towards them, or by the overtaking of a solitary donkey cart. Every twenty kilometres or so, they would drive through a one-horse town, where women in long, dun-coloured robes carried baskets of vegetables back towards mud huts and men in shabby clothes smoked idly at the roadside, watching them pass.

Rachel was sitting next to Gabriel. They had not spoken

for some miles, their minds elsewhere. The French boys were playfully thumping one another. The others were dotted around the ten rows of seats, enjoying a greater, if less comfortable, degree of personal space than they had on previous legs of their journey. Morag and Duncan were at the back, stretched out on the long bench seat, singing a song in high, Scottish voices: "The wheels on the bus go round and round, all day long…"

Rachel's thoughts drifted back to the square in Marrakesh.

"Why did the animals attack them?" she asked Gabriel.

"What?" Gabriel had been miles away. "The monkeys, you mean?"

"Yeah, why did they attack Inez and Carmen? Did that horrible guy *make* them do it?"

Gabriel shrugged. "Why did Adam get beaten up in England? Why were they after you in Spain? It's always been the same. Some people recognize us, know us by instinct, or from the stories their ancestors have told for many generations. And some *species* recognize us, like the bees. Others can't see us at all."

"What? You mean like the people who don't notice we're there, even when we're right under their noses?"

Gabriel nodded. "And of those that recognize us, some will help us, as they have always done."

"And the others?" Rachel pressed, already knowing the answer.

"The others want to do us nothing but harm." Gabriel turned and looked her in the eye. "They just want us dead. And usually, they win."

Adam walked along the beach. He did not know where he was exactly, but it was idyllic. Fine silver sand stretched out in a long white crescent into infinity ahead of him and crystal-clear water lapped gently at the shore. His feet enjoyed the contrast between the hot, soft sand beneath them and the delicious chill of the cool water that rhythmically splashed over them. It was a paradise where parrots and pelicans swooped and screeched overhead before landing in lush green palm trees which rustled in the gentle breeze…

Now and then, the classical music would push through his vision, and the shrill sound of the violins would bring him back towards consciousness. Then Adam would have to fight to return to the island in his mind.

He knew there would be scars – physical and mental – and he knew there would be pain to bear once he was on the other side: once this torture had ended … if it *ever* ended. All he could do for now, though, was focus and float in his subconscious, above the pain. The smell of singed hair began to bring him back into the room. Adam fought on in his mind … running away across the beach and out into the water, splashing across its surface to where the dolphins were playing.

He dived, deep into the cool blue.

* * *

Rachel was looking out of the window, daydreaming. A beach, crystal-blue water, somewhere nice… Chance would be a fine thing. Maybe one day she would get a holiday in a place like that…

Her reverie was broken as Laura sat down next to her; Rachel resented the intrusion that brought her back to earth with a bump. Gabriel had moved seats. He was talking to Inez and Carmen, who were nodding and smiling at him enthusiastically.

Rachel glanced at Laura.

"Hi," Laura said.

"Hi," Rachel responded sulkily.

"I think I'm building some bridges with your mum, Rachel."

Rachel shrugged and pushed out her lower lip. "You might want to think about building some with me," she said. "But to be honest, I think we're past that point."

Laura looked disappointed. "Rach…"

"Don't," Rachel said. "You are nothing but a liar. You just lie and twist and conceal, and you have done from the very moment I met you back in Triskellion." Rachel was warming to her theme. These were things she needed to get off her chest. "You might be a smart doctor and all that, but you have no real knowledge of what makes people tick. Morag and Duncan have more intuition in their little fingernails than you have…"

Gabriel and the Spanish girls stopped chattering and looked round.

"I'm not as sensitive as you guys," Laura said. "You're special. That's all I wanted to show."

"Show *who*?" Rachel spat. "Show your boss? Show the world? With you I'm just research, aren't I? A lab rat. We're all research, scientific proof. For what? So you can stick me in a cage and win a load of prizes?"

Laura looked down at the leg of her jeans and picked at the frayed hole that was developing across the knee. She knew that what Rachel had said was true. She *had* lied; it had become a way of life, working for the Hope Project. She was effectively a spy, a double agent. And Rachel's other comment had *really* hit home. Most of her own emotions had become so deeply suppressed that she really didn't know what made people tick. She realized that she had no close, personal relationships. Rachel and Adam had been the closest she'd got to loving anyone for as long as she could remember and now she'd lost them.

Lost two friends. Lost a mother's child.

She had let everybody down, including herself.

Suddenly she was crying like an infant. Her lower lip trembled uncontrollably and tears poured down her freckled cheeks. Her chest heaved, trying to contain the tears held in by years of self-control.

Rachel dug into her sleeve and handed Laura a tissue.

Laura turned to face her. "Thank you, Rachel," she said

between sobs. "Whatever you may think of me, how ever much you hate me now, I promise you one thing…"

Rachel waited for the crying to subside.

"No more lies."

47

The Englishman sat in his room and listened to the Atlantic crashing angrily against the town's ancient stone walls. The sea here was grey and unforgiving; far rougher than he remembered it.

He had visited the town many years before as a younger man, he and a group of his rich, spoilt friends. Their skin was bronzed and their hair bleached after many months travelling through India, Turkey and North Africa. He had stayed here for several months. He had spent hours listening to loud music in rooms filled with like-minded layabouts; the atmosphere heady with smoke and the pungent stink of incense. He had sat up late into the night and talked about changing the world, with friends who would grow up to be bankers and businessmen.

He had wasted far too much time.

Those were the days before he had found the path he was truly meant to walk. Before he had learned that there were ways he could really change things; that there was more to life than enjoying himself.

He smiled, listening to the roar of the sea outside.

There *was* enjoyment in this, of course, despite the pain and the disfigurement. Enjoyment in tracking these children down. And he looked forward to the overpowering sense of accomplishment that he knew would be his when he had taken the Triskellion from them. When he had taken *both* of them…

Even then, back in the days when his friends had been content to let their lives wash over them, he had been intrigued by the spirituality of this place. There was a dark and powerful history to which only he had connected. It was an ancient force that could not be denied, and lying in his darkened room, he felt it again now, filling him with strength as he waited for the children to arrive.

He sensed that the Newman twins and the other boy – the one who was guiding them – felt that coming here and uncovering what had been hidden for so long was their destiny. But it was *his* destiny too.

They shared it, as they shared other things.

History, and blood.

He reached for the jug of water by the side of his bed, poured out a glass and downed it to swallow his tablets.

There was not long to wait now.

They shared a destiny, but only one of them would be able to fulfil it.

* * *

Laura moved through the coach, past Morag and Duncan, who were curled up together, past the French twins and the two Spanish girls, and slid into the seat next to Gabriel.

"How long until we're there?" she asked.

Gabriel was staring out of the window. The sun was starting to go down; the sky was reddening above the expanse of scrubland on either side of them and the line of snow-capped mountains in the far distance. "Half an hour maybe," he said. "Can't you smell the sea?"

Laura took a deep breath. She could only smell the coach's exhaust fumes. "Listen, what we were talking about last night…?"

Gabriel turned to her. "You've got more questions?"

"Just a few thousand."

Gabriel smiled. "I'll do my best. One at a time, though."

"Where are you from? What's it like? How do you … travel?"

"That's three in one!"

"Sorry."

Gabriel thought for a moment. "Try to imagine a new colour," he said. "I don't mean a colour that's a *bit* like blue, or *almost* red. A completely new colour." He waited, saw the confusion on Laura's face. "It's impossible, isn't it? Like trying to think of a sound you've never heard before, or a smell. That's what it's like for me trying to give you the answers you want; that's what it would be like for you trying to understand them, even if I did."

Laura nodded. "I want to … learn." She shook her head. "I've been studying all this stuff for years, but now, sitting here right next to you, I feel like I'm in kindergarten."

"I'm not that special," Gabriel said.

"Yes, you are."

"There's a lot of us out there." Gabriel turned back to the window, leant his head against the glass. "And there's a lot of us still here. A lot of our … remains."

"The tombs?"

"We've never exactly been welcomed."

"I want to try and change that," Laura said.

"I hope you can." Gabriel smiled sadly. "I always thought it was an ironic name. The Hope Project…"

"Some of them think the same way I do."

"Not enough," Gabriel said. "They will try to stop us."

"You can beat them." Laura put a hand on his arm, glanced across at Rachel. "I've seen what these kids can do."

Gabriel closed his eyes. Laura thought he had gone to sleep and was about to get up when he spoke again. "What we *are*, how we live … it isn't complicated."

Laura laughed. "Thank God for that."

"You remember Honeyman, back in the village?" Laura nodded. "He understood. He saw it every day with his bees. For the hive to flourish, the bees must work for one another. As far as the rest of the world is concerned that sort of … harmony is almost invisible. Until there's a bee buzzing around your head on a summer's day." Gabriel looked at her, making sure she was with him. "If we're threatened, we *can* sting."

The coach rumbled on; Ali taking it slowly round the sharp bends as they began to descend towards the coast. Through the front window, Laura could see the grey expanse of the ocean ahead of them. The line where the waves broke, the ramparts and the red walls of the town nestling against the Atlantic.

"This place we're going…"

"The Watchtower," Gabriel said.

Laura thought for a moment and then understood. It was the ancient Phoenician translation for the town of Mogador. "And then?"

"Three or four hours on foot. Ali will take us. He's the last one who knows the way."

Laura dug deep into her memory, mentally mapping the area until she got it. She almost cried out with excitement. These were caves she had studied back when she was a student. She had read the archaeological reports a dozen times. She could have kicked herself for not working it out before.

"Thanks," she said. "For helping me understand."

Gabriel looked at her. "Wait until it's finished," he said. "You may not feel the same way."

Van der Zee leapt up from behind his desk when Mr Cheung walked into his office.

"Well?"

Mr Cheung was sweating and white-faced as he dropped his metal suitcase on to the floor. The instruments inside rattled and clattered.

"Nothing."

"*What?*"

"Either the boy cannot feel pain, or he simply does not know."

Van der Zee slammed his fist down on the desk. "You need to try something else."

"I've tried everything."

"There must be a way…"

Cheung shook his head. "I don't want to go back in there."

Van der Zee dropped back into the chair. "We're in big trouble," he said. "Unless we find out where they're going, we'll all be out of a job."

Cheung picked up his case. "That's fine with me." He walked to the door. "It's wrong… We shouldn't … I don't think I want this job any more."

Van der Zee watched Cheung leave, then sat, almost gasping for breath as the consequences of his failure rang around his head. He knew that the people in New York, or those in New Mexico, would be calling soon enough, demanding answers. He couldn't bring himself to think about what might happen when he failed to provide them.

His head swam with crazy ideas. Should he simply lie? He could tell them that Adam *had* named a place, then blame him when they discovered later that they'd been sent on a wild-goose chase. He could try to pin the blame on Cheung, or tell them that Laura Sullivan had been feeding them false information all along.

He could try to run...

He jumped when the phone rang, his heart thumping against his ribs. He felt sick as he reached for the receiver.

"It's Laura Sullivan." The line crackled. Her voice was low, barely above a whisper. "You need to shut up and listen."

"Go on..."

"I know where we're going. But there's one condition."

Now Van der Zee's heart was really pounding. "Just tell me where."

"We're heading for the Cave of the Berbers. It's ten miles north of Mogador."

Van der Zee scribbled down the details. "I'm grateful for this, Laura. Everyone will be grateful."

"I was right all along. It's where everything began; where the line started."

"So what's this condition?" Van der Zee was already staring at the map. It would not take long to mobilize the unit, to organize a transport helicopter. "What do you want?"

"You need to bring the boy..."

48

"Welcome to La Triskalla," the Australian behind the bar said. "Take a seat and I'll get someone to carry your bags up. Can I get you guys some drinks?"

They ordered water, Cokes, juices. Rachel sat down in a big, battered chair covered in a blanket and looked around the Triskalla Cafe. Tucked away up a side street, just within the town walls of Mogador, it looked like a bohemian sort of a place. She couldn't believe it when they'd arrived outside and seen the stylized image of the Triskellion hanging above the door. Inside, although incense was burning and a few logs crackled and spat in the grate, the air smelled damp and salty. Moroccan hangings fought for wall space with windsurf sails and fliers for kite-surfing lessons and camel treks.

Rachel looked across at her mother, who smiled wanly, and raised her eyebrows. A gesture that said how much she would have liked this place in different times and how Adam would have loved it; how he would have been racing off to sign up for windsurfing.

Rachel took her juice and got up to read some of the brochures that were tacked to the noticeboard. She looked at the photos of kids, not much older than herself, who had clearly been having a great time here in the summer.

Not a care in the world.

The Australian was standing at her shoulder. "Not the best time of year for windsurfing, mate," he said. "You should come back in the summer. Is it a field trip you're on? Isn't that what the guy who booked you in said?"

"Yeah, sort of," Rachel said. Ali had already gone into town in search of supplies for the following day. "Bit of exploring, you know."

The Australian nodded, held out his hand. "I'm Guy. But everyone calls me Jubby."

Rachel smiled at the funny name and looked at the young man's tanned, open face, the earrings, his matted, sun-bleached hair. He didn't seem like the kind of person to be caught up in their complex situation. Or anything complex at all. She liked his look and his easy manner, and was flattered by his attention.

"Where does the name come from?" Rachel asked.

"Jubby? Dunno, since I was a kid…"

"Oh, I meant the name of this place, sorry."

Jubby laughed. "No worries. Triskalla, you mean? It was the name of the place when we took it over. Apparently it's a really ancient symbol. The Moroccans use it as a charm to ward off the evil eye." Jubby widened his eyes at Rachel, making her smile. "But you get it a lot in Celtic designs, jewellery and stuff. You even see it in India. You been to India yet?"

"No," Rachel said. She was unsure whether she would ever see India, or anywhere else for that matter. Jubby pushed up the sleeve of his T-shirt.

"It's a great symbol, isn't it? Makes a gorgeous tat." He flexed his biceps and an ornate Triskellion in red and green ink twitched on his arm. He rolled back his other sleeve, exposing a circular design with what looked like two tadpoles contained within it. "I've got yin and yang too," he said, prodding the tattoo.

"So, Triskalla doesn't mean anything ... personal to you?"

"Nah, it's a good name for the cafe, that's all. We've only been open eighteen months and just hoped that it might bring us luck."

Inez wafted by, holding an empty glass, and Jubby's gaze followed her.

"Seems to be working!" he said, winking at Rachel.

Rachel felt a little deflated as she watched Jubby bound eagerly across to the bar to get Inez another drink.

Later, Jubby and his girlfriend, Rosie, joined them to eat. Rosie looked as put out as Jean-Luc and Jean-Bernard when Jubby monopolized the Spanish girls over dinner, telling them stories of great waves and encounters with sharks while showing off his tattoos. As soon as they had finished eating, Rosie sloped off with Kate to make up a room for Duncan and Morag.

Rachel sat on a floor cushion by the fire with Gabriel, the anticipation of the next day hanging heavy in the air.

"Bit of a coincidence, the name," she said.

Gabriel held up his hands in innocence.

Rachel found it hard to believe in coincidence any more, but maybe this place, like the village in England, had been named for a good reason. "Jubby seems to think it's good luck," Rachel said. She yawned, ready to sleep.

Gabriel watched her get up from the cushion. "I don't really believe in luck," he said. "Sleep well."

Rachel had had some disturbing dreams and visions since she'd first arrived in her grandmother's village.

But this was the worst yet.

There had been only the faintest slivers of early morning light coming through the window, but it was as though the man who had been sitting at the side of her bed had sucked all of it into himself. As though the darkness that seeped from him like sweat had overwhelmed everything around it.

He had been sitting there and watching her. Just sitting...

Rachel had been unable to scream or shout for help; unable to make a sound.

Now she lay on her side and stared out of the window.

She tried to shake it off, willing the nightmare to recede, listening to her heart race and waiting for her breathing to return to normal.

She turned over and found herself staring at him.

Her guts flew into her mouth. She could not see his face, which was shadowed beneath the hood of his robe, but she knew that he was smiling.

"What?" he said. "Did you think you were dreaming?"

It was the man they had seen on the Underground in Paris; the man who had demanded the Triskellion. She had not seen him since, but, looking at him now, she sensed that he had been with them all along. There had been many moments when she had felt as though she was being observed, and staring into the blackness, where a face should have been, she was in no doubt that he was the man – if he *was* a man – who had been watching them.

"I'd ask if you slept well," the man said, "but it's obvious that you didn't."

The voice was as cracked and low as Rachel remembered, and yet there was something else about the intonation that she recognized … but couldn't quite place. She slid away from him and pulled herself upright in the bed. "Who are you?"

"Well, this will all be over soon," he said. He raised his twisted hands, blistered and claw-like, and gently drew back his hood. "So I don't suppose there's any harm…"

Rachel strained to see in the half-light, then gasped.

Her hand flew to her mouth. She felt faint, but was unable to tear her eyes away from the man's face.

What was left of it.

What had once been his nose had been burned away, leaving a large hole in the middle of his face, divided by a sliver of bone. Taut wings of skin, that had once been the lids, dragged at the corners of his eyes. His mouth was a thin purple gash that widened when he smiled to expose the row of large, yellow teeth. The ears were completely gone, save for two twists of scar tissue on either side of his head, while all that remained of his hair was one or two long strands that caught the early morning light as they lay plastered across his skull.

As the man leant close to her, Rachel could see that the livid skin of his face still wept beneath a transparent plastic mask that added an artificial sheen to the raw and angry flesh. Knotted ropes of tendon appeared to be all that held the reptilian head up and, when he spoke, she could clearly see the cartilage of his windpipe move beneath a translucent membrane of freshly transplanted skin.

"I am Hilary Wing," he said.

It was nearly a minute before Rachel could speak. "But … you *died*," she said. "Back in Triskellion … there was a motorbike crash."

The purple gash of Wing's mouth widened. "Well, I think part of me certainly died," he said. "The strange thing is that, despite … everything, and trust me this is even more painful than it looks … I've never felt better in my life. Never felt *stronger*."

"What do you want?"

"We've been through this already, I think. You know very well what I want."

Rachel stared at the terrible face and tried hard not to let her eyes slide away to the corner of the room. To the bag that contained the Triskellion.

"I'm not here to take it," Wing continued. "Not now at any rate. I know that if I bide my time there's a bigger prize just around the corner."

Despite the terror that held every inch of her frozen, Rachel felt a strength begin to spread through her: the same sense of power she had felt when the Triskellion had burned through her skin in Marrakesh. "It doesn't belong to you," she said.

Wing leant forward suddenly. "You *stole* it," he snapped. "You took it from where it belonged and I intend to … restore the natural balance of things."

"You're a liar," Rachel said. "You talk about the Triskellion like it's some precious bit of family silver, but really you just want the power."

Wing sat back again. "Yes, if I'm being completely honest, I want what it can do. Triskellion was a village where people didn't get sick, where the crops never failed. It made us different … *special*. So, of course, I'm trying to imagine what *two* of them could do. That's one part of it…"

"What's the other?"

There was a sucking noise as the plastic mask tightened across Wing's face. "I need to make sure that you, and those like you, don't get it."

Rachel felt a little more power kick in; a surge of anger in spite of the fear. "It belongs to people like me. If the Triskellion… If both of them are family heirlooms, it's *my* family they belong to."

"Oh I know very well where these things came from," Wing said. "They're clearly capable of very wonderful things, but I'm afraid allowing your kind to exist is simply too dangerous. You can't be … tolerated."

"I think you're forgetting that we're actually part of the same family." Rachel smiled and could see that Wing was taken aback.

"I'm not forgetting anything."

"Your father; my grandfather—"

Wing jumped to his feet and raised a scarred hand as though he was about to slap her. "I am not the same as you. Don't make that mistake…" He pulled up his hood and moved slowly across to the bedroom door. "We may not get the chance to talk again," he said. "I suspect we'll all be rather busy over the next day or two."

"Get out."

"Where's your brother, by the way? Dead already?"

"Get out!"

"I'll put in a word when I get home," Wing said. "Perhaps

they'll lay on a memorial at the village church. Say a prayer for you both…"

He closed the door behind him without a sound.

Rachel counted to twenty before jumping out of bed and pulling on her clothes, the scream rising up from her before she'd even got the door open.

She tore down the corridor, past the rooms where the French and Spanish twins were sleeping. Laura stepped out of her room and held out a hand, but Rachel brushed it aside and raced further on, round the corner and into Gabriel's arms.

"It's OK," he said.

Rachel could not remember the last time she and Gabriel had been so close. She pressed herself against him as the tears came and, although he was no more than a boy, no taller and not much stronger than she was, she felt safe.

49

They were less than an hour into their journey and Rachel was exhausted. Lack of sleep made her feel light-headed and the terrible images from the night before haunted her, flooding her mind with horror, draining her of energy.

Ali had organized a couple of donkeys. One was loaded down with bags and the supplies that he had put together, while Duncan and Morag rode happily on the other. The first kilometre had been easy going, along a flat beach which had stretched out from the town walls of Mogador as far as the eye could see. Eventually, the beach had sprouted rough patches of vegetation – grasses and bushes – which in turn had swelled into windswept dunes, the soft sand making it hard to walk with any speed.

There had not been a great deal of idle chat as they'd walked, other than repeated comments about how hot everyone was getting, and Inez and Carmen reminding each other what a nice guy Jubby had been.

Ali was leading the expedition, coaxing the donkeys along through the desert landscape and whistling a strange, sad tune. He wore a long, deep-blue robe, with boots and camouflage-print trousers sticking out incongruously underneath.

"I like your top," Rachel said, by way of conversation. "Great colour."

Ali grinned. "It is the colour of my tribe."

"So the Berbers are not just one tribe?"

"No, there are many. We have tribes all across North Africa and beyond. But we believe *our* tribe is the oldest. We are where it all started." Ali closed his fist and thumped his chest, as if to demonstrate that he was the one who started it all.

"Started what?" Rachel was genuinely intrigued.

"Mankind." Ali said it casually, as though he were telling someone the time. "We believe that the Berbers were the original inhabitants of North Africa, long before the Romans or anyone else came here."

"How long are we talking about?"

"Prehistoric times. Like cavemen. Neanderthal man. We worshipped the sun, the moon and the rocks among which we lived."

"Really?" Rachel said. An image was beginning to form in her mind. "So how do you know how to find these caves?"

Ali tapped his head. "It's all in here. My father told me, same as his father told him. He didn't tell Mahmoud. Now you see why."

"I don't get that," Rachel said. "He seemed so nice, so …
generous."

"Oh yes, Mahmoud has very nice manners. And, of course,
he has plenty of money, which he earned in England. But
the way he earned his money … *not* so nice. That's why he
didn't earn our tribal tattoo. He got in with bad people in the
hippy days in Mogador. English people."

Rachel shuddered as she remembered the night before. She
thought about all the English people she had met, the worst
of whom was, without doubt, her own relative. But surely
Mahmoud could never have known Hilary Wing. Could he?

Rachel had not spoken of her horror, nor tried to explain
the monstrosity that had visited her in the night, to anyone
other than Gabriel. She had not wished to scare the others,
but she had also felt that Gabriel was the only one capable of
understanding, and of protecting them all from whoever
– *whatever* – it was that Hilary Wing had become.

Adam knew that they were on the move.

From inside his cubicle in the mobile unit, it was difficult
to get a sense of direction, or speed. But his instincts told
him that they were going somewhere, and from the subtle
changes in motion, he thought that they might be on water.

He looked down at his wrists. They were still strapped
to the gurney, but the bruises had nearly faded completely
and he felt almost smug about his rapid recovery rate. There
would be no marks.

He was pleased that they had not been able to break him. He had told them nothing, and he had felt no pain. The most horrifying part of his ordeal had been seeing the look of guilt on Mr Cheung's face as he had given up trying. A man whom Adam had once trusted and whom the Hope Project had considered their toughest interrogator. A man over whom Adam had gained the upper hand through his own strength of mind.

He was winning.

"Welcome aboard," Clay Van der Zee said, opening the door to the cubicle and releasing the straps from Adam's ankles and wrists. "Come with me."

He led Adam up on to the interior deck of a large motor launch. Adam had been right: they were on water, and his cell had been slotted neatly into the hold. He heard the engines fire up and glanced through a tiny porthole to see that they were motoring out of a harbour.

"Where are we?" he asked. "Where are we going?"

Van der Zee didn't answer immediately. They walked up a flight of steps to a control room, where several Hope operatives, wearing dark glasses and inhibitors, tensed as Adam entered.

"With any luck," Van der Zee said, "we're going to see your sister."

Adam focused, pushing out all other thoughts until, in his mind's eye, the image of a cave began to form.

* * *

As Ali spoke, the picture in Rachel's head was becoming clearer, like images from a dream coming into sharp focus: a cave, a beach, men in boats. She clutched the Triskellion that now hung on a leather thong round her neck. Then she became aware of another set of thoughts chiming with hers.

Adam.

Rachel's heart leapt and a warm feeling crept through her tired bones, renewing her energy. The connection was faint, but she knew now that her brother was alive and within her range. It was too early to raise her mother's hopes, but she felt sure that Adam was on his way.

They pushed on over scrubby desert until the landscape developed into sharp, grey rocks. Half a kilometre ahead, a craggy incline led up to a path that wound along the cliff top.

Ali pointed to the top of the path. "We can take the donkeys up that far, then we will have to leave them and carry the supplies."

The French boys grumbled, looking at the heavy bags on the donkey's back. Inez and Carmen agreed reluctantly, checking the soles of their flat shoes which would doubtless be wrecked by the rocky path that lay ahead. Laura and Kate trudged on, uncomplaining, while behind them Gabriel looked around to make sure that they weren't being followed, watching the sky as if checking his bearings.

All the while, in Rachel's mind, Adam's voice was growing stronger: telling her not to worry, that he was not far away.

She looked across at Ali. "You and Mahmoud are twins," she said, "so, are you … like us?"

Ali sucked his teeth and considered a moment. "I suppose so, yes, up to a point. There is a legend that says a man came from the sun at the beginning of time and created our people from the primitive cavemen."

Rachel nodded. She remembered the runes in Triskellion. They had told more or less the same story.

Ali pointed a finger skywards and cast a glance back towards Gabriel before continuing. "They say that the man from the sun accounts for the blond and red hair and the green eyes that sometimes occur among the Berbers. It is said that these people are a genetic throwback to the visitors who came to this coast."

Rachel was suddenly excited. Pieces of a bigger jigsaw were beginning to come together. "So you'd be genetically linked to the … visitors, the Travellers, who came here. Like we are to the one who came to England?"

"Yes, we are linked. But don't forget, the Traveller who came here and lived among the Berbers came maybe thirty thousand years ago." Ali spread his arms wide to demonstrate the enormous length of time.

"That's a long time for the genes to get watered down," he continued. "So by the time you get to Mahmoud and me, there's not much of the original DNA left."

"Enough for you and Mahmoud to have … special powers?"

"We sometimes have a sixth sense about what the other is thinking or doing, or when one of us was in pain." He grimaced. "That's how I saw what was in his head, and in his heart…"

"And now?" Rachel asked. "What do you hear from him now?"

Ali thought for a while. "Nothing," he said finally, flicking a thin branch at the donkey's rump to persuade it to continue uphill.

They spoke no further until they reached the summit of the cliff. Ali helped Morag and Duncan down and unpacked the other donkey. The rest of the party lined up along the cliff top. They steadied themselves against the wind and looked down at the grey sea that roared and smashed tirelessly against the ragged rocks below.

"So how does the legend end?" Rachel asked.

"I'll tell you later," Ali said. "We need to keep moving. We're going down there." All eyes widened as he pointed at the jagged coastline, and they began to pick their way through the rocks, down towards the sea.

Half an hour later, Ali had guided them between boulders, exposing narrow paths that zigzagged across and down the cliff-face, and they found themselves standing on a flat shelf that overlooked the sea. From this lower perspective, the coastline suddenly seemed familiar to Rachel. Looking thirty metres to her right, she could see where the rocks crumbled away and became a crescent of sandy beach. There was nothing of the modern world anywhere, and Rachel could see it almost exactly as it had been thirty thousand years before. In her mind's eye, she could see primitive tribesmen fishing from this beach. She could see them going out in their wooden boats, day in, day out.

"You were going to tell me the end of the legend," Rachel said.

Ali sighed. "The usual story," he said. "The stranger was taken away from his family and his brains were smashed out on a rock, but not before he had been forced to build what would become his own tomb. When the job was done, his body was left out till the gulls had picked it clean, then his bones were sealed up in the caves, where they could do no harm, and where nobody would ever find them."

"So how are *we* going to find them?"

Ali smiled. "When he built his tomb, he left a way in for those he knew would come one day. For *us*."

Rachel screwed up her face. "Why was he killed?"

"Because they were frightened of him," Ali said. "Frightened of his power. People have always been frightened of it. And they still are."

"Do we know where he died?"

"Right here," Gabriel said. He was pointing down at the flat table of rock on which they were standing, tears rolling down his cheeks. "This is the Killing Stone."

"Le Rocher des Tueurs," Ali confirmed.

Rachel looked down at the rock. Images of men

grappling – of one man fighting for his life – flashed through her mind. Vibrations tingled up through the soles of her feet and prickled at her scalp like electrical currents.

Gabriel was clearly feeling something similar. He dropped to his knees, his palms flat against the cold stone, his tears dripping into the cracks and fissures on the surface.

He began to howl.

The rest of the group gathered around him and murmured sympathetically. Kate and Laura stroked his head, while Rachel and the Spanish girls dabbed at their own tears. Jean-Luc and Jean-Bernard coughed and scratched their heads, and Duncan and Morag clutched at the adults, frightened by the powerful emotion that was being released from the boy they knew as Michael.

Gabriel's cries died as suddenly as they had started. He got to his feet, shrugging off the sympathy that was being offered to him, as if it was holding him up. "Come on," he said. "We have to keep going. We don't have long."

They hopped across the remaining rocks and down on to the beach, the damp sand a relief underfoot after the punishing rocky path. They dumped their bags and Gabriel led them forward. They walked away from the sea and up the beach until they could see, tucked under a rocky overhang, the long shallow arch and the down-turned black mouth that marked the opening of a cave.

"La Grotte des Barbares," Ali said. "The Cave of the Berbers."

"This is where our story began," Gabriel said.

Rachel looked at him. "And where it ends?"

"Only one way to find out."

And they walked into the black.

50

The sea was choppy and grey, and slapped roughly against the sides of the boat; against the pair of black, motorized dinghies lashed to the stern, and against the name painted in large white letters on the hull:

HOPE

On the uppermost of the three decks, Clay Van der Zee sat staring at the bank of screens and computer monitors on the wall in front of him. The boat's communications centre was every bit as well equipped as the one in the mobile unit that had been stationed in Gibraltar until a few hours before. Once word of the children's final destination had come through from Laura Sullivan, it had been a short voyage across to the Moroccan Coast, and once there, with the boat moored two kilometres offshore and out of sight of the beach, the command station had been quickly established. Now, Van der Zee was in constant contact with operatives at several different observation points and was able to switch easily between images of the beach and the entrance to the cave itself, both fed live from satellites orbiting the earth high above.

Like the rest of his team, Van der Zee was excited; almost breathless with nerves and anticipation. He had been since the message had come through a few minutes earlier.

They're going in...

Van der Zee checked in again – as he did every few minutes – with each onshore observation post, with every technician and member of the Hope security team on board the boat. There were more than a dozen of them awaiting orders, ready to move fast once the signal was given. To seize the four sets of twins as quickly as possible, to capture the boy – the outsider – who was leading them, and, most importantly of all, to take possession of what they had all come looking for in the Cave of the Berbers.

From the other side of the room, Adam sat and watched Van der Zee stab at buttons and bark orders into the microphone. Adam had been allowed to move freely around the cabin for some time, but there was no mistaking the purpose of the two security guards who had been assigned to watch him. He looked across at the blank faces; the dark glasses and inhibitors. He knew they carried weapons and that they would not hesitate to use them.

"You won't get it back," Adam said. "The Triskellion. You do *know* that, right?"

Van der Zee turned in his chair. "We'll see."

"You won't get *anything*."

"Let's just watch and see how this all pans out, shall we?" Van der Zee smiled, and pointed up at the screens. "You've got a ringside seat; you should just sit back and enjoy the show…"

Adam looked up at one of the screens, stared into the dark mouth of the cave. He'd seen Rachel, his mom and the others disappear inside a few minutes earlier. More than anything, he wished he was with them, but for now, all he could do was close his eyes and reach out with his mind. To let his sister know that he *was* with her.

To wish her luck.

Water ran slowly down the grey stone walls that rose up ten metres or more on every side before narrowing to a dark ceiling which seemed to shift in the damp shadows high above them. Each drip echoed as it struck the floor. A few thin shafts of light angled down from gaps in the rock, streaking the walls in pale beams, highlighting every detail.

Rachel, Gabriel and the others stood and said nothing for a minute or more, staggered by the size of the cavern. Then they began to move, slowly inching around the walls like a group of tourists, running their fingers across the rock and whispering in wonder.

"My God," Laura said. "These paintings…" Over the years she had seen hundreds of cave paintings, but none with anything like this degree of detail. There was an incredible level of artistry in every line carved into the stone, and something else too. There was…

"It's passion," Rachel said, reading Laura's thoughts. "This really *meant* something to him."

Rachel moved slowly around the walls, seeing … *feeling* the emotions that had been poured into every scratch and marking. There were images of bees and beehives, of falling stars and shoals of minutely detailed fish. And Triskellions…

She stopped in front of one huge wall and stared at a series of paintings that outlined the story Ali had told her. In swirling lines of black against the pale rock there were pictures of a boat and of a man being pulled from the sea. As Rachel stared, the dream came back once again, and suddenly she was that girl standing on the beach, watching a stranger being dragged from a fishing boat. A girl who had given birth to twin children and then watched as their father was dragged away to his death.

Waited as his body was reduced to a pile of bones.

While Rachel stood and stared, Kate and Laura moved to either side of her. Laura took a picture of the wall with the camera on her phone. She leant in close to Rachel. "Isn't this amazing?"

"What is *this*?" Kate asked. Laura opened her mouth to speak. "And keep it simple, OK," Kate said quickly. "We don't all have degrees in archaeology." She glanced across at Gabriel and the other twins. "Or special powers…"

Laura took a deep breath. "OK … I've always had this idea that something changed in the evolution of mankind thirty thousand years ago. Something that changed the Neanderthal into modern man – gave him the push to spread out across to Spain and into northern Europe." She looked at the wall. "*This* is where it happened. Whoever did these paintings is what *made* it happen."

Kate nodded, looking at the pictures. "The falling star isn't really a star, right?"

"I'm sure that's what the people who lived here at the time *thought* it was," Laura said. "And they wouldn't have had a word to describe who it was … *what* it was, they pulled from the ocean." She turned and looked across the cave at the three sets of twins as they moved around, pointing and muttering. "And it happened *again*, three thousand years ago, and since. More visitors arrived. In France, Spain, Scotland … and in Triskellion – in your own village." Laura watched as Kate reached for Rachel's hand. "And now, kids like yours, kids with these genes, can do the same thing that their ancestors did … can move human beings on to another level. It's *super*-evolution…"

Kate nodded again. She was beginning to digest the enormity of Laura's theory and the importance of her own offspring.

"Was that simple enough?" Laura asked.

Gabriel was standing behind her. He had obviously been listening. He smiled.

There was a shout from the other side of the cave and everyone moved quickly across to where Duncan and Morag were standing and pointing towards the ceiling.

"It's not shadows," Duncan said. "It's alive."

Morag grinned. "It's bees. Millions of them…"

Everyone stared up at the colony of insects that crawled across the roof of the cave. The bees hung in a moving canopy as though part of the cave itself; as if their low, insistent buzz was coming from somewhere deep inside the rock, like blood pulsing through a vein.

"It's like they're welcoming us," Morag said.

Then everyone froze, as another sound filtered down from above. A very different and more dangerous buzzing that got louder until it drowned out the noise of the bees. Until Gabriel had to shout to be heard above it.

"Everyone outside. *Now!*"

Clay Van der Zee rarely raised his voice when he was speaking to the man in New York, but he could not help himself. He had been as furious as he was confused since he'd first seen the aircraft swooping low across the cliff top a few minutes before.

"I did not *ask* for helicopter support!" he shouted. On the screen he watched the children spilling out of the cave and on to the beach.

The voice of the man in New York crackled over the speaker, filling the cabin. "That was my decision," he said. "You can't be too careful."

"What exactly are you expecting?" Van der Zee asked.

"If I knew that, there wouldn't be a problem."

"That's an attack helicopter," Van der Zee said. "It's armed…"

"These are not your worries, doctor." There was a pause and, for a few moments, until the man from New York spoke again, the only sound in the cabin was the distant clatter of rotor blades. "Are you still there, doctor?"

Van der Zee said nothing. He had spun round in his chair to look at Adam, and the expression on the boy's face had rendered him speechless. It was a look of horror at something that Adam had seen coming and could do nothing about.

The sound of the missile being fired was almost deafening.

Van der Zee twisted back round to face his screens and gasped at the explosion. "What the hell…?"

The speaker distorted as the man from New York shouted. "Who gave that order?"

Van der Zee watched the helicopter soar away and circle the cliff top as the smoke billowed skywards.

"I repeat, *who gave that order?*"

There were a few seconds of silence before another voice came over the speaker. The helicopter pilot sounded shaken as he identified himself and tried to answer the question.

"I don't know," he said. "Somebody … told me to fire. I *heard* him…"

Gabriel and the others picked themselves up and looked back at the cave. A dark cloud hung over the entrance, and black smoke poured from the point higher up the cliff where the missile had hit. Beyond that it seemed clear. Dust and debris were still raining down on to the beach and a solid column of bees swarmed out from the cave, circling the group, rounding them up like a lasso, guiding them back towards the entrance.

Laura Sullivan moved a few metres away from the others and took out her BlackBerry. She dialled a number. It was difficult to keep her voice down when she was so angry.

"What d'you think you're *doing*?"

"That was nothing to do with me," Van der Zee said.

"What?"

"I'm not lying, I swear."

"Just get that chopper out of here *now*."

"Listen, I promise you—"

"Did you bring the boy?"

"He's right here."

"Prove it," Laura said. She waited a few seconds. Then she heard Adam shouting out to her, telling her that he was OK.

Van der Zee came back on the line. "We've known each other a long time, Laura. You should know I'm as good as my word."

"I need to go…"

"Don't you trust me?"

Laura looked up at the helicopter that was still circling. "I don't trust the people you work for." She ended the call and when she turned back to the group, she saw Duncan and Morag staring at her phone. She slipped it back into her pocket as Gabriel stopped to address everyone.

"Well, they clearly know we're here," he said. "So I suggest we get back in there and get what we came for as fast as we can."

Rachel had seen the look on his face a few seconds before the missile had hit. Once everyone had started moving again, she ran to catch up with him. She pointed at the smoke, then up at the helicopter. "Was that you? Did you make that happen…?"

"Well, I didn't summon up the helicopter if that's what you mean, but I didn't think there was any harm in making use of it."

"I don't understand," Rachel said. "Why fire at the cave?"

"The cave's only the start of it," Gabriel said. "It's like the entrance hall." He looked up at the helicopter and shrugged. "I needed something to force the front door open."

Rachel smiled in spite of herself and helped usher the others back towards the cave as quickly as possible. At the entrance, Gabriel stopped and told Jean-Bernard and Jean-Luc to wait.

"You can't go back in," he said. The French boys tried to

push past, but Gabriel held out an arm. "No, you need to stay here. You've got a job to do."

"What job?" Jean-Luc demanded.

"It's important," Gabriel said. "And I think you'll enjoy it."

Jean-Luc and Jean-Bernard exchanged a look, then turned back to Gabriel and nodded. He thanked them, then followed the others, ducking through the curtain of dust and stepping back into the Cave of the Berbers.

51

The debris was settling on the inside of the cave. A wider crack had opened in the roof of the cavern and a shaft of yellow light cut through the dusty air. Laura was astonished to see that, although the main walls of the cave and the paintings remained intact, a large, triangular opening had fallen away on the far side.

"That's the front door I was talking about," Gabriel said. "Now, we'd better hurry up and get in there..."

They gathered around the exposed opening and, peering through, they could see a passage leading to steps that had been roughly hewn in the rock and which twisted away into the shadows. Gabriel led the way through the opening and they all tentatively followed him into a honeycomb of tunnels, alcoves and chambers burrowed into the side of the cliffs. The tunnels were lit by a pale glow that seemed to come from chunks of a glass-like material set into hollows in the rock face.

"Amazing," Laura said, stopping. She touched the glass.

"It's mica, or some kind of crystal. It looks like a system of lenses and prisms has been set up to direct natural light all the way from outside through to here. Sophisticated stuff. Not the work of your average caveman."

"Who ever said this was done by a caveman?" Gabriel asked.

"Tell me what you know about him!" Laura cried, but Gabriel was already pushing on, poking his head into nooks and crannies and moving quickly in and out of small chambers.

Laura and Kate turned into a room on the left while the others explored the one opposite. Laura picked up a bowl and gasped. It was metallic: silvery-grey and unlike any thing she had ever seen before. Unlike anything that had ever been discovered in a Neanderthal cave.

"I don't believe it," she said. "It's so modern looking." She laid the bowl gently on the ground and began taking photos. "This is thirty thousand years old and it looks as if it could have been made yesterday. It looks like it's been made on a machine. I mean ... I don't even *recognize* the metal. What am I talking about ... these cavemen didn't even have metal. Never, ever seen anything like it."

Kate stared at the bowl. "Is that what he's looking for?"

"Gabriel? No, I don't think so. This stuff is just a bonus. An amazing bonus. I think he's looking for a tomb..."

As she said it, the word suddenly sounded in Laura's mind like a tolling bell.

Tomb.

Years of tombs: finding them, studying them, digging them up. Laura looked closely at the chamber they were in. What she had thought were little rows of sticks drawn on the walls – perhaps some kind of numbering system – had, on closer inspection, turned out to have little heads and arms and feet. They were rows of bodies, laid out flat.

Had that been the purpose of this cave? Was it a burial site: one big tomb?

Her mind raced. What if Van der Zee was really double-crossing … *triple*-crossing her? What if he *had* ordered the missile-launching helicopter? She knew that he was certainly capable of pulling a trick like that. She also knew that there were people within the Hope organization whose agenda would be to get as many of the "special" people together in one place and blow them, and all those who protected them, to smithereens.

Was this labyrinth of caves going to be *their* tomb?

She felt panic rise within her. She had been stupid. She had been blinkered by her own research – research that would be no good to anyone if they were all about to be vaporized. In her blind enthusiasm to prove her theory, in her eagerness to do the right thing by Kate and return her son, Laura had helped set an elaborate deathtrap for them all.

"We need to get back out on to the beach," she said to Kate, the panic clear in her voice. She shouted into the other chamber. "Gabriel, Rachel, *everyone* ... we have to get out!"

Duncan and Morag scuttled into the room. They looked at the bowl and the figures on the walls.

"What have you found?" Morag asked.

"Never mind," Laura said. "We just need to get out."

"We can't," Gabriel said, calmly entering the chamber. "We only get one go at this, and the time is now."

"But they know where we are!" Laura shouted. "That's obvious, right? Now they'll be tracking our precise movements underground by satellite ... by infrared imaging. They'll have taken a position from my phone."

All eyes turned on her.

"I had to tell them where we were so we could get Adam back," she said.

Kate squeezed Laura's arm and smiled.

"I know," Gabriel said. "And you did the right thing. It's just that this isn't quite as straightforward as I thought it would be. We could do with buying ourselves a bit more time."

"Laura ... Dr Sullivan?" Morag tugged at Laura's sleeve. "Why don't you give Duncan your phone? He knows all the Hope passwords. He might be able to, you know, play around a bit."

Laura looked at Morag's innocent face, not understanding what she meant. This was hardly the time for games. Then she saw the smirk creep across Duncan's features and Morag's meaning became clear. If anyone could get into

Hope's system and mess up their tracking equipment, then it was Duncan.

"We won't get a signal down here, though, will we?" Laura said.

"Give it to me." Duncan took the BlackBerry from Laura and, as soon as it was in his hands, the signal went up to five bars. His chubby fingers moved fast across the keypad. Internet access came up on the screen, then a series of messages flashed past at lightning speed. He punched in number combinations, symbols, letters – his fingers becoming a blur.

"I'm into the mainframe," he said. Then, a few seconds later, he stabbed decisively at the "enter" key and looked up at everyone. "That should do it." He waved the phone at Gabriel, allowing himself an uncharacteristic smile.

"Good work, Duncan," Gabriel said. "Everyone has a job to do here, and that was yours. Now let's get on with ours."

"But they'll still know where we are, won't they?" Kate asked. She followed Gabriel as he led them down another of the cave's meandering, half-lit passages.

"They know where we are *approximately*," Gabriel said. "But they're working blind now. Whereas *we* know where we're going."

Laura looked across at Rachel and raised an eyebrow. In turn, Rachel squeezed her mother's hand and smiled.

The passages grew darker and narrower, the pale light from the prisms becoming even weaker the deeper they went. The air was cooler and damper, and the group quietened as the atmosphere grew increasingly tense.

Ali did nothing to make them feel any easier as he darted between them, waving a small torch around. He tapped the walls and the stone floor with a stick, muttering. He pushed his hands into deep fissures in the rock, then climbed up to feel for hidden ledges or checked entrances to other chambers on either side.

"What are you looking for?" Laura asked.

"The cavemen did not want this tomb disturbed." He pointed out huge rocks that hung precariously over their heads, each held in place by smaller stones: primitive booby traps to deter intruders trying to enter the caves.

Intruders like themselves…

They continued more slowly into near darkness and Morag began to whimper. Ali cursed, increasingly frustrated that they seemed to be getting nowhere.

"Wait," Gabriel said. Everyone stopped. "Ali, you need to be calm. You're confusing me."

"I am sorry," Ali said. His face looked old and worn in the light of his torch. "I have failed you; I thought I would have found it by now. I thought that once we got into the main caves it would be obvious. There should have been" – he made spikes with his fingers, searching for the words – "you know, stalactites, stalagmites…"

"You've done your bit," Gabriel said. "You got us this far. Now we need to stop panicking, and concentrate. Rachel?"

He reached out a hand to her and she stepped close to him. "I want you to think really hard. To focus…"

Conflicting thoughts were racing through her head. The dominant one was an increasing desire to escape from the caves. Sensing her doubt, Gabriel took her hand and squeezed. Rachel took a deep lungful of the damp air and, shutting her eyes, began to clear her mind…

At first, she was aware only of everyone's breathing, of Morag's nervous sniffs and the shuffling of feet. Then, as the noises faded into the background of her thoughts, another sound came: a low drone, a buzz. Behind her eyelids, a light began to spread and solidify, shaping itself into an orb that floated in her mind, golden and glowing. She tried to sense the direction from which it was coming and placed her hands against the cold wall of the passage. The ball of light drew her along, as it moved slowly back in the direction from which they had come.

"Can anyone see this?" she asked.

"See what?" Laura said.

Rachel followed the orb, ten … fifteen paces, until it came to rest, hovering against a flank of rock that angled down from the ceiling of the cave and widened at her feet. She touched the smooth surface as the golden light flashed left and then disappeared behind the rock. She took a step sideways and then, seeing the light appear again, stepped into a black space.

An entrance.

Concealed behind the wall of rock, as if hidden by a theatrical curtain, the entrance would have been impossible to see from the direction in which they had come. They had needed to stop at just the right point to find the angle of the opening.

By luck, or *someone's* judgement, they had stopped in exactly the right place. Rachel reached her hands out into the darkness and followed the orb, turning left into another chamber. This space was lighter: illuminated from high above by a bigger, domed version of the crystals that had lit their way to this point and which seemed to suck up the ball of light, until it faded to a speck and then was gone. Stalactites dripped overhead and, in the middle of the chamber, surrounded by a spiky fence of stalagmites, stood a rough, stone sarcophagus.

"I've found it," Rachel called. Her voice echoed around the chamber and reverberated back along the passage. "I've found the tomb…"

52

Aboard *HOPE*, the atmosphere had grown a lot more tense since the screens had suddenly blacked out. Van der Zee was desperately trying to find out what had gone wrong and the guards watching Adam were even more agitated. Adam did not know how it had been done, but he felt sure that someone in the gang was responsible for jamming the satellite feeds. One of the French boys maybe, or—

Van der Zee slammed his hands against the tabletop and bellowed into the microphone. "What is going on here?"

Adam closed his eyes and saw an image of Duncan beaming, holding up what looked like a mobile phone and waving it about triumphantly. When Adam opened his eyes again, his smile was as broad as Duncan's had been.

Van der Zee caught the look. "Did you do this?"

Adam said nothing, but kept on smiling, even though the guards on either side of him had taken a step closer.

From the speaker, the voice of the man in New York

echoed through the cabin. "What's happening at your end, Van der Zee? We've lost pictures here; we've lost tracking data."

Van der Zee reached for the microphone. "We're working on it," he said.

"Well, work on it faster!"

Van der Zee looked at Adam before waving a hand at the blank screens. "It doesn't matter," he said. "We still have visuals from the helicopter. We'll still be waiting when your friends get back above ground." He stared at Adam, letting his words sink in, then he turned back to his desk and hit the switch that connected him to the bridge. "Listen up. They know we're here, so there's no point hiding any more. Take us in as close to the shore as possible…"

Adam was rocked back in his seat as the boat began to move and pick up speed. He closed his eyes again and reached out.

He needed to let Rachel know what was happening.

The tomb was by far the plainest of the chambers they had found themselves in. The walls were white and undecorated. Though the roof was high above them, the space itself was narrow and there was barely room for the nine of them to squeeze inside.

"I'm cold," Morag said. The breath plumed in front of her face as she spoke. Laura moved across to take the girl's hand, feeling the sudden drop in temperature herself like a cloak of ice had been thrown round her shoulders.

Ali nodded towards the sarcophagus. It was brightly lit by
a beam from the crystalline dome of the roof. The stone had
flaked away in places and discoloured over the many centuries, but carved into the side was the unmistakable shape
of a Triskellion. "It's time," he said.

Gabriel nodded and stepped slowly across.

Rachel watched, still processing the information that
had come through from Adam. "Listen … Duncan did his
job with the phone," she said, "but they're getting closer.
They're on a boat—"

Laura nodded. "It's the same boat that Adam's on." She
turned to look at Kate, and was relieved to see a smile and
a mouthed "Thank you."

"We should hurry then," Gabriel said. He beckoned
Rachel across and they both squeezed between giant stalagmites and stepped over to the tomb.

"You OK?" Rachel asked.

"Yeah, fine."

Rachel nodded. Gabriel looked anything but fine. He was
pale suddenly and looked to be fighting something back:
rage or tears, Rachel could not be sure. "Only, I remember
how you were when they opened the tomb in Triskellion,"
she said. "I know it's upsetting…"

"I'm getting used to it by now," Gabriel said. "There are a
lot of bodies…" He stared down at the sarcophagus for half
a minute, and when he turned back to Rachel, his mood had

changed. He looked more determined than ever. "Let's get this lid off," he said.

Gabriel and Rachel leant down and began to push. It was not going to be easy. Morag and Duncan rushed forward, squeezed between the stalagmites and lent a hand, quickly followed by the others.

"I think it's moving!" Laura shouted.

Rachel closed her eyes and pushed with all the strength she had left, grunting with effort as the heavy stone lid inched aside, grinding against the stone beneath it and eventually crashed to the floor on the far side of the coffin, throwing up a thick cloud of dust and grit.

Without needing to be told, everyone waited until Gabriel had leant down and looked inside. Ali hummed the same sad tune he had been whistling since they'd left Mogador. Laura bit her lip, more impatient than she had ever been in her life. They all wiped the dust from their faces before moving forward to see what they had uncovered.

"They're yellow," Morag said. She and Duncan were on tiptoes, peering in over the edge of the sarcophagus. "I thought bones were supposed to be white."

"They are old," Ali said.

Laura could barely keep the excitement from her voice. "They're *really* old," she said. "Older than anything I've ever seen."

It did not look anything like a complete skeleton. What bones there were lay scattered in dirt, yellow and blackened in parts where they had been broken. A few brown teeth were still attached to half a jawbone, and the top part of the skull lay at one end of the sarcophagus, the ragged hole in the top of it clearly visible. Rachel knew perfectly well how this man had died – she had seen it in her dream and heard it from Ali – but it would have been obvious to anyone seeing what was left thirty thousand years later.

"They didn't leave much of him…" she said.

"Where is it?" Gabriel asked. He turned and stared at Ali. "It isn't here."

Rachel continued to stare down at the remains, but she knew what Gabriel was talking about. It was what they had come for.

The second Triskellion.

She reached up and took hold of the amulet that hung round her neck. The one recovered from beneath the chalk circle in the village that bore its name.

"I am not surprised," Ali said. "These people were frightened, and superstitious, and they almost certainly knew what it was capable of. They would not have wanted it buried with the bones."

"So where…?"

"My guess is that they put it somewhere it could not easily be discovered. Somewhere under lock and key."

Gabriel began looking frantically around. "How do we find it? I need your help."

"Not a problem," Ali said. He nodded towards Rachel,

who was still fingering the amulet, then back to the sarcophagus. "We have *both*…"

Rachel saw it straight away. She took the Triskellion from round her neck and stepped across to where the same, three-bladed symbol had been carved into the side of the sarcophagus. She bent down and blew away the dust.

Not a carving. A lock…

"The Traveller hid it! He knew he was digging his own tomb; that they were going to kill him," Ali said. "And he didn't want the Triskellion to fall into the wrong hands. So he hid it where nobody would ever find it or be able to use it. But before he died, he left *us* a way in."

Rachel looked up at Gabriel and he gave her a nod. She pressed the Triskellion into the stone. It was a perfect fit.

"That's incredible," Laura said.

Ali smiled. "Wait…"

The Triskellion began to glow and pulse, and from somewhere beneath the coffin, there was a series of clicks and the *"grind"* of something winding down. Everyone froze as the fence of stalagmites suddenly began sinking into the floor of the chamber. When the tip of the last one had disappeared, the light from the Triskellion died and the entire sarcophagus swung silently to one side, as if it were floating on a cushion of air.

There was a small square hole underneath: the entrance to some sort of well.

Rachel, Gabriel and the others inched forward and looked

down to see what the sarcophagus had been hiding. There were steps leading almost vertically down a dimly lit shaft. And at the bottom, a glimpse of something.

Turquoise, shimmering…

"Down there?" Gabriel asked.

"It makes a kind of sense, when you think about it," Ali said. "It was plucked from the sea thirty thousand years ago." He smiled. "Now you must do the same."

53

Rachel handed the Triskellion to Gabriel. He gave her a tiny nod in acknowledgement. She knew it was down to her. Gabriel had made it clear that everyone had a job to do and she knew, in her heart of hearts, that this was hers.

Kate hugged her daughter close. "You can't go down there, honey."

"Don't worry, Mom," Rachel said. "I'm a good swimmer." She kissed her mother. "Besides, it's pretty dangerous up here too."

"Inez and Carmen will go with you," Gabriel said.

The Spanish girls nodded and, having each kissed Gabriel on both cheeks, they joined Rachel, who was staring into the shaft at the water below.

"Please be careful," Kate said.

Rachel sat on the edge and swung her legs over the opening to the well. She pushed a foot out, feeling for a foothold and, finding one, started to climb down towards the turquoise water. Inez followed, then Carmen, both treading carefully and holding on to the gnarled surface of the wall. A few steps down and what had appeared from above to be a narrow shaft, opened out into a cavernous, underground grotto. The interior was completely covered in multicoloured layers of coral, worn smooth by the constant dripping of water and soapy to the touch.

Rachel slid on her bottom down the last few steps and stood up on the rim of slippery rock that surrounded the water. She looked into the pool. The water was crystal clear, and ripples distorted the pebbles and rocks that covered the bottom. It could have been one metre deep, or ten.

She looked back up to the entrance, now high over her head. She saw her mother and Gabriel silhouetted by the light that shone above them. She watched them wave, then disappear from view.

"We're on our own," she said to Inez and Carmen. She turned back to the water. "It looks deep. I don't know if I can hold my breath all the way to the bottom."

"We can help," Carmen said. "We have been diving since we were babies."

Inez smiled and touched Rachel on the shoulder. "That's what we're here for. To help you breathe."

Rachel looked from one twin to the other. "It's now or never," she said. "Guess we'd better take the plunge."

Inez and Carmen flexed their arms, then dived into the

lagoon with the grace of porpoises, barely making a sound as they broke the surface of the water.

Rachel watched for a second as they slid down through the water, their black hair flowing behind them.

Then she took a deep breath, held her nose and jumped in after them.

Gabriel had told Laura to make her way back through the network of caves and passages towards the entrance – they would rendezvous on the beach – but she was eager to gather samples and take photos as she might not get another chance. Ali was doing his best to hurry them all along, keen to get Duncan and Morag out. But Kate was reluctant to leave while Rachel was still inside the caves.

She hung back with Laura, waiting for her daughter to resurface. They moved from chamber to chamber together, picking up small artefacts: stone tools, pieces made from fish bones and other items, like the metal bowl, that were far more sophisticated in design. As they travelled further back from the grotto, the passage widened and the chambers on either side became progressively larger. They were covered in paintings and decorative carvings that were even more elaborate than those in the cave's main entrance.

"Look at this one," Laura said. "It's beautiful." She traced the outline of a large painting with her finger. "Looks like a mountain."

Kate nodded.

The mountain was flattened on the top and had been daubed with reddish pigment. Laura looked closer. "It could almost be Uluru in Australia," she said. She leant away so that her head did not cast a shadow across the painting. Above the mountain, a large star was painted. To the right of it were five smaller stars arranged in a diamond pattern. "And look at the stars ... Alpha Centauri and Beta Centauri ... if I'm not mistaken that's the Southern Cross constellation; you know, like the one on the Australian flag." She paused for a moment. "I didn't think you could see the Southern Cross from this part of Europe. Wait a minute…"

Her finger traced a line down from the stars to the base of the mountain. Animals had been drawn there. Animals that looked like begging dogs but with back legs that were too big, tails too powerful and front paws too tiny. "Kangaroos," she said. Her voice was trembling, her mind reeling with the implications of what she was looking at. "These are kanga-roos. This is Australia."

She turned round and realized why she seemed to have been speaking to herself. Standing and looking at the op-posite wall, Kate Newman was speechlessly pointing at the paintings that stretched out in front of her across the rock.

Unmistakably drawn out in black, sooty lines was a primi-tive rendering of the New York skyline. The Empire State Building was there as well as the Chrysler Building. There was a large figure with an arm held aloft: the Statue of Liberty.

"It's not possible," Laura said. Underneath the cityscape,

matchstick figures of a mother and two children were represented. The hands of the children were joined together by a Triskellion.

"It's us," Kate said weakly. She edged slowly along the wall, following the painting. Where the Manhattan skyline stopped, a painting of the sea began. A large white bird hovered over it, carrying two children on its back. Across the sea, a small triangular island had been painted, with a Triskellion in the bottom left-hand corner.

"It's our story," Kate said. "It's the kids' story. This place represents *us*." She turned and looked at Laura. "I don't understand. How could these cave people have seen so far into the future?"

The implication of the paintings made Laura's head pulse with possibilities and extraordinary ideas. She ran her hands through her hair as if trying to contain the thoughts bursting from her skull.

"I don't think it was them," she said. She nodded out towards the passage, towards the tomb. "Whoever those bones back there belong to … he knew we were coming."

54

abriel pressed his hands against the rough edges of the sarcophagus. He had wanted to be alone for this part. To gather together the remains of his ancestor. One day he would have recovered all his ancestors' remains, would have the chance to lay them to rest, as he had done with the hearts he had recovered from the village of Triskellion. As he had hoped to do with the hand of the "saint". He would keep them away from the probes and scalpels of the scientists. The less genetic material they possessed and could analyse, the better.

He had sent the others back. He needed this moment, and he needed to be near Rachel, who was swimming somewhere beneath his feet. He leant over the stone trough and looked down at the scraps of tooth, bone and skull…

The first blow glanced off the side of Gabriel's head, twisting him round and knocking him face-first into the gritty stone wall. The second blow landed squarely on the front of his skull, felling him instantly.

He could feel blood trickling into his eyes and he tasted something metallic where the force of the blow had driven his teeth through his bottom lip. Weakened as he was, he knew he had to lead his attacker away from the chamber, away from the entrance to the lagoon. Summoning every ounce of remaining strength, he got to his feet and rushed at the dark figure, the force of his attack driving the man back out into the narrow passage.

Gabriel held his hand up across his face and felt something snap as his forearm took the weight of another blow. He attempted to wipe the blood from his eyes and looked up to see the figure towering over him. A tall figure in a hooded cloak.

A figure with no face.

Supported by a heavy, black stick, Hilary Wing reached down and extended a twisted and scarred hand. Gabriel felt the claw scrape his neck as it grabbed at the leather thong, tugging until it snapped and gave way. The gold blades of the Triskellion glinted and swung momentarily in front of Gabriel's eyes, before disappearing beneath his attacker's cloak. The stick came raining down again and again, on ribs and arms and legs, sapping the remaining strength from Gabriel's limbs; battering him into submission…

Wing knelt down, and Gabriel could smell the rot on his breath and in his wounds. Gabriel blinked through bloody eyelids and stared into the hood of Wing's robe. Despite the lack of features, Wing's eyes shone out: cold and blue.

He smashed the stick down on Gabriel's head one final time.

The water was freezing at first, but as she floated down, feet first, towards the bottom, Rachel felt a current wash over her, as if somewhere a heater was pumping out warm water. Turning, she kicked her legs out behind her and pushed herself down through the water; down to where Inez and Carmen were swimming along the bottom, turning over stones and sifting through pebbles.

The main pool was lit by the glow from the tomb above, and tiny, phosphorescent jellyfish were caught in the beam. But there was another, stronger light that came from somewhere across the water and which gave the bottom of the lagoon an odd radiance, like a swimming pool illuminated at night. Rachel swam along with the twins and then signalled that she needed to go back to the surface to breathe. They swam back up to the top, treading water while they took mouthfuls of air.

"We should go towards the light," Rachel said.

Taking another breath, they all dived back to the bottom of the pool and swam towards the glow. It came from a tunnel that led into what appeared to be another cave a little further on.

Carmen signed that they should swim through. With her breath running short, Rachel swam after Carmen, pushed along from behind by Inez. The tunnel was longer than it had at first appeared, but became brighter and higher, and Carmen swam upwards. They broke the surface of the water and found their heads in a small pocket of air, just beneath the roof. The surface of the rock glittered with tiny crystals and brightly coloured coral. Rachel panted, taking deep breaths of the heavy, sulphurous air.

"I don't know if I can do this," she gasped.

"You must," Carmen said, pushing black strands of hair back off her face.

"You must rely on us to help you, Rachel," Inez said. "You can do it. You just need to relax."

"Relax?" Despite the circumstances, Rachel managed to laugh.

They took another breath and pushed on. After a few more strokes, the tunnel opened out into a wider underwater cavern. The white light was dazzling and seemed to come from above, like the beams of headlamps, flooding the water with light. Carmen swam upwards again and Rachel followed quickly, anticipating more air – but there was none. The water seemed to go on for ever and Rachel began to panic. The lack of oxygen was burning her lungs, and her limbs began to flail wildly in the water.

Don't panic, Inez said with her mind. *Don't be afraid of the water; breathe it.*

And suddenly, Rachel could breathe again, as though the water had become air. Inez pushed her onwards, upwards towards Carmen, who was floating above.

Carmen pointed into the light and, as she came closer, Rachel could see another colour emerging between the fragmented beams.

Gold.

She swam towards the gold, which was glinting and rippling through the blue water. She reached out ... getting closer.

Gabriel dragged himself across the wet floor. He knew he had been foolish to go it alone and allow himself to be caught off guard. If only he had managed to keep Adam and Rachel close, their combined power would never have allowed this to happen. It was one of the reasons he had brought them all together: to enable him to achieve things he could not manage alone. They thought he was protecting them, which, up to a point, he was. But neither Adam nor Rachel had realized that they were also protecting him.

Would he fail here, at the final hurdle? Beaten and destroyed by the brutality of men like Hilary Wing? Men who had murdered his ancestors and scattered their remains, so that now, tens of thousands of years later, Gabriel had been sent to retrieve them.

He could hear a shuffling further along the passage that led away from the tomb. He took a second to gather some strength. He could overcome the pain with his mind – that was easy – but the shock and the beating had drained his body of energy. He could not channel any of his usual powers.

He dragged himself to his feet and, staying close to the wall, moved along the passage. He followed the shuffling noise that echoed back along the corridor. It seemed to be coming from a chamber some way ahead – one that was concealed by a twist and turn in the rock, as the tomb had been.

Gabriel hugged the wall until he was outside the entrance to the room, then peered cautiously inside. It was decorated with paintings like the others, and there were several doors leading off to smaller, adjoining rooms. A carpet of bees crawled over the ceiling and buzzed lazily in and out of one of the side rooms. Many alcoves had been carved into the walls, each of which held metallic bowls, cups, bangles and lumps of clear crystal which glowed in the half-light. Hilary Wing was hunched over a pile of artefacts. He was stuffing as many as he could into his cloak, dropping priceless items on to the stony floor in his haste.

"I suppose you think these belong to you too?" Gabriel said weakly.

The hooded figure spun round, his scarred skull protruding from the hood like the head of a snake.

"Put them back," Gabriel said.

"Are *you* going to make me?" Wing hissed. "You can barely stand. I'm surprised you are still alive. They make you freaks out of tough stuff."

The irony of being called a freak by Hilary Wing was not lost on Gabriel. "I think the phrase is something about 'the pot calling the kettle black', isn't it? And while we're on the subject of who is and isn't a freak ... don't you think that there might just be a *little* bit of me in you?"

Despite the lack of expression on the papery skin drawn over Wing's bones, there was a sudden change in mood. A strange gurgle came from the back of his throat. "What do you mean?"

"I mean, how do you account for your amazing powers of recovery? Your ability to withstand pain? Anyone *normal* would have died in that crash ... and certainly from those burns. Perhaps you are more like us than you like to think?"

"Shut up!" Wing screeched. Dropping the remaining bowls, he flew at Gabriel, pinning him against the wall; his stick across the boy's throat, squeezing the breath out of him.

"They knew all about you," Gabriel whispered hoarsely. "Look on the walls..."

Wing's reptilian face twitched, the flesh tautening around his open nose cavity. The blue eyes broke contact with Gabriel's and widened, scanning the painting on the wall behind the boy's head.

It was all there.

Hilary Wing's life was drawn out in front of him. A big house the shape of Waverley Hall: his family home. Then the village: tiny little huts leading to a moor on which was painted a big Triskellion. Next to the Triskellion were twins and a man with long hair and a beard: Wing himself.

"What is this?" His eyes darted around the walls. He was keeping the pressure on Gabriel's throat, but there was panic in his voice. Everywhere he looked there were moments from his life displayed in swirls of colour against the rock. His eyes went to the picture of a man alone, seated on a kind of horse, with wheels where its legs should be. Further on, the "horse" was painted in flames, with the next image depicting a man in a hood, brandishing a long stick and looking like the Grim Reaper.

Wing seemed to recover his composure and turned his eyes back to Gabriel. "If that's supposed to be me, the artist has made me look like Death himself." He pressed down on Gabriel's neck and smiled. "Which, as far as you're concerned, is exactly what I am..."

55

Rachel reached forward into the thick, green seaweed. Rays of golden light were coming from behind the weed, fragmenting and flickering as they floated back and forth. She felt coral, rough and knobbly, beneath her fingers and then something metallic, like a blade. Rachel felt a buzz spread through her body; felt the strength return.

It's here! she said with her mind. *We've found it.*

The Spanish girls began to tear at the weed with their hands, exposing a niche in the rock behind.

For the first time in the tens of thousands of years since it had been hidden away under water, deep beneath the caves, a human hand touched the Triskellion.

The second Triskellion.

The blades glinted against the dark rock, held firmly in place, encrusted with coral and bound by weed. From out of the depths, one or two small silver fish swam up and basked in the glow of the blades. Five or six more followed: bigger, darting faster between the beams. Then ten, twenty more, until a whole shoal of fish wove between the rays of light and began to nibble and pull at the tangles of weed that had held the Triskellion in place for so many years. Aided by the fish, Carmen and Inez found small stones and sharp pieces of shell, and all of them worked at the coral and cut away the weed until, finally, the three-bladed amulet came free in Rachel's hand.

Rachel held the Triskellion out in front of her. The twin beams of light which still shone from somewhere deep in the gloom beyond, bounced off the blades and refracted into rainbow colours that cut through the water like lasers. The fish began to swim in formation, weaving in and out between the beams, like a fluid silver ribbon.

We have to go, Rachel said with her mind.

No ... you must go.

Inez's voice was loud and clear in her head. But as Rachel looked at her, the Spanish girl appeared pale suddenly: the vigour gone from her strong, swimmer's limbs.

Hurry up, Rachel pleaded with her thoughts. *We need to get back. We don't have long.*

We have all the time in the world, Carmen's voice said.

Come on! Rachel started to swim back towards the tunnel, then turned, aware that she was on her own. Neither of the Spanish girls were following her. Rachel looked helplessly from one to the other as they drifted away, surrounded by fish which darted around them and glinted in the underwater light. Both girls were now very pale: fading before Rachel's eyes.

Please... Rachel pleaded, her mind reaching out.

Their black hair floated about their heads like fine seaweed, their limbs swaying loosely with the underwater currents. As Rachel watched, they seemed to float further and further away from her, drawn deeper into the twin beams of light.

What are you doing? *You have to come with me!* she screamed with her mind, but all the time she could feel herself being magnetically drawn in the opposite direction: sucked back towards the tunnel.

The life was draining from Gabriel as the stick was pressed hard against his throat. "This time you *won't* get back up." Wing's voice was strained with the effort of trying to kill this boy who would not lie down.

Then Wing screamed.

A wild, animal yell reverberated round the cave as the treasured amulet round Hilary Wing's neck suddenly became white-hot. His claw-like grip loosened on the rod across Gabriel's throat and it dropped to the ground with a clatter.

An image flashed into Gabriel's mind: a girl's arm pushing upwards, breaking the surface of still, turquoise water, a shining amulet held triumphantly in her fist. With the little remaining strength he had, Gabriel reached out and grabbed the other Triskellion that was now hissing as it burned into the scarred tissue of Hilary Wing's chest.

Wing screamed louder as the amulet was wrenched from

his neck, just as he had torn it from Gabriel's. Suddenly, the cavern filled with a blinding white light and a howling wind rushed through the room, pulling Wing back. It threw him from wall to wall, smashing his face into the rocks painted with his own life story, before sucking his body into one of the small, dark chambers that lined the cave.

Gabriel gripped the Triskellion tight and felt its power surge through his body. He staggered across to the entrance through which Wing had just been dragged. A low buzz came from within but it was drowned out by Wing's screams. Gabriel stepped into the chamber.

It was the inside of a gigantic beehive.

Gabriel stared. The room was a scale model of the caves themselves. The walls were thick with layer upon layer of bees, and every nook and cranny was clogged with dense honeycomb. Yellow wax covered every surface and blobs of thick golden honey dripped from the ceiling. As Gabriel entered the room, the buzzing rose to fever pitch and a column of bees peeled off, swarming around his head, covering his face and hands. Gabriel smiled as the bees crawled over him as if tending his wounds, nuzzling and licking like a thousand tiny cats pleased to see their master return.

He turned at the noise from the far side of the chamber and stared at the hideous scene.

Wing had fallen, or been pulled back, into a deep pit of honeycomb alive with the maggot-like pupae of developing bees. He flailed around on his back, but the more he struggled, the deeper his limbs became stuck in the dense brown honey which shifted around him like sticky, sweet quicksand. His head was a helmet of bees, and his pale blue eyes shone out, terrified, from among the black insects, while their grubs feasted on his rotting flesh. His moans were momentarily drowned out by the drone of the bees, then rose up louder as the insects began to burrow into his ears, mouth and into the cavity where his nose should have been.

Gnawing their way into his head.

56

Adam knew that Van der Zee could see it in his face. The enormous wave of excitement, of exhilaration, that he'd felt from Rachel – that had passed straight from her thoughts into his – could only mean one thing, and Adam had been unable to keep it from his expression.

"They've found it, haven't they?"

"Found what?" Adam said, wide-eyed.

Van der Zee shook his head, impatient, and turned back to the desk. The screens were still blank. He grabbed the microphone to address the Hope operatives on the boat. "It's time to move," he said. "They'll be coming out of that cave any time, so let's get a welcoming committee up on to that beach right now…" The order was acknowledged. Van der Zee turned back to Adam and shrugged. "Soon be over," he said.

"I really don't know what you're talking about," Adam said. "What you think anyone's *found*." He took a step towards the control desk but was intercepted by the guards.

"Shame we have no pictures," Van der Zee said. "But you should be able to hear everything."

As if on cue, a voice boomed from the speakers. High and edgy – a New York accent. "Talk to me, Van der Zee."

Van der Zee turned back to the desk. "I believe the artefact has been acquired."

"That's good. Very good…"

"So I've sent in a team to intercept them. That was the plan, right?"

"Yes, it was." The man in New York paused. "But plans can change, doctor, you need to be aware of that. We're dealing with people who are not … predictable. You have to think fast, and be flexible. Do whatever the situation demands. You with me?"

"Yes, I—"

"Get back to me when they've come out."

Van der Zee was about to speak again when the caller clicked off. He turned the chair round slowly until he was facing Adam.

"What does that mean?" Adam asked. "'Whatever the situation demands'?" Van der Zee said nothing. "And what happens to me, when all this is over?"

Van der Zee stared at the floor for a few seconds and when he raised his head, he could not look Adam in the eye. "That's not my decision," he said.

Adam felt the words like a cold hand on the back of his neck.

He knew that there were men on their way to the beach. Rachel and the others would be walking out of those caves into big trouble. He knew that he was in trouble too, and he knew that he could not just sit back and let it happen.

He needed to make a move.

Gabriel unfastened the leather necklace and handed it back to Rachel. When she had threaded the new amulet on to it, he passed across the original Triskellion.

"They belong together," he said.

Rachel put the Triskellion back on to the necklace and turned so that Gabriel could fasten it behind her neck.

The moment the two amulets touched, they began to move, sliding across each other, singing against Rachel's skin.

"It's been a long time," Gabriel said.

It was as though the metal of each Triskellion had softened: as though one could pass directly through another. The blades kissed and twisted together, weaving intricate patterns, and the light glowing from them laced round Rachel's throat.

Then it was over, and the amulets faded and slowed until they hung motionless from the cord round Rachel's neck. They clinked softly when she turned to look at Gabriel.

"You've got something on your hands," she said.

"What?"

"Is it … honey?"

Gabriel wiped his palms against his trousers. "That creature you saw by your bed … he won't be bothering you again."

Rachel stared hard at him, then nodded, understanding. "That's a relief," she said.

"We need to go." Gabriel moved towards the steps that led back up into the tomb.

But Rachel had walked back to the edge of the water and stood gazing down into the depths. "Carmen and Inez," she said. She turned and looked imploringly at Gabriel, but even as she'd spoken their names, she'd known that they would not be coming back up.

Gabriel shook his head. "They knew all along what they would have to do." He held out a hand. "Come on. We need to catch up with the others and get out, fast."

Jean-Luc and Jean-Bernard were sitting on rocks, idly tossing pebbles at gulls, when they first heard the boats. They looked up and stared out to sea as the whine of the outboard motors grew louder, then watched as the two motorized dinghies came quickly round the headland.

The boys stood and rolled up their sleeves.

The two boats hit the sand within a few seconds of each other and six men piled out of each. They were dressed head to toe in black and all wore dark glasses and inhibitors.

They exchanged a few words and then began running

hard towards the entrance of the cave, quickly covering the few hundred metres or so between them and the two sixteen-year-old French boys.

Jean-Luc and Jean-Bernard stood and watched them coming. Jean-Luc glanced at his brother. "There are twelve of them," he said. "It's not fair."

"You're right," Jean-Bernard said. "The odds are terrible."

Jean-Luc grinned. "Well, maybe we should each have one arm tied behind our backs. Give them a fighting chance…"

The brothers stepped casually out into plain sight and waited until the last possible second to strike. The man who appeared to be in command signalled to his men that they should be careful, but it was clear from their reactions that they did not see the twin boys – "special" or not – as much of a threat.

Within ten seconds of engaging, two of the men were unconscious, two were nursing broken arms and collar-bones, and three more were spitting blood and teeth out on to the sand.

The group's commander gave the order to back off.

As Jean-Luc threw one man over his shoulder and slammed another into the wall of the cliff, he turned to his brother. "What about tying both arms behind our backs…?"

On the boat, Van der Zee was transfixed by the sounds coming through the speakers: by the grunts and screams and the frantic radio calls for assistance. He didn't see Adam's eyes flutter and then close; didn't see him slide down in his seat and then topple on to the floor.

"Doctor! The boy…"

Van der Zee turned round to see the guards pointing towards Adam's body. "What on earth happened?"

"He just collapsed. One minute he was fine, the next—"

They stopped and stared as Adam began to jerk and twist on the floor, as froth oozed from his mouth; as his body gave one final spasm and then was still.

Van der Zee jumped up from his chair and screamed at the guards as he lurched across the cabin, "Well, don't just stand there!"

The guards moved quickly and knelt down next to the boy. One of them picked up his wrist, feeling for a pulse.

"Nothing," he said.

"You sure?" Van der Zee asked.

The guard nodded and both men removed their dark glasses and inhibitors.

"What are you doing?" Van der Zee shouted. "Be careful he doesn't…"

But a second was all Adam had needed; a second to get inside their heads.

Then he had them.

57

Morag and Duncan should have been out of the cave and back on the beach ten minutes earlier. They were supposed to have stuck close to Ali, but they had somehow managed to wander off in a different direction and had become separated from him. Now, as they tried to find their way back to the entrance, they could hear Ali calling out to them from somewhere deep in the maze of tunnels and caverns. They could hear the anxiety in his voice.

"Ali!" Morag shouted. "We're here…"

But her voice bounced back off the high, damp walls and she knew that he would have difficulty tracking them by sound alone.

"An echo," Duncan muttered. "A sound wave that has been reflected and returned with sufficient magnitude and delay to be perceived as a wave distinct from that which was initially transmitted."

"Maybe we should stay where we are," Morag said.

"Also, the name of a character in 'Daredevil'."

"He can't be far away," Morag said. "He's bound to find us eventually." She turned to look at Duncan, but he had already wandered away again. She took a few steps in each direction and called out to him. When an answer finally came, she could hear something strange in her brother's voice.

"Morag … I'm in here…"

She turned left into a tunnel she had not seen before, then left again, squeezing through a narrow gap between a pair of upright slabs, into a small cavern. The walls sloped inwards and the ceiling was so low that no adult would have been able to stand upright. Every inch of wall had been covered in drawings, so that standing in the confined space, Morag felt as though she was part of it; as if she'd stepped into the middle of a painted scene.

Duncan was standing in front of a wall, his arm outstretched, pointing.

Morag looked at the pictures: a bank sloping down to dark water, a vehicle of some sort disappearing beneath the surface. She turned and followed the images round the wall, her little heart thumping in her chest.

Two small figures kicking towards the light.

Two larger ones carried away inside the vehicle; inside the car.

Four pairs of eyes: wide, terrified. And others, watching from high up on the rain-swept bank.

"It's us, isn't it?" Duncan said. "It's just like in my dreams."

Morag nodded.

"I don't understand. Did the person who drew this dream it too?"

Before Morag could answer, she heard Ali's voice, and this time it was coming from somewhere close by.

"Ali ... over here!"

"I hear you!" Ali shouted. "I'm coming..."

The children were each stretching out a hand towards the other, and both reached at the same moment. Morag buried her face in Duncan's bony shoulder while he did like-wise. They were both sobbing, keeping their faces averted from the pictures surrounding them – happy enough to cling together while they waited for Ali to find them.

"I've never seen anything like this," the helicopter pilot shouted. "It's like the sea's ... *boiling*, or something."

The amazement in his voice was evident as it boomed from the speakers above Van der Zee's desk. In the pauses, the cabin was filled with the clatter of the rotor blades, but beneath was a very different roar: the sound of water rushing...

"It's the fish. They're just under the surface: thousands of them ... *hundreds* of thousands of them. Silver fish ... not sure what kind. The entire shoal is moving in the same direction. It's like they're forming themselves into some sort of shape... God, it's just incredible."

Van der Zee stopped listening. He did not need telling

what kind of shape the pilot was trying to describe.

Something three-bladed…

"Is there anybody receiving me?"

Van der Zee said nothing. He was finding it hard to concentrate with two guns pointed at him. "So what happens now?" he asked, looking at the two guards. They stood, unblinking, one on either side of him, their weapons trained on the man who only a few moments earlier had been giving them orders. Their minds were now completely subject to Adam's control.

"I haven't really decided," Adam said.

"Well, I don't think you have very long."

"Really?" Adam said. "Looks to me like *you're* the one who's running out of time."

Van der Zee tried to look casual. "Come on, it's not like you're going to shoot me."

"I don't have to shoot," Adam said. He looked at the guards. "I just have to tell *them* to."

"Are you both all right?" Ali asked.

Morag and Duncan separated and stared across at Ali, who had just about managed to squeeze into the tiny cavern. His head was wedged against the ceiling and, if he were to stretch out his arms, he could have touched the walls on either side.

"What's the matter?"

Morag tried to speak, but nothing came out.

Ali held up a hand to let her know that it was OK. He was already looking at the pictures. He had his answer. "These are your … parents?"

Duncan nodded.

The parents he and his sister knew only from vague memories and vivid dreams. The parents who had been snatched away by the same people who now threatened their own lives.

Now it was Ali's turn to be speechless. He swallowed down the lump in his throat and beckoned to the children. "You need to come now," he said. "The others will be waiting."

He ducked down low, backed out carefully between the two slabs of rock and turned out into the tunnel. It was darker suddenly, and, feeling his way along the wall, his hand brushed against a small, smooth rock set back in a hollow. Ali knew at once that he'd made a terrible mistake, but it was too late.

A booby trap…

He heard the ancient mechanism whirr into life and the grind of rock against rock as the huge boulder was released and began to drop. He tried to press himself back against the wall of the tunnel, but there was nowhere to go, and even though he managed to twist his body away from the impact, the boulder fell squarely across his legs, crushing the bone.

His scream echoed through the maze of tunnels and caves.

Morag and Duncan were no more than a few seconds behind and dropped to the floor next to him. They heaved at the boulder but there was no shifting it. They tried pulling Ali by the shoulders, but that did nothing except increase the volume of the screaming.

"I'm sorry," Morag said.

Ali took a gulp of air and managed to spit out three words on long, laboured breaths. "You … must … go!"

Morag shook her head firmly.

"We want to stay with you," Duncan said.

Ali grabbed the boy's arm and squeezed. "You must go…"

Morag got to her feet. "We'll try and get help," she said.

"No…"

Duncan shook off Ali's hand and stood next to his sister. "We won't be long," he said. "I promise."

Ali groaned and reached out a despairing hand, but it was too late. He was just able to turn his head and watch the two children running back in the direction from which they had all come: back into the labyrinth of tunnels.

He let his head drop back into the dirt; the pain in his heart every bit as terrible as the pain in his legs.

58

Laura and Kate emerged, blinking, into the sunlight. They had become lost in the maze of passages and, by the time they had been able to see the afternoon light shining at the end of the tunnel, they had fully expected to see everyone else gathered on the beach, waiting for them. Laura looked wide-eyed at the team of beaten and bloodied Hope agents crawling from the beach and helping their walking wounded back into dinghies.

Jean-Luc and Jean-Bernard ran back up the beach to meet the two women, apparently eager to get into the caves themselves.

"I see you ran into a bit of trouble," Laura said.

Jean-Luc smiled. "Nothing we couldn't handle."

"Where are the others?" Laura asked. "Morag and Duncan should have been out ages ago."

"No," Jean-Bernard said. "You are the first."

Laura and Kate exchanged a worried look.

"Rachel's still in there," Kate said. The panic clear in her voice as she turned back towards the cave. "I'm going back in to look for her."

"I'll come with you," Laura said. "And we'll look for the little twins too."

"Wait!" Jean-Bernard shouted, grabbing Laura's arm. "They are fine."

"Rachel is coming back," Jean-Luc added. "She has found what she was looking for."

"How do you know?" Kate's voice was high and strained.

The French twins tapped their heads simultaneously.

"You wait here," Jean-Bernard said. "And we will go and bring them out."

Fighting the strong instinct to go and find the three children for whom they were jointly responsible, Laura and Kate watched the energetic French boys pile into the entrance of the caves, whooping like Apaches.

Rachel and Gabriel ran back, trying to retrace their route to the entrance. Gabriel moved fast, dragging Rachel behind him. Distant noises echoed through the passages; random shouts and cries hung in the air. Rachel was not sure whether the noises were all around her or inside her head. Although she had the Triskellions safely round her neck, she felt a growing sense that something was going wrong.

One of the noises – a high, whooping sound, like the scream of monkeys – was getting closer and closer. Turning a corner, they ran, headlong, into Jean-Luc and Jean-Bernard, who automatically tensed, ready to fight.

"Easy," Rachel said.

The French boys smiled and dropped their guard.

"Any problems on the beach?" Gabriel asked.

"No sweat," Jean-Luc said. "You gave us a job to do" – he shrugged – "we did it."

"Good," Gabriel said. "Now turn round and go back. We have to get out."

"But what about the kids?" Jean-Luc asked. "Morag and Duncan."

A worried look passed across Gabriel's face. "They're not outside?"

"No. Only Laura and your mother." Jean-Bernard nodded to Rachel.

"But I told Ali to get them out quickly."

"We have to find them." Rachel began to pull Gabriel back, but his eyes told her he was not about to be pulled anywhere. That he would be making the decisions.

"Gabriel," she pleaded.

"*We'll* find them," Jean-Luc said.

"So where are Inez and Carmen?" Jean-Bernard asked. The look on Rachel's face told him everything.

"No!" he shouted. "No! No…!" He pulled back his fist to hit Gabriel, but his brother stopped him; spoke quietly and firmly.

"We will find them, Jean-Bernard. We will bring them

back." He grabbed his brother's trembling arm and they ran off together, down into the twisting void of the darkening tunnels.

Clay Van der Zee's eyes flicked nervously from side to side. Both gun barrels hovered millimetres from his temples and it was making him sweat.

"Still waiting, Van der Zee," the metallic voice crackled again over the speaker. "Update, please."

Adam nodded. Van der Zee licked his dry lips, preparing to answer: trying to sound in control.

"As you know, the artefact has been found," Van der Zee said. He looked to Adam for approval and got it.

"And the ... targets?" the voice crackled again.

Van der Zee's eyes questioned Adam.

"Tell him everything's OK," Adam whispered.

"Everything's under control," Van der Zee lied. "I'm awaiting a final report from the landing party."

"I'm getting conflicting reports here, Van der Zee. Are the targets still in the caves? I have to make a decision ... now."

Adam shook his head. Van der Zee did not know what to say.

"Can you hear me, Van der Zee? *Are the targets still inside?*"

Adam switched off the communications button. Alarm bells were ringing in his head. He looked across at the distant shore. Heard the helicopter circling above. "Targets? What did he mean by targets?"

Van der Zee shrugged.

"Who is he?" Adam shouted close to the doctor's face.

"Even I don't know his real name. He's Head of Operations for the Flight Trust – the organization that owns Hope – in New York. I only know him as Max."

"So who does he answer to?" Adam's voice was getting louder. "Give me a name."

"They don't use full names, Adam." Van der Zee looked serious, and scared. "It would be too dangerous."

"OK, here's the deal," Adam said calmly. "You're going to order that helicopter down, then we're going to take this boat into shore and pick up my family."

"We can take the boat wherever you like, Adam," Van der Zee said. "But, I'm afraid, I'm not the one who controls the helicopter."

Gabriel's mind darted from chamber to chamber, down passages and corridors as they made their escape from the caves. Duncan and Morag were nowhere to be found. Finally, they could see the light from outside as the sun lowered in the afternoon sky and shone directly into the mouth of the cave.

They ran out on to the beach, hoping to see Ali, Morag and Duncan reunited with Kate and Laura.

Rachel scanned the beach. She saw her mother, crouching with Laura behind rocks ten or fifteen metres away. She called to her, and Kate jumped up, waved and started running towards the cave. Gabriel looked frantically from side to side.

Duncan and Morag had still not emerged.

A large, black motor launch sped into view on the horizon. Rachel watched it churning up a wake of foam as it began to power towards the shore. She could hear the roar of its engines and then the sound of another motor, high above them, swooping down, black and insect-like out of the sun.

Everything seemed to move in slow motion as the snake of smoke shot from beneath the helicopter, and a second missile exploded into the cave behind them.

The blast knocked Rachel to the ground, and as she looked up, dust and debris fell around her. Her mother stood, shocked, frozen to the spot. She could have been turned to stone, save for the terrible screams that came from her. Rachel turned to see Gabriel lying flat beside her. He raised his face, sooty from the blast.

"You did this!" Rachel shrieked above the fading clatter of the helicopter blades. "You opened the door ... and now you've closed it again."

"No..."

"You've deliberately sealed it up so that nobody can get inside again. Well, you've sealed Morag and Duncan and the others up with it."

Gabriel shook his head feverishly from side to side. Tears streaked his cheeks, washing clean lines into the soot.

He scrabbled to his feet, holding his hands to his head in anguish.

"I didn't do this," he said. "It wasn't me. Rachel, it wasn't me..."

Gabriel turned and sprinted back towards the cave. The missile had struck just above the opening and Gabriel watched, helpless, as rocks rolled down the cliff-face and tumbled on to the beach, blocking the entrance. Only a small gap remained where the mouth of the cave had been.

Gabriel ran.

He dived though the small black gap, back into the cavern, a second before the cave collapsed in on itself.

59

Rachel screamed and began to run towards the cave, but she was firmly pulled back by her mother.

"Leave it," Kate said. "He's gone…"

"No!" Rachel shook her head, tears streaking her face. "He can't just … go." They stared at the entrance. There were still smaller rocks rolling down on to the sand; dust was rising in a black cloud that drifted back towards them on the breeze.

"I think it's time to leave," Laura said.

Rachel did not move. "But Morag and Duncan are still inside. Jean-Luc and Jean-Bernard…"

Laura laid a hand on her arm. "Nobody else is coming out of there, Rachel."

As the rumble of collapsing rock died and the helicopter wheeled away across the cliff top, Laura became aware of another sound. She turned to see the motor launch still racing towards the shore. Men with dark glasses and automatic weapons were standing on the deck. After the beating handed out to their unarmed colleagues by the French boys, the next wave of Hope operatives would clearly be taking no chances.

"We have to get out of here *now*," she told Kate and Rachel. "We—"

All three of them turned slowly to face the ocean again, their faces suddenly wet with spray as the water rose up from nowhere and roared.

"What's happening?" Kate screamed.

They stood and stared as, thirty metres or so offshore, the surface of the water began to spin at incredible speed. At first, it looked as though a giant whirlpool was forming, but then it lifted, hovering above the water and growing into a monstrous tornado, its funnel over twenty metres high.

Laura was almost blown off her feet, and sand was whipping up into her eyes. "Get down!" she shouted.

They all dropped to the floor, just as the spinning column of wind and water began to move. Just as the helicopter reappeared, swooping in from behind the cliff top. It was moving too fast to avoid getting caught in the vicious tower of water which rose up to meet it.

Adam stared at Clay Van der Zee. It was as though the doctor had resigned himself to something, though to *what*, Adam could not be sure. The man's face was impassive, even though there were still two guns pointing at him. Even though the anguished voice of the helicopter pilot was filling the cabin.

"I've lost control ... there's nothing I can do..."

The noise of the rotor blades was suddenly much louder and Adam knew that the sound was not only coming through the radio.

"The instruments will not respond!"

The chopper was close. Way too close...

"I can't bail out," the pilot screamed. *"I can't bail out!"*

Adam released his hold on the minds of the two guards. They snapped into life, like men woken suddenly from bad dreams, took a few seconds to work out what was happening, then ran from the cabin.

"I have to try!" the pilot shouted.

Adam ran to the porthole, craned his neck and struggled to look up. It was hard to see anything at all with the whirlwind throwing water hard against the glass, but he could just about make out the dark shape that was getting larger, fast.

"The boat ... I have to try and get clear," the pilot's voice screeched.

Adam turned just in time to see Van der Zee drop back into his chair and close his eyes. From the speaker, there was nothing but screaming through the crackle of static.

"I think this is probably goodbye," Van der Zee said.

From the beach, Rachel, Kate and Laura watched as the helicopter was caught and held tight in the tornado's grip. They saw it thrown around as though it were a toy,

The aircraft rolled over and twisted inside the dark funnel, the blades *"whop-whopping"* to no avail as the pilot tried his best to regain control.

"It's like it just reached up," Kate said. "Like the wind just plucked it out of the air…"

The sense of horror quickly grew, until each of them felt it like a blow to their stomach; until they realized that the helicopter was going to crash, and exactly where it was going to come down.

When they saw just what the point of impact would be.

Laura's hand flew to her mouth. "Oh my God!"

There was not even time to turn their heads away…

It was like a rush of wind, just for a moment, and then the full force of the explosion broke across them, throwing them on to their backs. The noise was unbearable, and by the time it had died down sufficiently for them to get back on their feet, the fireball was already climbing high into the air. Debris was crashing down into the water on all sides and they could no longer see anything of either the helicopter or the boat it had destroyed.

Rachel stood and watched, and for those few seconds before the realization – before the grief – hit, she was looking through a different pair of eyes.

She was a young girl who had rushed from a cave to that same spot thirty thousand years before. When another vessel had fallen from the sky. When a fireball had risen from the ocean and smoke had blacked out the sun.

The scream brought her out of it.

Rachel turned to see her mother dropping on to the sand like a dead woman and Laura rushing across to offer what little comfort she could.

"Adam!" Kate shouted.

Then Rachel understood. She saw the smoke continue to rise and felt her world fall away as she went down.

"Adam was on that boat."

60

Rachel clung to her mother and their tears mingled, their cheeks pressed tightly together. No words, no gestures could express the trauma of the past hour. As their shadows grew long in the late afternoon sun, they stayed on their knees in the sand and wept.

Laura paced up and down at the water's edge, shaking her head, trying to make sense of the burning wreckage floating offshore. Cinders and particles of smouldering boat hissed as they floated down and landed in the sea in front of her. The vortex had subsided, but a kilometre out, the sea still rolled and boiled...

Rachel got up and wiped away the sand stuck to her cheeks. She spat bits of grit from her mouth and strode towards the sea after Laura. She caught up with the Australian and launched herself at her, grabbing at her sweatshirt, pulling her down into the water: thrashing and punching wildly. Laura tried to restrain Rachel, but she had been caught off guard and the two of them tumbled into the cold, grey Atlantic.

Kate saw what was happening and ran in after her daughter.

"Rachel … no!"

Laura and Rachel were waist deep by the time Kate reached them and attempted to pull them apart. She held each of them by the neck of their shirts, like naughty children. As they struggled, the three of them fell into an awkward, wet embrace, clinging to one another for comfort, their tears coming again.

Then Rachel felt something else…

…Something which at first she mistook for a hard knot of grief, tightening in her throat. But the feeling became warmer, a vibration, and, as a new warmth spread through her, she realized that the twin Triskellions were pulsating against her chest.

"Can you feel it?" she asked.

Laura nodded.

"What is it?" Kate asked.

The feeling grew, buzzing, filling Rachel's head with sounds and voices. "It's … *hope*," she said. "I think it's a good sign."

She looked upwards. Instead of cinders, a fine mist of raindrops was falling from the sky. They all raised their heads; the warm rain soothing their stinging, tear-stained faces.

Gabriel? she called out with her mind.

Silence, save for the roar of water out at sea, but in her

head, Rachel could see Gabriel, Morag and Duncan, close together and moving away from her into a darkness thick with dust. Were they still alive, or was it no more than a wish?

"Adam…!"

Her mother's scream wrenched Rachel away from the vision. Laura and Kate were splashing through the water along the shore, towards a wet figure that had been washed up on the beach. Rachel rushed towards the body of her brother. The three of them attempted to pull him up the beach, hauling his dead weight on to dry sand.

His lips were blue and his dark hair was plastered across his forehead. Kate covered his cold cheeks with hot kisses.

Rachel thought he looked beautiful. She held his limp hand.

And then Adam coughed. His body lurched and jolted. Spasms passed through his limbs and a jet of salt water spewed from his mouth on to the sand.

He slowly opened his eyes.

"Hi," he said.

61

Rachel stared out across the water, her eyes drifting up from the vision of horror and destruction that still smouldered and smoked out at sea. Up to the single, bright star that had begun to glitter high above the ocean.

How had she described that feeling to the others?

Hope...

Adam, Laura and Kate appeared at her shoulder. Rachel turned. "You ready?" she said.

Adam shrugged. "For a trek across the desert with no idea where we're going? Yeah, sure."

"Well, I don't think anyone's going to come and pick us up," Rachel said. She tucked the twin Triskellions down below the neck of her sweatshirt, then hoisted her backpack up on to her shoulders.

The others did the same, and they began to walk.

epilogue

It was long past the hour when darkness should have fallen but it was as though the sun had stopped sinking. Instead it hung low in the sky, blood-red, just above the sea. The dark water was veined with pink streaks which stretched all the way to the shore, spattering the sand and the rock face with a strange light.

The light was even more unnatural as a result of the huge arc lamps that had been set up along the beach. They fired powerful beams against the cave's entrance, where mechanical diggers were still working to remove the fallen rocks. As half a dozen generators hummed and rattled, people swarmed across the sand like ants: rescue workers, medical personnel, and others whose roles were a little harder to define.

Men and women who seemed answerable to no one, who wore dark glasses, despite the absence of conventional sunshine.

A makeshift office had been quickly set up a little further down the beach, along with an emergency room, where the staff were getting ready to receive wounded, or worse.

There was just as much activity a hundred metres offshore, where boats manoeuvred through the wreckage of a vessel called HOPE and the helicopter which had crashed into it. The explosion and the fire that followed had been intense and pieces of both craft were still smouldering. Lights from the rescue boats cut through a thick curtain of smoke which hung across the surface of the water.

Already, aviation experts were arguing about exactly what had caused the tragedy, but it seemed likely that the freak tornado, reported by local weather stations, had sucked the chopper down and caused the pilot to lose control. It was just unlucky that the aircraft had crashed directly into the boat – an accident no one could have predicted.

They had searched in vain for survivors, and now divers were working to recover bodies.

It was far quieter on the cliff top. It was darker here too, and a variety of night creatures had begun to move around, poking through the scrub and grass in search of food.

Lizards, rats, snakes, a small fox...

A gentle wind danced through the long grass where, eight or ten metres back from the cliff's edge, a small patch of soil began to shift and fall in on itself. A large beetle scurried quickly for cover as the movement increased and the soil gave way.

And a fist punched its way up from the earth.

Out in the open, the tightly clenched hand seemed to glisten in what little light there was. After a few moments, the first insects started to settle – mosquitoes and gnats – drawn by the sickly sweet scent. But they were gone again as soon as the fist began to move.

Once the blistered, honey-covered fingers had started to uncurl and claw at the cool night air.

author's note

In 2007, while excavating a group of caves on the Atlantic coast of Morocco, an international team of archaeologists discovered the remains of a Neanderthal tribe. The scientists were astonished when further research showed that some of the specimens' teeth and bones were those of a different species: more like *Homo sapiens*, who were previously thought to have arrived long after the Neanderthals had died out. The evidence suggested that in North Africa, this new species of human had coexisted, and possibly bred, with the Neanderthals.

Archaeologists continue to argue about what caused the genetic and behavioural shift, but all agree that *something* happened to trigger the development and spread of modern man across Europe.

Some kilometres south of the caves, in the town of Essaouira (formerly known as Mogador), tucked away in a narrow backstreet, there is a cafe called La Triskalla. The sign of the Triskellion hangs outside. They make delicious crêpes…

Read an exclusive extract from the next
book in the TRISKELLION series.

Available spring 2010

Triskellion 3
prologue:

Western Australia

Molly Crocker stared across the yard to where the boy was working, cursing herself as she spilt the lemonade and reaching for a cloth to clean up the mess. When she looked up again, the boy had moved out of her line of sight and there was a large bee butting gently against the window from outside.

Zzzzz ... dnk. Zzzzz ... dnk.

Molly thought it was a bit early for bees, but it wasn't a complete surprise. Everything was going haywire with the climate these days. Global warming was never out of the news.

She was careful not to spill any more as she carried the lemonade outside, down the steps from the porch and out across the front yard to where the boy was painting one of the fence posts.

"Here you go," Molly said. She handed the cold drink across. "Looks like you could do with this."

The boy, whose name was Levi, had been working at their place for the last couple of weeks. He'd mended the roof on one of the barns, fixed the gate on the paddock where Molly's horse was kept and done some basic plumbing inside. He was sixteen, Molly guessed – about the same age as she and Dan were – and according to their mother, the Aboriginal tribe he belonged to had been living in the area for over forty thousand years.

Levi drank half the lemonade in one gulp. "Thirsty," he said.

While Molly waited for the glass, she stared around the compound. It was isolated for sure – their closest neighbour was seven kilometres away and it was half an hour in the truck to the nearest shops – but it was a nice place to live. They were only ten minutes from the sea and got to go surfing after school or ride horses in the hills whenever they fancied it.

Debbie, their mum, and Mel – the woman who shared the house with them – reckoned they were lucky.

That they all had a pretty good life.

Molly wiped the sweat from the back of her neck and tried to remember how long they'd been here. Was it two years? Something like that...

Levi handed back the glass. "Thanks, Rachel."

Molly blinked. The glass slipped from between her fingers and shattered on the ground. "Excuse me?"

At that moment, Dan waved from the other side of the yard as he walked back to the house. Levi waved back enthusiastically. Called out, "Hi, Adam."

Molly watched as her twin brother stared back, confused,

and walked back to the house a little faster.

"What did you call me?" Molly asked.

"I called you by your name," Levi said. "Your name is Rachel, but you've forgotten. You've forgotten everything."

Molly stared. The boy was making no sense, and yet … something was swimming forward from the recesses of her mind. Something was struggling to come into focus.

"I think maybe you should go," Molly said.

Levi didn't move. "It's good that you forgot; that you all started a new life. It was the only way you could stay alive. But now it's time to remember again."

"You're crazy," Molly said. She turned at a noise from the house and saw Mel and her mum marching quickly towards them across the yard. Dan was walking nervously a few metres behind. Mel was carrying the shotgun.

"What's my name?" Levi whispered.

Molly stared, held by the boy's intense green eyes – funny how she'd never noticed that they were green before – and saw a beach.

An explosion and a boy running. Rocks falling and a ball of flame rising high into the sky. She felt desperately sad for no reason, and the word came out of her mouth without her brain telling it to. "Gabriel."

The boy smiled.

"Hey!" Mel was shouting as she, Dan and Molly's mother got closer. She raised the shotgun. "Get the hell off our land right now. And don't come back."

"You'd best do it," Molly said.

"I need you," he said. "You and Adam."

"Need us for … what?"

Mel and the others were only a few steps away. "Didn't you hear *me*?" Mel screamed.

"There are people in the shadows," the boy said. "They've stayed hidden for a long time, working quietly to destroy you – all of you."

Molly nodded. She could feel the danger and remember the urgency and the pain. She remembered running and running…

"You've been hiding for a long time, Rachel, but it can't go on for ever. It has to stop. It's time you came out of the shadows."

"Why?" Molly said. She hadn't been aware of the clouds gathering, and the first fat raindrops felt cold and heavy. "Why now?"

The boy's eyes darkened. "Because they're coming…"